Jo-Anne Richards comes from the Eastern Cape and now lives in Johannesburg. She is a journalist. *The Innocence of Roast Chicken*, her first novel, was an instant South African success, topping the bestseller lists for fifteen weeks.

Praise for *The Innocence of Roast Chicken*:

'Jo-Anne Richards has the writer's eye, the natural ability to sniff out the telling detail and the right word. She is a delight to savour – one of the freshest voices to emerge from South Africa in years'          Peter Godwin

'Jo-Anne Richards displays a wonderful feeling for place and period . . . her prose is sharply evocative, and she conjures up the child's powerful feelings with a vividness intensified by nostalgia'
                              Margaret Walters, *The Sunday Times*

'This book has pace and tension – shot through with the terrible beauty of the South African landscape and the efforts of a child to stave off gathering evil'
                                                          Gillian Slovo

'[A] rapturous and tactile evocation of dust, food, noises and a childhood domain, rendered with a marked empathy for the child and the magical properties of a child's stamping-ground'          Elizabeth Buchan, *The Times*

*Also by Jo-Anne Richards*

The Innocence of Roast Chicken

# Touching
# the
# Lighthouse

Jo-Anne Richards

review

First published in 1997
by REVIEW

An imprint of Headline Book Publishing

First published in paperback in 1998
by REVIEW

10 9 8 7 6 5 4 3 2 1

ISBN 0 7472 5521 0

Printed and bound in Great Britain by
Clays Ltd, St Ives plc

HEADLINE BOOK PUBLISHING
A division of Hodder Headline PLC
338 Euston Road
London NW1 3BH

# Touching
# the
# Lighthouse

# 1

I was in search of my life. I was in search of something which could still the rustle in my heart and the rattle in my brain. That was why, running just ahead of disillusion, I first went there – to that city of the wild and the possible.

But this isn't supposed to be the story of me – the offspring of Eastern Cape respectability, with all its wholesomeness and grass-banked suburbs.

What I set out to tell was the story of Maud. But she is also not the kind of person whose life would have been chronicled, had it not been for us. If it had not been for all of us, and the way she bound our lives that year.

I was there. And although I cannot claim to have been purely an observer – I wish I could – I was never decisive in that strange saga of extraordinary times, and the extraordinary people who were formed by them.

Even now, I have the same feelings about my life. I am still in the wings. The central characters – the successful businessman and the two bright, truculent teenagers – are out there on-stage. I, the mother, have no part of my own, beyond all my clamouring behind the curtains, to be sure they dress the part and give their best performance. My life's work, God help me: I seem to have made them my life's work.

But that makes me no different from thousands of other women. It's not as if that year ruined my life, or anything. My husband says that what happened to me is called growing up. He is impatient with the whimsy of my sensibilities, and says he is amazed only that it took me so long.

But, you see, it was that year which started the trickle of all my tears and youthful juices, loamy with life and musky as soil after a night's rain. And once that leak begins, it can't be dammed – until

1

one day you look out at the landscape of your life, and it has the aridity of the smattering of dust which settles after a Berg wind.

I didn't intend it to be like this. I don't think one ever does, in those vigorous days when one is special and destined for life's wonders. But it was that year, and what we did with it, that set the tone for what I did with my life. And it was Maud, with the things she set in motion, and the people she brought together. But still I cannot blame her. The only people I can find to blame – and, oh, I've searched – are the girlish two of us, Susan and I.

When we meet, rarely now, Susan never lights my cigarette for me. We cordially sip tea and inquire after each other's children. Our chat is as desultory as the strands covering our friendship and we leave again, with dry kisses on cheeks and unmeant promises to send news in a Christmas card.

It's funny how clearly I can remember every detail of how it began – each step of the hope drenched way, from the sea at Storms River, claiming for me the world beyond the Eastern Cape. From the depths of the Knysna forest to the rush of wheat-green tedium, impatient to be gone, to be Cape Town.

I wonder what it looks like now. I wonder, as the grey sky leaks the whisper of snow. I wonder if the rain still mists across the heathery mountain, leadening the sea. But of course, it will be summer there now. As it was when I left Port Elizabeth that April to drive to the Cape.

I can see with absolute clarity my small grey Datsun, and how the journey gave it the wind-rushed effect of greater speed than it was capable of. I remember that I sang, the radio and I competing with the rattle and clatter, and the roar from the open window.

'Forever young, I want to be forever young. Dur-dur-dur-dur-dur-dur-live forever. Forever, forever young . . .'

I dragged on my cigarette and allowed it to dangle from my fingers as the heel of my hand beat in time with my exhilaration. I remember that I ignored the strands of hair which flurried around my mouth, seeking the words I flung into the gusting car and whipping them away.

I was trying again – trying to find again that ardour I had been in danger of losing; that sense that my life would be perfect and time-appointed.

I wandered over wavelike hills, each one higher but each the same as the last. Up and unending over, up and over. My Datsun strained and slowed on the umpteenth up, struggling to mount the next swell as a white Mercedes swished past on the solid white line and silently disappeared over the brow. I turned the radio off as the car filled with the pumping fumes and clanking growls of tip-trucks labouring in the other direction. And then they were gone, leaving just the wind-whistled silence at the top of Sir Lowry's Pass.

It fell away. The earth fell away so suddenly that I clutched at my breath with the sense of running headlong to the teetering edge of a cliff face. Beneath me the world collapsed into another, far below. It was a new world, bounded by mountains and outstretched sea and, at the far end, Table Mountain. Hackneyed in the expectation of its beauty, it was in reality all elegant splendour and blue-black mastery of its surroundings.

I had arrived in that place of promise, where being grown-up would truly begin. There it was, stretched before me. I had but to plunge down this Pass, faster and faster in the joy of being there.

But at its foot, Cape Town seemed removed again, its siren mountain holding it just that distance ahead of me, inviting but remote.

I rattled along the grey road, the snap of loose gravel from roadworks clicking at the car doors. The maelstrom of excavation, with its struggle of bulldozers and confusion of laboured trucks, brought me to a gravelly stop behind the same white Mercedes, the driver's silhouette slapping its hands impatiently on the wheel. A road worker leant into the stop sign he held, his arm draped around its neck like a lover. He was yelling backward to a man resting on the roadside, his free hand signing its affirmation of his words.

'. . . *Andazi . . . uzoya nini emsebenzini?*'

In the opposite direction streamed a line of cars, as closely driven as a convoy. I heard the echoed yell from the other end of the deviation.

'OK . . . OK *hamba ngoku.*'

The man twirled his sign to display the green 'Go'. The Mercedes spattered stones with an aggressive clatter and was gone, weaving the muddy deviation and bounding ahead on the straight. I plodded the straight road, expecting Cape Town.

The mountain floated aloof at the far end of the barren Flats.

And the road, hypnotic in its rigidity, crept unwaveringly on towards me.

I wasn't a baby anymore, to be leaving home. I would be twenty-five next birthday. When I had finished my law degree, I had accepted the offer of articles from a friend of my father. In my home town, for God's sake. Oh, I could justify it. I could tell people how prestigious it was to do articles with a firm of the Eastern Cape's foremost attorneys. I could also explain earnestly that in smaller firms, in the smaller towns, you were given more important work as a clerk.

But then I would also have to confess that I seemed to spend much of my time delivering summonses and ferrying my boss's children while his wife played tennis. Each day, instead of filling me with the keen bite of enthusiasm, weighed on me with its lack of challenge. And I was given testing tasks so seldom that they always retained the sharpness of fear, never mellowing through experience.

And when I was tired, it seemed easier to drive to my parents' and eat supper there, rather than struggle to cook in my cold, dark cottage, the bed still unmade from the morning. So, most evenings saw me there, as much a child as I'd ever been. We never managed, my mother and I, to negotiate the terms of new adulthood. The contrapuntal scolding and sulky rebellion of childhood never left us, as we, two women, obscured ourselves behind the shields of mother and daughter.

The two exclamation points of the cooling towers brought the buttressed Table up close, and then, suddenly, I was in Cape Town, sweeping with the freeway around the grassy skirts of the mountain.

I think that only if one has come into that city for the first time, following that road, can one have a sense of what that sweep of mountain, city and sea did for me – a girl nurtured by squat towns and barefoot streets. A girl who had gently prised at her squashed hopes and carried them tenderly there. It could do that. All that indecently unfettered beauty could seem to deliver from you, all at once, the wild desires you hardly knew were growing within you.

The sun-sparked sea glowed with the glare of ships, and the counterpoint of dark fishing boats and tugs. In rhythm with the winding road and scalloped slopes, intoxicated by the vivacity of the bay, I easily forgot my intended course and went too far. I backtracked when I saw the bare patch of what must once have been District Six, before it was cleared for being too mixed and too motley.

I twisted my car back through the tiny streets, easing past the down-at-heel dignity of flower-boxed terraces. Through roads packed with parked cars, I came at last to our road – the place I was to meet Susan and find my new home. It was filled with the unmistakeable badges of all that was new, and all that my mother would disapprove of. Battered combis, roof-racked Beetles decorated with surfboards, guitars leaning on balconies, the sounds of UB40 and Juluka, and incense wisping through wide sash windows.

Crown Street, just below the railway line, in the heart of Observatory – this was the coolest place we could possibly be, Susan and I. And she had found it, pretending nonchalance as she described it over the long-distance line, affecting not to care for the trendier-than-thou sight and smell of the place.

And there she was, I remember, pretending she wasn't waiting for me. Crouched on the *stoep*, her blonde hair wisping into her eyes as her face screwed up for the tough suck she always gave her cigarette. She held her small body taut, as she always did, fielding the world from her innards – a protective goalie for her delicate parts. She clutched her knees with her arms, as achingly strung as she had always seemed. All through our university years, I had listened, heart in mouth, to her high notes, waiting for the strings to snap, for that beautifully carved neck to crack.

She looked up as she saw me struggling to park in a tiny spot two houses down. Her mouth twisted into her one-sided smile, but she didn't rise.

'Well, you got here.'

'Oh, Suze, this is the most incredibly beautiful house. I can't believe you found something so absolutely perfect.'

'Well, it's a house . . .'

We sat in silence, our legs dangling from the *stoep* to the narrow pavement, I savouring the friend smell of her.

Screwing her eyes in contemplation of the chimneys across the road, Susan drew her cigarettes from her lap. I watched this old ritual of ours take its place now on the sun-heavy *stoep*. Placing

5

two in her mouth, she lit them both and placed one between my lips.

'Come, I'll introduce you to Auntie at the café,' she said, her grin softening the lines of her face, allowing the vulnerability of her inner lip to peep through the guardianship of her teeth.

'Going over to see "Auntie" and "Uncle" by the café, are you?' An old man stood, leaning on the *stoep* rail of the house next door. His speckled face gaped open suddenly, freeing a surprisingly youthful yell of laughter.

'Yes, Mr Kennedy,' Susan called. 'This is my friend, Jennifer. My sister actually – but not a blood sister.'

'Your sister, hey?'

'Well, yes, in a way.'

'They're fighting again . . .' the voice rustled across the *stoep*. I hadn't noticed the black bundle, which I was drawn to now with the fascination of distaste. An ancient sack of human parts sunk on a metal-legged chair, her head swung in a metronomic shake, flakes of skin sifting from her scalp.

'Who, Mrs Kennedy?'

'The lipless mouth widened. 'The "Auntie" and "Uncle" by the shop. It's the money again. It's always the money. He can't hold on to it past the Tote. She's as tight-fisted as an old clam.'

Her speech wobbled in rhythm with her shake. 'You two go on in there. See what you can hear. But don't forget to come tell the old people. We can't move around like we used to. And we can't hear so well. *Ag*, twenty years ago, I could of told you every word they yelled. *Ja*, I could hear them make up too, in that bedroom up there. It's the one with the lace. I can't hear so much any more. They don't shout so loud as they used to.'

The ancient body heaved in a sigh. 'And not many of the old folks's left here now. These young people round here, not many are friendly like you. They look quite strange, the lot of them, not nice and ordinary girls like you. Most of them never bother with a "How d'you do" for us.'

'OK, bye Mrs Kennedy, Mr Kennedy.' Susan was wearing her twisted smile as we crossed the road and walked towards the café.

'Oh God, how mortifying.' I wailed as we moved out of earshot. 'Surely we can't still be "nice ordinary girls"? And here I thought you'd chosen this cool spot for us because it was our natural element.'

6

'Don't get carried away, dear. It doesn't escape notice that you're still wearing the shirt your mother bought from Woolie's at least three years ago.'

'Bitch! Look at you – still wearing your sensible teacher's cardigan. You can talk.'

'Well, I don't have a problem with the way we look. I just don't have any illusions about fitting in. D'you know, somebody here told me – I can't remember who – that Mrs Kennedy's had twenty-three children. Can you believe that?'

'Jesus, no wonder she looks half dead. How horrific. Is that possible? Well, I suppose if she started at twenty, perhaps . . .'

'. . . But she'd have to've had about one a year, give or take. That means she would have spent all the best years of her adult life pregnant. It's barbaric.'

We entered the café single file through the old corner door. The interior was dark, its only natural light squeezing through the entrance behind us. Wooden shelves lined the wall to our left, packed with dusty baked-bean tins, single toilet rolls, pilchards and baking powder. The huge counter to our right, wood-framed, lit its innards with a yellow glow, bilious on the cheese, bacon, polony and chocolate slabs.

The large woman behind the counter stood poised, her head fixed away from the door. Arms folded aggressively, she ignored us as we approached the counter and waited. Still bearing the imprint of last night's rollers, her head strained towards the floral curtain which raggedly covered a doorway to the interior. From behind it, I could hear the sounds of cricket commentary and a competing yell.

'You've never wanted me to have any fun, you old bag. You moan and pinch and . . . and . . . you bloody nag at every cent I spend. And who makes it, I'd like to know?'

'Who makes it?' The woman swung her pendulous arms down in outrage, before bringing them up to lean her elbows on the counter. She brought her eyes around to view us as she continued. 'I do, that's who. Who the bloody hell d'you think's serving customers now, while you sit there listening to the sport?'

She smiled at us and in a transformed voice said: 'Nice to see you, girls. Is this the one's come to stay with you, lovey?'

'Yes, this is the one. No doubt you'll be seeing a lot of her. She smokes like a bloody chimney.'

A burst of laughter cracked from her mouth. 'Nice to meet you, my girlie. We're a nice neighbourhood . . . Who're you calling an old bag, you lazy old fart . . . We've been here sixty-something years. All our lives . . . Oh shut up, these girls don't want to hear your bladdy rubbish.

'You're in the end one of the terrace, hey my girls? It's a nice one.' She leant her floral bosom against the counter and narrowed her eyes at us meaningfully as the light from the door was blocked, shadowing her face. Glancing backward, I caught the approach of three white-faced people, their hair slicked and unnaturally black. They jolted into the café in their curiously sprung walk, two boys and a girl, identical thin legs encased in black pants. Two wore black T-shirts, the third a black leather jacket, scuffed and peeling at the edges.

'Twenty Camel, please Auntie.' They didn't smile. Smiling was very uncool.

Auntie reached behind her and slapped the cigarettes on the counter, her eyebrows raised, drawing us into her little conspiracy of normality, where neither of us was very sure we wanted to be. Susan raised her eyes to the ceiling, sighing to show her utter exhaustion and inattention to the scene in the shop. I, well, as usual I scuffed and blushed and half-smiled at Auntie so as not to offend her, and apologetically half-smiled at the black-clad figure replacing the change in his pocket. He swept both of us with vacant eyes and the three bounced from the shop on the balls of their feet.

'Your neighbours, hey!' Auntie jerked her eyes at the door. 'Hmm. You know . . .' She leant forward again, beckoning us to bring our heads closer '. . . I think they must be satanists.'

'No, Auntie,' said Susan, bringing her eyes down from the ceiling. 'I think they work in advertising.'

As we wandered slowly back across Crown Street, they were draped over their *stoep*, a few doors down from ours. Even when I was wearing my cool stuff – even when I wasn't wearing the shirt my mother had bought from Woolie's – I felt an awkward awe at that ease of trendiness; I with a face that showed an uncool eagerness, and reeled my emotions across it in shifting display.

At university it had been the same. I had arrived with such liberal fervour, passed down from generation to Eastern Cape generation – proudly worn as if it placed me beyond all condemnation. During my first Political Science tutorial, it had crumbled about me like an ancient cloak brought out of its lightless chest. I had cloaked up then with new-found Marxism, worn with such flamboyance by my activist tutor. And I prepared myself for political service, for gaining entrance to The Left, that sealed mystical group practising their mysterious rituals. But they wore their Stalinist cloaks with the same awesome ease that I recognized in my new neighbours. And I was always so bloody eager, with the jolly nice speech of my young ladies' school. They terrified me in their ritual ease with slogans. They intimidated me with their cleverness. And I never did quite manage to read Althusser.

*Uuhuuh-uuhuuh, uuhuuh-uuhuuh*

The hoarse, flat blast of the fish-horn burst its painful way through the mellowing street. Rattling after the blare it sent as its herald, the covered truck raced past the terraces and skidded to an abrupt stop shortly before the café.

'Fish for you?' The men were grinning, cocky sun-tangled faces wide with good nature and audacity. 'Come buy a lovely fish for your supper from Achmat.'

The men laughed. We grinned back, shaking our heads. The man who had spoken, in his upward-tilting Cape speech, pushed his cloth hat aside to scratch his head, and cudgelled a look of perplexed innocence across his wicked face.

'You gooses fancy our truck? We'll *mos* give you a *lekker* ride.'

'Bladdy skollies.' Auntie's voice shrilled through their bursting laughter. 'Sell the bladdy fish and leave the white girls. They're nice girls.'

The men threw their heads up in unabashed laughter. '*Middag, Antie. Bietjie vi-is?*' The man who had spoken leapt from the truck, wiping his hands across his faded blue chest.

'*En wie se Antie is ek nou?* Cheeky bladdy skollies . . .' She wiped her hand ineffectually at his knitted cap. The man grinned at her and she frowned back, hands on hips. '*Gee my mos 'n bietjie galjoen,* Achmat. Is it nice today?'

'*Ja,* it's *lekker* fresh, Antie.'

'*Antie*! It's "Madam" to skollies like you. *Dankie,* Achmat. And leave the nice girls alone, you hear?'

The street seemed muted and evening-mellow as the mélange of rattling laughter and squeaking springs faded.

We were sitting on the *stoep*. Susan had fetched a bottle of wine, which we savoured deliciously, watching the late sun gild the chimney across from us. The cramped street, with its crimped Victorian sides, had faded to darkened geometry. Above our heads, the sky still had colour and the sun flamed across the roofs.

'I'm going to find my life here.' Our cigarettes wisped whitely into the darkening. She paused before answering.

'You mean you haven't had any up to now? Could've fooled me. I thought we'd done the odd bit of living.'

'No m'n. I mean real grown-up life. Not that raging we used to do – when we still had time to postpone what we should be doing with our lives. *Ja*, no I mean that here, perhaps we can find the kind of lives we should be living. And maybe where we belong.'

'So, you didn't find your political heartland working in the Eastern Cape?' She was mocking me, and all my pompous excuses for taking my previous job.

I acknowledged the tease with a grimace. 'Look, that was my home town. How could I become a proper grown-up when the pharmacist always asked if I still had that trouble with worms and the bookshop automatically charged things to my father?'

'But I thought you told me the Eastern Cape was the place to be – the very cauldron of the political world?'

'Well, that's what I thought. But it didn't seem to find me.'

I sipped at my wine and paused while I one-handedly lit two cigarettes and placed one between Susan's lips. I dragged, and watched Susan blow the smoke rings I was never able to perfect.

'Thanks Sister.' She used the term which had become meaningful to us after much jested use. We were the Sisterhood of Women who had felt self-mockingly brave for periodically dispensing with men.

'But this now,' I said. 'This is the best place to get more meaningfully involved ... don't sneer, Sister. It's very unattractive.'

Eyes scrunched in habitual scorn, her expression mocked my pretentions. But I knew she felt it too, the need to be part of it all. Part of the glory, part of the great sweep of anti-apartheid, anti-imperialist, anti-classbound, anti- ... well, all those things, anyway ...

'Oh Sister, fuck off. It's just that I'm so chuffed to be here. I love this house, I really do. It seems such a great setting . . . well, for anything.'

'By the way, I've taken the front room. I was here first . . . Well, at least you're predictable. You've always had that fucked up, romantic view of the world. I can't actually believe you're still in law.'

'Well, I had to do something practical, didn't I? My parents told me, rather inconsiderately I thought, that they didn't want to support me for ever. But I suppose I always thought I could do something worthwhile with my life. And that it would give me a taste of other people's existences. I've just never done or seen a thing my whole life that might help me to feel part of things.'

'Oh, I know what comes next. You're going to give me the my-childhood-was-so-easy-while-others-were-suffering angst.'

It was just beginning to chill the upper arms, the breeze which swished through the darkness. I laughed with her and she poured the last of the wine into my glass.

*Ka-latter ka-latter ka-latter, ka-latter ka-latter ka-latter skkrree-eee-ee*

The suburban train scraped and clanked and screeched its way past the back of our houses.

'I'm sorry about your divorce, Suze,' I said. 'I'm glad you got out, but I'm sorry you had such a rotten thing to go through.'

'No, don't ever say: "Sorry about the divorce". The divorce was great. I loved the divorce. It was the marriage that was rotten . . . Anyway, I suppose it's all experience, as you would say . . . Do you remember me talking about Maud? She used to char for me while I was married. Anyway, I'm not sure how, but she traced me here. She asked if she could char for us, so I felt bad and said yes. She's very fierce and she hardly does anything around the house. But I didn't know how to say no.'

'That's OK. You know I don't notice untidiness anyway.'

That's what I remember about my first day in Cape Town. The rest I remember mostly in fits and starts. It wanders wistfully through my memory. Except for Maud. Maud's days I hold trapped, pinned and framed.

*Kalatter kalatter kalatter, kalatter kalatter kalatter skkkreee-ee-ee*
K   I heard a key in the front door in the long silence after the
train. The door slammed and footsteps moved through the dining
room at the foot of the stairs, and into the kitchen. Kettle and tea
noises followed.

'Come down and meet Maud,' Susan yelled through the wall. I
had to go down anyway. The bathroom was beyond the kitchen –
tacked on to the house as an afterthought during some renovation
or other.

Maud was tall. Her unsmiling eyes, backlit by the kitchen
window, were higher than mine, and appraising. Perhaps it was
her height, or her years of charring for those younger than herself,
with less substance, that gave her eyes the wrinkle-braced strength
never to falter.

'I don't do floors,' she told us. 'And I don't bend to do cupboards. I don't bend to do the bath. It is my back. My doctor says it
is bad.'

'Well, OK,' I said, flinging tentative glances at Susan, who leant
against the broom cupboard, gazing steadfastly at the nails she
was picking. 'That's OK with me. You must just do what you
can.'

I couldn't really do this. This was an assured, grown-up thing to
do – discuss terms of employment. And I couldn't do it with this
fierce, intimidating woman whose large hands were now tugging
and folding a loose end of her turbaned *doek*. Susan, I thought,
help me here.

'Susan? Would you like to negotiate a salary with Maud? I'm
sure you'd like to have some input.'

Maud interjected before Susan could raise her head. 'The
Madam knows what I get paid for a piecework.'

'Oh God Maud,' I said. 'You can't call us "Madam". I'm Jennifer – or Jenny – and she's Susan.'

That word, that sign of all that our parents did wrong in relation to their maids, cringed about us, an insidious nudge that perhaps we were not so very different, after all. And from Maud, with her strength of grip, and her strength of gaze, it sounded obscenely obsequious.

She showed no sign of having heard me, but remained standing in silence. Was she waiting for something? Did I forget to mention anything? Was she offended?

'Um, Maud. Is there anything you need?'

'I will give you a list.'

'OK, we'll get anything you want when we go shopping. So, OK. Are Saturdays and Tuesdays all right for you?'

'That is good. I start today. Now I will sit to have my breakfast. Where is the kitchen chair, Madam . . . Jennifer?'

'Oh, sorry, Maud. We've just moved in. We'll buy one.'

'I will use a dining-room chair for now.'

Maud still stood, her eyes moving between me and Susan, who had begun to edge towards the door.

'Your husband is very angry . . .'

We were both stalled in our escape for the door. Susan's stiff little step cemented to the floor in the entrance to the dining room. I watched her eyes fix themselves on the pine floor at her feet.

'Do you still work for him, Maud?' Her casual question unravelled as she asked it.

'I still work there – but one day, not two.'

I was fastened on Maud's eyes – those unbending watchers, those cores of fierce dignity. They had been annexed suddenly by the eyes of another being. Eyes with a narrow gleam. Her cheeks shone from the window's silvering, and their surface broke as she smiled. Not a happy smile. All I could think of then was that it was a devouring smile. It was a smile which got the better of us. Her voice, deep when she spoke, cackled now in her sudden laughter.

'Why do you say he's angry, Maud?'

Maud gleamed her triumphant look at Susan. She moved away, playing the line, knowing she had hooked us. Slowly she reboiled the kettle, opened the cupboard and placed a tea bag studiedly into a mug. Lumbering past us, she fetched a dining-room chair and lowered herself, creaking and shifting. With the tea bag still in her milky tea, she strained the heat through her teeth.

'Maud?' Susan was desperate. I could see her biting at the slightly bloody edge of her thumb.

'Oh, he says to his mother . . .'

'His mother was there? What did she say?'

'She says to him that you are a "no-good, selfish little climber".'

'Jesus, what a cheek. Me, a climber! What's there to climb in his family? What else, Maud?'

Maud sucked her tea through her teeth, pausing to add another spoon of sugar.

'Your husband, he says you take everything and leave the house empty. He says he has changed the locks now, and that he has nearly called the police.'

'I was entitled. It was mine. Every single thing I took was mine when I moved in or it was a wedding present. I took nothing of us . . . nothing!'

I could hear the high keen of her strings, straining against Maud's roughly held bow. Her hands pinched at her lip, pulling at small pieces of skin. My stomach biled at the sight of her eyes, tearing at the room, at us and at her absent ex-husband.

'Suze? It's OK, Suze. Of course he'll say that. What does it matter?'

She took a breath and closed her eyes to stop their shredding movements. I felt shaky with the effort of bringing that sound down, of calming the whine which hurt the ears and vibrated in the gut. I glanced at Maud, her half-smile quelling.

'He's changed the locks. Now I can never go back and get my last few books.' She sounded plucked, a defeated little twang, deadened in the air.

'He has a new woman there now. She gives me a lot of trouble. *Ka-cha*, hm-hm-hm-hm-hm.' The reverberating click of Maud's tongue clattered her disapproval into the room. Susan didn't say anything. I could see the tight sinews of her neck.

'What does she look like . . . not as pretty as Susan?' I wanted to give her something, a small present to place in the hands she clutched in her lap.

'Not good, not bad. But clever. A clever woman. Cleverer than you two.'

There was silence. And then I felt the laugh in my chest – foamy laughter, slippery with tension. Susan's burst in small gulps, painfully fighting its way past her throat.

'How on earth do you know that, Maud?' I asked, feeling a second wave of fizzing mirth. 'How can you possibly tell she's cleverer than us?'

Maud was appraising still, her eyes sparking amusement. She didn't join in our laughter.

'I can just see. I can see many things.'

'Maud?' Susan cleared her quavering throat. 'Maud? Please will you tell me what she does there? Will you keep telling me what he says?'

'Yes, I will tell you things. This is my main piecework. I will tell you what is happening with that husband. I will tell you everything.'

# 2

'It's not as if I didn't know, Sister. Though it's what I keep telling people – that I didn't know, and that we married so quickly I hadn't had time to see what he was really like. But I did, Sister.'

I lit two cigarettes in Susan's hung pause, leaning away from her to guard the small flame from the whip of the sea breeze. The sea gleamed at us, its brightness aching behind my eyes. I watched her shift on the hump of rock, pulling her protective arms more tightly about her legs, the wine bottle clasped between her feet.

I remember, oh I remember us there. I can picture our small figures on the hunched Camps Bay rocks – one of us huddled away from herself, from the sight of what she was, and had become. The other, well, I was soaring with the newness of things, with the wild thrill of seagulls. But I hunkered there with her, clustering my defences to hold the flying pieces of her.

She sucked at her cigarette and lifted the wine bottle, her tight little hand darting up to wipe at the rim, first this way, round and round, and then the other.

'Only once or twice, but I did see it before we married. That . . . that sensitive soul of his . . .' Her face twisted its self-deprecation. '. . . it floated away with all the wine, and left only some mean spirit in its place.

'But then, when all that ugliness was gone again, I didn't want to remember it. I thought it couldn't really have been there. It was like a . . . a troll under the bridge that I tried to stop believing in. And . . . and he said his soul had been dried up by all those tough women he'd been with before. He said it was different now – that I had changed him.'

The seagulls whirled and keened their mourning sound. Wisping smoke, Susan's hand clutched itself over her screwed-up eyes, defending them from the sand's cruel white. Not from me. I still

17

don't think – the way we were then – that it could have been from me, although my eyes chased hers, trying to catch and clasp them, to give her my warmth. She needed it, I knew she did, even though she sometimes feigned to find it irksome.

Just a hint of winter was there that morning. I can remember it because summer was still so much with us. But it was there, waiting to be acknowledged, in the tugging edge of cardigan over shirt front, in the cold pull of hair to be free.

I knew how to do this. And I needed it, my part as her defender. When I think of it now, my parts were so disparate, my pieces so scattered. But alongside her, well, she gave me solidity, and a wholeness I didn't really have. I felt that if I could just stand spread-limbed before her, I could prevent her fall.

This was the way it had always been with us, even back in our university days. I remembered that time on the circus ground in Grahamstown, the morning after the circus had left. We had wandered over the trampled grass and elephant droppings, exclaiming over the treasures left by circus-goers, feeling the spirit of the people who had dropped their ticket stubs and the young girl who would not find her sequinned belt when she came to ride her ponies, or fly the trapeze, or . . . We had spoken of all these things, my spirit swelling with the need to hold myself before her fraudulent toughness, to cushion her with my defence. But we had not spoken of the psychology student. We had not mentioned his random cruelty in choosing her to try out his tentative heterosexuality before finding himself, thankful to be gay, in his joyful inability to find her attractive.

But that day on the Camps Bay rocks, at least she was talking. At least she was breathing the pain from her stress-strapped body. Not easily. Words never poured from her as they did from me. She heaved over them, purging her mouth of them, struggling over the quick streams.

'So why did you do it, Sister? Why did you actually marry him?'

'You don't know how many times I've asked myself that, Sister. It was . . . part of it was for him. His art, when he got around to it, was so brilliant compared with my small canvas smears. *Ag* Sister, I don't know why I suddenly saw myself as some handmaiden. But I think it was because I felt so useless, like I didn't have the talent to be an artist in my own right. And . . . and that all I could be was his muse, the protector of his talent. He wanted it all, he wanted my talent. He . . . he wanted to use it for himself.'

I watched a cormorant displaying its wings, waiting for its waterlogged feathers to dry in the morning sun, before it could fly again.

'Are you painting, Suze?'

'I can't . . . I can't paint. But I s'pose he was right. I was selfish too. I wanted to get it easily, that creative satisfaction. I wanted to get it from him. I suppose that means I never did have much talent. I'm a teacher, an art teacher. I can give it to others, but I'm ordinary. I have to remember that, and make an ordinary life for myself.'

I remembered her painted poetry, her huge scrawled canvases. Some were graceless, some sparked with brilliance, but all had the anger and the thread of fiery madness that burnt its narrow lava streak through her. They were never nondescript. Nothing she ever did had ever been vague or even normal.

'You'll paint again. You've never been ordinary. Don't do that to me, Sister. You've always been the exceptional one of the two of us. What have I got to believe in and look after if that's all there is to you? And what does that make me, if even you are ordinary?'

Susan lifted her eyes and twisted her small smile. 'See that ship out there, Stuff-up? Where do you think it's come from? Tell me a story.'

Sometimes I thought Susan couldn't see my swelling goalie spirit. Or it didn't convince her of her safety – as if it were like some inflatable giant, floating and twisting with the buffeting breeze.

'Well, its last port of call was somewhere incredibly exciting and exotic, somewhere where the likes of you and me, with our South African passports, are never likely to see. Perhaps it comes from Zanzibar, and the cabins haven't yet lost the faint whiff of frangipani and cloves. Or from India, carrying pods of cardamom and the waft of coriander. Or, Sister, yes this is it. From Morocco, where a young nomad, prince of the desert, holds his white steed and listens to the wind. He's listening for the wind to tell him his questing sailors have found the two brides he seeks – one fair and pale as the jasmine blossom, the other dark and full of figure, his night and day, his flower

19

and his gypsy. Soon they'll see us here, Sister, through their telescopes, and they'll hurry to find us' . . .

. . . We sat in Crown Street, the shadows falling fast around us, tumbling into the narrow street to escape the glaring sunlight over the roofs. We were sipping wine again, spying – without appearing to – on our neighbours.

We idly watched the old man wander slowly all the way down the street, stop briefly to watch the advertising-satanists, and then come to us. He stood for some time, silently staring at Susan with his head on one side.

'I did have a wife, I did. She left while I was in the desert.' The old man's face, cunning as a manipulative child's, hunched in over its toothless mouth. He put his head on one side, surveying Susan as she sat by my side, her feet bare and scattering sand from our morning on the beach.

'Lily,' he whimpered. 'Li-li-ly.' It built to a wail as we watched, fascinated by his long-fled passion, that 1940s figment of his past, or of his trapped mind. 'She stood here, here in this street, and she waved to me. She said she loved the way a man looked in uniform. She bought me some tobacco and some biltong and she waved to me. *Ja* . . .' He sighed and munched his gums, staring at Susan.

'You look like her. You're pale, just like her. Only you don't have her red mouth. In the western desert, it was hot in the desert, I remembered her red, red mouth while she waved to me. She was smiling.'

'Wasn't she here when you got back, er . . .?'

'Uncle Willie,' supplied Susan, raising her tight, amused eyes from the toes she was picking.

'Gone, go-one, I never again saw that smile. Go-one'

'Wi-llie, Wi-llie!'

'Yes, Mr Kennedy.' The wail had vanished from his voice. He straightened, arms at attention, only his eyes straining sideways to the house next door. The Kennedys' was the first free-standing house after the long terrace.

'Come on now, Willie,' Mr Kennedy's voice came to us from his *stoep*. 'Leave the girls now . . . Just ignore him, ladies, he got the shell-shock in the war. He just walks up and down here talking nonsense . . . You hear, Willie? They don't want to hear your stories. They've got more important things to do' . . .

. . . 'What amazes me,' Neil said, pausing with drinks in both hands, 'is only that someone out there has nothing more important to do with his life than to spend his time seeking out these tramps and *bergies*.' He moved then to hand out the drinks, his eyes concerned and inward, still musing on the sheer profundity of his pronouncement.

'Now you girls . . .' Susan's eyes met mine. Her mouth was all twisted up. '. . . Now you girls know I'm not a racist, but you know there's an element in me that can't totally condemn the man's actions. I mean these *bergies*, they're the very dregs, a drain on society. It's decent people like you and me who bear the cost of these people lying around drinking meths.'

'Jesus, Susan, you know these people?' I said, a wash of ammoniac amusement tincturing my hostility. 'You brought me to dinner with people who think it's OK to shoot *bergies* for kicks? It's just lucky he's not a racist.'

Neil turned to me quizzically, his furrowed forehead struggling to help his brain decide whether I was joking. He reminded me of a child whose earnest, protruding tongue was a necessary aid to rope-climbing. Rope-climbing didn't come naturally either.

'I know, it's humiliating, isn't it?' Susan answered me, two fingers busy at her nails, picking and picking. 'But then I work with his girlfriend. She teaches these wholesome values to well-to-do southern-suburbs children.'

'Oh, you sillies,' Jane cut in. 'You know Neil is only teasing you two because he knows what sort of views you hold. Now don't go taking him seriously and ruining my dinner party, just because some weirdo's been going around shooting the odd vagrant.'

'Five odd vagrants.' I should shut up, I knew I should accept the smoothing of Jane's pastel mouth. I hadn't even really been invited. I came as an added extra because Susan hadn't been able to face coming alone.

I could see why she hadn't been able to refuse the invitation outright, to sneer at Jane's patronizing sweetness. Behind those pinked cheeks and alice-banded hair, a genuine kindness had prompted her to hold a being-nice-to-recently-separated-colleague dinner party. It was a caring that Susan had to face each day in the staffroom. It was hard to turn it aside without seeming ungracious.

21

But anger still burnt at the back of my tongue. I was irritated by the serenity of Jane's ignorantly calm hands, creamed and pink-nailed, as they lay in her lap. And by the pouting of Neil's self-indulgent mouth, the sureness of his grasp on the whisky glass. He turned to face me, his aristocratic head blond and well-cut, his Aran sweater arrogant in its certainty.

'So, you come from the Eastern Cape, do you? I see the foreign press's still stirring it up there since last month's shooting in Uitenhage.' Was he trying to cut free that monstrous fury within me? Or was he just too stupid to see?

'Stirring it up?'

Susan was silent. Her mouth had lost its twist but she was terribly pale against the tiny ooze of blood from the torn cuticle she raised to her mouth.

'Well I just think things are never as bad here as they make them out to be overseas. And overseas people just don't understand our kind of problems. They stir it up when we should just be left alone to sort out our own issues.'

'Oh I see. And how could it be worse, Neil? Genocide? Forty-seven unarmed people were shot by police, for God's sake.'

'Well, the police say they were attacked. And I really don't see why they would shoot if they weren't. It stands to reason. These people are trying to make the country ungovernable. People like you think you're all very liberal, but when the chips are down, if the blacks took over, you'd be the first out the country.'

'Oh, for God's sake, Neil. That's pathetic. Every witness has denied the police version. So, who would you believe?'

'Well, I just don't know . . .'

'Exactly, which is precisely why there's an inquiry being held.'

'And I can't understand . . .' Susan cleared her throat and finally raised her eyes, '. . . how the government expects to continue . . .'

She placed her damaged finger in her lap and tenderly covered it with her other hand. 'I mean, there's protest and fighting in almost every township . . .'

'Oh come on now, you people.' Jane was squirming in her chair now, her blue eyes mixing her unease with something else – excitement, anticipation, something like that. 'I'm just so sick of politics. Can't South Africans talk about anything else? We're fixated. It makes me sick.'

Neil turned to her, his acorn eyes turning musty. Tenderness, I noticed, slackened his chin, which he habitually held in a jutting pout. 'Sorry, Honey-love. This is boring for you. I'm just sounding off to your two radical girlfriends here. What do you want to talk about? What's in that gorgeous head of yours?'

To my slightly repelled fascination, Jane's serenity crumbled into reddened giggling, her pink fingers wriggling before her face, her eyes coyly seeking Neil. 'Don't you notice anything?' She was meaning Susan, surely. What could I possibly notice? I'd never met her before.

'Oh, girls,' she said in mock-schoolteacher exasperation. 'Look at my hand!' She wriggled her fingers in the air before us. 'We're engaged. See my ring?'

'Oh, goodness me.' Her face turned earnest, as she stared from one of us to the other, our faces gripped in immobility by her display. 'Oh, Susan, I do hope I haven't upset you. Oh dear, you're remembering, aren't you. Oh, I'm such a wally. I should have realized. It's so very sad when a marriage can't be saved.'

'I don't think it's sad, I think it's the happiest thing that's happened to her in recent times.'

I don't know why it happens to me. It's as if the froth of gushiness, of too much niceness, has a chemical reaction on my body. It turns me to salt, unmoved and sharp. I can even hear it in my voice, deadened by the weight of statuary.

Jane ignored me and gazed her vacant blue into Susan's blank face. 'You'll meet someone else. You'll be married again soon, I'm sure. A sweet girl like you.'

I glanced at Susan and my throat tore for her. There was always something in her which so badly wanted to fit. I think she felt life would be easier, the air wouldn't breathe so hard into her aching lungs, if she could just be more like Jane. If she could want those things, and nothing more. If she could fence out life, and interior-design it to her specifications.

But I could see the other thing now, which so often made that impossible. I watched it rise from her belly. I wished I could tell her it was all right. I wanted to tell her: it's that wildness in you. That's what draws our two selves to dance their dervish dance – the dance which unsettles people and respects no boundaries.

Well, anyway, that's how we saw ourselves, in those frantic, febrile times. But it wasn't all merely posing. It was there, a part of many of us I think now, a product of our times and of that place.

'I can't marry again.'

I watched Jane's soft chin settling over her bosom as her eyes displayed their look of caring. Susan paused, ripped at a nail, and continued: 'I couldn't be trusted with a nice man. I'd tear the fucker's throat out and munch his intestines for breakfast.'

Her bloodied nails brought a touch of real horror to her wild eyes.

A small gulped giggle from Jane drew the loudness of the room's silence to manageable levels again. 'Really, Susie,' Susan hated the diminutive. She couldn't stand being reduced, made inoffensive by that nickname. 'I never know when you're teasing. Sometimes I wonder if you're being half serious.'

'Dead serious, Jane. Dead, dead serious. But don't worry about it. Congratulations on your engagement. I hope your marriage will be everything you deserve' . . .

. . . We were sitting on the couch. It was the right place for us, sitting in the dark, watching the glow of our cigarettes. We'd always had such ritual places – the *stoep* for wavering hope and cool savouring; the couch, that dull, brown couch for wallowing, for drinking and joints, for serious *dronkverdriet*. We'd bought it in Grahamstown and it had travelled to Cape Town before me, and stayed with her while we had lived apart.

'I suppose it wasn't only that, you know Jen, that made me marry him.'

'No, I know. I suppose I always thought it was all somehow connected to your mother. Wasn't it?'

'*Ja*, I suppose. But in that perverse way that makes both you and me do such idiotic things periodically. You know, I still fear that my mother couldn't love me . . . no, that's not really fair . . . But it's as if she can't see me, as if I'm behind a soundproof screen if I'm not following the accepted path: courting, preparing for marriage, marrying, having children.'

'So how's she coped with the divorce?'

'I suppose remarkably well. She was even supportive in her way. But she's just blotted it out of her mind. It's gone. She still talks about divorcees in that tone of voice. She says it was a mistake and I'm back to square one – virginity restored, and all that. I can begin the game again.'

Susan sounded exhausted. She paused and I watched the burning ember travel upward and its colour flare briefly, before travelling down again.

'But, you know, I'm such a fuck-up. Even though I go and do the right thing periodically, I can't bear to do it properly. I couldn't bear to do it as they did, to surrender to their . . . um . . .'

'Yes, I know. To your parents' type of suburban contentment.'

'Mm, so he was my small rebellion.'

'Well yes, I suppose a several-times divorced alcoholic could be construed as a statement of some kind.' The tips of my spread fingers touched hers on the couch. Susan's voice shook with a small laugh.

'Well, I thought he was romantic. I thought that, at least, that level of intensity could never be boring. I don't think I ever realized how very boring genuine misery is, day after day.'

'Well I understand you. Thousands wouldn't.' We laughed together, allowing the laugh to build and draw tears to our eyes. 'Did you see Jane's face, Sister, when you said that about eating intestines? Oh shit, you're a crazy woman. Oh, I can't bear it, the thought of her, it's just so funny.'

'I know, now she'll steer around me in the staffroom every time I reach too abruptly for my tea.' Susan was gulping, her laugh running out of air at the silent end of each breath.

'And you, Jen?' She recovered at last and we were sniffing, wiping our eyes with our hands. 'Are you looking for a man? For a husband?'

'Well, I don't know. I do want to do the marriage thing, I suppose. But eventually. Not now. I want to be, you know, like a together person first. I want to feel kind of fulfilled first' . . .

. . . The sunlight brought a wakefulness to the workbound train. Breaking through the drowsy shadows, its glimmer touched my window just as we rumbled through Salt River and headed for Woodstock. Warming my cheek and the top of my head, it felt like a benediction from Cape Town. A wanton gift of herself, to mark the morning when I truly felt that this was my place, by acceptance if not by birth. It seemed then that I was the first person to feel this way; the first girl who couldn't pack her soaring desires into her stubby, tomboy home town, and who brought them here to see them swirl about the lightening mountain.

Through the shaking window of the train, I avidly grasped each piece of Cape Town's ragtag mix; its ease of spacious beauty, its blockhouse poverty; its wildness, its black-*doek*ed devoutness; all its cosmopolitan trendies and all of its women whose privation and disappointment were stamped on raisin faces. I was part of them, the business suits, the T-shirts splotched with paint, the way-out ballet skirts, and the old couple who climbed on at Woodstock – I was part of them too. The mark of long-ago Eastern Europe still sealing their speech, they huddled together in crumpled suit and dress. But they had also chosen this place, they too were Capetonians.

From the station I wandered down Adderley Street, tasting the fresh breeze of morning, the sun still random brush strokes over shadowy shapes. I was early, early enough to dawdle at the edge of Parliament, warily watching the gun-strapped police. I was early enough to wander into the main avenue of the Botanical Gardens to watch the striding workers ignore the scurry of squirrels; the arch of oak trees leading to the khaki of mountain solidity behind.

But I knew what I wanted to do. If I wandered up Wale Street I would reach the arched road leading to the Supreme Court. After I had been there, I would find my new place of work. Right now I wanted to absorb the feelings of the court building. With my sanitized life, spirit washed down with detergent respectability, I wanted to take away the building's aura of all the human souls who had been there, the imprint of their stories. I wanted to feel the weight of its symbolism and its power in the life of people.

A crowd was gathered outside the Supreme Court. The sparks of massed excitement flew, embedding itself in the bellies of passers-by. Some, mainly white, saw the dark group, smelt its power, and baulked, hurrying away. Others ran to embrace it. One or two jittery policemen – large Alsatians on leads – inexpertly herded the crowd into a boiling mass while running youngsters and genteel-*doek*ed women still dodged and ducked to join in.

*Boom-boom-boom-boom*

In the midst of the mêlée was a yellow prison van, an indistinguishable mass of dark prisoners just visible through the mesh sides. Beating the vibrating mesh, they were joined by the fearful rhythm of the *toyi-toy*ing crowd in the street.

*Boom-boom-boom-boom*

'Ya-ya-ya-ya-ya', from a hundred joined mouths.

Fingers wormed through the portholes in the mesh, touching those of the people in the street. The police were edgy on their feet, eyes darting to each other and back to the crowd. They allowed their dogs the slack to lunge, and pulled them up short again with strangled snarls. The truck was waiting for the court gates to open, and the police kept glancing at the high, impervious entrance. They could see, and the knowing crowd could see, that they were ill-equipped to deal with any further delay.

*Boom-boom-boom-boom*

'*A-ma-ndla!*' A single cry from a lyrical, heartfelt throat.

'*Awethu!*' The roar of massed response.

I could see the owner of the small corner restaurant across the road fumbling with his doors, shoo-ing his wife inside, pulling them closed with a clank.

'*Ma-yi-buye!*'

This time the police caught sight of the arm, sun-gilded fist rigid at the sky. Two lunged forward, their dogs causing a screaming wave through the crowd. But he was gone, disappeared into the anonymous mass as its deep roar echoed through the arches at the entrance to the street.

'*i'Afrika!*'

The gates swung open suddenly and the truck jerked forward. People scattered from its path while others laid their hands flat on the mesh or stretched fingers through the holes, grabbing at the fingers which scrabbled for a touch of the outside. And then it was gone, the powerful gates swung to against the crowd.

'*Julle mense het tien minute om hierdie straat te verlaat.* All you people, you have ten minutes to disperse or we will take action.'

The sinister hump of a yellow Casspir had drawn up on either side of the crowd. As the policeman growled into his bullhorn, the crowd-body broke up into separate beings, recognizable and human. Some ran, some sauntered, scattering the crumbs of the crowd through the diluting streets.

'Who were they?' I asked two young girls, smiling and chattering still with exhilaration, glancing warily towards the police. They looked at me briefly as though I had flown in from another planet. But they smiled.

'The Kakaza accused. The case's going on again today. It didn't go on this last month again. You're not from here?'

'No, I just moved here over the weekend. But I've read about the case. It's from last year's riots in Langmanskraal, isn't it?'

'Yes. "Oupa" Kakaza. He is a big man to the townships here.

The people love him. He is a leader in the Cape . . .'

What else do I remember after that, about my first day at work? I remember my anticlimactic office, its partitions glassed in on either side of the door. I remember the buff pile of housing-and worker-dispute files passed on from my predecessor. Oh yes, and I remember meeting the dark young partner who headed the firm's new 'public interest' section.

'I'm Philip Wainstein. How d'you do? From the Eastern Cape, are you? Lot going on down there right now, what with the Uitenhage inquiry coming up. Interesting place to be, I'm surprised you've moved here. Oh well . . . I see you've joined in a good month.' He laughed, a raspy gurgle. 'You just begin and on Friday it's Easter. Hope the weather'll be nice for you.

'And I see you've got your files. Heather left you a pile of notes about the cases before she left.' He turned away, but stopped and turned again, his face vague and harassed, his hands spilling papers. 'The Kakaza case's going ahead again. Accused Two, Three, Four and Five are our clients. They're all young guys – of course you know who Accused Number One is? Vuyisile Kakaza, "Oupa" they call him. Clarke-Featherstone are his attorneys. They're overseas-funded of course, as we are. So're the next few accused. The last few have *pro Deo* counsel, a pretty inexperienced guy. But we try to help him a bit where we can.

'Anyway, I did all the preparation. It's a very stop-start affair, but looks like it's going to be a marathon. It's an important trial. I'll want you to do a lot of sitting in. They need an attorney present. Take notes, see where we need to find more witnesses . . . you know the drill. OK then. Ask if you need anything.'

K*alatter kalatter kalatter, kalatter kalatter kalatter skreee-ee-ee*
I waited in the silence after the train. Even the birds had quieted. There it was, the key in the door, the clumping footsteps to the kitchen, the kettle and tea noises.

Susan was already down there. I had heard her taut bounding on the stairs much earlier. I followed her down and found them in the kitchen. Maud was settled solidly on the dining-room chair which seemed now to have moved permanently into the kitchen. I knew we'd never get it together to buy a kitchen chair.

'Morning Maud.'

'Yes, hello Jennifer.'

She slurped her tea – tea bag still in the cup – through her teeth. She was watching me but, with eye movements she could have learnt from our mothers, holding Susan in check at the same time. Her eyes were already avid, her mouth amused. I could see she was ready to talk.

'It's a pity I never have time to chat properly on Tuesdays.' Susan was gulping at a cup of coffee, her book bag clutched under her arm. 'I'll be late for class if I don't leave exactly now.'

She took another gulp and made as if to put the cup down on the central table. But I could see she wouldn't leave.

'*Ag*, Maud, please just tell me quickly, what's been happening over the other side. Just quickly because I must rush.'

'Well, the Greenpoint Madam . . .'

'No, no, I don't have time for her today. I want to know about my ex-husband. Save the Greenpoint Madam for another time.'

'Well . . .' She was teasing, playing Susan along. 'It's all the same. To talk of the one this time, I must talk of the other.'

Susan was instantly arrested, her cup held midway to her lips. Maud turned back to her cup, humming softly.

29

I couldn't bear it. '*Ag* Maud, tell her. What's going on. Who's the Greenpoint Madam?'

'The Greenpoint Madam is my Monday-and-Thursday Madam. She is very beautiful. More beautiful, much more beautiful than you. She has a very good job.'

'Yes but what about her and Susan's ex?'

'She has a much better job than you – beautiful clothes, much nicer than yours. But that husband of hers, *ka-cha* hm-hm-hm-hm-hm!' She shook her head. 'No good, he is no good, that one.'

'No, I'm really going to have to go, Maud. Can't you be quicker?' Susan was edging to the door, still holding her cup. Her eyes were leaping at Maud.

'His mother, she is gone.'

'And the woman? The clever woman?'

'She is gone, but on holiday. She says she is going home to her mother. So after she is gone, that husband he says: "Is this Greenpoint Madam so very beautiful as you say, Maud?" So I tell him: "Hm-hm-hm-hm-hm. Very beautiful." So he says: "Can I have the phone number, Maud?"'

'Jesus, that man is unreal.' Susan sounded amused, but her head was turned away from me, to the front door where she wanted to, but couldn't bear to, escape.

'So I say: "*Ka-cha!* You are no good for her." And I say no. But I leave my book on the hall table, just so.' Her hands squared the shape of her address book on the table. 'When I come back, the book is so.' She shifted her hands diagonally.

'So!' she said, her covetousness spent, her hands satisfied, folded in her lap.

Head down, Susan strode her tense-legged way to the door.

'Bye you guys. I'm late.' She didn't look back. When I turned to Maud, she was fearsome again. Her pride rose with her large body as she stretched her back with her two hands.

'There is a big mess here, you girls have left. There are many plates and glasses on the lounge floor. I cannot bend so far.'

'Jeez, sorry Maud. I'll pick them up quickly. We won't do it again. It was my first weekend, OK? We were celebrating.'

# 3

'Oh Mo-ther. Don't you know anything?'
    I am silent now, as I contemplate them, my blonde-tossed girls with their giggled sighs. They are still such children.
    'Golly you know, even Audrey's mother knows it's OK to go to those clubs.'
    I always marvel at their beautifully rounded vowels, still slightly alien to my South African ear.
    'It's not as if we're going alone you know. What on earth do you think will happen to us?'
    He says it too, in the pact of their father–daughter smiles: Oh, leave them alone. They're just children. But it makes me angry when he says it – as though he is expunging all their responsibility, handing it over for me to lug with the mother goods in my arms – three jerseys, three pairs of shoes, three books, hats, tissues, guilt.
    These days, I find myself gazing at these curious adolescents. If they would let me, I would like to trace their features with my fingers, to search for some part of me, for a trail which leads from what I was, to this life I live now. They are just children, these girls of mine. But somehow, in becoming flesh, they have transmogrified the ghosts of my past and of my youth. Their hope, their truculence, even sometimes their sweetness, drag me increasingly back through it all, from the time I was like they are, to what I am now.
    'I don't really know . . .' I say now. 'I suppose I don't really know what I think, but it's the idea of the two of you, alone at night . . .'
    Big sighs, with confident little hands fluttering upward to lift gouts of blonde hair over collars and down backs.
    'We've to-old you, we will not be . . .'

'OK, OK, you won't be alone, but you're just going with other kids. You'll be without grown-ups, is what I meant. I'm still not sure . . .'

It's amazing how their gestures mirror each other's, and their father's. How often have I watched him lift his thin-fingered hands, just so, and run them through all that barely grey hair? A small display of victory over life, it seems to me, as I watch, and love, and resent the level of certainty it implies. He finds it so easy to be so sure of everything – even of me, with his amused glances and barely affectionate gestures.

'. . . um, perhaps you should ask your father when he comes home. I still don't know . . .'

Both pairs of lips, moulded from their father's peremptory business face, twist in impatience and both pairs of blue eyes, in which I had no part, roll upward.

'Oh Mother, can't you ever make your own decisions?' That's the younger, my baby. 'We want to know now. We need to tell Audrey, you know. Why must Dad always make up your mind for you?'

Because, I feel like saying, he has no apparition of failure to bring doubt to his every decision. You and he act decisively, knowing you have brought your educated minds to bear on the problem, and knowing, just knowing, that you have the God-given, family-provided right to have things turn out just as they should.

Somewhere inside of me, that buoyant identity must still be there. But I suppose I trap it there because I fear it will cause harm. I can't allow that – even if it is just to the established way of things. I have no right, you see. How can I rebel against the run of our lives here, when all I have is the certainty of having failed at the only important thing I was ever called upon to do? They're probably right – these villagers, these neighbours, this family of mine. What good did all that edge-living do me, or those around me? No, they're probably right.

'But really, Mother.' That's my first-born. 'I'm sixteen. What on earth do you imagine will happen to us? Or do you think we'd fall into bad company and go on a murdering spree?' . . .

. . . 'On the 15 and 16 June the accused, together with other persons, assembled at various times in the Roman Catholic Church and the

*Kumalo School and various other places in the area of the Langmansk-raal Squatter Camp. Many schoolchildren were present since they had been told to attend meetings in honour of the anniversary of the June 16 uprising of 1976. After several speeches had been made, the accused, together with other persons, proceeded to Langmanskraal Road. During the course of the day many vehicles were stoned or set alight; petrol bombs had also been manufactured. The South African Police on many occasions instructed the crowds to disperse and also they fired tear gas at the crowds. However, as soon as the gas lifted, the crowds gathered again. Upon arriving at Langmanskraal Road, they placed tree stumps, car tyres and other objects across the road, thereby impeding the free flow of traffic; various cars were stoned and at about 16h40 on 16 June the first deceased, Mr Cahill, was stopped at the barricade. His car was stoned and set alight and he was assaulted; he died of his injuries. A short time later Mr Lodewyk's car was stopped. It was stoned and set alight and he was stabbed; he died of his injuries. The stoning of cars continued that day and the next. Police vehicles patrolling the area were also stoned.'*

'Weren't we at university together?' She interrupted my reading. Still lost in the case summary, I gazed at her blankly a minute.

'What're you doing here? I see you've got the Kakaza papers with you.'

Too early still for the trial, I was leaning against the pillar at the edge of the Supreme Court steps. I had come here to read the court papers, needing the salt-laden breeze to freshen the burgeoning heat of morning.

'Yes,' I said. 'You did journalism.' I felt a trickle of wariness, a sudden defensive shuttering of my hopeful self – recalling how every conversation I had ever had with her had brought intimations of my own stupidity.

Her clothes still drooped their second-hand status, as they always had. And her scuffed shoes, on feet mapped by dryness, were handmade leather.

'Yes,' she said. 'I'm covering the Kakaza case for the *Cape Times*. I'm the Supreme Court reporter actually, but the Kakaza case is the most important thing going on right now. Jilly, Jenny, Joey ... What's your name again?'

'Jennifer. And you're Ilsa. Impossible to shorten, isn't it?'

'So you're the new attorney? Well, don't get so hung up on all the legal crap ...' Ilsa lengthened and snorted the word 'legal',

'. . . that you don't recognize the immense, like, significance of the case for the community.'

We were walking into the building together, I clutching my papers to my chest to protect myself from her cleverness and her scorn. 'Well no, of course it's an important trial . . .' I stopped and turned to wait for her beyond the security-entrance checkpoint.

*Be-eep*

She was turned back by the woman in charge of the metal detector. She clunked her keys down and walked through again.

*Be-eep*

'Oh for God's sake, you see me here every morning. What do you think I've got stuck up my jack? An AK-47?'

The woman did not shift her pebble face.

'*Gaan weer deur asseblief.*'

'It's probably my loop, you know that?' A young advocate behind her blushed and ducked his head. But he was smiling.

This time she didn't beep.

'*Ja*, so what were we saying?' she asked.

'Yes, I said I know it's important. And it's legally interesting too. It's just that . . . well, I wish that what my clients did wasn't quite so awful. It's just . . . it's not so easy to deal with.'

'God,' she said, halting her stride. Her blue eyes were incredulous, rather exaggeratedly so, I thought. 'I always thought you were a liberal.'

I flinched inwardly and felt the rise of colour to my face. I always opened my mouth, didn't I? Words always gushed straight from my troubled brow, before I could form a measured, Marxist response. She put her hand on my arm. I could see the lecture forming behind her eyes.

'You can't make an omelette without breaking eggs, you know – or did you think there was another way?'

'No . . .' I trailed behind her as she turned and strode through the domed foyer. 'I know that. It's . . .' I knew I should shut up, but out it poured. '. . . I suppose it's just the individuals I can't help thinking about.'

I knew what she'd say next. I just knew it. God, couldn't I ever keep my mouth shut?

'Those white guys were victims of the Struggle – not of the individuals. It's tough . . . it's just one of those tough things . . .

And those young black guys, they're the arm of the Struggle. You can't go seeing them ... God, but you are a liberal, aren't you?'

Ilsa stopped briefly at the double-sided doors of the courtroom. Turning, she allowed her certainty to press her point home to my evasive eyes. Then she swung around, shoving at the doors to enter before me.

Panelled with dark solemnity, the courtroom breathed with the life of my new existence, the one I would find here. It stirred with a depth of human experience I was greedy for.

I could never express myself to people like Ilsa, who always managed to intimidate me into shambling incoherence. I wished I could have told her that, in fact, I did understand the anger. I even thought I understood the violence. But for me it could never be a broken egg.

I had to shift things in my mind before I entered that courtroom. I remember so well how I rearranged my small-town values to make room for those accused. I had never even seen them, but I shifted busily, redecorating and dusting off old ideas, chucking out what could never fit the new scheme of things.

As I passed through the double doors, I began to see them haloed by dragon battle. I so badly wanted to believe in the formula. That, fired by the violence and vilification they had seen, they had become what they were now – heroic young men, with tragic eyes, battling the system and brutish cops. I needed it, if my teetering arrangement of acceptance were to hold.

How young I was. How hurtingly young. In going back over it all, I find that I must remember these things very gently, so as to avoid bruising the tender flesh, of my memories at least.

'Is this my new attorney? Thank you, thank you God, or Philip Wainstein I should say.' The young advocate was big and dark. He hitched his black robe up higher on to his shoulders and moved towards me, scrunching his face into a grin.

'You're supposed to appreciate her for her skills, you know,' a tousled blonde advocate threw over his shoulder.

The dark one broke into raucous laughter, and stretched out his right hand. 'You think I don't? I can see how skilled and organized she is. And besides . . .' he said this to me '. . . you have nicer legs than Philip. No, seriously though, we're very pleased to have you. You'll brighten our lives during the interminable

35

trials-within-trials which seem to pop up every few weeks. I'm Jeff Halloran.'

'Jennifer Pringle' . . .

. . . The boy knuckled his face, streaking tears and snot across his cheek. The old man beside him addressed a quick stream of Xhosa at him before turning his gaze, serene and dignified, back to the coat of arms above the judge's Bench. A large man in a safari suit, a wodge of dark hair flopping to his eyebrows, turned then and frowned.

'Hey, Halloran. Can't you take care of your own accused? Can't you see the boy's distressed?'

Halloran turned, emerging from the row of black-backed advocates, scuffling with papers. He struggled to stand, dropping files, and pushed towards the aisle. I stood too, but hung back, uncertain.

The safari-suited man was there before Halloran or I could reach the accused benches. 'What is it, china? Hey, come on Jackson. What's the deal? Come on, you guys. Help me out here. What's his case?'

'The boy says he is ill, Big Baas.'

'*Ag* come on now, Oupa. I thought we were finished with this "Big Baas" shit. Knock it off, man.'

The old man never shifted his eyes from the coat of arms. But his mouth turned up at the corners and his body stirred with a tremor of silent laughter.

'You'd better ask for another postponement, Jeff,' said the figure in the safari suit. 'I'd better cart the kid off to the hospital. Oh, by the way, who's this addition to the team?'

'Oh, let me introduce you. Jennifer Pringle. Jennifer, this is Captain John Muller, investigating officer, giant of the CID' . . .

. . . I was leaning against the wall swirling my glass of cheap red wine. Susan was cooking – something she did occasionally when she wanted to feel homely.

'So,' she said, turning her frilled apron to face me, 'How was your day, dear?'

I laughed. 'OK. Oh . . . you know who I bumped into? Ilsa.'

'Ilsa . . .'

'Don't you remember? Yes, you do, Sister. She was the one who gave us hell that time, for handing out money to beggars.'

'Oh, you mean old "liberal guilt won't transform society" Ilsa?'

'The one. The very one.'

'And she spoke to you? I'm amazed, enthralled.'

'Well, I suppose it was a tough job, but somebody had to do it. She felt she had to lecture me on the significance of the Kakaza trial.'

'Oh, fuck her! I hope you suggested she stage one of her little feminist walkouts – right out of your sight.'

'Of course, O Brave One . . . just like you would've done, I'm sure.'

She went on stirring busily, her hair pulled back from her face, her teaching clothes protected by the apron.

'Don't for one minute ever think that I'm as intimidated by the heavy Left as you are. I never had quite the romantic vision of them that you did. And I know very well that, if they'd have you, it wouldn't matter a fuck how elitist and exclusionary they've been to people like us, you'd jump and grovel at the chance.'

Her words trailed into the bathroom as she disappeared to wash her hands. When she reappeared I could see her 'uncomfortable' signs returning. Shaking her damp wrists, she strode to the table, her movements jerkier than they had been. She had looked quite soft earlier, watercoloured with the serene wash of respectability.

'Oh,' I said, 'And of course you wouldn't!'

She shrugged. 'You know we've never been ascetic enough to fit in with them. We'd never be able to give enough time and effort to agonizing – even if you've never quite faced that. We could never sustain it – we'd always trail off into drugs, sex and rock 'n' roll after a while . . . not to mention drink.' She lifted her glass and swigged exaggeratedly.

I stuck my finger into the bowl she was stirring. Without looking up, she cracked the spoon down on my knuckles. I laughed and held my injured fingers, trying not to show that she'd really hurt me.

'Actually, I think it worked the other way round,' I said. 'I think we were always kind of hedonistic because of the rattle inside us. In a way, I think it's because we could see no place for ourselves.'

'Oh for God's sake. Speak for yourself. I don't rattle.'

'You?' I laughed and wrestled the spoon from her savage grasp. 'You rattle more than anyone I know.' I slowly and deliberately licked the sauce from the spoon as she swatted ineffectually at my head, trying not to look irritated and, dare I suggest it, rattled.

'And you?' she said. 'I couldn't believe you were for real when I first met you. Such a precious little child – you pictured yourself on the barricades, demonstrating away apartheid. And then, shamepies, you discovered it was more complicated than that. And you tried desperately to memorize famous French communists. Pathetic!'

I aimed a couple of light kicks at the aluminium table leg. I knew this was my role as defender of Susan's soul. We both knew when her jerkiness had reached the point, usually the gentle point, when it became necessary for us both to turn on me. Then our mutual mocking of my eccentricities and my idiocies would be used to calm her.

But sometimes she took it further than our ritual token. Sometimes I wished she'd shut up. I knew, though, that if I were to show my hurt, it would take her by surprise. She believed so little in herself, she used to say, that she never expected anyone to take her acid words to damaged heart.

'Well,' I said, a poised petulance there in my lower lip, 'I wasn't always so intimidated, actually. And I did get involved in things once.'

'You mean, you grovelled to the heavies and threw out the names of dead theorists . . .'

'It wasn't like that. You know there were one or two projects I really tried to be involved in. But the thing is, I always felt left out. Like we were doing this stuff, but they always seemed to be doing more – more than I could be trusted to know about.'

'Well, what did you really expect? You've even got the face of a liberal, dear Stuff-up. No matter how you try and try to be a Marxist, you'll always say the wrong thing and get purged.'

'Oh, excruciatingly funny.'

She was still laughing at me, but it was gentler now, with a fondness there in her mocking.

She paused and then added: 'God, but you found it all so rousing, didn't you just.'

Her teasing had become bearable again. It was aimed, really, at both of us and only partly at the ranks of the Left. We knew ourselves well enough to recognize – with a rather forgiving self-irony – how much we revelled in passionate sloganeering.

'Well,' she continued. 'You're really going to love this place. Obs even has a street committee.'

'How come? I thought you only got them in the townships?'

'*Ja* man, but this is Obs, you know. Well, actually, it's called an Action Group. They hold house meetings, in the street one down from here . . . By the way, have you still got your Che Guevara poster?'

'No.' I laughed now, in the warmth of her quizzical gaze. 'I wasn't sure it would be cool here.'

'Well,' she said. 'I'm surprised that that would even have registered with you, Stuff-up.'

'Anyway, my poster doesn't have quite the same appeal when I can't horrify my mother with it' . . .

. . . I remember it all now, as I sit by my window watching the thick grey pelt of the sky leak its moistness.

My girls have gone out, flouncing from the house in teenaged turmoil. They blame me, I suppose, for the guilt they feel, despite themselves, about leaving me alone here. And they rebel against having to feel it at all. I can feel their reproaches over the fact that I have so little of substance to occupy me, besides them. And so it passes on, from generation to generation – as I blamed my mother, when I was young, for having no intensity to hand me in the sunlit shallows of our small town.

But it was that year which taught me that searching for life could be dangerous. I learnt then that it was safer in the long run just to hide behind the lives of others.

I remember that, instead of holding my watchful gaze on my own existence, all my attention was fixed on those courtbound boys. That first week in which I saw the Kakaza accused, I wished to suck the vicarious juice of their experience; to soak up their lives. I should have taken care of my own . . .

. . . 'Mr Halloran, I see that Accused Number Two is back among us. Can I take this as a sign that you are ready to continue again?'

'Yes, My Lord. The accused is better now.'

'And what seemed to be the problem, Mr Halloran?'

'Well, My Lord, he complained of severe abdominal pains on Tuesday and he was taken to Somerset Hospital. It seems, according to the hospital report, that he was suffering from a hysterical reaction brought on by the stress of the court case.'

'Well, I'm certainly pleased we can get going again. Mr Erasmus, please call the State's next witness.'

'Certainly My Lord,' said the prosecutor. 'And I'm sorry that Accused Number Two's delicate sensibilities seem to be so upset by these allegations that he committed murder and conspired to overthrow the State. He must be a very sensitive soul, as I'm sure the evidence will show.'

'That is quite enough, Mr Erasmus. Please call your witness.'

'Yes, My Lord. As your Lordship pleases. I call Agnes Twako. And we will need the services of the court interpreter.'

The interpreter rose and, tugging at his gaping jacket, placed himself alongside the frightened young woman. His self-important stomach strained against the buttons of his shirt as he led her through the oath, her quiet voice shaking, her eyes darting around the room – to the roof, the floor, to the accused and quickly back to the roof.

'Please tell the Court where you live?'

'*Uhlala phi*?' the interpreter said, his bored eyes on the back of the courtroom, his arms folded. He did not turn to the young girl as her tentative voice paused.

'I live in Langmanskraal Squatter Camp,' his voice reported.

'Please tell us about the afternoon of June the sixteenth, the afternoon in question.'

'I was walking towards Langmanskraal Road. My mother asked me to buy milk for the baby.'

'And then what happened?'

'And then I heard the singing. I heard there were freedom songs, so I went to see.'

'And then, Miss Twako?'

'So then, when I saw the crowd, I joined it and we walked down Langmanskraal Road.'

'In this crowd, did you see any of the accused that are here in this courtroom today?'

'Yes, some of these accused were there in the crowd that day.' Her eyes came to rest, finally, on the rows of boys and men. The old man sat, as always, with a half-smile, his eyes fixed somewhere over the judge's head. The woman stared at them before jabbing her finger again and again.

'Let the record show that the witness has indicated Accused

Number Two, Number Five, Number Fourteen, Number Fifteen and Number Seventeen. And then what happened, Miss Twako?'

'And then a car driven by a white man was stopped. The people in the crowd, they threw stones at the car. The white man tried to go back but too many people were behind. He could not go forward. Big pieces of branches and old tyres were in the road.'

'And then? Could you see what happened next?'

'Yes, then I could see the people in the street push the car. And the car was rocking and rocking. And then they pushed it over on its roof. I heard the boys shout that the white man must get out the car, but he did not come out. He stayed in the car.'

'And then?'

'And then the car was lit with a match.'

'Did you see who set the car alight?'

'Yes. I know him from school. Jackson Langa. Accused Number Two.'

'And then? Did you see any more?'

'Then I couldn't see for the pushing crowds in front of me. And then suddenly I could see again. I could see the white man sitting in a pool of water in the road. He was splashing water, trying to put the flames out on his body.'

'Orderly, could you take this photograph to the witness, please? Miss Twako, is this the white man you saw that day?'

She nodded. Her hands were fluttering about her face, and I caught the glint of tears, runnelling beside her nose. She used the back of one hand to rub at her cheeks and across her eyes.

'Could you please answer the question for the record, Miss Twako.'

Her small voice murmured. 'The witness has answered yes, My Lord,' the interpreter said.

'She said: "Yes, that is the man".' His arms still folded, he was gazing at the door at the back of the courtroom.

'Thank you, Miss Twako. That is all.'

'We will now take the tea adjournment before the cross-examination of this witness,' the judge muttered, closing his notebook and rising.

I remember the feel of my leaden legs as I pressed the pins and needles from my ankles. I felt submerged, caught in the wash of her story. I watched her leave the witness stand and stumble

41

slightly. But she seemed unreal to me, like the spectre of a past horror, appeared here before us.

The advocates rose, chatting and laughing among themselves. I caught pieces of their separate conversations, but in scattered, broken shards.

'So where did you stay in Arniston?'

'And so I said to the old fart: "My Lord, I am indebted to Your Lordship for Your Lordship's input." '

But beyond them I caught sight suddenly of the dark, bent head of the young advocate, the inexperienced one who was acting *pro Deo*. He was scribbling on his yellow pad, his intensity evident in the whirlpooling of hair about his head.

Alerted perhaps by my gaze, his head jerked up and he stared through me. Then, with a small twitch, he brought his eyes up short to meet mine. And he smiled. I watched him drop his pen and bring both hands up to rub viciously at his face, through his hair and scour at his nose – to take, I thought suddenly, the smell of that death from his body . . .

. . . The bodies lay strewn, spreadeagled in careless heaps across the square. We had been walking, he and I, in search of lunch when we saw them.

His name was François and he was that peculiarly Cape-bred creature – the left-wing Afrikaner with Huguenot ancestors, and utterly French cultural sensibilities.

We'd gone through all the conversation-markers of a first walk together. The 'How long have you been at the Bar?' and the 'Are you new to Cape Town?' and the 'What do you think of the accused?'

As we reached Greenmarket Square we saw the blood-smeared clothing and splayed limbs.

And then we heard the laughter from the mix of humanity standing around the cobbled square. The bodies were dummies, skilfully blooded and displayed in awkward death.

'What's going on?' I asked the paint-spattered boys and girls leaning on lamp-posts and laughing with proprietary ease.

'We're from the art school,' a dungareed girl told me. 'It's Guerrilla Art.' I smiled at her. Warmed to expand, she became animated, talking with her thin fingers and vibrant face. 'We believe art should also be relevant, like involved in the socio-political sphere. We're, you know, protesting against the shooting of all those people in Uitenhage. Last month. It's to mark the start of the judicial inquiry this week.'

A police van tore to a halt, scattering the languid crowd. The art students quietly mixed in with the amused gatherers.

'Who is responsible for this?' The policeman shouted through his bullhorn. No one replied, but laughter rustled through the crowd. '*Dis nie 'n grap nie*. This is not amusing. This is a waste of police time. The persons responsible should now come and clear this up, you hear!'

United beyond their differences, the crowd took courage from each other, glancing into the faces of others, feeling the common joke against a common enemy. Tentatively, they touched each other's humanity beneath the dark and the light skins, the ragged and the designer clothing. They nodded to each other, shaking with uncomplicated mirth.

The policeman lost his cool. He strode from his van, slapping his rubber baton against his thigh. François, wanting to join in with the crowd, but unable to step too far beyond his intensity, smiled and ran his fingers through his already disordered hair.

'Jesus, I hope he doesn't now create an incident here. That would be typical of the bloody *boere*.'

The policeman made a tentative swipe with his baton but the laughing groups tilted their bodies from his fury. He bent and manhandled one of the dummies, but was eluded by her impassivity. The crowd roared, urchins ducking through the gathered legs to catch a glimpse of the *boere* humiliating themselves. The policeman, his teeth gritted, bent and grabbed at her again, but dropped her in confusion as the hilarity became tinged with hysteria – at the sight of a policeman grabbing at a dummy's breasts.

'*Ja*, so take one of those home with you and give your wife a rest.'

The wicked lilt of Cape speech gave added mischief to the comment. The policeman, a trickle of sweat making its way from under his hat, stared into the crowd to locate the offender. Beside me, a woman in a sweating, flowered dress shook with ribald laughter. She slapped my shoulder, before turning again to the bending figure:

'If you can't come right with a dummy, *hoe gat jy regkom met a ware dol*? *Ag ja*, that's how his mummy looked when she made him. That's why he's such a dummy. She suits you, *Konstabel*. You make a lovely couple.'

His eyes furious, the policeman caught sight of her and made a small rush towards us, his baton raised. The woman shrieked and, still laughing, the crowd melted her into their midst.

'*Jou ma se moer*,' yelled someone from the other side of the crowd and the policeman whirled. Then, seeming to see the futility of his humiliation, he strode to the van and slammed himself into the cab. Revving wildly, he reversed over the slippery cobbles, spattering small stones. And he was gone. The laughter drifted into the colonial stolidity of the square and languidly floated away. The crowd, like the melting of ice cubes, trickled slowly away from its solid centre.

'That was incredible, hey François?'

'You must be from the Eastern Cape,' he said, smiling suddenly, and I heard the tell-tale echo of my pitched accent.

'*Ja*, and you?'

'I'm from here. But I've spent a lot of time in the Eastern Cape. I was an activist there for some years, you know; did some important work and narrowly missed getting detained. That's why I finally came back.'

In my momentary cringe, I felt the approach of distant disappointment, waiting to pounce on my expectations of him. Surely there must be some irony hidden in there somewhere.

'Oh, OK. But you grew up here, did you?' I asked him.

'*Ja*, my mother's Marie de Villiers.'

'The political writer? Wow.' I felt the disappointment recede slightly, its batwings furled. 'What does your father do? I've always wondered about your mother.'

'My father left us when we were little. I suppose that's why I'm more comfortable with women, really. I've always admired my mother for her strength – I really have empathy with women.' I felt the dark shape fade still further into the distance. We walked in silence a while.

'Have you seen Cape Town from the mountain yet?' he asked.

'Well, yes, when I was little we came here and went up the cable car.'

'No, I mean at night?'

'No, I haven't. I suppose it must be something.'

'There is something so incredibly spectacular about this place at night, it's almost unreal' . . .

. . . The night sky lay thick with stars and the damp smell of salt. Susan's date was late, not outrageously so, but enough to tempt us into the wickedness of a quickly rolled joint on the *stoep*, its smoke wisping into the dangerous outside air.

'He thinks I'm incredibly straight, you know. Like some kind of Miss Priss.' She said this with a hint of wild challenge, and I got an inkling of why she had suggested the joint.

'Well, most people do when they first meet us. I suppose it's because we don't project ourselves according to stereotype. We don't even dress as misfits . . .'

We often played this game of deadpan self-irony. We both revelled in it, and in our half-serious image of ourselves. '. . . I suppose that's an element of our madness, an extreme form of sociopathy – that we care so little, we don't even care to be recognized by other misfits.'

The laughter bubbled in us and danced in starbursts about our heads.

'But you know,' she paused while I used my insignificant nails to hold the roach to her lips. No matter how insignificant mine were, they were always better for holding roaches than her battered fingertips. 'You know, I've discovered people go through a process with us. At first they classify us as dweets, and they treat us accordingly.'

I could feel the night sky whirling, the profundity of our lives and our hopes swirling there about the *stoep* and the chimney pots over the road.

'And then,' she continued. For a moment, it seemed so long since she'd spoken that I couldn't recall what we were talking about. But I remembered as she went on. 'And then they get that bewildered look and don't quite know how to treat us. And then it dawns on them, we're not dweets, we're just certifiable.

'There's someone who teaches with me, you know? For a long time, I could see she thought me really straight. But every time I commented on something she got that perplexed look. Then one day, she turned to me and said: "My God, you're really sick, you know!" And she said it with such intensity and relish.'

We were laughing wildly when his car drew up and he wound

down his window. He had a nice face. Too nice for Susan. Or for me, I suppose. He had those acceptable-to-mother looks. Thin blond hair, nicely cut and spread evenly over his scalp. Firm chin. A touch of the effete about his polo shirt and pale blue eyes.

'Well, this is a jolly sight. You must be Jennifer. How do you do. I'm Jonathan. Are you two ready for the fireworks? I believe they're going to be quite spectacular – they always are for the Cape Town Festival. Isn't it a nice way to start the Easter holidays.'

We drove to Sea Point and had to park miles from the fireworks. There seemed to be hundreds and hundreds of cars, parked everywhere. Wandering along the seafront, we watched the dark-nosed kelp treading water and nudging each other. I was glancing at Susan, watching her struggle with the part of herself which so longed to be taken home to his mother. Against it was pitted the fiendish fighter, her dark creativity which tugged and fought to be free, and to fly against all the prevailing winds which tried to drag it down.

We watched the fireworks smear across the star-struck sky, jolting through our bodies with sharp retorts. Jonathan stood protectively by, defending us from elbows and guarding us from assaults against our virtue. I watched Susan wrestle, her small face white against the black of the sky. I watched her want that, longing to sink into his easy hands. But I watched her begin to feel the crush of them on her exotic wings. And as the last spattering flowers fired across the sky, I heard her whisper and felt her cold fingers on my palm.

'Let's swim.'

'Are you mad?'

'Yes, oh yes. Let's swim.'

'Naked?'

'Of course. How else?'

And we ran, our laughter wisping and dancing about us in the wind. We left Jonathan standing, his brow perplexed, his protective spirit anxious. He took a few running steps after us, but remained on the promenade as we discovered some furtive, dark stairs to the rock-filled beach.

We felt our bodies wild and silver as we shucked our clothes. Smeared with moonlight, we shrieked and clutched at each other, dodging the salt spray which stung the eyes and iced the nipples. We could smell the fecund musk of the drying kelp, and that of our own wildness.

*Kalatter kalatter kalatter, kalatter kalatter kalatter skreee-ee-ee*
K The train cut through my sleep, bursting its brazen presence into the quiet. I waited, trying not to move my head on the pillow.

Crash. I winced at the slam of the front door, and each crushing step she took towards the kitchen. I lay a while trying to doze, but I could hear the kettle and tea noises. I listened to the shuffle of Susan getting out of bed and digging under the pile of clothes on her desk for her dressing gown. I gave in and, trying to hold my flinching head steady, descended the stairs very gently, and with great dignity.

Susan already had two cups out. She was spooning coffee carefully, steadying the tremor with her other hand. Maud was ignoring us, slurping her tea, her eyes furious with dignity. She was staring through the window into the blinding white of the kitchen courtyard.

'Morning Maud,' I tried tentatively. She grunted.

*Ka-cha.* Her click resonated disapproval across the room. I joined Susan in the safety of our solidarity over the coffee bottle. Susan pulled her mouth down in an expression of terror.

'The attack of Maudilla the Hun,' she muttered, but very quietly. My giggle was hardly noticeable, just the smallest sound of breath escaping.

'Are you angry with us, Maud?'

*Ka-cha*

'Well, you'd better tell us,' I said. 'I can't bear the tension any longer. What have we done?'

Susan had lit two cigarettes and she placed one now, with shaky fingers, into my hand.

'*Ka-cha.* The lounge. I never see such a mess. Never! Food and plates, lying on the floor. Empty wine bottles dripping on the carpet, and the smell of wine all about. And the smell of the smoke. And – *ka-cha* – I know what is there. Hm-hm-hm-hm-hm.'

'Ah, jeez Maud. Sorry, hey. Look, don't you worry about the lounge. We'll clean it up later. It was a holiday yesterday, you know? We just didn't feel like going out.'

'Good Friday is a holiday for Jesus. Not for drinking all that wine. And I know what else there is. I know the smell of *dagga*. I see those big ashtrays. I have sniffed at them. I know it is *dagga* in that ashtray, in all those *stompies*.'

We began to shake with giggles at the thought of Maud, so unyielding in her gravity, bending at the waist to sniff at ashtrays. Susan mimed her sniffing, with pulled-up nose, behind her chair.

Despite our shakiness, I remember that we felt very bold that morning; intrepid in our role as batterers at boundaries. Over our coffee, we exchanged the collusive glances of our rebellion, allowing Maud to catch just a glint of them. That was much of our pleasure in it, after all – the brazening of our ritual wickedness before all the mother figures in our lives.

Maud was silent, her gaze stolid in its disapproval, eyes holding the injured dignity of suspected mockery. She turned away from us, to the sink.

'Oh Maud,' I said, appealing to her stiff back. 'Oh, please forgive us – come on. We had a bad night on Thursday night. We were up late and Susan's new boyfriend was cross with her. We just wanted to sit in here all day and froust. We couldn't bear the thought of going out and being healthy.'

I watched her back relent slightly. She sat in silence, slurping at her milky tea.

'OK, I will tell you about your husband,' she said at last. And when she turned, the transformation had taken place. Her body had slumped out of its rigid form and been taken over by that other, sly spirit.

'On Wednesday, I go there, to his house like usual. But he is very strange. "Morning Maud," he says, but he is smiling. He is never usually smiling in the morning. Usually he is like this.' She put her head into her two spread hands and groaned. '*Ja*, like you two this morning.'

We smiled but neither of us spoke. I wondered if Maud could feel Susan's flying-apart tension beneath the giggles she had mustered since I had joined her in this house. I watched her anxiously and saw Maud's eyes flicker over her. Of course she knew. That was part of the peephole charm of our lives for her, and part of her mastery.

'I see he is looking at me, as if to say he is cleverer than me. As if he thinks he can get the better of old Maud. So I go up, quietly, quietly, up the stairs. And I look in his bed and I smell at the pillow, and I can smell the Greenpoint Madam's perfume. She lets me use it sometimes. It says Channel.'

'Yes, she would have Chanel.' Susan's lips were bloodless from the hold of her teeth. Trying to draw her into comforting sneers at the Greenpoint Madam's expense, I was throwing her a lifeline. But she would take it only if she felt like it. Sometimes she would prefer to go under, again and again, losing her breath, her heart and her hope.

'You don't have nice perfume for me to use like that.'

'No, but then we don't have the kind of charms that get us bought stuff like that – and while she's married *nogal*.' Susan was still ignoring my desperate line. But then I saw her small shake, like a dog from water.

'*Ja*, she certainly sounds like a nice virtuous woman, Maud. Just the sort you would approve of, especially in the week of Good Friday.'

Maud turned slowly to Susan. *Ka-cha*. 'That Greenpoint Madam's husband hm-hm-hm-hm-hm. He is no good. On Thursday he comes home again with his friends. He is drunk, while the Greenpoint Madam must be out at work. "Help, Maud help!" they call to me. I say *ka-cha*: "I will not help you. He is drunk." But they cannot manage. So then I take him like this . . .' She stood and gestured, with her rough hands, the grabbing of his shoulders, '. . . And I throw him on the bed. "Maud, Maud, I am thirsty," he says, but I get him nothing.'

'You're cruel, hey Maud?'

'Cruel! Ha! He is no good, that one. No good for the Greenpoint Madam. But your husband, he is also no good for her.'

'So, did you say anything to him?'

'So I say, "Hm-hm-hm-hm-hm. You like the Greenpoint Madam?" So he says: "Sh, sh, Maud." ' She mimed their conspiracy, her eyes darting to and fro. 'He says: "Maud, a man must be free to find himself – especially after that frigid thing I was married to." '

49

Susan did not move, but in my gut I could feel her inward flinch. I couldn't touch her. She would have hated that, despised its intimation of pity. But inside, I grew great abounding arms and wrapped them around her. There was nothing else I could do. I didn't know how to make Maud stop. And if I had, Susan would just have told her to continue. She was determined to hear everything, no matter how each word slashed at her.

'So your husband he says to me: "Maud, this is our secret, hey?" He says: "You mustn't tell the Greenpoint Madam's husband." And I say: "*Ka-cha*. That one. He is no good. I say nothing to him." So he says, "Good. And Maud, you mustn't tell that ex-wife of mine, or my girlfriend, when she comes home."

'So, when he says that, I say nothing.'

# 4

His stomach lay gently rounded, the flaccid belly of a small child, held uncaringly loose before him. Tenderly, he cradled it in his arms.

It was all gone. In just those insignificant few minutes in the early hours, it had disappeared – the grail we had sought through the charged evening, twining our hands and our fantasies, joining our mouths to taste the shivering sweetness of anticipated touch.

François had fetched me in the dusk-deadened street and driven me away.

'It's a surprise,' he told me, and flung his quick one-sided smile over at me. 'We're not going anywhere usual.'

But I knew. As we turned up Kloofnek Drive, I knew. His gift to me that evening, our first date, was the heartbeat of my girlish romance. Frail from frequent flight, it was still alive that night, as we headed for the foot of the moon-fed precipice. We were going up the mountain.

The spirit of his offering seemed almost feminine in its subtlety. And at that moment, I hoped. The warmth of it mingled in my mouth with the taste of stirring excitement so that, as he parked, I leant across and gently kissed his gaunt, serious cheek.

The cable car, jostling with couples, lifted us through the dark. François placed an arm about my shoulders as the breeze chilled the ears and teared the eyes. And below us, far beneath, a skein of silver wandered across the water toward the lights, which glimmered and flickered in life-affirming miniature.

We ate dinner in the stone and thatch restaurant. And we talked – but it was of the Kakaza trial. I felt the inappropriateness of bringing the flame of those deaths into this place, but François, so sensitive in gesture, seemed unable to let go of his taut and serious hold on the world.

51

'Well, I have to somehow deal with the common purpose aspect. My guys were just part of the crowd.'

He paused to pour me some Cabernet, and silently watched me take my first sip. He had frowned to make the choice of wine, conscious in his feline way of every signal, every unspoken marker to match tonight's carefully placed stars and delicately arranged dusting of lights beneath the mountain.

'Well, what're their versions?' I asked. 'I bet they weren't even there. Haven't they all developed sick mothers and aunties who required urgent visiting on that day?'

He smiled his lopsided grin. I was going along with him only because of my hopes of him and because I liked him. I wanted to talk of nothing, of the stars and the sea. I wanted to begin the tentative display of dreams and fears, of loves and hates. I wanted to touch the person he was, beneath the lean asceticism. But I still had the need to impress that little bit, to show I could match him, conversation for conversation. I competed with him stride for stride, fearing to repel him with my feckless side.

'I think most of them will be placed at the scene by the State witnesses. And, as you know, there's precedent in other political trials for convictions of murder on the basis of the common purpose of the mob. They've got an even easier job proving Terrorism. All you have to do is sing a few freedom songs, raise a few fists, and *voilà*!'

I was dying for a cigarette. But I saw no sign of cigarettes about him, no agitation of fingers at pockets, no bulge under his jersey. I ran my fingers through my hair and fiddled with the salt cellars, building small towers and dismantling them again.

'So what do you intend to do?' I asked. 'I'm sure you'll be able to shake a few witnesses in cross-examination?'

'*Ja*, it's a possibility. But I also have to attack the common purpose idea – show they were caught up somehow, that they weren't really intent on murder and mayhem.'

'Mm. Oh François, look at the lights of that plane over the sea. Isn't this just the most special place?'

'Yes, I thought you'd like it. How do you think I should handle the common purpose?'

'Well, I suppose you could ask them if they'd felt intimidated by their wilder peers – scared to break away. Or maybe . . . well, I always think, if I was in that situation, I'd probably get caught up by the crowd out of curiosity, and I probably wouldn't even see what was actually going on.'

He smiled at me then. Reaching across the small checked table, he brushed my hair from my ears with his two hands and kissed my nose, very softly. It felt damp, but I feared to rub it away with my hand.

The food arrived. Never, in my English life, had I tasted a *waterblommetjie bredie*, and so I had ordered one on that night, I thought, of portent. But as with so many things which sounded romantic when I was young, it was curiously ordinary. It tasted not so very different from the stew eaten in the suburbs every Thursday – the night the maids were off and the mothers cooked.

'Tell me some more about you. What were you like as a boy?'

He looked surprised. 'Well,' he ran his fingers across his forehead, mussing his hair devastatingly. 'Well, I suppose I wasn't a typical South African male child. I couldn't be, with my mother around. She thought South African men were probably about the worst scourge of the earth . . . I suppose her opinion wasn't improved much when my father moved out to live with his twenty-year-old lover.'

'Oh Jesus, I'm sorry.'

'No, it's fine. I hardly remember him. I didn't really miss him. My mother's more like two parents anyway. She's incredibly strong and she's developed her own way. I think some people see her as a little eccentric. I didn't have a conventional upbringing, that's for sure.'

'Well, you're lucky for that. Mine's just plain boring.'

We wandered to the queue of nestling couples waiting to go down. He seemed to tease me just a little, there with his skew smile.

My decision, still unmade, burnt the palms of my hands. It was a first date, and my mother's warnings wormed their malevolent way into my mind. But this was a liberated man, who expected nothing less than equality. On the other hand, would we spoil it, miss out somehow? And then he lifted my chin with his two hands and brushed his lips, hardly touching, over mine. And my decision was made.

Crown Street was gently lit and muted behind windows drifting incense. Susan had left the lamp on in the lounge. She must just have left the room – the couch still held her warm imprint and the air the faintest whisper of her smell. I could hear her quietly moving about the bathroom, but I knew she wouldn't come through – I would do the same for her, were the situation reversed.

We had one bottle of liqueur, so we poured and drank, silent in the shyness of knowing why we were here and of not knowing enough of each other to know how to begin.

'Night-night Sister,' Susan called from the stairs. The lilt in her voice danced over the words, carrying to me her smile and two metaphoric hands, victory-clasped above her head.

I smiled and turned to François. 'Good,' he said quietly and rubbed his face into my hair. I could feel his pulse beating through his pores, vibrating in the air between us.

'Let's go to bed.'

'Are you sure? Do you really want me to?' he asked. I smiled and nodded.

We slipped quietly up the stairs. I switched off the light, but left the curtains open to draw in the yellow glow from the railway station and the light from the illuminated mountain. Dark skin shimmering in the ethereal light, he slid over the silent bed. His tentative hand stretched flat towards my breast, but withdrew without touching.

'Let me kiss your eyes,' he said quietly and I closed them for him, concentrating my nerve endings to catch each tiny touch through my skin.

'No,' he said. 'With your eyes open.'

'What do you mean?' They were open now, but my head had drawn to the side, guarding its wary parts.

'You must trust me.'

'No, not that much.' That first shivering of nerve endings was gone now. Disappointment drew a caustic tone to my answer.

'Yes, my mother used to do that. She'd make us hold our eyes open while she kissed our eyes. We weren't allowed to blink. She said we had to be that close and trusting.'

I shook my head and closed away the crouched sight of him.

'Just hold me rather,' I said, desperate to draw him through the mist of his mother's madness, which I seemed to feel gathering about us.

I stretched towards his chest, glowing with the radiation of his flesh. But as I felt his penis harden against my thigh, so I felt his spirit soften. His body slackened against mine and he whimpered.

'Oh, but I want you. I'm sorry.'

'I want you too.' I didn't know how to shock him from his sinking miasma.

'Oh no, how can you? How can you want me? I'm not worth it – in the end, you see, I'm just like the other men. I just want your body. I want to take you and use you.'

'I don't care. It's OK.' I was fumbling with the revulsion of his melting manhood – of this spawning of his mother's hatred in her son's self-loathing.

Eyes closed, face twisted with agonies, he brought his nudging penis into me. He whimpered as he withdrew and I watched him – I, still and withdrawn with the aversion I could feel crawling to the back of my throat.

'Oh God, don't let me hurt you.' I was not part of this. I wanted just to breathe, and to have him done. To have my bed again.

'I'm sorry,' he said, and then he came.

'I'm sorry,' he gasped as I twisted my face from his sweaty head. He lay heavily against me until his breathing quieted. Lifting himself, he gazed into my face, too close.

'I'm sorry. I'm just not . . . I suppose I'm not what . . .'

'Oh for God's sake, please stop saying "sorry". Why be sorry? I invited you here. It's my fault.'

My body curled like the convulsive closing of a hand.

'OK,' he smiled and submitted to my whiplike words. 'I just can't stand that about men. No matter how sensitive they are, in the end they want to use women. I couldn't bear to do that to you.'

He brought his wheedling face nearer, too near my shuttered eyes. I curled away from him, holding myself inside the tranquil shell of my own belonging.

'Oh but my tummy's so sore.' He rocked over his cradled stomach, soft now with the muscle-slackened transformation into infancy.

My forehead prickled with the awfulness of his weirdness, smeared now in contaminating wetness through my body. I hoped he might leave but, at last, he lay quietly and slept with the ease of a nestled baby. I crept from the bed and quietly opened Susan's door.

'Tea, Sister,' I whispered, and I heard her duvet rustle. She gave her tight little sniff and felt for her gown.

'Why are you so disappointed?' she asked as the kettle boiled.

'You should know there are countless maniacs and arseholes out there.'

Her eyes squinted slightly as she watched the ends of the two cigarettes catch and glow. Her hand, held too taut, was tremulous as she placed one between my lips.

'In fact, don't think it's better here. They say there're seven women here for every man, and all the good ones go to Jo'burg. It stands to reason, if you find a man, he'll either be married, gay or a lunatic – or a combination of all three.'

We carried our tea through to the lounge and sat on the couch in the dark. Hunched over my warm cup, with a hand spread beside me on the rough brown fabric, my posture echoed hers, claiming a solidarity, clutching at her companionship.

'I don't know why he disappointed me so much,' I said. 'I couldn't have been looking for a "suitable husband" in that devilish look of him. It must have been his intensity. I think I was wanting some kind of great passion. That feeling that it would just take over everything else and suck me into it.'

'Well, that's us OK – always seeking some kind of sensation or some bloody outer edge.'

'But this time, I sought and all I came up with was some monster baby, like that huge duck – what's its name? Huey?'

'Ooh Sister, I must go to bed. Mummy, but I'm so tired, and my little tummy's so sore, Sister. I want to be tucked into my little bed.'

We laughed, with the hysteria of emotion overturned. We clutched at each other, racked with the hilarity of feelings transmuted and the pure funniness of the scene viewed from the bottom of the bed. We felt the absurdity of our lives, from the perspective of the great cosmic joke beyond us all.

I awoke with rampant light pouring past my open curtains. His clothing was gone, thank God. But then I heard sounds of coffee-making from the kitchen and I knew it would never be Susan, out of bed at this time on Easter Sunday.

She was sitting up in bed, naked, eating the Easter eggs her mother had sent her. She didn't look at me as I curled on to her bed, but hunched over the chocolate, obsessively pressing pieces – one after the other – into her mouth. I picked up her other egg and bit it, scattering crumbs and splinters.

'That's not how you eat chocolate,' she said, still not looking up.

'You should start at the top. I've never seen anything so outlandish – biting an egg in the middle. You're just compulsively otherwise, you know that?'

The telephone began to ring. Our chewing stilled and our eyes joined. Hearing the heavy footsteps moving towards the phone, we both leapt from the bed and ran for the stairs, colliding in her doorway.

'Don't you dare touch that!' Susan yelled, crouching to shout at François through the carved uprights of the banister. His hand stopped and his eyes moved up the stairs, in something approaching awe, to the crouched naked stranger.

I was racing down, three stairs at a time, my open gown flying like Superman's cape behind me.

'Hello?' I gasped as I grabbed for the phone. 'Oh, hello Mom. Yes, happy Easter to you too.'

'Well, thank God it's yours,' Susan said, and I saw her suddenly appear ridiculous to herself. She rose with dignity, her thin arms clutched over her breasts as she darted for her bedroom. She came down the stairs again slowly, mummified by her tightly drawn gown.

'I phoned last night but you were out,' my mother was saying. 'So you went on a date already? Anyone nice?'

'Well,' I said, glancing at François. '*Ja*, OK I suppose.'

'What's his name?'

'François.'

'Oh yes? Afrikaans is he?'

'Yes, Mother. Afrikaans.'

'Well, don't get too involved. Remember that a marriage is ten times harder with a difference of cultures.'

'It's not like that, Mother.'

'Oh, and how can you know that for sure? You went out with him, didn't you? Anyway, I must tell you I'm just pleased you've gone to Cape Town. It seems quieter there. I can't tell you what a mess Port Elizabeth is – all those naughty kids marching everywhere, and *toyi-toy*ing, right where everyone can see them.'

I sighed.

'It's all very well for you to sigh. But you should just see what it's like. It's just impossible to drive up Heugh Road with all the nonsense that's been happening in Walmer Location. They're rushing around and fighting each other, left, right and centre. All you can see there is smoke and burning tyres. And I'm sure those so-called students are involved. Those ones you were helping while you were here.'

'I wasn't helping them, Mom. They didn't need my help.'

'I blame their leaders, those UDFs and ANCs and things . . . Anyway, all I can say is I'm glad you're not in the middle of this. And don't you dare go and get yourself involved with more of those black political types down in Cape Town, you hear?'

'Yes, Mother. OK Mother. Have a good day too, OK? Yes, I do too. Bye.'

François, drinking coffee against the door frame, had regained his satanic flair but, now that I had viewed it face-to-face, I couldn't stop seeing the lost child battering behind his eyes.

'I can't believe two liberated women like you were so afraid of a man answering their phone in the morning,' he said, his eyes squeezed with amusement.

'Well, I would think you would understand people having a weird relationship with their mothers,' I said, flinging just that one mean dart to punish him for my own disappointment.

'Anyway,' said Susan. 'Don't you know that's the way of the world? We'll do anything and go anywhere as long as our mothers don't know. That's the Eighties' liberation.'

He laughed. 'So what're you two liberated women doing today?'

'We have an appointment,' Susan leapt in, knowing I was slower to form my lies and more fumbled with my delivery, than she was. 'It's very important. We've had it a long time. And we can't take anyone else. Sorry.'

I walked him to the door as Susan disappeared upstairs.

'Don't forget you promised to come to the Stellenbosch film festival with me next weekend.'

I'd forgotten that he'd asked me during dinner. 'Oh, did I?'

'Yes you did, and I have tickets.' He smiled and leant forward to kiss my nose. This time I wiped it dry. 'I want you to spend the night on the little farm I live on, just outside Stellenbosch. It's the most beautiful place in the world.'

Oh God, how awful. But I had absolutely no clue how to extricate myself, and I had never developed the self-possession which could brazen out a frank withdrawal.

'Um, well, OK then. But I can't leave Susan, you know. Do you think we could take her too? You can see she's not well. I don't like to leave her for so long. She's still very depressed by her divorce.'

'You know, I just can't stand what men do to women. Yes, it shouldn't be too hard to get extra tickets. I'll see if I can bring my friend along, OK? He's a bit weird, but that shouldn't bother her, should it?'

'No, I don't suppose it should' . . .

. . . I watched the grey meerkat raiding the dustbin on the edge of Signal Hill, the small scene somehow easier to watch than the vastness spread there beneath us.

Susan was bent to rummage on the floor of her car for her khaki hat. 'So why must I always be the raving weirdo, that can't be left alone?' she asked as she settled it, very precisely, on her head.

'Oh, but you do it so well, Sister.'

'Oh really, and who is it who's irresistibly drawn to every loon this side of the Equator . . . Come here, Sister. Open your eyes and let me lick your eyeballs.'

Our laughter was loud in the rarefied air, so far above the silent sea. Table Mountain hunched beside us, its arms around the city, which lay crawling with dinky cars, draped with tinselled mist.

Susan tied a tracksuit top firmly about her waist and took off ahead of me up the path.

'Just remind me now. Why are we doing this again?' I called after her.

'We're living in Cape Town, OK? People do healthy outdoor things here. They don't sit on the couch all day drinking cheap wine and smoking dope.'

'You could've fooled me, from the look of Crown Street,' I yelled at her steadily climbing back.

'We're not students any more. It's time we grew up.'

'Oh I see,' I said. The sun was too hot on my head. I should have brought a hat. I didn't quite recognize this new Susan. This one must have developed here in Cape Town – I hadn't met it before. Its walk retained Susan's stiffness of arm and leg, but its stride swung more purposefully from the hip. And the hunched, protective back had straightened.

I wanted a cigarette. It wasn't that I didn't want to do this, or that I couldn't enjoy this immensity of beauty, I thought, as I watched the tight figure ahead of me. It was just that – with this other Susan as my guide – this new fixation had to be entered into with such intensity. I strode awhile, trying not to think, matching Susan's severity of purpose. Struggling up the stone-strewn path, I just felt for a while. I felt the detachment of the silence, and the sun which heated the back of my head and itched at my armpits.

I had dressed inappropriately as usual. I was very hot. It was lovely, this place, too lovely just to wash over me. I would have liked to stand absolutely still, to marvel at the vast dark mountain, frowning over the vitality of the city. I could have spread my arms out and allowed the tenuous breeze to cool me. And I could have gazed and gazed at that sea, freckled with fishing boats. I could have narrowed my eyes against its glitters, and absorbed the summer hum of insects clustered around daisies. I wanted to close my eyes and listen to the *crrr-crrr* of doves and the *wheet-wheeio-whee* of who knows what. If this new Susan stuck around long enough, we'd probably have to learn all their names and classifications and things.

I caught up with Susan. She had stopped her assault on the mountain briefly, to allow her girl's body to fight the breath into her tight chest. Viciously, she tugged the pale hair lankly behind her ears.

I always thought of them as The Alien, these characters which would people each new obsession and compulsive interest – the beings she created to fit herself to the parts she set herself. But, in fact, they weren't altogether like that, because she sought them out. She took her unguarded self and searched, like a hermit crab, for another shell to cover her. Each one she tried could never quite fit. It could never have enough angles to take in her bursting creativity, her wild heart and her bitter mouth. There on the mountain, I watched her fearfully as she squeezed and pressed her prickly crab self into that unwilling shell.

I never knew how to relate to the new being. It interfered with my role as her protector. None of our unspoken rules, gently devised to hold her parts together, applied to her new self. The only way I could deal with it was slowly, slowly to coax them apart.

'Wait, hey, just wait a minute,' I called as she grappled with the path just ahead of me.

She turned. I had to make it my fault, this stopping. She would never countenance an appeal based on her own white face, or the asthma spray which she puffed on as she turned.

'I'm exhausted, Suze. Rest a sec. Please. If we're walking, Sister, surely this is also important. Perhaps we can just sit on this round rock a minute and look at the view.'

'Ja, OK. But tell me when you feel better.' A small shred of Susan was beginning to winkle its way through.

We sat in silence. I watched the mist wisping over the ethereal rim of mountains beyond the city. This was almost too much, this overstated loveliness. In the Eastern Cape, beauty is dry and stunted. It is the aloe-strewn earth, the colour of dust, the struggle for survival. Here, every view was lush with easy loveliness, green and golden with birdsong.

I could smell Susan's sweatiness beside me on the round rock. She even smelt different today. I couldn't locate her musky, agonized smell beneath this new Susan's smell of roughly pulled heather.

'Hey Suze, what are all those little purple-spiked flowers?'

'Don't ask me.'

'And those yellow and white things?'

'How do you expect me to know?'

'Oh, sorry. I thought that if we were becoming walkers of the Cape trails, we were supposed to know all that stuff.'

'Ja, well shit, we're only just beginning, you know.' But I caught it, before she turned aside. I saw the tiniest smile of Susan, who would laugh with sharp irony at the two of us, and all our little quests. I pushed a bit, digging in there for Susan.

'Oh Sister, listen to the call of those large grey birds, and notice the nesting habits of those small, yellow ones. Please notice the fertilization of those funny spiky flowers by those buzzy insect things.'

'Fuck off, Sister.' But she was smiling. A twitch of sadness, at the loss of what she thought she could be, twisted itself around the edge of her smile. But she was back.

'Hey, Sister, let's go back down for a cigarette. And let's eat our picnic. I'm starved.'

'You know, Pringle, you never let me find myself. You always have to drag me back to my same old life.'

'I'm trying to save you from yourself.'

'No,' she said standing, stretching her back with her hands, and curving her shoulders forward into Susan's protective slouch. 'No, it's your totally stuffed-up inability to grow up into a real person. So you can't let me, either.'

I grinned as she aimed a small swipe at the top of my head. This we both knew, we'd choreographed it so long ago. We could fall into it like a stately dance we'd learnt as children. It was the turning on me, the mockery of all my insecurities and eccentricities, for the safety of her loosened pieces. She needed the time, while we wandered back down the path, to put herself back together.

At the bottom, just beyond her car, a tiny Muslim shrine perched on the edge of infinity. I led her there now, feeling instinctively it was where we should go. We removed our shoes and slipped inside. Near the windows at the far end, a man in white robes sang with the wild virtuousness of wanton spirituality. But of course that says more about me, with my childhood diet of Methodist worship. We sat in silence, allowing the rapture of his reverences to calm us. I knew she ached. I ached too – burnt and stung with the hardness of things. But I knew, listening to the silent zing of her tautly strung mind, that she also sometimes soared. When we didn't ache tiredly, when we didn't crush ourselves into tiny shells, we could sometimes take off and fly with the fish eagles.

'Morning,' said the man, smiling as he passed us and left.

'Morning,' we answered, and sat awhile in the deep silence before we too stood to leave.

We sat on twin boulders looking out towards Robben Island. We drank wine and ate all the deli goodies we had bought with the hedonistic delight we took in food. And I had packed it this morning, hoping we could smother our senses in it, without the ascetic disapproval of the mountain-climbing Susan.

The small breeze whipped at our dark thoughts and waved them about our heads, where they scorched into ashy insignificance.

'Oh well, Sister,' I said. 'If we never grow up, and if no one ever loves us for ever and ever, at least we'll always have each other . . .

. . . My husband, that handsome almost stranger, arrives home as I sit where I nearly always sit at this time of day – pressing my face and my life against the glass which cages the leaden sky.

I can hear the stair-racing squeals of our girls.

'How're my girls?' I imagine his fair face filled with a tenderness that I used to see when he turned to me.

It's not his fault. I know that. I know that I am the one who has created our relationship as it is. I seem to have been so fearful of having things taken from me, that I rip myself from them before they have the chance.

I would like so much, one day, to explain to him about the rough textures of the life we lived, about the lights and darks, the rights and wrongs. But I wonder if he, from his placid provenance with the texture of damp lettuce, could ever see the contrasts we were rubbed against. And could he ever, in his exasperation, understand that most of my fears and manic withdrawals have to do, not with myself, but with a fear of causing damage? I have learnt, in so hard a way, that while I thought we were kids, while I thought that we merely played at life, I was capable of causing cataclysmic changes.

I can hear his heavy steps, surrounded by chatter, and I imagine his greying hair, the way it flops over his forehead as he climbs. He's very aware of his hair, though he pretends he is not. Very careful to maintain that contrived frivolity in just the one aspect of him, emphasizing rather than lessening his dour purpose. I can hear them approaching, closer now, bouncing and measured, bounding and sober.

My girls explode through the door, their faces mimicking his symmetry of feature, but with their own firecracker bursts of vivacity. They halt just inside the door, as they catch sight of me on the window seat, a cigarette in my hand.

'Oh no Dad, Mom's smoking again. Can you believe she didn't stick to her resolution again?' That was my elder, eyes rolling up to meet her father's.

'Well, I've given up with her,' he says. 'What can we do with a mother who is supposed to set rules for the family, but then sets us all a bad example.'

He sighs. 'Oh, well. Good evening, dear.' And he nods to me, a slight irony there in the bend of his head.

I mumble hello and turn back to watch the London commuters, shrouded now by the darkness of the village street. There, through the glass of their entrapment, I keep my small collection to watch each day – the dark-suited one who lives two doors down, and that salesman type who lives above the Rose and Crown. Each day

I watch them, but each day I know I am really just waiting. I wait and wait through the winter for every crack in the lowered sky, which will show me just a hint of sunshine.

I drag on the cigarette, ignoring my family's continued badinage. My one small rebellion, and they can't resist worrying at it. My one little statement that exclaims for me – where I cannot – that a personality still beats within this pale person.

'Oh, by the way, Malcolm,' I say to him. 'The plumber came today and he said those old pipes of ours are . . .'

'So how was your day, girls?' His smile scrunches blue, tip-tilted eyes. I glance at their close little group, clustered around the couch – 'sofa', he always corrects me. And then I return to the life beyond the room. I can hear the murmur of all those girl-child details they love to give their father – the awful, awful teacher, the hockey team's new goalie, the boy in the village.

'So, Jennifer, how was your day?' His voice is suddenly distinct from the haze of mumbling around the couch.

I shrug, but turn from the window. I can tell from his perplexed expression that my face is now the still pool it becomes when it has rinsed away all sign of hurt. It is my own small triumph that, at this age, every slight no longer rushes unbidden to tear-filled eyes.

He takes a long breath, holding my gaze. I think the blankness of my face, and his inability to reach me, must fill him with a helpless fury. I can see it forming in the sinews of his neck.

'Oh come on, Jennifer, there must be something. You can tell us about your day, surely to goodness.' His children catch his irritation of inflection, as I sometimes feel he intends them to. They are sighing and giggling, long hair and arms entwined around their father's neck.

I am desperate suddenly. What can I say? What on earth can I possibly say that won't just infuriate him further, after the useless afternoon I spent with the time-wasting plumber? The one who somehow sniffed out the pecking order in this house and ordered me around, summoning me from the bedroom to hand him a spanner, and calling for tea every half an hour?

'Well, I had to go back to the church hall this morning. We didn't finish sorting for the white elephant stall last night.'

'Oh my goodness, yes. The bazaar. I'd forgotten. Oh, the wild excitement of village life, yes indeed. Out two nights running with the vicar's wife. And here it comes. The event you've all been waiting for. The whi-ite ele-phant rock 'n' roll.'

The girls are shrieking with laughter and he is loving it, tickling them in grappled horseplay – his irritation spent in minor cruelty. I think it is only with me that he loses his tight control on life and his emotions.

I wonder what first attracted him to me, over glasses of wine – not South African wine, God forbid. The time wasn't yet right for that. We were at some party or other – I remember I'd been dragged there unwillingly by another ex-South African – shortly after I'd arrived in England. Perhaps it was the contrast of his unquestioning contentment and my angst.

I know what it was about him. I so badly wanted his sureness. I wanted, vicariously, to absorb his constancy. He was so very unlike any South African man I knew, and that was what I needed. I felt he could make me emotionally safe. But, God forgive me, with his British passport as grail, he could also keep me safe from having to return to the place whose pain and guilt I had escaped.

He tried. I do think he really tried with me, as far as he was able. But slowly, over our years together, I have watched his inability to understand me turn to impatience. And my inability to put it all behind me, as he feels he would have, feed his exasperation.

I watch him there, still absorbed in horseplay. They're largely the reason he's stayed, I'm sure – his adored girls. And perhaps his abhorrence of failure. But I sometimes think there must still be some small spark of our early relationship, or surely we wouldn't be capable of hurting each other as we do.

'Oh, by the way, Jennifer, I forgot to tell you.' He stops tickling and looks at me. I'm still hurt and I squash out my cigarette without lifting my eyes. 'Your friend Susan called two nights ago when you were at the vicarage.'

My eyes have sprung to join his. 'Did she say why she called?'

'No, she didn't.' His eyes are back on the tickled tangle of bodies.

'Well, I should phone her then.'

'You can't,' he says, his voice flat with lack of interest. 'She said you could only phone her until yesterday, that she was going away or something.'

'Why, Malcolm?' My voice is shrill with all the tears I suddenly find clamped in my throat. They burn their unshed acid at the back of my eyes – for my disappointment. And for my hurt, that he cared so little and bothered not at all. 'Why didn't you tell me?'

'I can't believe this. Don't you go on at me, just because I forgot a stupid message. Jesus.'

She phoned. How long has it been since her last phone call? And I didn't phone her back. She will think, in her tightly bound pride, that I didn't care to, or that my life is too busy to include her. I can see my family gazing in fascination at my burning, glassy eyes.

'Oh, come on, Jennifer. She's just someone from the past, for God's sake. You have your own family now. Besides, it costs money to phone South Africa. And it's not as if you're exactly close.'

I find myself damp with tears. I haven't cried in such ages. I watch the dark of the village evening cover the common. It will still be sunny in Cape Town now, its warmth splintering off the glaring sea . . .

. . . The sun was a gentle caress on warm hair and eyelids – a day to lick ice cream and watch lazy seagulls glut themselves around fishing boats. Tugs burped their way across the harbour, as Jonathan guarded us and ushered us gallantly through the crowds beside the Harbour Café.

The last day of the Easter weekend, and we would spend it as Cape Town demanded, in the indolent enjoyment of her charms. Jonathan had offered to bring us to the harbour, for the fish *braais* dotted all along the quay.

After finding us a good position, he left us, earnestly seeking the drinks we'd demanded. He struggled through the clustered crowds, his decency shining like scrubbed skin. We waited for him. The sun had become a magnifying glass, aiming the light at our heads, wisping and charring all the darkness from our brains. This was Cape Town, with its laid-back indifference to the violence which was crashing about the ears of the rest of the country.

'Let's go over there – see how they gut and scale those fish,' I said to Susan, and we edged through the clotted groups towards the *doek*ed and aproned women, fisherfolk by their sun-knotted faces and deft-fingered hands. Working rapidly through the pile of fish at their feet, they called their raucous jokes, almost incomprehensible through the sing-song of their English-Afrikaans mix.

I took Susan's shoulders and manoeuvred her through the

people. I was happy to be role-bound again – as the stronger, the more practical. But then we laughed at the absurdity of it, at our joint uselessness, as we stumbled against the wine glass of some yacht-club type, in white pullover and sailing shoes.

'Oh Suze,' I said, nudging her. 'There's Jonathan. He's searching for us. Shall I yell or wave or something?'

'No, not quite yet. I can't cope with him every second. Let him search a little. He'll find us soon enough.'

'Shame, Sister, he looks so beaten-down and bewildered.'

'Yes, he pulls his forehead down like this . . .' She scrunched her small face into a caricature of perplexed stupidity.

Jonathan searched through the crowd, hunching slightly to protect the sloshing glasses he carried. His forehead and upper lip were sheened with the effort and responsibility. Amused by our own little circle of cruelty and solidarity, we sniggered as he pushed a harassed path through to us.

'*Ag*, it's such a nice boy, Sister. What do you want with it?'

'Oh I don't know,' she said. 'Maybe it was the contrast, you know. I thought he might make a change for the Sisters.'

I could see her pain beating its wings in her head, as she rubbed the stiff blade of her hand across her eyebrows. I could see exactly why she had been attracted to him, and why she wanted to want him. His goodness shone so silvery beside the batwing darkness of her ex-husband's psyche. But I think she already knew that it would never work – she could never crush her eagle span into the neat weave of his finch's nest. His TV-screen vision and sit-com morality already chafed at her. But I also knew that I shouldn't prod at that knowledge yet. She was still in the stage of pretend-pretend. The truth was there deep down, but she hadn't decided to turn and look at it. It still felt too sad. And she didn't feel like being sad. Not today, not in this sunlight.

Jonathan reached us at last, sagging with the release of breath held while balancing our drinks across the quay. A fast-fingered fisherwoman grinned. She had enjoyed, with us, the small comedy of Jonathan's approach and our nastiness. Lifting her head from the fish, she looked straight into his face.

'*Ag*, what a nice boy you've got,' she said. 'A *nice boy to take home to Mummy*.' Her voice lilted over the words and her companions joined in her laughter. Jonathan didn't smile. His face blazed with the heat in his fair skin. Desperately, he tried to turn the subject from himself.

'Er, er, um, you're very good with your hands, you know? Very fast with those fish.'

'You think I'm good with my hands?' Her fingers flashed forward and gripped him briefly, and he buckled in momentary shock. When he straightened, traces of fish remained on the front of his cream, pleated pants. All the women were shrieking with laughter, beating slippery hands against aproned thighs. Jonathan was gasping.

'Let's, uh-hrum, let's go and see the tugs,' he said to Susan, stopping to clear his throat. Susan had a detached look of faint amusement about her, a look that should strike dismay into the heart of any ardent suitor.

The harbour had the smell of all harbours, of fish and smoke and a tarry smell I could never identify. And today, it smelt sticky with candyfloss and holidays. The gulls screeched stridently above the *braai*ed fish, blackening and smoking on countless fires.

We backed away from the group and Susan, unable to resist the alliance of women we had formed with the fish-gutters, turned once more to say: 'You can have him if you want. I think he's too nice for us.'

'*Ag* thanks dearie. But he'd never last the ride with a real woman. I think maybe he needs to find another blond boy, just like himself.'

Two young men, who had been watching the gutting alongside us, burst into laughter at Jonathan's outrage and discomfort.

'My God, she thought I was a *moffie*,' he said, choking slightly on his wine and bringing tears to his pale eyes. 'And those *moffies* were laughing. I just can't believe this.'

'Oh come on Jonathan,' said Susan, her irritation rising from the dankness of that truth, deep inside her. 'What does it matter? Why do you care that someone thinks you're gay?'

'Because it's perverted. It's unnatural and I don't like things that are unnatural or . . . or decadent.'

'Oh dear God, but sometimes you do come across as a wimp, Jonathan. Someone needs to shake you up a little, show you a little decadence . . .'

'I know you're just trying to shock me, Susan. Can't you ever be serious? Can't you ever just be a nice girl? I know you really are.'

*Kalatter kalatter kalatter, kalatter kalatter kalatter skreee-ee-ee*

K I brushed on a touch of blusher, listening to the birdsong in the silence left by the train. As I lifted my hand to brush my hair, I caught the sound of the key and the clumping footsteps. I had pulled on my jersey and grabbed my bag when I heard the tea noises.

Susan was already downstairs – she took a long time in the bathroom each morning. It was always a struggle for her to choose what to wear. I thought that she couldn't decide which pieces of herself to appease by pandering to their scattered tastes. The only time she seemed to dress all of a piece was when one of her domineering other selves was in residence. Usually, after trying and rejecting, in scattered frenzy, crumpled, silky shirts and twisted linen skirts, she always appeared with that slightly out-of-kilter look. What began as a perfect study in school-marm, would end up with one wild touch of call-girl. Or, out in the evening, I would watch people frown in bewildered inability to decide what made her sexy outfit seem eccentric, rather than sultry.

This morning, she had somehow managed to filter into her outfit, for all its sophistication, just a whiff of Platteland farmgirl.

She was making coffee when I came down. As I joined her, she lifted a just-lit cigarette from the ashtray and placed it between my lips.

'*Ja* Maud,' I addressed the large back bunched over the slurping tea. 'How're you today? Did you have a good long weekend?'

'Long weekend! *Ka-cha*! I must work yesterday. I have no holiday for Easter Monday. *Ka-cha!*'

'Oh shame, Maud. Who made you work yesterday?'

'I went to the Greenpoint Madam. The Greenpoint Madam's husband says I must work because the Greenpoint Madam must also work. She says she has lots of work.'

Using her sturdy legs to bolster her, she scraped and juddered the delicate dining-room chair around to face us. I watched in fascination as her disapproving face scrolled away leaving, beneath, that spectre of her Peeping Tom self.

'Yes, lo-ots of work.' She laughed, a slow chuckle full of covetous delight. 'I think she must have had a lot of work – with your husband.'

I dragged on my cigarette and watched Susan bite at the skin around her ravaged nails. Her hair hung palely beside the face which sometimes, too early in the morning, showed every frail vein beneath her skin. Maud was watching her too, with the shrewd, sideways glint of her eyes.

'Oh,' I said. 'So the paragon makes you work on Easter Monday, Maud?' My small dig was as much to bring an amused twist to Susan's mouth as to thrust peevishly at Maud's great regard for the Greenpoint Madam's every virtue. The poor contrast we made left us hungry for bitchery about this woman – tall brunette, sleek with tight skirt and sports car. I don't know why I imagined her this way, this woman we had never met.

'No *ka-cha*! It was not her. "Sorry hey, Maud", she says to me. "You know how men are". And I say "Yes. And yours is no better." So she laughed and then she left. But she gave me that wink by the door, you know?'

Maud was up now and, as she contracted from her Maud-form, her shoulders moulded into just a hint of piquant shrug. Her peeper's personality scrolled off the screen of her mobile face and, there before us, was the flirtatious wink of the vivacious Greenpoint Madam, made sympathetic by the sad downturn at the corners of her smile.

'Like this, you know? And then she says, "Oh Maud, you know I shall work so very hard, don't you?" And she laughed.'

Maud trilled the Greenpoint Madam's sparkling giggle.

'And then she says: "Just watch all those men for me, will you Maud? You know that all they can do is play cards when they come around – they can't get on without one of us. Keep them happy, won't you . . . So they don't wonder about me, hey?" And so she left. And the Master, ooh *ka-cha* hm-hm-hm-hm-hm.'

Maud sank heavily back into the creaking chair, its joints heaving and shifting as she shuffled herself into a comfortable position. Susan was lighting another cigarette. She didn't light me one – she knew I could never stomach two before breakfast. I couldn't see her eyes. I would have to keep watch, to guard her splintered selves, keeping a lookout for cutting edges with which she could slash at herself, or those around her.

'So,' said Maud, her eyes darting between us. I think she was a little disappointed in her audience – Susan showing more interest in her nails and her cigarette and I, well, I was tired of the bloody Greenpoint Madam and her fucking. I was more interested in holding Susan together during the dark wave which always seemed to emanate from talk of her ex-husband.

'So, the Greenpoint Madam is out for a long time, most of the day, so . . .'

'OK Maud. The thing is, I must go,' said Susan suddenly and, as she lifted her head, I could see the sickness of the Greenpoint Madam's evoked activities hovering about her white upper lip. 'I'll be late for school if I don't go.' She stubbed her cigarette out viciously.

'No wait, wait, you must hear. This is a big story. Just hear one more time. This is not your husband I speak of now,' she said, shrewdly gauging Susan's need to leave.

'So these men with their beers . . .' Maud was up again, toting imagined six-packs, and before me I saw a group of *manne*, red-faced and rough-mannered. 'So they are now the friends of the Greenpoint Madam's husband. So in they come and, the whole morning, they play cards in the dining room and drink beer. Hm-hm-hm-hm-hm, but they drink so much beer. I never see so much beer and they sit in there with the cigarettes – the Greenpoint Madam she doesn't smoke . . .' Maud lifted her upper lip at Susan's ashtray.

'No, but of course she doesn't,' I heard Susan mutter. She was pulling on her jacket – tailored linen, a pale peach, under which she had a frilled white blouse.

'So,' said Maud, her raised voice pinning a truculent Susan to her place beside the table. 'So, they play and they play at the cards and the curtains are closed. And I must bring them food and chips to eat.

'Hm,' she said. 'Hm-hm-hm-hm-hm.' Her disapproval was back, tightening her features in indifferent nobility. 'And they start to swear at me when I don't come quickly. And they call for me, all day. So in the end, I just stay in the kitchen. I don't listen any more.'

'So is that the end of your story, Maud?' asked Susan, really quite timidly. 'I really should be . . .'

'So then they go outside later,' she continued as though Susan hadn't spoken. 'The husband of Greenpoint, he . . . I think he sees his friends out. They have drunk, mm-mm-mm, such a lot.'

The story seemed to have wandered away into a meandering stream of insignificance. I was smiling at the sight of Susan's impatient face, poised near the door.

'So then,' she said, her voice rising and lifting in triumph, so that we both stopped and turned to listen. 'So then, the one friend he says to me: "Maud, Maud, come help, Maud. The Master is sick, Maud."'

We were silent. Susan had turned in the kitchen doorway, her eyes on Maud. Exultant with the power of her performance, Maud knew she held us in avid attention.

'So I say to him . . .' her voice dropped a fraction, 'So I say: "Ha! He is drunk. Why should I help you?" So he says: "No Maud. No, he is sick Maud. Quickly, help me with him." Her voice cracked in fear and I could see, in her face, the man's dull, beer-drenched features grow fractured with dread.

We didn't say a word as she paused for breath. She glanced at both of us.

'So I say: "Never! *Ka-cha*! He is just drunk. I don't carry drunken men." So then he says, "Please, Maud. Damn you! Come on Maud! He is really sick Maud. I think . . . Maud, *ag* Maud I think he is dying. Please Maud."'

Through this gifted medium, we watched the agony of the terror-struck man, holding his dying friend on the pavement, his hands futilely clutching at his friend's slumped arms.

'So then I say, "OK. But he is just drunk. He is falling down from the liquor. I see this often." But I help him to carry the Master to his bed. When we get to the bedroom, I drop him on the bed, like this. So I say: "It is not right for me to have to carry a man when he is drunk." But the other Master, he calls the ambulance and then I see the Master go blue. And then I listen, like this, to his chest and I hear no heart.'

Maud turned from us, her story seemingly complete. We stood, held in the web of her tale. Maud sucked at her tea and settled back in the chair. Dropping the characters of Greenpoint, she returned to herself, and her serene dignity.

'And so?' asked Susan. 'So? He didn't really die, did he?'

'Yes. When the ambulance come, they say he had a heart attack. He was dead.'

'My God!' We still stood, gripped by the final vision of someone we had grown to know so well. I watched Susan, until the quirk of her mouth's edge began its twist. And then it came, that perverse giggle of hers which sought the humour in the outrageous, the cynical laughter at the offbeat.

'My God, Maud. He died. I can't believe it. And you threw him on the bed. While he was dying. Jeez, I can't believe it.'

Maud drew her prim back straight. Her mouth formed its offended clam line while her eyes threw outrage.

'Well,' she said, with great dignity, 'I was thinking he was drunk.'

# 5

'Miss... Miss... Please come here Miss. Miss, can we talk with you?'

At first I wasn't aware of his call. His voice swept gently across the backdrop of the courtroom, while I stood rooted in other things.

How significant each of these small events seems to me now. Then, I didn't notice at all how those desiccating days were leaking me of youth and stretching me out to dry.

I find myself marking all the small significances which I didn't notice then. As the quiet 'Miss... Miss' swept past me, I was thinking about something which swallowed my attention to the exclusion of everything. Strange that now I cannot recall what on earth it was.

Someone tugged at my sleeve. And in my startling, I pulled my arm away defensively. The boy fell back, watchful and wary, deferring to my seeming distrust. He stood in the dock looking down at me – what was his name again? Jackson, that was it.

'Miss?' he tried again. At the time, I found it odd that he should look at me with so much unease. I still couldn't truly comprehend these boys, and what they had done.

'Yes?' I answered, embarrassed at having jerked and seemed to fear him. 'Were you talking to me?'

'*Ja* Miss.' The boy tousled his feet in disarming scuffle. Running his forefinger across his nose, he ducked his head and said again: '*Ja* Miss. Miss? You're our lawyer Miss, aren't you?'

'I'm yours, yes. Along with Numbers Three, Four and Five. Are you worried about something? Is there something you want to know?'

'No Miss. Oupa explains what we don't know. And sometimes the advocate, Mr Halloran, he tells us what he's doing. No, Miss.

Miss?' he ducked his head again. 'My friend accused Number Five, he thinks you're nice. I think you're nice too.'

I stared at him a moment and then smiled. I didn't know what to say. Why on earth couldn't it have been one of the others? One of the young boys caught up in the emotion of that freedom-singing day, accused now of having the common purpose to kill, merely through being there. But this one . . . he seemed so very guilty.

I kept seeing the man in the photograph in the court file, kept thinking it must have been taken just before he died. I kept seeing his photographed torment as he doused the flames on his body in that meagre puddle.

I had tried, and I supposed that I could understand the forces that had formed them. But I couldn't fit this flesh-and-blood youth into my view of how he should be. He should be an avenging crusader as I had recreated him – not this kid before me. Kicking at the benches, he had a dimpled smile which would have seemed fitting at a Sweet-Sixteen party.

'Thanks,' I said. We smiled at each other shyly, not knowing what to say.

'Are you OK, in the jail?' I asked suddenly, remembering his snivelled anxiety and the cramps which had tortured him a couple of weeks before. 'Is there anything you need?'

'We . . . yes, it is fine. No problem. We . . . my friend Accused Number Five and me we like to read James Hadley Chase books. Please, if you can, Miss, can you bring some books for us, maybe some sweets too?'

'Yes . . . I suppose. I don't see why not.' I was aware of the bulk of the investigating officer looming beside me. The blue of him filled me with that prickle of primeval disquiet which always seemed to accompany the sight of safari suits, camouflage gear or yellow police Toyotas.

'What's this? Is the little bugger worrying you, Miss Pringle? Hey china, What d'you want with the prettiest woman in the room, hey?'

'No, really,' I said. 'It's OK. He's my client. He wasn't worrying me.' I glanced at Jackson so as to catch the expected flash of fear. But he looked . . . well, head on one side like that, he looked impudent.

'*Ja* Big Baas. She is very pretty. Too pretty for you.'

The dock erupted in boyish laughter. The large policeman laughed too, his face glistening with the unwholehearted laughter of embarrassment.

'Hey, hey, hey,' he said. 'Come on china. Enough with the "Big Baas" shit, OK? What, you think you're going to chat her up in your position? Ha!'

'No,' I said. 'No, he wasn't. Captain? I'm going to bring them some things to court. Like books and sweets, OK?'

'*Ja* sure, why should I care? Just show them to me, OK? And they can have them.'

Oupa was watching him closely. '*Ja*, Big Baas? And then you'll wet-bag the boys' heads and take the sweets, *nê*?'

'Ah bugger off, Oupa, man. Come off it.'

The old man was staring straight ahead again, his body jerking with his silent mirth. I didn't laugh. I wasn't sure what the game was here, what cynical convention they adhered to, the two of them, with this mention of police torture.

'Well,' the old man said, turning again slowly to the discomfited detective. 'Well, the young lady she knows about you. You have no chance there, Big Baas. She knows about the wet bags and the electric shocks. She can see how nicely you can get confessions out of these boys, with a bit of a shock here and there.'

'*Ag* Oupa, man. Bugger off, will you?'

I watched this formality of steps between the two, riveted by my own superstitious disquiet at Oupa's audacity. He was using what should never be used in these circumstances. Here, in the presence of base power, he was mentioning what should never be mentioned. The old man was busy with his silent laughter, as he gazed before him at the coat of arms.

'Ah come on, man,' said the detective, red-faced now, strangely caught between amusement and irritation. 'You know for a fact that, when I'm in charge, I never let any of that shit happen. I can make a case good enough without any of that crap. That's lazy detective work, that's my view. It's for guys who can't be bothered to learn a decent investigating technique.'

'Not even a little lack of sleep to help you, Big Baas?'

'*Ag* cut the shit with the Big Baas, man, Oupa. Bloody hell, you even saw that, through the other shit, some of the guys said in their statements I brought them hamburgers and Coke when they were hungry. I don't torture people.'

The old man's silent laughter was breaking into a breathy rasp as he gazed at the wall above his head.

'*Ag* Oupa. You're not fair, man. You know, I never said anything to the guys when they said things about me. Even when everyone who reads the *Cape Times* now thinks I'm a child-torturer, just because they wanted to withdraw their confessions ... *ag* Oupa, stop laughing, man.'

'*Ja*, Mr Detective, Cap-tain John Muller, you lose your sense of humour when a pretty girl is around, *ne*?'

I think that was when Captain Muller wandered off. After that, I remember only that dull police officer followed dull forensic expert. It was hot – the judge called for fans – and I remember that he called for quiet as the boys in the dock began kicking each other and giggling quietly ...

... I let the phone ring while I count slowly – nine, ten, eleven ...

I can hear my daughters closeted in my bedroom, giggling over the clothes which have, while I ceased to care, grown outdated and eccentric.

Twelve, thirt—

'Hello, hello?'

'Yes, hello. Is that Cape Town? Is that Susan Grant's house?'

'Yes. But Susan is not here.'

'Oh. Can I please ... Can I reach her anywhere, please?'

'Susan has gone away for a while.'

'Yes, I know. But do you know where she is?'

'She has gone overseas.'

'Overseas? Where? Do you know where? I'm phoning from overseas.'

'Overseas. I only know that she has gone overseas.'

'Please help me. Do you know which country she is visiting? Do you know where she's staying?'

'No, she never says where she's going. She only says she'll be overseas.'

'OK. You're sure she never said where? She didn't mention the name of her hotel, which country?'

'No, she never tells me that. Sorry.'

'OK, thanks. Thanks very much for your help.'

'OK, bye.'

'No, wait. Wait please. Listen, if she phones. Please, if she phones tell her Jenny called. Please ask her to phone Jenny in England.'

'Joni?'

'No, Jenny. OK? Please don't forget. It's very important. Or ask her what her phone number is, so I can phone her? Thanks.'

'OK, bye.' . . .

. . . The street was washed with grey and quietude, edged with gilded chimney pots. Mellowed by evening and wine, it was gentling our jangled day.

'You old bastard, there's no way you can do that any more.' Auntie's voice shrilled through the silence of the diagonal space between the corner café and our house. 'Don't pretend you're such a hotshot suddenly.'

Dangling our legs over the edge of the *stoep*, we could see Mr Kennedy's torso straining over his balcony rail next door.

'Are they fighting upstairs?' called Mr Kennedy, his tortoise face tightened into a grin.

Although he lived directly opposite the café, his *stoep* provided the worst fight seats. His house faced the café's blank side wall – the entrance was on the corner. Our position for Auntie's café fights was just as bad, but we were ringside for their lace-framed bedroom fights.

'No, Mr Kennedy,' I leant forward to call back. 'I think this one's in the café.'

'What is it? What is it?' Mrs Kennedy's voice cawed from behind him.

'It's another fight, Mrs K,' Mr Kennedy turned, twitching with excitement. 'No, I can't quite hear yet, my dear. They don't seem to fight as loudly as they did when they were young, hmm?'

'You bladdy old phoney,' Auntie's voice abraded the soft evening. 'Don't you tell me you can still do it. I'll tell you bladdy different, and I should bladdy know.'

Mr Kennedy was leaning out over his rail, his hands twittering with frustration.

'What is it, girls? What's the fight about? Can you hear?'

'Oh yes,' Susan yelled without turning to look at him. She paused, taking a terse draw and blowing the smoke luminously into the dusk. Mr Kennedy twittered, leaning still further out on sinewed arms.

'Yes? Yes, girls? Is it the money again?'

'Oh no, not this time,' called Susan, looking at me. Her mouth carried a smile, but with just the tip of each sardonic corner turned down.

'No, Mr Kennedy, I don't think its the money. I think . . .' her voice had grown louder, 'I think it's about . . .' her voice fell away again and she mumbled the last few words, '. . . It seems to be about the sex.'

'What?' yelled Mr Kennedy, as we fell into giggling. 'What, girls? What did you say?' He was spry with energy, his mouth gaping for information.

'No, nothing Mr Kennedy,' I called, feeling suddenly sorry for him in his need for this small excitement, after so many years. 'No, we can't really hear what it's about. Really!'

*Uuhuuh-uuhuuh, uuhuuh-uuhuuh*

The hoarse blast of the fish horn sliced through Mr Kennedy's next question. His head twisted from side to side like a wizened meerkat's. The truck rattled into the street and skidded to a stop.

The men leapt from the back of the truck to jostle and laugh around Mr Kennedy as he bent to choose his fish. I recognized Achmat, his face ruddy with sun and laughter.

'Fish, girls?' Mr Kennedy called.

'No thanks, Mr Kennedy,' I called. 'We don't know how to gut them.'

'Come, come here now,' Mr Kennedy said with the sudden authority of superior ability. 'Come, I'll choose you a lovely piece of galjoen. I'll gut it now quickly for you and fillet it, and you girls can have a lovely piece of fish, fresh from the sea, for your supper.'

We followed his bandy figure across his *stoep*, as the retreating *uuhuuh-uuhuuh* carried the truck out of Crown Street.

'Evening Mrs Kennedy,' we mumbled, repelled and fascinated by her embodiment of crumbling dereliction. Her skin appeared to disintegrate before us as flakes drifted down over her black dress in time with the shake of her head.

'Evening girls,' she said through the lipless mouth that appeared hardly to move.

Their passage was dark with stained lino and agony, which breathed down from countless gore-filled icons. The passage twisted narrowly past three closed doors to the kitchen.

'Where d'you think they put all their twenty-three children?' I whispered and Susan shrugged, her eyes rolling upward.

The kitchen was clearly the room in which their family living – all their eating and talking, all their crying and laughter – must have taken place over at least four decades. This was where children must have crushed together to do homework, to discuss boy- or girlfriends while their mother stirred pots on the ancient stove, where the Kennedys must have been brought small glittered angels from school, and where they would have heard of deaths and impending marriages, and perhaps of teenage pregnancies. All the joys and disappointments and fears of their Observatory-enclosed lives had been lived out and absorbed by these smoky walls.

In the centre stood a wooden table, dented by cutlery, gouged by pencils and penknives. Against the wall was a sagging couch and, alongside it, a wooden ball-and-claw chair. On the couch sat a pale girl – so young, it seemed to me, even then. Long sandy hair straggled about her freckle-framed eyes. I watched her glance up briefly and incuriously, intent on jiggling the large baby which niggled and pushed with its plump hands. She sighed and opened her blouse. The baby, I remember, was frightening in its voracious assault on her slight body, seeming to suck her dry, seeming to bruise the delicate youth of her.

A young man watched her, sitting backward on a kitchen chair. They took little notice of Mr Kennedy and he ignored their presence. Lifting a large knife with a home-carved wooden handle, he held one fish by its tail, slashed and gutted it with the speed of flashing steel. Wrapping our fillets in a sheet of newspaper, he left the fish gut sliming the table, where a tabby cat leapt to sniff and investigate.

'Now you can have nice fish for supper, girls,' he said, grinning at us. Seeing Susan's eyes move from the young man to the girl and her nuzzling parasite, he said: 'That's my youngest son. You can see he's not much older than this one, and she's my granddaughter.' He gave a quick laugh, a sudden *ha*! 'She went and got herself pregnant, so she came to stay with us. Her father wouldn't keep her.'

The girl ignored us all, and showed no sign of hearing her grandfather pour out her shame to strangers. The young man didn't move. Chin sunk on forearms, he watched the baby suckle.

'So how many children have you got, Mr Kennedy?' Susan

asked as we wound back through the dark passage.

'Thirteen,' he replied. 'Two are dead now, but we have . . . let me see . . . I think we have thirty-one grandchildren.'

'Oh well,' Susan muttered to me, giving an ironic little shrug. 'Thirteen! I was only ten out' . . .


. . . 'My Lord, the State requests that your Lordship make a ruling that the identity of the next witness be protected, and not revealed in any press reports. My Lord, we would further request that your Lordship please clear the courtroom of all onlookers, except the press, for the duration of this evidence.'

'Please enlighten me, Mr Erasmus, as to the reason we are holding this evidence *in camera*.'

'My Lord, the witness is entitled to the protection of the court since she is to give some evidence of sexual assault.'

'Very well. Orderlies, will you please clear the court. Very well, thank you. And now, Mr Erasmus, I presume you are ready to continue.'

'Yes, My Lord. I call Margaret Thandeka Mdoda.'

The thin woman moved haltingly to the witness box. She was young, and so fearful. Her large dark eyes flitted about the courtroom, flinching from the dark robes and the vast coat of arms which seemed to batter her fragile youth.

'Place-your-right-hand-in-the-air-do-you-swear-to-tell-the-truth-the-whole-truth-and-nothing-but-the-truth-so-help-me-God-say-I-do-so-help-me-God!' gabbled the judge's clerk.

'I do, so help me God,' said the young woman, her eyes painful in their perplexity.

'Right Miss Mdoda. Please state for the court where you were on June the fifteenth, last year.'

'I was at work in town. I am the tea girl in the office of Mr Reynolds and Mr Jacobs.'

'Yes, Miss Mdoda? And what happened to you on that day?'

'Yes, so . . .' her eyes filled with tears, but she blinked them away, staring at the grey-haired judge who was nodding encouragingly. 'So you see, Mr Jacobs he ask me to stay late to serve drinks. He was working late that night and he has customers for drinks. So then . . .' She paused, and bit her lip, shifting in the witness box. The light struck her from the side and the shine of her youth was silvered suddenly in her tears.

'Yes, Miss Mdoda?'

'So then I say the buses they will all be gone by that time and I must get home because the next day it was the sixteenth of June. I must be home for Soweto Day or my family would be in trouble from the students . . .' She ran her forearm across her nose, smearing the trailing tears. 'So Mr Jacobs he say he will drive me home afterwards in his car.'

'And so, did he do so, Miss Mdoda?'

'Yes, so by eight o'clock Mr Jacobs he was driving me home to Langmanskraal Camp. When we reach Langmanskraal Road, we drive along and then, we turn where the road bends. So . . .' She paused to drink from the glass of water the orderly had passed her, at the judge's gestured behest.

'So then, the car it is stopped by the crowd. I can see the stones coming from all sides. They hit the car. Then the people, they try to open the front door and drag Mr Jacobs out. I was very frightened and I open my door and crawl out while the people are busy at the front door.'

'Let me just stop your story there a moment, Miss Mdoda. The crowd around Mr Jacobs's car – could you recognize any of them?'

'I was too frightened to see the most of it. But I remember that I see my neighbour and my neighbour's friend. I remember because they don't look like themselves. I was scared because I know them and suddenly I don't know them. They look . . . they look . . .' She ran her arm across her face.

'Take your time, Miss Mdoda,' said the judge. 'Take as much time as you need.'

'You were saying, Miss Mdoda?' The prosecutor's face was struggling with the attempt at hangdog sympathy. 'You said they looked . . . What did they look like?'

'They look like animals, like dogs when they have caught a cat in the street.'

'Objection!' Jeff Halloran and François spoke at the same time, François leaping to his sprung feet, Jeff listlessly half-rising.

'Yes, yes,' said the judge. 'Sustained. Mr Erasmus, kindly remember that your witness is not an expert in the psychology of facial expressions. Please do not encourage conclusions like that.'

'As the court pleases. Now, Miss Mdoda? Do you see those two young men in the courtroom?'

'Yes.' She pointed twice and then twisted away from the sight of them, her hands covering her streaked face.

'Let the record show,' said Mr Erasmus, 'That Miss Mdoda pointed out Accused Number Two and Number Five.'

Jackson again. Jackson, sitting now with his face serious and undimpled, his head stretching sideways towards the comfort of Oupa Kakaza's shoulder. And Jackson's best friend, also one of ours. I flipped through my pages quickly: yes, Thomas Silinga. He and Accused Number Six, seeming unaware of the witness or her evidence, were shoving at each other, giggling quietly as they tried to stomp on each other's toes.

'And then what happened, Miss Mdoda?'

'So then, I run to some people and I ask them to help me. Two men, they take me into the bushes and . . .' She laid her head on her arms and sobbed.

'Do you need to take a few moments, Miss Mdoda?' asked the judge, raising himself from his seat to lean over the Bench. She didn't reply. The judge shuffled his things. He gazed at her solitary figure, silhouetted by the window-wrought aura which clung to her. She wouldn't look up at him. His face jerked with the effort to keep its spread of understanding as he stretched still further, struggling to reach his sympathy across the breadth of the courtroom.

'Miss Mdoda? . . . Miss Mdoda? Shall we adjourn the court to give you time to recover? Yes, I think we will give this witness a few minutes to compose—'

'No,' she said suddenly. 'No, s'OK. I am now all right.' Her body, haloed by glowing light, stretched to its full avenging height. Her youth disappeared into the fullness of her angry voice and regal bearing.

'No. They take me, these men, in the bushes – these men I ask for help. They push me down in the bushes . . .'

As she paused, my professional self lifted its dry head above the wash of drama. I glanced at the struck face of the judge's assessor, before grabbing my yellow pad and scribbling: *Jeff, isn't this inflammatory – is she implying it was one of the accused???*'

'The one man, he hold me down . . .'

'Just what I was thinking,' Halloran hissed.

'He hold my hands above . . .'

'Uh, My Lord?' He rose in his languid style. 'Uh, is there some relevance to this, uh, evidence, or is my learned friend merely intending to be inflammatory?'

'Is there an objection in there somewhere, Mr Halloran?'

'Yes, my Lord. It seems to me that this young woman's evidence, heartrending though it is, is being tendered merely to be inflammatory.'

'I don't think I'm inflammable, Mr Halloran.' The judge looked at him quizzically.

'No, my Lord. I certainly didn't mean to imply that your Lordship was. But I would certainly like to know whether it has any relevance at all to the State's case.'

'Mr Erasmus . . .' The judge turned his head slowly towards the prosecutor. 'Where is this evidence going? Has it any relevance to your case?'

'Well, my Lord . . .' Mr Erasmus ran both hands through his hair. '. . . Not directly, My Lord. But it goes to show the general anarchy and mob rule in play that day.'

'Well then, I'll let it run but I'll make a decision on relevance later.'

'As the court pleases. Miss Mdoda, could you continue please? You said these two men . . .'

'Yes, the one he hold me down and the other he rape me. Then they change.'

'Did you know who these men were, Miss Mdoda?'

'No, I have never seen them before.'

She shivered, as though the cold of that midwinter's night had whispered suddenly through the shining windows . . .

. . . A breath of waterlogged winter thrust its way through that autumn night, licking at our eyebrows and dampening our hair. There was something that drew Susan to stand out in the wild of the foggy night, something that appealed to her in its lashing cold. We stood on our *stoep*, I watching the wildness in her that wheeled and whipped with the wind. There was a greater darkness to her since our university days, like a depth of herself which she had sunk to touch before rising again for air. There was more to the jitteriness she had always shown. Now it was tinged with despair.

'Have you ever been to the foghorn?' she asked me, her eyes dark with feral depths.

'No, of course I haven't. What for?'

'It's in the Mouille Point lighthouse. Come!'

'Why are we doing this, Sister? It's freezing. It feels like winter. Are you mad?'

'Of course! Just come.' And she was rushing through the wind to her car, leaving me as usual to the practicalities – the locking, the switching, the grabbing for cash.

We drove to Mouille Point where the great sea pounded at our ears, obscured by the pulp of the fog. Susan sat still a minute, eyes closed. Jerking forward, she struggled with her door, wrestling the wind and the flailing spray. I scrambled to follow, fearful of losing her in the night's grey flesh.

My clothes slapped and winnowed about me and I was gasping at the thick salt air when I joined Susan, flattened against the hulk of the Foghorn building.

'Sister, for fuck's sake, this is a very weird thing to be doing.'

'I know.' Her laughter was wild and it wisped about us in the swirling fog. 'But then we are weirder than other people.'

'Oh come on. We're not as weird as some – not as weird as our "satanist" neighbours.' I was shouting above the sea's roar, struggling to bind her to the earth, to curb her flying sea spirit which frightened me just a little.

'Oh,' she yelled back, laughing still. 'Much weirder, Sister. All their weirdness is displayed in their clothes. Ours . . . ours is deep inside, the most dangerous kind. Ours is about boundaries. About exploring – pushing things as far as they will go . . .'

In the next instant, my body was hit by a force so powerful it was shocked into blind rigidity. The foghorn's blast, jolting through my splintering frame, spasmed my limbs in reflex recoil. Released again, they were swamped by adrenalin in rushing waves. And we ran, racing the wind and the chasing blare, our screams unheard above the agony roar.

'There now,' said Susan as we reached the car. 'Don't you feel good now?'

'Good? I feel crazed. I feel blasted and tingled all over. I feel high.'

'Exactly' . . .

. . . 'OK,' said Captain Muller, 'just let me have a small glance inside so it's all right and proper. OK then . . . Jeez woman, are you trying to drive them crazy? Look at these books. They're all covered in half-naked women.'

'I know,' I said blushing. 'But it's what they asked for. They specifically wanted James Hadley Chase novels and sweets. And tobacco.'

'And I can see why.'

I smiled as the eager boys pulled the books out and passed them around.

'Um . . . Miss?' It was Jackson again. Perhaps this time he'd ask for *Das Kapital*, if only to keep my illusions in straight stereotype.

'Miss? Jennifer? Thomas and I have written letters for you.' He thrust them into my hand and the two clustered together, giggling and glancing at me. I found my place in the benches and opened the first.

> *Pollsmoor Max Prison*
> *P/bag X4*
> *Tokai 7965*

*Dearest friend Jennifer*

*Great is my joy for this opportunity of writing this letter for you. In reference to health I am highly in progress, and my wishes are to hear the same for you too.*

*To start with, when I'm alone I think about you. Maybe it's because you are a person who likes other people because you are a friendly human being. Therefore I ask you to think about me and pray for me to have success in my trial.*

*My wish is for our friendship to continue when I am outside. I do not believe this is just a dream because it's my first time to think about a person like this. There are many things which I want to ask you. But on this present moment I cannot. Maybe at the end of this case I will try to ask.*

*I have a friendly message from Number Nineteen, that is my co-accused, he says if you can buy for him also some James Hadley Chase books and also some sweets he can be very glad. What I believe is that you wash my hand and I must try by all means to wash yours too. That's why we say in life a hand washes another hand. Please reply as soon as possible. Pass my greetings to all at your home and the Comrades.*

*from Jackson (Accused 2)*

I glanced towards the dock, where the two sat whispering among the other accused. I felt chilled. This doomed child still thought he would be freed – free to talk to girls and hold hands and grow up and walk through the sunset. He thought we could be friends.

I opened the other envelope.

> *Pollsmoor Max. Prison*
> *P/bag X4*
> *Tokai 7966*

*Dear friend,*

*Great is my joy for this opportunity of saying these few words to you. In reference to health I am very excellent, hoping to hear the same from you too. I am only short of words to express my feelings, but at any rate you know about my situation. I can be very much more than thankful if I can receive a letter from you.*

*I hope and pray that when this case is over I can work for you, maybe as your garden boy.*

*I only hope and wish that the Almighty will secure our souls until the aimed goal is achieved.*

*Kindly permit me to pen off here. Pass my kindly greetings to all at your house and the Comrades.*

*Bye-bye now,*
*from your friend*
*Thomas Silinga (Accused No. 5)*

'Jennifer . . . Oh sorry. Didn't mean to make you jump like that.' Ilsa's feet were planted, her tattered leather bag slung from her shoulder. With her other hand, she swept the tangling strands of dark hair back from her face.

'Um, I couldn't help noticing that you were, like, very close to the accused.' I looked at her blankly, still lost in the innocence and tragedy of my letters. 'I'm sorry that I lectured you last time. When I was going on at you, I was just trying to tell you how important this trial was. These men are really figureheads, you see . . . I wanted you to see that, if you were working with them, you know? But anyway . . .'

I didn't know what she wanted me to say. I was filled with the absurd urge to laugh crazily. Here in my hand I held a scrumpled note which asked if this figurehead of the Struggle could work as my 'garden boy'.

'. . . So I wondered if you'd maybe be interested to come to a UDF meeting – well, a UDF-affiliated group – in Obs next week? Over the weekend.' . . .

. . . Wishing it were elsewhere, the evening sun laid its languid arm across François's car and let it lie there carelessly, before drifting away from us, out of sight.

In the sudden dusk, I felt the loss of its flitting dance. In that car, where I so little wanted to be, I feared the disappearance of the sun's easy grace. In its leaving, it had peeled me of my Eighties bravura and left exposed my core of primeval fears. I feared the dark and the night. I feared, as humans used to do, that in spite of our blind faith, the sun might not rise again. I feared this man and his transformation into damaged child. I feared, oh I feared that I might be left alone with him.

His car irritated me. Why had I not noticed on that first date how showy it was of him to drive that rusted Beetle? He was driving while he boasted. Oh hell, I know I was awful to him. I remember how Susan and I rolled our eyes and enjoyed our wit at his expense. But everything, absolutely everything about him, seemed to irritate.

'Now you're going to see Stellenbosch, the most beautiful university town anywhere, where members of the real white Left went to university,' he said. 'Us Afrikaners, you know, make the best Marxists because we're naturally ascetic. Not like you bunch of wishy-washy English liberals.'

I remember that Susan and I didn't bother to reply. I was rigid with fretful tension. All I could see, with a crawling aversion, was the hand which crept across my seat to stroke or pat or squeeze. And it seemed that the further we descended into the cutting wastes of monosyllables, the greater became François's self-abasing attempts to impress us.

By now he was a guerrilla – well, nearly. Oh the great dilemma of the committed. How should he fight – law or bombs, from within or from without?

'Well,' muttered Susan, 'I don't know that anyone will notice, either way.'

From his cubby hole he had snatched a Guevara beret and set it over his saturnine face. It can still make me cringe to remember the way he humiliated himself, the way he strutted and postured, setting himself up before us to be ridiculed.

'I've always had a great affinity for the Struggle in Namibia. I think I'll go up there sometime. I could be a great asset to Swapo. I've done my army service, you know. I'm sure that could help them. But also, just imagine. A lawyer. I could handle all those cases against Koevoet for them.'

'Oh-oh, poor Swapo. That's the end of their Struggle,' said Susan to me, no longer bothering to murmur. 'They may as well surrender.'

'Yes,' I breathed through giggles of tension. 'Koevoet's secret weapon. Plant François in the forces of the enemy.'

'Oh, you two,' he said. He was silent a moment, and then gave a soft laugh to show he didn't take offence. 'All you can do is tease.'

The film festival was just awful as I'd imagined. The movie house was filled with nouveau lefties, all in sandals. It was, of course, a French movie. There were subtitles and I think it had something to do with lesbians.

My anxiety over being left alone with him had drifted, with the smoke from the joints we had shared in the car, through all my phobic limbs. I clutched Susan's arm as we entered the cinema, slightly paranoid in the face of the alien crowd.

'When you said Susan would come . . .' François said, apology seeping from him, '. . . Well, I really did try to get another couple of tickets, um, but I couldn't. So, well, my friend – he's a really crazy guy, you mustn't mind him – anyway, he said he'd rather meet us afterwards. But, it doesn't matter here about only having two tickets. People sit all over the steps in the aisles. That's OK here, you mustn't feel out of place, Susan.'

I looked at Susan. I had infected her with my fears and she quivered now like a harp string. 'No,' I said. 'No, she can't leave me.' The absurdity of my reaction settled on us and we began to giggle, our mouths thin with grimaces.

'Well, OK.' François's eyes shadowed, but I could see he had been cowed by the fury of the Sisterhood. He would never stand up to it. 'OK, I'll sit there. I'm used to it.'

We sat through the wash of French angst, our knees clutched to our chins, Susan's nailless fingers denting my arm. François was lost among the people who clustered the steps.

As the film edged to its agonized crisis, we both started convulsively as a snore rumbled from the aisle. Ripples of superior laughter followed as another snore rollicked around the cinema with acoustic ease.

'Oh my God, it's François,' said Susan, her voice high-pitched. I raised myself slightly to see and began to giggle hysterically at the absurdity of the foetal figure lying on the steps, beret tipped over face, hand cradling his cheek.

The film ended and François lay unmoving. The very ordinariness of his figure had shrunk our terrors so that we felt able to walk from the cinema without tremors.

'Step over him,' said Susan. 'God, this is humiliating. Only for you would I do this.'

But he awoke as we passed, nudged by sandals or urged awake by sniggers. Grappling with his fallen beret, he bounded through the solemn shuffle.

'I must have fallen asleep,' he said, unfazed by the narrowed eyes and smirks. He laughed and grabbed us both by an arm. 'Come, let's go meet Etienne.'

Etienne was a ponytailed accountant, unsettled and unfitted for any of society's expectations. Neither Afrikaans nor English, he derided the Afrikaans students, still leaking from the cinema, and mocked us for our Englishness. He had about him pockets of loose pills, tablets and capsules which he examined, one at a time, frowning at the palm of his hand while he spoke.

'So, what we gonna . . .' he scowled at a capsule, held it up to the sparse street light. 'So where should we go, china?' he asked François, tossing the capsule into his mouth.

'Well, I'd like to show these Sisters . . .' he smiled, to show how user-friendly a man he really was '. . . my farm cottage. I live on someone's farm, you know? I thought we could have drinks there.'

There was something strange about Etienne's grass, which we bottlenecked under those grasping oak trees. Or perhaps it was the night, with its heaving shadows and possibilities of unnamed ghastliness. But we thought it was the dope. We always told it that way.

I turned myself around in that puttering Beetle, clamping my eyes on the headlights of Etienne's car, in which Susan was travelling. But, as we turned into the twists of a farm road, I knew that we had lost them. The lights travelling behind us swept past, illuminating an unfamiliar car, before leaving utter darkness.

A thin layer of hysteria resurfaced as François showed me into his cottage, fresh with the smell of rush matting, and served me good wine.

'Don't worry. They'll find us,' he said with a good cheer that irritated – and slyly placated, it seemed to me. He sat on the arm of my chair and invaded my space. I couldn't take my eyes from his hands, damp as frogs, as they reached for either side of my face.

'Oh no. Oh Jesus Christ,' I said, my voice rasping past the coating of dread in my throat. 'Oh God, François, I'm so worried about Susan.'

That held him at bay for an hour, the minutes seeping slowly through the silent cottage. I could hear only the clock and my own breathing as I watched François swirling the wine in his glass, his face anxious . . . understanding . . . or was he leering at me, looming over my fragile body?

'Well, we can really do what we like,' he said. 'We'll hear them the minute they turn into the farm road.' I suppose he was tentative. I heard him as menacing. I looked down at my translucent, insect's body and felt detached from it, but protective of the dark organs and nameless innards pulsing inside their thinly drawn skin.

'Oh Jesus, François.' I had to draw his attention away from me, or he would take me to his bed and I would split. I would tear and my inner workings would spill over the rush matting. 'Oh, I'm so worried. Something's happened to them. They've crashed and they could be lying bleeding in the road. They could . . .'

My horrors, communicated through shaking lips, crawled up on him. 'What should we do?'

'I don't know. Jesus, I don't know.'

His fear was real now and he began, at three in the morning, to phone the hospitals, and the ambulances. I don't know that I believed in Susan's danger, but it kept him away from me. Finally, I heard him phone Etienne's parents, and infuse them with the early-hours magnitude of fearful possibilities.

'Mrs Malan? Sorry to phone you at this time, Mrs Malan. I just wondered if you'd heard from Etienne' . . . 'No, they haven't come here yet, Mrs Malan' . . . 'No, well, he was with my girlfriend's friend, Mrs Malan. She's worried about her' . . . 'Yes, I know he's married Mrs Malan. She was just keeping him company in the car' . . . 'Well, it's just that we thought they might have crashed and we wondered if you'd heard' . . . 'No, it's just that they haven't got here yet' . . . 'OK, Mrs Malan, we'll phone as soon as we hear. Sorry, Mrs Malan.'

And then the phone rang.

'Yes? Hello? François speaking. Oh, Etienne. We were so worried' . . . 'How could you have lost me?' . . . 'But did you look for the farm?' . . . 'Ja, it can be quite hard in the dark' . . . 'So are you back at the girls' place . . .?'

'Oh God, tell them to come back,' I shrieked.

'He says it's an hour's drive back from Cape Town, should he bother?' François asked me, his hand over the receiver.

'Yes, yes, I want them here! They must come now!'

The hour trickled by. Every minute or so, I heard myself say: 'They'll be here any minute, any minute.' François left me alone, phoning Mrs Malan and mildly absorbing a stream of abuse which I could hear from my chair in the corner. 'They'll be here any minute, any minute.' François went to make coffee.

The sky was lightening when the car drew up, the majesty and strength of the sun daring us not to have believed it would return. But I was too fragile for it. I feared its pounding on my silkworm limbs. Susan crept through the door, her eyes aching and haunted. Without a word, she came for my chair and squeezed her thin body alongside mine. We clutched at each other, that armchair seeming the only safe haven in the immensity of the outside world.

'I feel that I'm a cardboard cutout,' she whispered to me. 'Look at the back of me and check that I'm there.' But the beginnings of fearful laughter were there now, as we could face, side by side, our night dreads.

'You're all there,' I said. 'Well, as much as you ever were.'

'Come girls,' said François, wanting at last to show off that limitless farm. He flung the window open. 'Come look at the baby calves,' he said. 'They'll suck your whole hands. Come see this incredible horizon.'

But we huddled together in that one chair, giggling at our ridiculous position, too fearful to face the enormity of the world.

'No, François, leave us alone,' I said. 'We're safe here, the two of us. We're not ready for the real world.'

K*alatter kalatter kalatter, kalatter kalatter kalatter skreee-ee-ee*
  We heard the train as François dropped us home. We were
happy to be safe, and back there. Making coffee with the stolid-
ness of no sleep, we heard Maud's key-clatter, slam and the heavy
footsteps from the front door.

  *Ka-cha!*

  'And a very good morning to you too, Maud,' said Susan. We
were full of bravado now, full of the absurdity and the silliness of
the night, and its fears.

  *Ka-cha!*

  'I'm very well too, Maud. Thanks for asking.'

  'You two have not been in bed. I can see.'

  'Blast, so you mean all that racing up the stairs and ruffling our
beds was all in vain? You could see all along?'

  *Ka-cha!*

  'Ah come on, Maudie,' I wheedled. 'We just got lost in Stellenbosch. Don't be angry.'

  'Hm, well, I can smell all that smoke, so much smoke, on your
clothes.'

  'Well, what can we do? We're smokers.'

  'It is not cigarettes I can smell. I smell *dagga*. You have been
smoking *dagga*. Hm-hm-hm-hm-hm, but it is bad stuff.'

  '*Ag*, Maud,' said Susan, trailing her thin hair behind her ear. 'We
were just trying the stuff. But ugh, we hated it, didn't we Jennifer?
Ugh, did nothing for us, did it?'

  'Absolutely nothing,' I said, my voice tremulous with suppressed giggles. 'Hardly felt a thing. And we didn't even inhale.'

  Susan handed me my cup, which I clutched between two cold
hands. She perched on the kitchen table, her coffee in one hand,
chewing at the nails of the other. Maud was pouring milk into her

mug, swishing her tea bag around with a teaspoon. The chair heaved and squealed as she wriggled herself on to its *riempies* and scraped its legs closer to the kitchen table.

'So, how's the Greenpoint Madam making out?' Susan asked, still ripping at her nails. We watched, fascinated, as Maud's narrator began to seep, like so much ectoplasm, through her dignified elder statesman.

'The funeral was yesterday. On Thursday I was helping to make cakes and pies for the people.'

'What did she wear? To the funeral, I mean.'

'Oh she look very beautiful . . . She is much smarter than you . . .'

'Well, we know that by now . . .' said Susan, her teeth gritted over a stray piece of fingernail.

'She wore a beautiful black dress . . .'

'Above the knee or below?' I asked, slurping at the comfort of my coffee. My head was beginning to wince in pain, as much from lack of sleep as anything else.

'Short dress. She has very nice legs. She is thinner than you . . .' she said, nodding towards me, '. . . but she has more flesh than you.' She was nodding, with a look of distaste, at Susan's fragile-boned frame.

'Oh, she would show off her legs at her husband's funeral. She just would, wouldn't she, Susan?'

'*Ja*, well I wonder if that pathetic ex-husband of mine was inappropriate enough to go?'

Maud's narrator swelled with the enormity of the information which she gathered, constantly and voraciously, from her environment.

'Your husband is gone from her life, she tells me.'

'What?' said Susan. 'That must be a blow for him. Her husband dies and my husband's ditched.' She gave a dismissive flick of her fingers.

'*Ja*, and particularly in view of the fact that the little Merry Greenpoint Widow sounds like she has money for Africa,' I was carrying my empty coffee cup to the sink, under the watchful eye of Maud's elder statesman. I had seen it appear, just peeking through the eyes of her narrator, at the sight of the dirty cups and toast plates.

'She says to him . . .' She cackled suddenly with the sly humour of her narrator. 'She says he is not good in the bed and she says she will not need him again.' She cackled again.

Susan's vulnerable lip, released from her teeth, turned up delicately at the corners. She carried her cup to the sink under Maud's monitoring eye.

'When I go to your husband to work there, I say: "So, no more Greenpoint Madam!" '

Susan had turned at the sink, riveted by Maud's audacity. Maud stood and, as we watched, she shrank into the intense, lurking form of Susan's ex-husband.

'So he says: "What do you know about it"?' We could see his drink-spattered menace. Susan jittered, threading strands of hair between her fingers.

'So . . .' Maud grew again into her large body. 'So, I say to him: "I know what I know!" '

We watched her shrink again, the darkness spreading through her eyes; the desolation of too much intensity crossing her face. 'You know too much, you know that?' We could hear the threat in his quiet voice. 'You live off other people's lives. You carry stories . . .' We could hear the impotency of his rage. 'You carry stories to everyone – even to Susan. Don't you? Don't you?'

'And he pushes at me, like this, with his hand.' She rose to the righteous height of her elder statesman. 'And then he says I am fired, just like that.'

'Hha!' Susan and I gasped simultaneously. 'On the spot, Maud?' asked Susan, her hands suddenly still.

'On the spot!'

'My God,' she said. 'The fucking hypocrite – fucking little arsehole pretends to be a socialist. Surely he gave you a month's pay, Maud?'

'Nothing,' she said, her composure aggrieved, her hands folded in her lap as she sat again. 'No, he says I never did my job. He says I never clean the house nicely anyway. Ka-cha! Now I must search for another piecework on his day.'

We were quiet as Maud allowed herself, just for a moment, to relish the piety of victimization. I sidled up to Susan and, lifting her hair, whispered very quietly: 'Well, he is an appalling arsehole, but you have to admit he's right about the amount of actual charring that gets done.'

Susan smiled. Maud slurped her tea through her teeth, the tea bag still floating in the mug.

Ka-cha!

# 6

I can picture the sea almost exactly as it was that salt-edged day. Strangely, that's how I always conjure it. Not wild with spray, or dark with tumult. It is always that calm sea which glints and glistens before my eyes, now grown so weary of grey. And it is that day, sated with sun, and sand, and the pink juice of lamb chops, which stubbornly appears just beyond my window.

There was nothing significant about the day. Nothing particular that happened or should have happened. But I suppose I remember it for what it was. It was showy Cape Town, flouncing her colours and flashing her sea. I remember looking and feasting, and thinking that I should encapsulate the gut-warming heat. I felt a slowing of time, that day.

It was a day free from everything – from the dank gathering of violence, and the building of forces that we wanted to be part of, but had no place in. From the battle that we cheered with quixotic zeal, and yet feared, for its unknown end. It granted us a time out of time from the remorse of living each deceitfully normal day while knowing that each of us, by living our lives, allowed things to be, which should never be.

But Cape Town had a way of removing herself, on days like this. In her green and her softness, she had a way of denying her Africanness. She had none of the severity which gave depth to the continent she clung to. There was no struggle in her beauty, no battle for survival.

We drove to Gordon's Bay – it must have been a Saturday. We stood watching the sea, which basked in the sunlight, too leaden with laziness to heave its waves.

By coming to the Cape . . . I was watching the horizon misting at its morning edges . . . I supposed that we had made it easier to be African. Our choice mocked all our ambivalences to this land of life-sacrificing vegetation. Here, as the sunlight danced with the sea, you could open your eyes and hardly see the poverty and ferocity, stretched just beyond us.

'Do you ever think,' I asked Susan, 'that it wasn't so very cool of us to come to Cape Town?'

'What on earth are you on about?'

'Don't you ever think that it's just an easier place for suburban refugees like us to feel like lefties? I mean an easier place to cope with . . . well, things?'

'God, you're weird sometimes! I don't know what you're rambling on about. But whatever . . . Everything is supposed to be more populist here, I mean the Left, you know?'

She sucked at her cigarette and twirled her hair around her fingers. I watched her, always fighting the words from her taut mouth.

'Anyway . . .' She crushed out her cigarette and retrieved a peppermint from her pocket. '. . . I know someone who went to a mass rally here to launch the UDF. She said it was the first time she felt she really belonged. No one haggled over who was a liberal or a Trot, or had read Oblivitskovitsky.'

She looked like a waif, hunched over the hand she was chewing on. I thought I saw glimpses of another Susan, the universal daughter-niece-grandchild. Her clothing, worn over her frivolous bikini, was little-girl, but as usual, just slightly offbeat. Her princess-collared shirt was that bit too small, outlining her nipples and swelling a cleavage where usually she had none.

We'd been invited to join her uncle and aunt, and I think it was her great-aunt, for a *braai* on the beach. This lesser Susan had risen to greet them. I didn't mind it so very much. We all had a child inside, to some extent. Her child persona seemed younger than mine. Just as well. Mine hung around, haunting the *stoep* of my childhood home. A twelve-or thirteen-year-old, it burst between absolute childishness and blasts of adolescent truculence.

'So, will you come with me to Ilsa's UDF meeting?' I asked her.

'*Ja*, why not. When – this evening? *Ja* . . .' She sighed. '. . . Let's go and see if we're still insecure enough to be frightened away. Oh, listen Sister . . .'

I was unwrapping the plastic from a new packet of cigarettes.

'Listen, here come my aunt and uncle – Jeez, that's lucky! At least I managed to get the meeting place right, for once. Listen, please don't offer me a smoke in front of them.'

'I cannot actually believe this. You. You've been divorced, had a million lovers, and you're not going to smoke in front of your auntie and uncle.'

'Well, I just can't. She's my mom's sister.' She shaded her eyes to watch the red Mercedes pull up alongside her battered Morris. 'Just relax. It's not as if I see them that often. But they're so jolly normal . . .' She pulled her tangled fingers from her mouth and gave a tight little wave. '. . . I think we both need some normality, just for a day.'

They were wonderful. I loved them for the serene warmth they brought, along with their picnic basket, beers and lamb chops. And Fortris for Penny, their lank-limbed daughter, which we drank in pure nostalgia, sucking through our teeth the taste of after-school snacks and peaches with the down still on them.

They gave us a day of purity – freed us from the business of growing up. And from all of our tense reaching for hopes, as the romance we read into life changed its ending, again and again.

The old lady was splendidly bigoted in a way impossible to take badly. She knew she made us all laugh and, in a way, I think she caricatured herself for us, her hawk-nosed Wasp prejudices and her colonial views.

'Come and sit, girls. Let's settle the blanket up here above the sand, under the trees. My goodness, just look at that sea!' That was Aunt Meg, comfortingly proper in her spotless linen shorts. I watched her peel them off to expose her Viyella one-piece. I wondered if her daughter had told her she had to wear it. It was so similar to my mother's – the one she had bought with tear-sheened eyes the day she turned forty. She had turned to me for reassurance, in the fostering of some mythical mother–daughter chumminess. Only that once. And I had told her she was far too old for a bikini, anyway.

I found Meg so motherlike that day, but without the rub of my own abrasive adolescence, just past.

I remember the smell of meat, mixed with the breeze-brought tang of seaweed, as we soaked our languid bodies and giggled on the sand. And we listened, sucking Fortris through straws, to Great-aunt Dorrie telling us about the family.

'Of course, I think she did very well for herself,' she articulated in her low voice. 'Meg? Did you hear that? I said you married well.'

'Dorrie . . . I'm just ignoring you. I know you're about to say something absolutely dreadful.' She smiled her rounded smile at the old lady, who pursed her lips.

'I don't quite know, Meg, why you should make an assumption like that. I was about to say it was clever of you to marry a Jew.'

'Oh Dorrie!'

We gasped into outraged giggles and I threw a glance at Ben, Meg's husband. He was smiling serenely at the meat he was turning with *braai* tongs.

'Well of course I think so too,' he said. 'But it's funny, Dorrie, I got the distinct impression you disapproved of me once.'

'She was always hopeless with money, that girl, just hopeless! And they're so talented with money, you know – the Jews. Look how well he's done in his business.'

Ben roared with laughter, lifting the chops into a waiting pan.

'Aunt Dorrie! I can't believe you can be so anti-Semitic,' said Penny, staring at the old lady with the severity of her youth.

'Nonsense,' she said, turning the full magnificence of her raptor nose on the child. 'I didn't say I didn't like Jews. I admire their traits. I think they're clever.'

We ran – the three children, as we were that day – and belly-flopped our hot, laughing bodies into the water. It was almost too warm to refresh us. And we ate, dripping with salt and meat rivulets, which ran down our arms and mingled with the watery pools on our thighs.

'Well, now I have you captive . . .' said Great-aunt Dorrie. She didn't elaborate for a minute and we felt too lazy to ask. We watched as Ben settled himself on the blanket, beat a towel into shape under his head and closed his eyes. Meg was reclining on a beach lounger, immersed in her Joanna Trollope. It was covered in plastic – obviously a book-club book. I'd seen it in my mother's book-club basket too.

'I was saying . . .' Dorrie's voice rose to attract our attention. We were lying on our towels, heads propped on elbows. 'I was saying that you can't swim or run around for at least an hour after your lunch, so you girls can read to me from the newspaper.'

I sat and unfolded the *Cape Times*. I really didn't feel like it today. Not today.

'Well, what would you like to hear, Aunt Dorrie?' I asked. 'The front page is interesting. It's all about how the laws banning interracial sex and marriage are being scrapped.'

'Good show!' called Ben, his voice muffled under the hat he had drawn over his face.

'Now, why on earth do you think I want to hear that rubbish?' said Dorrie. 'I've never had the least inclination to marry anyone but one of my own. Read me something interesting.'

'Well, there was a fire in a soccer stadium in Bradford . . .'

'Goodness, child! No one I know would play soccer – a game for hooligans. And I don't care much for those soccer-mad Pommies, either.'

'OK, well . . . that certainly cuts down the news options a bit,' I mumbled to Susan, who lay giggling, her face – for once the calm face of her childhood – platformed on her two hands.

'Well I don't suppose you'll be interested, Aunt Dorrie, but I'll tell you anyway: "Three UDF sympathizers, including an eleven-year-old, were detained . . ." '

'No, no. I can't be bothered with these UDFs and Cosatus and things. Read on.'

'Here's one for you, Aunt Dorrie. Bruce Springsteen married secretly.'

Susan and Penny burst into laughter, their bodies bouncing on their towels. Their legs were sticking up in the air, twining around each other's, jostling in cousinly competitiveness.

'And here . . . woah, now here's something you'll like, Aunt Dorrie. The cliffhanger in *Dynasty* has brought the country to a standstill. Everyone is bursting to know who was killed in the final episode, when they were all mown down in a massacre.'

'Oh yes,' said the old lady. She perked up a bit, but sniffed her aristocratic nose to show it was all a bit beneath her. 'I think I saw that programme. Go on, girl.'

'Well, this one isn't for you. A crowd of between 30,000 and 50,000 gathered for the funeral of Andries Raditsela – he was a unionist, Aunt Dorrie. There were work stoppages and prayers and . . .'

'Go on, go on. I don't want to hear about all their stoppages and things. Any excuse will do, it seems. What did he die of? Was he necklaced?'

'No, Aunt Dorrie. He died just after being released from police custody . . . Oh, here's one you'll like. A dieting model had been starving herself and she went on a binge of eating, and she died.'

'She died? From eating?'

'*Ja*, gutsed herself to death. Just like that.' I snapped my fingers together and refolded the newspaper.

Dorrie sighed. 'There's nothing in the papers any more. Just violence, and more violence, and shootings and stoppages and funerals. And then they get themselves shot at the funerals and then it starts all over again.'

Penny sat up and pulled a large white shirt over her bikini, lifting her wet ponytail out of the collar with two graceful arms.

'Did you make that shirt in home economics class?' I asked her, wanting really just to deflect Dorrie from reflections that would dull this child-centred day.

'Does it show?' she asked, and giggled.

'No, it's just that all things made in school have one side that's better than the other – that's where your mother sat up all night to finish it before it was due.'

'That's fairly accurate.' Meg's voice came from behind Joanna Trollope.

Penny was giggling. 'Well, absolutely everybody's mother did . . .'

'Of course, what else are mothers for?'

'. . . Well, all except Bernice, of course.' Her voice slid into a sneer. 'She said her mother didn't do anything on hers. But she's a prefect.'

'Oh no, a prefect,' I said. 'Well, that accounts for that.'

'I know . . . but you know, she even has a deportment girdle.'

'Well, never mind. She'll come to a bad end. My old head prefect's ended up playing guitar in a happy-clappy church – deep in small-town Eastern Cape.'

The two of them gasped in horror. 'No, surely not,' said Susan, suitably hushed.

'Yes,' I said, elaborating. 'And I think she leads a Brownie pack . . . You know, you can always tell those girls who're going to be prefects. You know how everyone always sings the end-of-term hymn with such gusto:

'Lord dismiss us with thy blessing . . .'

I sang the first line and they both joined me boisterously on the next line:

'. . . Thanks for mercies past received.

'Well,' I said, portentously, 'and, you know how everyone just mumbles their way through assembly on the first day of term?' I conducted while we sang, in exaggeratedly tired voices:

'Lord receive us with thy blessing,

Once again assembled here . . .

'You watch out for who's bursting with song. They'll be prefects. And they never get caught wearing *tangas* in bloomer inspections.'

We spent a long time talking of school, stories of being caught taking the stairs two at a time or who was expelled for smoking in the loo. We were killing ourselves laughing, bursting with the winsome spirit of our schoolgirl selves.

While it was still midday-hot, we curled under the trees and read Penny's old *Bessie Bunters* and *Archies* and *Caspars*. And, as the sun dipped over the sea and threw the shivering shadows of trees on the sand, we played with the elastic Penny had brought – knotted together for break-time games. We made her mother and father stand, feet astride, holding it taut. We vied with each other to remember our most intricate steps, running over the elastic and around the grown-ups. And silly hopscotch, as the sun dulled with the exhaustion of the day, smearing the sky with washed-out pinks. We played it on the beach, drawing the squares and circles in the sand. Even Meg joined us, but Penny and I cheated by rubbing the lines off the sand when it suited us.

Only once that whole day did I see Susan's stress return, when Dorrie said: 'So do you think you have finished collecting husbands now, my girl? Will you settle down properly now?'

But Meg shushed her, as she poured our tea from thermos flasks and we slurped it from blue plastic cups. 'Leave the child,' she said. 'She's had her troubles, but thank the Lord, she's looking much better now.'

That was, as I remember it, the last true day of summer, the last day that I ever remember being truly young and full of sun-ripened juices. As the sun fell and spilt itself over the sea, we sat, swinging our feet on the grassy edge.

We drove back in our chugging way, falling further and further behind the Mercedes. Suddenly, spread beside that monotonous national road, we came upon a vast, *toyi-toyi*ng crowd, singing and chanting and ululating. We drove alongside them, held up by the cars which crawled in apprehensive crocodile, windows firmly closed, eyes in front.

Yellow police Casspirs were placed strategically along the gravel verge. Very young policemen in riot gear held rifles, their faces blank with fear. We felt a ripple of foreboding at the sight of those confronting forces, held in check by a thin, taut line of command. But I remember there was exhilaration too. And that we both wanted so much to roll our windows down and throw a thumbs-up ANC salute. But that would have been silly – trying to grasp at some solidarity through one small illegal act . . .

. . . 'So how long have you been in Cape Town?'

I mumbled something like, 'Couple of months', and listened to someone going on about sharing resources and skills, and something about consciousness-raising.

I had embarrassed myself, at the entrance to the small Obs semi that Susan and I had struggled to find in the narrow streets.

'Um . . .' I said, as the earringed young man opened the door. 'We're looking for a meeting.'

'Are you looking for the Odag meeting?' he asked, opening the door a little wider, but looking us up and down nonetheless.

'No, um, Ilsa told us to come. She said it was a UDF meeting.'

And then he smiled, but in that patronizing way that brought the heat to our faces, as we stood in the whipping south-easter.

'Well, it is of course,' he said. 'The UDF is an umbrella grouping of democratic organizations.' He peered at us, one eyebrow raised. The wind whirled around our legs and brought our arms protectively about our chests. 'One of those organizations, of course, is our very own Observatory Democratic Action Group.'

Oh Jesus, but we could make ourselves cringe in those days. I saw him later, chatting to a small group of people across the room, smiling beatifically at his own cleverness. A young woman had linked her arm into his. She wore her jeans so well. God, I was jealous. It always seemed so easy to be a leftie if you could wear jeans so well. Just tight enough and just loose enough to wrinkle attractively at the knee. Not too tight, mind. That wouldn't be cool.

Alongside me, someone was saying something about Pete, who's 'not really committed, you know. I think it's his background'.

'I know what you mean about him,' someone answered. 'You

know, like, in some ways, the greatest enemy of the bourgeois-born Left is their own families. Of course my family isn't truly middle-class, but I understand . . .'

'Aw, fuck, Melanie. What shit are you speaking?' A bearded young man lit a cigarette and blew a very precise smoke ring into the silence he had created. 'What d'you mean you aren't middle-class?'

'Well, my background isn't. My grandparents were Lithuanian immigrants – they were very poor, you know.'

'Aw fuck off, Melanie. Everybody's grandparents were Lithuanian immigrants once. Jeez, but you're full of shit. Why can't you all just accept that you come from bourgeois backgrounds – you can rise above that, can't you?'

And then I spoke. Even as my mind was telling me to shut up and blend in, I could feel the words spilling from my uncommitted mouth.

'Ja, I agree with you,' I said. 'I think it's quite pretentious to make out that we don't. What else can we do? My family is such 1820 Settler gentry they raise the Union Jack in the backyard and salute it every night while whistling "God Save the Queen".'

I don't know why I always did that sort of thing. Yes, I suppose I do. It was a wilful degradation, of myself and my caricatured family. It was an ironic offering of my background as a bribe, so they would laugh and like me despite it.

The bearded man laughed, quite unashamedly. I wondered how he came to be so confident that, in the silence of that mass disapproval, he could align himself with us by laughing.

'I don't think,' said Melanie, narrowing her eyes at me, 'that you should actually be so proud of a background like that.'

'No,' I said, 'I thought you would . . . Well I thought it was funny. I'm not . . .'

'Leave it,' said the bearded man, still laughing, 'let's sit down.'

'Ja,' Susan said, squeezing against my arm as she lit two cigarettes. 'They've had their sense of humour surgically removed.'

I blinked at the heat behind my eyes, sweeping them around the room to stop them from filling. The gathering was mainly white, but a smattering of dark faces crayoned in a certain credibility. In the centre sat a young black man, withdrawn from the chatter, conspicuous by his air of studied relaxation – arms folded over his chest, feet crossed on the coffee table. People talked around him, giving him space while others were jostling for seats. He raised his eyes and they met mine – mine burning with humiliation. His – I couldn't tell. But fancifully, I remember thinking that they seemed filled with too much for his slim, young body to hold.

'Who's that?' I asked my bearded man, gesturing with my chin.

'Oh, well spotted,' he said. 'He's about the most important person here. We only know him as Mandla. He's said to be the Botswana connection.'

'For the ANC? OK. But what does he do? Does he fight? Does he carry messages? What?'

'God knows. And he certainly wouldn't tell you, so don't go asking, in that quaint way of yours. How did you get to be here, by the way?'

We were smiling, relaxing into his acceptance of us. Susan offered him a cigarette, eyes flitting about her.

'Ilsa asked us,' I said, and our eyes sought her out, floating in the background. Never drawn into the fervency of discussions, she flirted with corners, whispering to people, nodding, whispering again behind tilted, silent heads.

'So, you know the bigshots here, hey?'

'Oh really?' said Susan. 'We never know what's really going on. Shit . . .' she ripped at a fingernail, her jaw taut with effort.

'*Ja*, rumour has it she's a member of the party – does important work.'

'You mean the ANC? Shit, and we just thought she was some fuckhead type who never did much.'

He laughed. 'Well, maybe that's her cover, the harmless fuckhead thing. And no, I don't mean the ANC. I mean a little to the left – like the communist party.'

What else do I remember? We were there to discuss the delegate to the UDF national congress in Johannesburg. It seemed to whizz past us: the proposal, the 'Yeah's, the 'Sure, she's really committed's.

And: 'Do we have consensus?' Yes, of course we did. Who on earth was going to argue with that wave of decision?

Propping his long confident legs on the coffee table, our bearded man said: 'The punting of the Stalinists! That was neatly buttoned up before we got here. Feel useful? Feel you're making grand democratic decisions? I'm Mike, by the way.'

We giggled, drawing attention to ourselves.

'Um,' said the woman who wore her jeans well, 'uh, I'd just like to say that I find it offensive that Mike over there has his feet on the table. That's really typical of your male domineering attitude, Mike.'

'Aw shit,' he muttered, lifting his legs to the floor with his arms.

'*Ja*, you're always the same. Your body language like expresses your belief that you're in charge here.'

I waited till they were busy with the next point of discussion. Very inconspicuously, I whispered: 'So why did you get shat on and not that Mandla?'

'Don't be crazy,' he whispered back, chastened now.

Not so long ago, searching for something to do between the polishing of Kentish surfaces and the tidying of white cupboards, I found my old suitcase. And, almost of its own volition, it still held everything I had once wanted to keep, the small trappings of my life. There I found the crumpled resolution which was taken that day.

So many words. As I look at them again, I remember that someone argued against using the words 'democratic forces', which he felt had a militarist flavour.

'Perhaps we could say the "oppressed peoples" instead,' he said. But, while the gathering appreciated the sentiment, they felt his words implied an acceptance of the apartheid mythology that there were different 'people plural'.

'OK, OK!' he said. I can no longer see his face, but I can still play back the anxiety in his voice. 'So let's say: "the oppressed men and women".'

And Good-jeans leapt in, confident of her position in the in-group: 'My God, surely you mean "women and men"? Can I be hearing this patriarchal bullshit . . .?'

'He's about to be purged,' whispered Mike. 'Can you tell? Probably a Trot!' . . .

. . . 'Who're you phoning?' my husband asks, arriving from the office and passing me without a touch in the passage. 'Aren't you about to serve dinner?'

'Oh, no one important. Just something I have to do. Could you pour yourself a drink? I won't be long.'

'Well, yes. Fine. But I've had a long day. It would be nice if we could eat fairly soon. Who are you phoning? You're not still chasing after that Susan, are you?'

My hand jerks guiltily as I redial the South African number. But he is gone, too intent on the sitting room's girlish esteem to notice my reaction. How does he always manage to see through my small deceits, to place his cool, controlled finger on exactly what I am doing? I suppose I so seldom make phone calls. I make so little effort to involve myself closely with other people – beyond the merely polite or the shopper's greeting – that it isn't that hard to guess whom I might be phoning.

'Hello?'

'Hello, is that Aunt Meg, uh, Meg?'

'No, this is Penelope. I'm afraid my mother's not available. She's not well. Can I help you?'

'Um, Penny, I don't know if you'll even remember me. This is Jennifer – Susan's friend, from Cape Town.'

'Oh . . . yes. Vaguely. Gordon's Bay, wasn't it? Did you want my mother? I'm afraid she's going through radiotherapy – that's why I'm home. She's having a hard time with it. Was there something you wanted?'

'Oh God, I'm so sorry. Please give her my love and tell her I hope . . . I hope she gets better. I often think about her. She was so warm, so . . . I always thought of her as such a . . . well, a mother I suppose.'

'Yes, we're still good friends. I hope she gets through this. But she's a fighter . . .'

'This seems so unimportant now. But I'm trying to reach Susan. We lost touch . . .'

'Yes, I heard . . . My parents always used to ask after you. Strange, that. You were so close, weren't you?'

'Yes, and now . . . well, now I just need to see her so badly. I miss her, you know? And . . . And I need to come to terms . . . well, I just need us to talk about things.'

'Yes. I think I understand. But I'm afraid . . . well, it's not that we ever see much of her. But she came to see my mother when she was diagnosed. She said she was going overseas with Rodney on this business trip. I think they've shoved the kids in boarding school in a kind of last ditch attempt to save the marriage.'

'So what's he like – Rodney? Do you think he understands what she's like, Penny? Does he ever encourage her to paint?'

'Rodney? I don't think he knows one end of a paintbrush from the other. No, he's a company man, through and through.'

'And so? Do you think they'll split up?'

'Who knows? He may be ordinary, but you know, I don't think he's necessarily bad for her. In some ways I think he stabilizes her, but . . . we'll see. She's always seemed to be carrying so much baggage.'

'Yes . . . I suppose me too. Maybe that's why I'm phoning. I'm living in England now. I was hoping I could meet her while she was here.'

'Well, perhaps you could try Rodney's London office, Alcon. I'm afraid I don't know the number.'

'That's OK, it should be in the book. Thanks . . . Thanks for everything, Penny. Good luck. And please, I really wish everything of the best for your mom.'

'Thanks Jennifer. Good luck finding Susan. Bye.'

As I replace the telephone, I realize that I have forgotten. I have been too absorbed in my own needs to ask her about herself, about how she's ended up, about what kind of grown-up she's become . . .

. . . Now it has come – the time when I must think through that Sunday, the day from which my mind has constantly ricocheted. Now I have to think about it, if I am to understand the effect it had on the spiralling events which formed us.

We were so imprisoned, that day, by our bubble-enclosed view of ourselves. Beyond its rainbow perspective, we could see nothing of Jonathan, nothing at all of his feelings and his hurts.

I suppose it started with the tequilas, that afternoon which no one else has ever heard about, which my mother never knew of, which – in that orgy of pre-marriage disclosures of lovers and friends – never was spoken of.

That was the time when Susan and I still vacillated over who we were. We were still young enough to agonize over our wavering image as innocent experimenters, as decadent sophisticates, as young girls in search of love, as New Women, or as promiscuous sluts. Now, of course, I think that I was never arresting enough to be given a label, and so I was none of them. And Susan? Susan was special.

It began with Jonathan, who picked us up for a late lunch while the wind gave its banshee yell past our house. I remember the shampooed niceness of him. And I remember that I could feel trouble that day. I could smell it in the entanglement of his soap-scrubbed essence and Susan's wild redolence of mossy depths and twining roots.

I shouldn't have let her accept his invitation. I had heard her cry in the night. I hadn't gone to her – her pain was too dank and fetid to be warmed by me. But I think she knew. She knew I could hear, and that I sat with my cheek and my hand pressed to the wall. It was the picnic I think – with its desolate picture of enclosed serenity – and, in a way, it was the political meeting, in all its excluding intensity, which made her regurgitate the churning depths of a marriage which sat rank in her gut.

Oh hell, I should just look at it head-on now, and consider it in perspective. Back then our excesses never stemmed from boredom. It seems to me that we whirled through those wild and dangerous years, untouched in body but not in our hearts, by the violence which howled its fury about us. Flung to and fro by our vision of ourselves and how we wanted to be, by our rebellious desires to be everything that our mothers were not, and yet earn their love in the only way we knew how, we fluttered uncommitted where we most wanted involvement. And in the end, the forces we thought did not affect us, caught us in their grasp and flung us into this desperate hedonism and dervish nihilism.

We insisted on the Speakeasy, the restaurant where Susan and I would go periodically to gorge ourselves in an orgy of pasta and cold white wine. Susan was being outrageous. She was challenging Jonathan to be more than he could be.

'Jonathan? Tell us your kinkiest fantasy.'

'Oh Susie . . .' Susan winced at the diminutive. 'I'm not really a great one for that kind of thing, you know. For me, it's an expression of love. I can't . . .'

'Oh come on, don't be a dweet.'

That's how it went on, while we drank more and more and Susan's eyes dilated in unleashed tension.

'Let's have tequila slammers,' she suggested at last.

'Oh really, Susie, I don't know if I could stomach . . .'

'Oh Jesus, you are a lame prick. Come Jennifer, let's go share a joint in the loo.'

# Touching The Lighthouse

I looked back at him as we made our way through the tables, mopping his reddened face on his serviette, twisting it unhappily in his steady hands.

We left the restaurant late, Jonathan trying to make light of our tequila glut and our challengingly open smoking of joints.

'Well, it's lucky I'm driving, isn't it?' he said, with a desolate chuckle.

We were silent as he drove us home. Perhaps he wanted to leave us then, I don't know. But Susan was reluctant to let him go. She wanted to make sport of him in his symbolic aspect of Nice Young Man. She wanted to test him, knowing he was bound to fail her. He opened her door, as she knew he would. And brushing her belly against his, she dragged him into the lounge and poured him wine, which he didn't want. In perspiring discomfort, he shielded himself from our drug-loosened gaze.

'Oh come on, Susie. I don't know how to react . . .'

'Oh? How do you react to this?' she asked him, rubbing her belly and breasts against mine, as I hovered uncertainly in the doorway.

'Oh God, Susan. Don't.' He gulped at his wine. Choking suddenly, he brought tears to his eyes.

Putting me aside, Susan strode to the hi-fi and snatched an album on to the turntable. I can feel it still, that music she chose, the spice-tinged swirl of North Africa, and the carnal beat of virility and war.

It pounded through the walls, thrusting itself at our bowels. We began to move with it, Susan laughing wildly at the ceiling. Jonathan made no more attempts to leave, staring slack-mouthed at the swooning together of our pliant bodies. And I? It's hard to say how I felt in the heat of that room, with the memory of tequila in my mouth. I was fascinated by my unwilling arousal from Susan's touch, at the forbidden quality of her lissome dance. And by Jonathan, daring us with his agonized excitement.

Susan was using me as her foil in this punishing display, taunting the goodness in him which so irritated her. But as we camped it up for Jonathan, stroking each other's soft flesh, our gasped breathing and small faked cries became the reality. As we paused briefly to look into each other's eyes, our chests were heaving with the heat of each other's mouths. Falling to her knees, Susan rolled my short skirt upward and ran her hands up my inner thighs, laying them to rest on my sweat-drenched under-wear. I pulled her up and, without looking at her eyes, pulled my dress over my head. I looked again and she was naked. And then, so was I.

I vaguely remember Jonathan. I think he held his hands to his face. I know he was there to the end, but he, whose presence had caused what happened, became unimportant to its culmination.

We swayed together, feeling the unaccustomed softness, learn-ing the lust of searching nipples and the cave feel of our deepest insides. Still the music burst through us, moving us through the narcissistic stroking of our own bodies, displaying them for each other with arched backs and spread thighs. We moved, and our movement became our own ritual dance, celebrating a pagan taboo.

'Oh God, I can't take this.' Jonathan made a small move to leave, but Susan pushed him back, unwilling to let go of this voyeuristic power she had, watching what should never be watched – this corruption of an innocent soul. He didn't try to leave again.

As Susan turned back to me, all feeling I had had for him was muffled by the feral smell of our arousal. I pressed against the skin of her chest and pulled her to me, my hand in the damp hollow of her back. She pressed her mouth to mine, tasting of sweat and smoke and tequila. I felt her forbidden tongue in the secret darkness of my mouth. And then I tasted the sulphur of her wildness catch and flare and I, who was too close to her in many ways, felt my own catch and flare.

'Lick me,' she whispered, pulling back from me. 'Get down and lick me.' Her eyes, darkened by wild pupils, clutched at me. I was suffused by my own excitement, and a dread that was close to nausea. Slowly, I found the petal feel of her. She tasted clean and sea-like, redolent of kelp. Filled with primeval fears, I sucked at her until she came in a rush of wetness on my chin.

Pressing me to the ground, she rubbed her alien breasts over my belly. And then she spread my thighs apart with those tense, capable hands and lifted me to her mouth until, wavelike and relentless, my body was flung into its own spasm.

We lay still, the record ended, our breathing labouring its echoes through the silence of the room. We didn't look at each other, but lay – naked limbs entwined – as we heard Jonathan shuffle from the room. We heard the front door slam.

# Touching The Lighthouse

I wanted to ask her if she was OK, if her fragile mind was holding on to all its parts. But I didn't want to bring my harsh voice and plodding fears into the room. I wanted everything still to be OK, the balance of our friendship intact, with no shame to mar our closeness.

We didn't speak of it. As I lifted my head she ran her finger down my face. For once I felt unable to read her smile.

There were many aspects to that afternoon – and to my relationship with Susan – which shaped that year and all the things which happened. It had a wild and innocent aspect, the unfettered experimentation of children. The touching of cousins in the blanketed night, while the grown-ups talk next door. And it had the darkness of Susan's pain, and the decadence of pushing back all our boundaries to experience all of the hidden depths of life . . .

. . . Susan and I, sitting on the couch, spoke in that momentous way we had, about the passages of our lives. I watched her match flare in the dark as she lit our cigarettes and placed one between my lips. We had been to work that day, but I can remember nothing of it. A Monday, I suppose, like any other. Susan and I were gentle with each other as we poured our wine and scavenged in the fridge for leftovers – eaten out of the pot with two spoons.

'The reason we are different from other people,' she said to me, 'is that we see each passage as an adventure. It means that some things don't mark us the way they do others – we don't see things as irrevocable or that they have to change our lives.'

'But some things,' I said, thinking of her pain and the shattered pieces of her, 'some things hurt us more deeply than they do other people, because we don't expect them to and we open ourselves up to each adventure.'

'Mm.' Her spread fingers just touched the tips of mine. We sat in the darkness smoking, sipping at the cheap red wine which reminded us of the uncomplicated strands of our university times. 'But that adventuring, you know . . .' I watched her struggle with her words, spreading her expressive hands to show me our universe. '. . . It also means that we do push the limits, sometimes to the edges of our sanity.'

I saw the stretched wires of her soul, singing with the intensity of her threatened reason, and with the beauty of her strung mind. And I feared for her. I feared for me too. But I feared for her more.

I wanted to expand again and stand before her brittle talent, protect her from all that could pierce that surprisingly open spirit. Her body tried to do it, with its clutching arms and bowed, protective shoulders. But it wasn't enough.

'I suppose,' I said to her, 'that, in society's terms, we should be looking for husbands. We should be doing something our mothers can understand. Then perhaps they'd be close to us, instead of tolerating us with great patience.'

'You can understand it, I suppose,' she said. 'Getting married and having children was their life's work, which is ruined if we don't do it too.'

'Well, I suppose that sometimes I do want that. But . . .' I sucked at my cigarette, grasping for my concepts. 'But I also know that we don't seriously look for those things, you and I. Because otherwise, how could we do it so badly, how could we perversely seek out the losers, the psychopaths, the arseholes that we do?'

Susan's laugh lilted through the airless room, its windows closed against the howl of the south-easter outside. 'We do, don't we? But I suppose it's addictive – the intensity and the edge-living.'

*Kalatter kalatter kalatter, kalatter kalatter kalatter skreee-ee-ee*
      I was nearly dressed, wetting my stubborn hair and twisting it to add some body. I waited, and there they were, her key and clumping steps. I entered the kitchen at the same time as Susan, just as Maud switched on the kettle.

'Morning Maud.'

'Morning Maud.'

She ignored us, standing stolidly before the sink, scrabbling in the upper cabinet for the mug she preferred. She poured her milk in first, added the tea bag, and watched as its swirling brown was coaxed out by boiling water. We stood expectantly while she sat herself heavily on the dining-room chair, which lived here now. She stirred in three spoons of sugar and slurped at the mug.

'Aah,' she said. 'Yes. Life is not always easy.'

'Well, that's true,' said Susan, popping bread into the toaster and pouring just-boiled water into our instant coffee. 'But surely not for our own Merry-Greenpoint Widow-Madam.'

Susan was insatiable still for news of her. Perhaps she wondered if the grand post-funeral break-up was final, or perhaps she just masochistically wished to draw out stories of Greenpoint's beauty, her wealth and her charm.

Maud gave a flicker of a smile. 'Well no, the Greenpoint Madam – it seems her life is good without that no-good husband. She has a good job. She is not poor like you two.'

We waited for her sparkling narrator-person to take over, for our telescopic view into other people's houses, and other people's lives. But she remained subdued. Her eyes were screened, not opening on to the Greenpoint Madam's next Act. We waited, but she held to the heavy curtain of her dignity.

'And so?' asked Susan, twitching, unable to bear the waiting.

115

'What's she doing? Has she got new clothes?'

'Oh yes,' said Maud. But she remained sitting, planted before the mug, while she sucked her tea through her teeth. 'Oh yes, she always has new clothes. Very pretty clothes. Nicer than yours. She gives me her old ones.'

She lifted her eyes momentarily in stolid reproach, but dropped them again to her tea.

'She has a new boyfriend . . .' she said, as if in afterthought. Our fingers stopped stirring and both our faces turned to look at her, where she sat in indifferent pride.

'Yes?' I said. 'Who is he?

'His name is Manie. She says she met him at the work. He is a big buyer – he buys all the stuff she sells at the work.'

I glanced at Susan. She was a little tight-faced this morning. I think she wanted me to do the asking. But she was as intent as I to have Maud bring him into the room so that we could picture him, hear him speak, and to get a sense of him.

'What's he look like, Maud? Handsome? Nice man?'

'Well, he is big man. Very big man.' She held her hands as though she were holding two pumpkins, to give us the impression of great, rounded buttocks. But her heart wasn't in it. Her eyes didn't glint with the appreciation of her wickedness. No smile larked about on her features. 'He has a big car,' she added, nodding appreciatively at her mug. She sighed. 'But I have seen him only once. So I cannot tell you much.'

'Is something wrong, Maud?' I asked, unnerved by this change in her. We didn't want her to change. In our expectations of her, she kept us rooted in the reality of life and ordinary people unaffected by ourselves. She marked for us, in her expected way, each changing week, each lowering season.

*Ka-cha.*

'Is it us, Maud?' I asked.

Susan whirled on me, pointing at me with the knife that was now covered in Bovril.

'Dear God, Sister, but your paranoia knows no bounds. You do that with me, you know. It's really, really irritating. As soon as someone's a little down, you have to think it's you. You have to seek reassurance. Shit!' She swung her stiff figure back to her spreading.

*Ka-cha.*

116

'Maud?' I said quietly. 'What's the matter?'

'*Ag*, it is the piecework I got in the place of her husband.' Maud jerked her head at Susan, as if it were her fault that her ex-husband had fired her, and caused her this sorrow.

Susan tightened her lips and made a small '*Ag-gg*' noise. She was viciously attacking the nearly empty Bovril jar. Oh God, she worried me. She had always erupted now and again, seeming so filled with amorphous resentment that it vomited from her – usually over something inconsequential like my shoes left on the kitchen table. But it had always had the amusement of familiarity, the wry irritation of too much closeness. Not this cold, bitter taunting of isolation. I watched her brittle movements for a minute, before turning back to Maud. Resting her forehead against her palm, Maud emptied her teacup and stood to place it in the sink. She scuffled busily with the taps and the dishes.

'Where is the piecework, Maud?'

'In Woodstock. Not so very far from here.'

'Oh yes? And are they awful people – messier than us?' I began to laugh, but quietened in the silent room.

'They tell me they sometimes do things at night, and then after, I must clean.'

'Like parties, you mean?'

'Like those operations.'

I frowned into my coffee mug, unable to understand, yet hesitant about questioning her further, as I saw the fury she was venting with the pot scourer. We had left dishes in the sink, and for once, she hadn't chided.

'Like . . .' I waited for her to supply the rest, but she was silent. Susan poured another cup of coffee and stood with her back to us, facing the glossy emptiness of the kitchen cabinet.

'You mean, like . . . like what sort of operations?'

'When I go there, I can smell the blood.'

'Jesus, Maud. What kind of operations? What goes on there?'

'It is young girls go there. I saw one. She knocked on the door, crying, begging for help. They tell her to come in the night, another time.'

'You mean, like they do . . .'

'They take the babies out.'

'. . . abortions?'

'In the kitchen, there is a big wood table with straps on the wall

117

for the feet. And a big light hanging down, dirty with flies. Hm-hm-hm-hm-hm. Dirty. Walls are dirty. Hm-hm-hm-hm-hm. But when a person must look for a job, then life is very hard.'

'Oh God, Maud. Was it awful? I'm so sorry.'

'Blood. Too much blood. Blood on the big table and on the floor. And flies sitting in all the sticky mess.'

'Shit!'

Susan still had her back to us. I peered round the side of her. Her eyes were closed and her face white.

'They say I must clean all the blood. Too much blood. And old. Old and hard and sticking to the floor. I say: "No, this is too much for me. I am leaving." But the man raises his hand to me, like this, and he threatens me and says I have come to work, I must work. So, I must scrub, with my old back and these knees, I must kneel and I must scrub at that blood until it is gone.'

Susan walked out without a word to either of us. I heard her pause to pick up her bag, before the front door slammed. I didn't know what to say to Maud, or how to comfort. I felt inadequate in my bloodless life, in having no frame within which to appreciate what she had gone through or give her my support.

'But Maudie, you mustn't go back. You can't, surely. You don't need that piecework that badly, do you? Maudie?'

'I need it very bad for my grandchild's schoolbooks. But I will not go back. I will never do that, scrub on my hands and knees at the blood. Never.'

'I'll . . . I'll tell people you're looking for piecework, Maud. We'll try to find you something.'

*Ka-cha.*

# 7

'I call Silas Lizo Ntloko.'

Oupa Kakaza sat in straitened dignity, pressed by unruly boys, captive to the stares of the crowds. Gazing at the coat of arms on the wall, he seemed to take his mind, wrapped in its own gravity, beyond the sweat of the courtroom, beyond the whirring flap of the fan.

'So help me, God,' said the young man in the witness box. His dark face was disfigured by a smear of white flesh – perhaps a burn scar. Would a burn scar look as this did? Perhaps it would be taken as a sign, I remember thinking – that creeping of white from beneath the black. The mark of Judas, in this turnabout country where white was never pure, never sanctified by symbolism.

'Yes, My Lord, we are ready,' said the interpreter, straining his self-important stomach against his buttons. He looked at the witness, frowned and shook his head. The young man, Lizo, was lifting one leg and then the other, rubbing at his shiny face with his sleeve. He swept his gaze towards the long benches of the accused, but seemed to flinch from the sight of them.

I felt terribly sorry for him. I had never been called upon to make such a choice. Never. Strangely, I remembered a girl at my school, her vibrant red curls always an affront to the headmistress. She had been punished for them, made to stand on the school hall stage to have the forbidden perm brushed from her head in ritual humiliation. Only, it wasn't a perm. As the headmistress pulled and, in growing fury, tore at her lovely hair, that girl clicked the rebellious drawing pins in her shoes against the floor, lifting one foot and then the other, in unbeaten triumph.

But they had cowed her in the end. She had been the only girl who had refused to scuttle under the tables when caught in Carlo's Coffee Bar. So out of bounds was that smoky café that we schoolgirls could be expelled just for being there.

Offered the choice of ratting on her companions to save her place in the school, she had held out – through the sarcasm of the headmistress, through the clucked tongues of the prefects. But inevitably, she had given in at last. She gave in, the truculent click of drawing pins gone, when her parents came to school and wept over her in the quadrangle. I wonder what became of her. I think it would have ruined her, crushed her living spirit while her body, obedient as the undead, went through the motions of completing matric and emerging into useless adulthood.

This boy would be ruined too. Dear God, but I was incorrigibly suburban. Please let nobody ever know I equated that girl's gymslip story with this young man, who had weighed jail and gallows against the spectre of the informer's death.

'. . . Yes, I attended the meeting called by Oupa . . . Yes, I see the man known as Oupa. There . . . the old man with the Number One in front of him.'

'Let the record show that the witness indicated Mr Kakaza,' the prosecutor said. 'Now, Mr Ntloko, what was the purpose of this meeting, called by the man you call "Oupa"?'

I watched the rapid exchange between the thin young man and the bulging front of the interpreter. The interpreter turned slowly back to face the judge, rocking on pompous feet and tugging at the sides of his jacket.

'My Lord, we went to the meeting to discuss the preparations for June the sixteenth. We, the youth leaders in the Langmanskraal Squatter Camp, were called to listen to the old man to prepare ourselves for the events on the day.'

'And which events were those which you, the youth of the Squatter Camp, were expecting, pray tell us? A few dead whites, perhaps?'

'Objection, My Lord.' Oupa's advocate was on his feet remarkably fast for his bulk. 'My learned friend is being unnecessarily inflammatory. And his question, My Lord, in any case, calls for conjecture. It is common cause that, certainly in public, there were no comments to this effect.'

'Yes, sustained. Please, Mr Erasmus. There is no jury here before which to waste such outstanding hyperbole. My assessors and I are entirely unimpressed by your dramatic ability.'

'Yes, My Lord. As the Court pleases. Mr Ntloko, can you

remember anything of Oupa's speech that day, to the youth leaders of Langmanskraal?'

'Yes. I remember he said that "One day, and it won't be long away, we the oppressed people will take back this country." He said: "It is the time for us to fight, the time to take a stand against those white people who think they can hold us under their feet for ever and ever." '

' "Time to fight", hm? And how did the people react, Mr Ntloko?'

The young man rubbed at his face, breathing high in his chest. 'Well, My Lord, they got excited. There were many people with their fists in the air. I think, at the back, there were some who called "Kill them. Shoot the whites as they shoot us." '

'Oh yes? And how did the kindly Oupa react to this?'

'Objection, My Lord.' The advocate sounded weary of the necessity, tugging at his languidly slipping gown.

'Yes, sustained. Please control yourself, Mr Erasmus. No more of your ironic characterizations, if you please.'

'As the Court pleases. Yes, Mr Ntloko. What was Mr Kakaza's reaction?'

'He held out his hands to make the people silent, like this. And he called "*Amandla*". And the crowd shouted "*Awethu*". And then he went on with his speech.'

'Did he tell them that there shouldn't be any killing on the day? Did he tell them at all that they should be non-violent?'

'No, he said nothing like that. He said we should show them in our protests, on the day of our greatest sorrow, that we are unbowed. That we will soon make it so they cannot govern us. He said: "As you prepare for this day, remember that this is your country. It does not belong to the whites." '

'Thank you, Mr Ntloko. No further questions.'

He was taken through it all again in cross-examination, and I think he admitted to having attended hundreds of meetings before and after that day. I think he acknowledged that he remembered this one in such detail only because he had been told to by the prosecutor. And he did admit before them all that his evidence was paid for – by the dropping of the 'murder by common purpose' charges against him. That had he not stood before us and said these things, he would be sitting where the others were.

My mind didn't stay on that cross-examination. I wasn't calm that day. I was jumpy with fears, frantic with fantasies which haunted and delighted, which shamed and pleasured.

Yes, of course it was that. I couldn't get Susan from my mind, and what we had done. What we had done to Jonathan, and to each other. And whom he might tell. And what it would mean. I shivered with truant pride at the bravery of our cross-boundary explorations and I burnt with the image of what this would do to me, of how men might flinch from the shade of homosexuality. But mostly, I feared what it would do to Susan and me, and whether we could ever go back, or forward or whatever, without recoiling from mistaken touches, and without the elaborate avoidance of misunderstood caresses.

I still struggled with the wrestled mess of myself. I swung between notions of blasé sophisticate and innocent infant touching that which she didn't understand. Or perhaps the wild child who thought she was running headlong into life, but was running away, faster and faster in whirling, dizzy retreat.

I couldn't face those fervent young men in the accused bench. I couldn't chat to them of things, of life, of why I had forgotten their books again. I waited, head down, for them to be marched down to the cells, before I could face the combat in the railway station, the flurry and scrum on the train home . . .

. . . She came home late, brash with the tobacco and whisky smells of those tough girls she knew from her home town. She met them in the evening sometimes, for their raucous laughter and their arm-wrestled reminders of her less-than-genteel side. They made me uncomfortable. I hated their hard-girl image, and could never join in with their loud vulgarity. But Susan could. Susan's tough-girl self could smother her waif parts in planted elbows and mean-mouthed jokes.

She clumped in on feet which could have planted themselves astride at the hot-rod track on a Friday night.

'I've cooked some supper. Can you believe it?' I said, wary of this alien being. 'I've tidied too. Aren't you impressed?'

I must have seemed so irritating to this sure Susan – laying myself open, begging in pathetic puppiness for everything to be as it was before.

'Jesus God,' she said, striding to the fridge to deposit the six-pack of beer we would probably never finish, once she had returned to herself. She opened one, watching the manipulation of her arm muscles.

'Can't you fucking ever do anything without fucking reassurance? Can't you ever be a normal fucking grown-up? Fuck it!' she said as her hand slipped and she scraped it on the bottle-top.

She had been snorting amyl nitrate. Each time she turned or brushed past me, I could smell it – the reek of her betrayal of all that we were to each other. She and I had tried it before – I anxiously, she flinging her head back and declaring 'This is kid's stuff.'

It was part of how we saw ourselves, that we were willing to try almost anything, then. But it had always been together.

'What do you want from me, huh?' she asked into the silence. 'What do you want me to do? Thank you for cooking and cleaning? For doing something your fucking mother should have taught you to do in between her fucking decorating bursts.'

I know now, I think. It was her way of coping – to inflict the hurt which was to become an ulcerous ache in the gut of our friendship. It was a fearful withdrawal from the vulnerability the weekend had brought, and from her exposure to a threatened rejection which could lead to the final splintering of her inner self. But how was I, in my oversensitive skin, to know it then?

'Well, I thought at least you could have thanked me,' I said, petulance masking my hurt. 'And why do you have to bring my mother into this?'

'Oh? And who else is responsible for the pitiful fucking little cow that you are? Your mother was too busy decorating and redecorating her lounge, to teach you how to behave. You think you're such a fucking little Eastern Cape aristocrat. Well, I'll tell you. The only reason your mother was so filled with the need to redecorate all the time was to cover up her deep desire for flying ducks and copper animal plaques.'

That's when I shut down. Glassed into my mind's rational side, I watched with interest how easily the words came to her suddenly. She had always carried anger – a bitter fury at her ex-husband, and at herself for not being the kind of girl who could make life easy on herself. And she burnt with the injustice of having the parents to fill her with suburban expectations, and the talent and individuality which prevented her from realizing them. And now this. This new anger at having put herself at risk with me and made herself vulnerable. It filled her store of rage past the overflow mark.

I could reach down and almost touch the hurt she had inflicted. The worst was that she had pushed my own cruelty about my family back at me. She knew. She knew that the stuff about my family was off-limits. That I gave my family in mockery as a hostage, so people would like me and leave my background alone. She'd done the same with her family – the overstating of faults, of pretensions, of small-town views grown narrower with age and time.

'Oh, Jesus fucking Christ. How I hate the way you always gape there at me with those little-girl eyes just waiting to cry. You drive me mad, every day of my life. Can't you ever say anything – can't you fight back? What's the matter with you?'

We stood there, the day sliding us towards winter. I was locked in the enclosure of my mind, unable to clash kind with kind, or use the flashing swordplay of bitchiness – the school-perfected skills of bitter-tongued duel.

She swigged her beer. Her hair hung lank about the desolate toughness of her face. Unable to speak, I reached out for her, but her shoulders shrugged away from the touch. My hand grazed her breast and I tugged it back, fearful suddenly of what she might think. Her mouth, twisted with inner bitterness, split open and spilt her words at my feet.

'You fucking little freak. Scared, are you? Scared I'm going to jump you? You have no fucking idea, do you – you actually think I want you. Let me tell you now that if I wanted a woman, which in actual fact I don't, it wouldn't be you. I don't know how I've stuck you so long. The way you speak irritates me. Your stupid pretensions, the way you can't leave me alone. You must always creep up to me, you can't be on your own . . .'

She stopped on a burst of expelled air. I can still picture her, sucking at the cigarette she had lit for herself.

'And you're dull as fuck . . .' The burn of her words felt so real that I glanced down at my belly. '. . . You're so controlled, aren't you? We talk about boundaries, but you can't do anything with abandon. Most of the time you can't even let go enough to come.'

She . . . I know she was trying to make me fight back. The infuriating submission of my silence goaded her to say the worst possible thing she could think of. But that's what I know now.

That last was the very worst. I think she realized it, because she turned suddenly and made for the stairs.

Everyone needs to feel the safety of their own bathroom, to know that their garglings and hawkings, their whispered secrets in the bath about inadequacies and orgasms, that all these things are safe from the outside world. And that they will be kept there – warm with moist air and friendship. I stood there alone, struggling to breathe.

I can't remember moving to the front entrance, but of course I must have, because I can picture myself sitting on the *stoep*, legs clutched to spasmed chest. I sat and watched as winter fell over the street in a drowsy shroud. Winter was just there, not even caring enough to show me the quicksilver flash of season's change.

I caught no sign of the clashing of forces which, that day, had ended summer. Winter was just this dense curtain which had dropped suddenly over Cape Town's glow. I put my hand up to my face to feel the wetness, as I sat in the grey drizzle . . .

. . . I can't remember what the evidence was that day, as my swollen eyes still leaked their hurt. I hid my face in my files, avoiding the boys and young men whose James Hadley Chases I had forgotten again.

I felt no connection with them suddenly. I had thought them my umbilical cord to the beating heart of reality. My tie to real life, as it had never been lived in the small yards which had squared off my life. But that day there was no room for them. Nor for anger. All I could feel was a throbbing sense of loss. It was an intimation, a preview of the emptiness which lay beyond our friendship.

It had been us, always us. Standing shoulder to shoulder we could mock them, the people who lived life as we were expected to. We could stand and laugh at all the nice young men we should have taken home to our mothers. We could revel in our difference – the difference we had fostered and taken pride in – because there were two of us.

I had never really been strong. But alongside the shattering pieces of her, I had felt the stronger of the two. I had become strong in my task as guardian of her parts.

I had feared, after the episode with Jonathan – but nothing like this. I had been fearful of living our lives on constant guard against mistaken touches, and kisses whose innocence was still lingeringly redolent of sex.

I had seen Susan briefly that morning. I had crouched at the top of the stairs and watched through the banister rails as she, swollen-eyed as I, collected her things and made for the door. Her tough other self was long gone, and I could feel her hovering sense of desolation. But I had said nothing. She could never have responded to someone about whom she felt shame.

Years before, she had accused a girl we knew of telling stories about her to a boy that she liked. She had come apart, her pieces flitting about the walls. And she had never spoken to that girl again, even when she found she had been wrong – especially because she had been wrong, she confessed to me.

That morning on the stairs, I understood that she had come apart. And, still shattered myself from the truths and half-truths she had used against me, it would have to be me, her fixer, who patched her up again.

While oaths were taken in court and earnest men made decisions that would affect the lives, and possibly the deaths, of boys and men, I sat brooding on the gift that should be my offering.

'My Lord, I object. My learned friend is leading the witness to say that Mr Kakaza . . .'

What special thing could I tender? She had always seemed a princess to me, a forest creature whose sparkling talent had given me a sense of life's vitality. What could be worthy, what could draw her back into the circle of witchery that we had created about ourselves?

I always find it strange that, on those days when you can deal with nothing beyond the emotional burdens you already carry, the great cosmic sense of humour lumbers into play. It would be that day that Muller, the handsome policeman, chose to catch me as I was slipping quietly from the court for the lunch adjournment.

'Listen man, uh, I was wondering, um. I've got some tickets for the ballet . . .' He reddened, embarrassed by his own softness. I think he must have bought those tickets for me, thinking that I should be pleased by the gesture. Or perhaps I'm stereotyping him. Perhaps he often pressed his safari-suited body into the theatre and sighed over tutus and tights. I don't know. I don't know because I never really knew him. And that day I didn't have the resources to deal with his expectations or his hurts. I remember that I gazed at him in perplexity, unable to take in what was happening here.

'I beg your pard—' Could I buy her a book? But then, what? She hardly ever read novels. 'I mean, um, what . . . Are you asking me out? On a date?' Perhaps music. Music always had ritual meanings for our whole Sisterhood thing.

'Yes, actually, I am. Something wrong with that?'

'Um, no.' I know. I could buy her a new tape of Tim Hardin. We had sat on the couch, talking of things – so many things – to the sounds of his music for ages and ages, until the tape had died.

'Well?'

That was what I would buy her. And maybe a book as well. 'Well, what?'

'I'm asking you to the ballet. Do you want to go or not?'

Yes, a book too. A tape wasn't enough. 'Er, sorry? Oh yes, a date. Oh no, I'm really sorry. I couldn't. I don't think I could. You see . . . well, I'm sorry, I just can't.'

'It's because I'm a policeman, isn't it?'

'Sorry?' I was already making for the door, but I stopped then, held by the bitterness in his tone.

'I said . . .' He paused for emphasis. 'I said . . . it's because I'm a policeman. Why did I think you were different? Man, I'm a detective. I just catch criminals. I don't do the government's dirty work. But to you I'm just a bloody policeman. And you wouldn't like your fancy little friends to see you going out with a dirty bloody policeman.'

'No, well . . . I don't know. It's . . . Look, I'm really sorry. I can't really deal with this right now. I don't really know why. I don't know what I should say . . .'

'No, please don't say anything. You've made yourself clear.' He strode away, leaving me standing in the foyer. And then François came through. Oh God, I thought, my mind on books and bookshops, not this too. It wasn't that François hadn't accepted – well, he seemed to have – that nothing was to come of our relationship. But he found it necessary to show off each time he saw me, to impress me with his leftiness in an attempt to show me how worthy he was. I found him exhausting, as I was forced to counter his small, by-the-way academic observations, or his throwaway intellectual views on life, each time I bumped into him on the stairs or in doorways.

'So, how's this trial, hey Jennifer? It's really hotting up, isn't it? I think it's becoming the most important political trial of the decade. What do you think?'

'Yes, I suppose it is. François, excuse me, won't you? I must—'

'Incredible, isn't it? We're really privileged, aren't we? To be part of this. One day, all these guys will be seen as figureheads of the Struggle.'

'I suppose. But I still just find our guys kind of confusing. But anyway it doesn't matter now. I really should be—'

'Of course, much of what's happening in this trial is just an exercise in "rounding up the usual suspects" and symbols. I think they're especially keen to have Oupa out of the way now that things are coming to a head . . .'

'François, much as I'd love to stay and listen to your lecture, I—'

'Oh, come on Jennifer.' He laughed and gripped my shoulder in a chummy fashion. 'Come on. I'm not lecturing you. Can't you just stop now and again for a little discussion? I won't be here much longer, you know. When the trial's over I'm off to Namibia.'

'I'm sure Swapo will be thrilled. Listen François, I would just love to sit and discuss political significances with you, but I don't feel very well. I have an errand to run, and then I think I'm going to go home. I really don't feel well at all.' . . .

. . . 'Alcon Holdings. Good Morning.'

'Yes, good morning. I wanted to ask someone about Rodney Grant.'

I have a headache which has been pounding at my brain all day. In fact, these days I seem to wake with it, and go to sleep with it. I am pathetically superstitious about it too. I won't take an aspirin. It seems to me – I feel it so strongly, that stupid belief – that it will stop aching when I find Susan. I feel that my body is reminding me of the gravity of my quest, and that if I take a tablet I will be betraying my task and then . . . then I will never find her.

'I'm afraid we have no employee named Grant . . .'

'No, I know. He's the MD in South Africa. In Johannesburg.'

'Well then, if you'd like the Johannesburg number . . .'

'No. No, you see they're coming here, to London I mean. I want to find out when. And where, I mean, where they're staying.'

'Certainly Madam. I'll make that inquiry for you. Would it be possible for you to phone back later today? It's our lunch hour, Madam, and most of our executives are out of the office.'

'Yes, OK. Thanks.'

I lost Susan that year, in the winter which howled its north-westers and flung its icy rain about our ears. I lost her in the destructiveness which followed our fight, and the lust over which she had lashed me. We saw each other in the years which followed, briefly and without contact, but we never came back from damaging each other, with our blame, over the currents which led us to Mandla, and the destiny we brought him.

I crept unwilling into adulthood, pressed into a wallflower life in an attempt to do no more harm. And in a country established and settled, where the actions of girls, or the church bazaar rummagings of inconsequential women, could have no wild and cosmic effects. And I did so without Susan, without her ability to paint our lives for us, to colour them in vistas of vivid magenta, and the spiritual yellow of sunlight.

I so want her now. I want to glue her pieces, to love and accept all her raging aliens. I want to stand before her, protect her eagle self from life's traps. I want to hear her say: 'Well, Stuff-Up, you neurotic little arsehole. You've really fucked up your life without me to look after you, haven't you?' Because that was our way, when things became too much, to turn on me. It was part of my duty as guardian, and I want that again.

I need it to make me strong again. And I need her to paint again, to smear her colours all over my life. I have wasted far too much . . . time, life, whatever. And perhaps squandered the important things which I have been granted, and wanted to love, but been too afraid to accept. I need to get rid of the grey. I need so badly to cover every patch of grey . . .

. . . 'You're not a journalist, are you?'

'How can you tell?'

'You're dressed too corporate – too much grey.'

'Corporate! Hell, that's impressive. I thought it was just a mismatched mix of Woolie's sale and Mother's gift.'

I hadn't been able to stay in Crown Street. Waiting and watching were not within me. I had laid my delicate gift in the centre of her bed, adjusted it slightly, and left it there.

I felt good about its choosing. I felt it would speak for me – the tape to remind her of our evenings on the couch. And the book of walks in the Western Cape, a sign of my embracing her many enthusiasms. But more than the things themselves, she would see – in its wrapping and its laying before her – a propitiatory offering to Diana, to curb her moon-howled wrath.

I caught the train back into town, to the Press Club at the Café Royal, where lawyers were tolerated, but where I should be unlikely to meet any tonight.

I had a reckless, hyped feeling of anticipation over my gift. But I was running also, from the desperation of knowing that I might one day lose her more irrevocably, at a time when I had nothing else. When we had jeered and sneered at all the nice things our mothers had wanted for us, and when it was too late to go backward.

I was jittery. I drank my wine fast in compulsive gestures. The pub was dark, old-fashioned plush and red-velvet-padded. It suited me that night because it soaked up my intensity. It had its own intensity zinging about me. It was a place of people who had known each other, perhaps too well, probably for too long and too incestuously. Among those severed and unsevered emotions, and in the criss-crossed relationships I could make out in overheard snatches, my chain-smoking went unnoticed.

The man who bought my second drink was confident in the warming manner of the man who likes women and knows he is seldom rejected. He wasn't good-looking, not in my former schoolmates' rating system, anyway. He was stocky and dark-eyed and hairy – an earthbound man, untroubled by fancies.

I had seen him across the garrulous chatter, sitting backward astride a bar stool. He had been part of a group of journalists – and yet slightly apart.

'No, no, that was nothing,' a loud young man had been proclaiming over their laughter. 'Shit, Chris, don't you remember how green you were – excuse the pun – at the time of the Laingsburg floods? You should have seen him. He'd never seen a dead body before and he bloody near puked when he saw a dog's corpse floating down the river. That was the only time I've ever seen him put off his beer . . .'

The dark man had been laughing with them, but his eyes had been on me. They had watched me solidly, while mine had skittered across the room, glancing off groups, rebounding off couples, and each time falling back on his unmoving gaze.

'Another Castle for me, please Solomon, and another of what she's having.' He was very close as he leant across to bring the drinks closer. I could smell the spicy smell of his shirt, still damp from the drizzle outside.

'So what do you do?' he asked, placing his foot on the rung of my bar stool.

'What do you think?' I asked. 'You ... You're clearly some ... some bookkeeper in a government department. I can see it in your fearful, mole-like demeanour.'

His eyes narrowed in a crumpled smile. He ran his hand across his beard as he caught up with the game.

'But of course,' he said. 'I can tell what you are – it's that vacuous expression and perfect nails which give you away. You're a beauty consultant. Of course! Your life is one big worry over ingrown hairs. How do you cope with the stress?'

His words fell quickly, without gravity. He was a man who was comfortable with his cleverness and used it as a tool, without ostentation.

'But really, strange-eyed naiad who's turned up in our jaded midst,' he said, lighting my umpteenth cigarette. 'Don't think I can't see right through you. You're a lawyer, of course.'

'How can you tell?' I spoke fast too, but it was the quickness of my skittish need for this flirtation.

The great-stories-I-have-covered crowd roared with sudden laughter so that I wasn't sure, for a moment, if he had heard me. He leant forward, brushing my frivolous wisps of hair aside to speak directly into my ear. I could feel the heat of his breath against my cheek.

'Well, perhaps the clothes a bit. But you're the kind of girl who'd have a profession. Daddy'd have seen to that.'

'Well of course. But you must understand that a profession – while important – shouldn't be taken too seriously. It's something "to fall back on" if I need to, isn't it?'

I glanced at him quickly. His mouth was impassive, but around his eyes, a faint crinkling had gathered. I liked this man. I liked his solidity in the face of my flightiness. Oh, how badly I needed it, on that night that I felt so adrift.

'Well,' he said, 'having something to fall back on is a good idea,

I always think. I always like to make sure I have something to fall back on.'

'Yes, well,' I said, dampening my anxious mouth with the tip of my tongue. 'Myself I've always thought a girl should make sure she's covered for all contingencies.'

'Really,' he said, 'I think that's very sensible. And it's always a good thing to find someone reliable to cover you in emergencies, you know.'

He ran his fingers briefly across his lips and replaced his hand, absolutely at ease, on the bar counter. His fingers lay blunt-edged, comfortable with their stillness, seeming to hold the ingrained memory of soil in their prints and earth against their palm. My lips felt dry. I ran my tongue over them again. Glancing up, I saw that he was watching me, his eyes glittering with laughter.

He moved his hand to cover mine. In the reddened light, my hand looked very pale against his tan and fluttered in fey nervousness against his palm.

'So tell me more,' he said, 'about being a princess, and why she needs a profession.'

I could feel his warmth being squeezed into my chilled hand. 'Well,' I said, my eyes flitting here and there. 'It's very important, you know. 'It's something to tide me over between husbands, should one inconsiderately die on me.'

'Oh, to die on you! I can think of nothing more delicious at this moment.' He ran his fingers lightly down my taut neck, allowing them to rest briefly in the hollow at the base of my throat. I felt entangled by his quick-breathed force. It webbed about me, strung by his warmth and the power of his sureness. And something else. Something that surged from one to the other, that parted our lips and made each finger's touch erogenous.

'So, are you a successful lawyer?'

'Oh God, no,' I said. I was talking fast, wanting him to think me funny. And I was doing it again – throwing out my family's neuroses as bait, to seem amusing rather than predictable. 'Don't you know that to be a successful princess I should have found myself a nice young man at university – God, waste of money that was.'

'A nice young man like me?' He shifted his feet, placing one arm across the back of my stool so that I was aware of the substantial body of him – rough-edged in its plainness, unsophisticated in its warmth.

'You don't qualify as a nice young man. I don't think my mother would have rated you at all.'

'Why ever not? What beastly mark could your mother detect about me, hm?'

'Well, you just wouldn't be right . . .' He was having his fun with me, forcing me to come out with all his qualities which were disagreeable to mothers like mine.

'Hm? What is it that disqualifies me from being a debutante's swain?'

'You're just all wrong . . . She wouldn't like you. You're too dark. Too sexy. You . . . you have the wrong job. More?'

'My God, what more could there be? But then, of course . . . aren't those exactly the qualities that make the heart pump in that little princess-ish chest?'

I could feel his arm across my back, caressing my arm. The rush of our words, swelled by adrenalin, was no longer merely flirtatious. In the darkened crush of the bar, it had somehow left the realm of flirting, and become sex – the rutting of voices, the fucking of eyes and of fingers which spread fingers and probed damp palms.

'Let's get out of here. I'll give you a lift,' he said. And we walked to his car, pausing in doorways to suck each other's fingers. We leant against cars so he could lick my collarbone, and I could press my face into his beard. Reaching his car, he guided me into my seat, allowing his fingers to trail, pixie-like, across my thighs. Then he moved to the driver's seat and leant to kiss me.

'Jesus, this is strange . . .' he said, cupping my face in his hands. Did I catch a glint of gold? See it and ignore it? I just remember that he kissed me. '. . . Here I am, a happily married man with three children . . . Oh God, you didn't know. I've shocked you. Oh shit, I thought it was obvious – I wear a ring and everything.'

I don't think it was the moral aspect. The way we were then, I don't think I felt responsible for his relationship. It was his sudden removal from my fantasy. It was to do with my vulnerability and the intimation that one day, some time, I would inevitably lose Susan altogether. It was all to do with my need for his earthy cleverness to twist my flightiness around, and bury myself in his grounded sexuality.

'Well, it's your decision,' he said. 'I won't push you now. I'll phone and ask you, perhaps we can lunch together, in any case.'

He drove me home and we sat outside my house, listening to the wind-driven drizzle, the slamming of doors and the strains of Talking Heads. Then I left him, almost without a word, and went alone to my door.

I did sleep with him – not that night, but some time that week. I acted sophisticated and said we'd end our relationship with a bang rather than a whimper. But it was nothing special, filled as it was with the sadness of my unfulfilled need. It was planned and orchestrated, with none of the web-like power that had been in our eyes, and our fingers and our talk, that night in the Café Royal. I found I watched his ring, glinting as he caressed me, and was hurt by his obsessive need to wash the smell of me from his body . . .

. . . 'Don't you ever look for rings?' she asked me, spreading her fingers on the brown fabric, but stopping them short of mine. 'Not that it matters. But it explains a lot.'

We were sitting on the couch, our knees drawn up – consciously, very purposefully – in postural unison, our hands trickling smoke into the darkness. We drank wine as we listened to Tim Hardin, and allowed the tears to fall, for what suddenly seemed our sorry crossing into adulthood.

She had opened the door as I reached it and placed her arms about my shoulders. My head had drooped to her shoulder, oozing tears which had refused to flow past the tightness of my throat.

'Oh Sister,' she said, rubbing at her face with the palm of her ravaged hand. 'Oh Sister, I'm such a terrible person.'

And we had taken our place on the couch, except that our fingers didn't touch.

After a while, we moved to the kitchen where I sipped wine and leant against the wall to watch her cook. Frilly and young she looked, with her apron and her hair tied back – but pale. She was so pale that I felt momentarily fearful of her skin's ability to protect her innards. She held her mouth toughly, but she was still so small, seemingly too small to be wielding that great knife, and cutting that onion with such ferocity.

'Ja, you fuckwit, so why did you refuse the policeman?'

That was our way. That response was in its place and as it should be. Everything was as it had been. Really, it was. It's just that . . . it was just that I couldn't hug her. Her bony shoulders were suddenly a barrier. We were playing through the rituals, trying to find our place again. And I think we would have, had we been given time.

'I . . . I don't really know, Sister,' I said at last. 'It's weird. He actually looks quite a nice guy. And he seems to get on really well with the accused and everything. It's just that he's a policeman. How can you ever really get past that? Whether he wants to think so or not, in this country that taints him.'

'But don't you see,' she said, turning with the knife in her hand, 'don't you see that that's one of those boundaries? We should be breaking through boundaries.'

She stood still a moment, and then turned, scooping the onion into the pan. I sipped at my wine, watching her chop the chillies which had been in the fridge for two weeks and were beginning to look pitted and slightly fungal. She fried up the chicken pieces – God knows how long they had been in the icebox of our little fridge – and added the sloshy mush she had made from peanut butter and chicken stock and all those spices she used so well. A scattering of cumin, a pinch of cardamom, a bunch of coriander she had insisted on buying fresh, with the chillies. It too had become drooped with age. In the kitchen, over her cooking pots, Susan was competent, truly at home. Though we were lazy and cooked seldom, I think it gave her a oneness of her self with her upbringing. It was the only place they came together . . . and I think it gave her peace.

'Well,' I said at last. 'You may think it just one of life's boundaries. But I don't know that I could cross it. And, yes, he's right. I would feel ashamed if people saw, I mean people like Ilsa. Just imagine . . .' Susan turned, but she didn't giggle with me. I think perhaps she was too immersed in the run of her own logic.

'You should just get past the horror,' she said, placing a lid on the pan so that it would simmer. 'I think I would have. And I think I might have fucked him, just to see what it was like. Yes . . . I think I would have taken it further than you.'

There was something which chilled me, in the steamy warmth of our ritual cooking, something in the challenging thrust of her small chin, in the hardened wildness of her eyes as she turned

135

from her pots to look at me. As we sipped our wine, waiting for Susan's African Chicken to cook, I could smell an unease in the nervous sweat of her body, I could hear something in the tense rasp of her voice – something which jarred against our ceremonial edifice.

I suppose I knew it then, or rather sensed it. But it is only now, after a lifetime spent contemplating that time of vivid heat and wild winter, that I can try to put that sense of her into words.

I have to take some responsibility for it, in allowing what had occurred between us and what it did to her – for not protecting her from her untamed spirit. The things she did later and the choices she made were so inexorably twined in time, to what had gone before.

Right up until that afternoon when summer was still with us, I think I had been her only refuge. So many expectations she faced. I think her spirit shuddered beneath the prying eyes of all those hopes – except when she was with me. But now, in letting her cross one barrier too far, I had taken away her last refuge. Her mother, her brothers and sisters who had not gone to university, each man who slept with her, or was attracted to her, or wanted to take her home – everyone wanted something from her. And now I too. I wanted her to behave in a certain way, to make everything OK for me.

That night in our kitchen, I think she felt the burden of the sex we had shared and the gift I had offered her, and the expectations they placed on her. Now – I sensed it in the swing of her winter-spawned mood – she would play the limits, flirt with edges, before me too, and wilder and further than me. It was no longer a joint game, played by partners, to expel all the burdensome eyes. Now it was her solitary game, played to challenge me too. Robbed of her refuge, she would play it even here, proving she wasn't bound to me, and that she wasn't vulnerable.

But it was only a sense of this I had that night. And then the chicken was cooked and we got stoned and ate the entire mound of food, scraping the last cold scraps from the pan with our fingers. Before we went to bed, we sat on the couch again, listening to the tape I had given her. In the dark, she lit two cigarettes and gave one to me, but our fingers didn't touch.

We talked awhile and then fell silent. Finally, shoulder to shoulder on the couch, we wept quietly, in the maudlin aftermath of emotion. It wasn't just for married lovers, or for romantic hopes. It seems to me that our tears came from a deeper, darker place, encompassing all that we were, and all that we were unable to be.

'Oh Sister,' she said, 'what is to become of us?' . . .

*Kalatter kalatter kalatter, kalatter kalatter kalatter skreee-ee-ee*
I lay in bed and thought that things were together again, and all in their place. Each time I thought it, a small disquiet would flash peripherally at the edge of my inner vision. But each time I tried to examine it, it fluttered just beyond my reach.

I heard Susan's bed creak and I imagined her rising and tugging her dressing gown about her. I heard her door open and her footsteps on the landing. She paused outside my door, but then I heard the stairs bearing her down and away.

I followed her, anxious to complete all the rituals and be as we had always been.

'Sister,' she said as I entered the kitchen, and she placed a cigarette between my lips. We drew on our cigarettes, Susan coughing as the smoke hit the back of her throat. We were spooning coffee into our cups when we heard the key. The door slammed and Maud's heavy footsteps advanced along the passage. We had stopped mid-spoon, our heads alert to catch her familiar arrival. We smiled to each other.

*Ka-cha.*

'And good morning to you too, Maud,' said Susan.

'Hello Maudie, what have we done this time?' That was me, always so anxious not to offend.

*Ka-cha.* 'Such a mess again. Bottles and glasses in the lounge, pots and dirty dishes in here.' *Ka-cha.*

'I'm really sorry, Maudie,' I said, scurrying to gather the scraped plates and empty the ashtrays.

'Hm, well,' Maud said, mollified by my display of willingness. She moved heavily, her face a display of satisfaction. In her ponderous way, she found the mug she wanted and went through her tea motions – milk first, then the sugar and the bag, and lastly

138

the water, which swirled the brown of the tea through the milk.

'Maud,' said Susan. 'Have you found some more piecework? I've been asking all the teachers at my school, but I haven't found anything for you yet. Have you left the abortion place?'

'I have left,' she said. 'I have never gone back. I have found a new piecework, a good piecework. It is a good place to work, with many things to see.'

I watched, not wanting to hurry her, as her gravity was gradually overtaken by the troubadour. Taking her first sip of tea, sucked as always through her teeth, she slowly became the storyteller. In her eyes, I thought I saw the jester, with his glinting amusement at the follies that surrounded her. But the pull of her power held us still.

'The Greenpoint Madam got me this piecework with that boyfriend of hers, Master Manie. The big one, you know?' As her hands sketched his substantial buttocks, her eyes burned with the joy of her craft and the appreciation of her own wickedness.

'So,' said Susan, exhaling smoke and little snorted breaths of enjoyment. 'Single guy, is he?'

'He lives alone, but he has a wife – an old wife.'

'Oh *ja*? How do you know?' I asked, waiting for the curtains to rise on Manie's life.

'Hm-hm-hm-hm-hm. But she is a mad one. Very angry with him. She comes to the house. She comes when Master Manie is at work. First she phones him.' Her hand became a telephone receiver. "Who is this?" she says to me. I tell her that I am Maud. So she says: "Listen! Is the Master there?" So I tell her he has gone to work. So then she comes round, in her big BMW, still in her exercise clothes. With that band round her head and stockings with no feet.'

She stopped to slurp at her tea. We said nothing as she drank again and gravely replaced her cup. She needed no prompting. Standing, she pushed her chair to one side as her face took on the perky, vacuous appearance of the ex-wife. ' "So Maud," she says to me, "So, is the Master good to you?" So I say yes, he is good. So then she stands there in the kitchen a bit . . .'

Maud was bouncing her large body lightly on imagined gym pumps, flinging hanks of envisioned hair over her shoulders.

'So, then I am working, see?' And Maud became herself, stolid with dignity, washing dishes at the sink. 'So she says to me: "And is there another woman comes here, Maud? See, I'm his wife, well really his old wife. But really I want to know, you understand, hey, Maud?" '

I could see her, pouty with anxiety, wrestling the pain of emotional rejection from her lean, muscled limbs.

'So I just keep quiet,' said Maud. 'And she goes on talking and talking and I just keep quiet. So in the end, she says, "Oh Maud, I am so glad there hasn't been a woman around here. Thank you so much for setting my mind at rest." I just keep quiet again. I do not lie for the Master. But I do not tell her about the Greenpoint Madam sleeping there.'

'How d'you know? Did you see her there?' asked Susan. We were ardent now, drawn into Act One of their relationship.

'That same day, early in the morning when I come in, I see the Greenpoint Madam's car. So, I make my tea and then I go through to see to the house. But outside the bedroom, I hear a funny noise, like "Uh-uh, uh-uh . . ." So I think that something funny is going on here. So I go, quietly quietly, up to the door . . .' Maud was herself now – the collector of lives – her face glowing with acquisitiveness. '. . . So I bend down, very low like this . . .' She mimed the door, peeking around it at the level of her knees. '. . . So, if they hear a noise and look up, they will look up to where a head should be, not to where I look in.'

She sat, seemingly spent, and swallowed the remains of her tea. We stood mute with stunned delight at her audacity. Exchanging glances, we began to giggle.

'What's the matter?' she asked, accustomed to our involvement in the story. 'Why do you laugh like that?'

'Maud, you didn't!' said Susan, shuddering with the force of the laughter she was struggling to suppress. 'You didn't really, did you? You didn't peep into their bedroom!'

'Yes, I did,' she said, an edifice of righteousness. *Ka-cha*. 'I must see! I must clean the house. That is my job. I must see what is happening there if I cannot go in to do my job.' *Ka-cha*.

'So, Maudie?' I asked, a wheedle in my voice, to draw her back to her tale. 'So, Maudie, what did you see? Could you see anything?'

'Oh, yes.'

She was instantly appeased by my interest. Throwing one outraged glance at Susan, she focused on me. And as she darted her tongue out to dampen dry lips, she allowed the stateliness to slump from her body and the piety haze from her eyes.

'Oh yes, I can see. There is the Master on the bed with the Greenpoint Madam. There they were. Ve-ery busy! Oh yes, ve-ery busy.'

She paused, her empty mug still clutched in her fist.

'But I do not tell the old wife that. And I do not tell Master Manie what the old wife does next, after asking me all the questions.'

'What did she do?'

'She goes to his cupboard, and she searches his things. I let her stay while I clean and, slowly-slowly, she goes through his clothes, sniffing at the smell of him and searching, I think, for woman things. Then she finds letters, and you know, bills and notes and things. And she reads them.'

Maud rose, favouring her knees by pressing down on her thighs. She moved to the sink with her empty mug. Her back to us: 'So, by round about lunchtime, she goes home. She doesn't say goodbye but I watch her through the lounge window. When she gets into her BMW, I see she is crying.'

# 8

'That one,' said Susan, licking the bean curry from her knuckles and gesturing with the roti she had been nibbling. 'That one, I want to tell you, is a real loser. He is major bad news.'

She dropped her eyes so as not to draw his gaze. But he saw us anyway. He had driven to the Bo-Kaap considering takeaways, he told me later, but had changed his mind when he sensed the restaurant's dark curry fragrances, swollen with warmth and fruit and incense. Fate, he said. I said nothing.

And afterwards, when he was gone, I thought even less about Fate. I hated to see it the way Susan did – as some cosmic joke just waiting to belly-laugh at our belittling. I didn't like to think it was Fate that twisted the events which brought him to us. I liked to think perhaps it was more prosaic, nothing more than the damp chill that brought him inside, and perhaps the thought of his mutton curry congealing on the road to Llandudno. That's where he lived.

'I hope you two're stoned,' he said, with his raucous laugh. 'It's really the only way to enjoy this joint properly – excuse the pun – considering you can't drink here.'

He spoke that bit too loud, and we both winced as scarved heads turned and the dark eyes of Muslim diners contemplated us gravely. He joined us without asking our permission – he was like that.

'Move up, Suze. Can't you see I can't fit in this space?' As he jostled into the tiny space between Susan and the wall, I wondered if it were a gift or a curse in a person, that inability to consider their importance to others might not be as great as they assumed.

'How'd you find this place?' he asked, pulling his long legs on to the floor cushions with his arms. 'Not everyone knows about it. Did I tell you about it?'

'Not everyone,' said Susan, whipping her scathing eyes across his face, 'needs you to guide them to all the cultural highlights of Cape Town.'

We sat, as the other diners did, cross-legged before low tables. We had removed our shoes at the door and we ate, as everyone did, with our fingers. In the red-hued darkness, I covertly watched the bird-like fingers of Malay women, picking their way delicately over grains of rice and fruity, spiced meat. Susan and I, struggling to imitate, were gravied to our wrists, licking at our palms and sucking our fingers.

'I'm Martin,' he said to me. 'I don't think I'll shake your hand, if you don't mind.' He blurted another laugh. 'I don't think I've met you before. Are you also one of the art crowd? I've known Susan for years, you know.'

'Mm, more's the pity,' muttered Susan. He ruffled her hair, ignoring the way she ducked from him. I told him my name and found that I was smiling. It took me by surprise. He was everything I didn't like. He spoke too loudly, he laughed enormously, he had no sensitivity to speak of. Susan – well, I could see that she despised him. I could see it in the flip of her eyes, disdaining to rest on his face. But, so entrapped by other people's opinion of me, I think I recognized an immensity, a glory even, in his inability to conceive of anyone's disliking him. Bred of an innocent disregard, it gave him a brash charm.

'. . . Well, so that's how I got to Cape Town, and now I'll never leave. I know everything there is to know about this place, every nuance, every bay, every inlet. So, Jennifer, anything you want to know about . . .'

He spoke for most of the evening. We listened a lot, Susan tearing at her nails, her mouth in its cynical twist. He was a lecturer in graphic design.

'Not a field renowned for its depth,' added Susan, while he affected to beat her frail shoulder. 'That's why it suits him so well. Everything is surface, airbrushed to niceness. Yes Martin, no one ever accused you of being a serious artist, did they?'

'Yes, that's what my second wife used to say. She thought I'd end up a famous artist or a bigshot in an ad agency. When I just stayed a lecturer – well, because I like it, you know? And it gives me time for my diving and shit – well, she used to say I had absolutely no drive to speak of. Mind you, that was nothing to what the next one told me. She – little bitch, she really had a way with words – she used to say I'd always be a nothing, my whole life . . .'

'How many have you had?' I interrupted, fearful of losing the chance, as he paused to sip his Coke.

'How many what? You know in a way you remind me . . .'

'Wives,' I said.

'Three,' he said. 'Some Bluebeard, huh? Except that it was they who killed me – financially, that is. Well, no fine.' And he laughed, a belch of sound.

Strangely, he had a look of intensity about him, in the planes of his face, the cutting lines of his cheekbones and the working of his jaw muscles. But it was deceptive. It went no deeper than the words which spilled from his soft mouth, as red as a child's. His air of intensity was as fraudulent as the dissipated weariness which gathered in the lines about his eyes. He was an innocent.

'Stop biting your nails, Suze!' he said, grabbing at her hand.

'Fuck you,' she said. 'Why should I?'

'It looks ugly. Men don't like it.'

'Oh Jesus.'

'So, how do you two know each other?' he asked, ignoring Susan's rolled eyes. 'Have you been friends for long?'

'She's my Sister,' said Susan, partly, I think just to confuse his view of us. But I hoped, oh I hoped, it was also a rebuilding of our cobweb bond.

'Not your real sister, surely?'

'Not blood sisters, no.'

I wanted to weep at the fragility of the filaments we had spun – and perhaps could spin again. I wanted to weep for the sticky hurt which still clung to the scars of our fight and to our stilted touches. And I wanted to weep for my weakness in turning slightly from her, in my pain and my fear, and for wanting something else to cling to, at least with one hand.

'You mean sort of like a coven?' he asked.

'Absolutely,' I said. I wanted to show her that I was wholly part of our rituals and that we were shoulder to shoulder, backed against the wall. 'With our moon-spun witchery, we are the scourge of ordinary people.'

'Ooh,' he said. 'Scary.'

'In our wild clutches, men writhe in thrall to our sorcery.' I was holding his eyes with the feigned fervour in mine. But I felt Susan's hand creep across the table and I felt her fingers just touch mine.

'. . . They are not our equal, poor creatures of the surface world. And we, spell-wrought by spirits of changing sea and unmoving mountain, we fly unchained through the prosaic world. We are the heart and gut of nature, forged from the force of life itself.'

I was flinging my head back, camping it up for him. But deep down, we really believed in that stuff, Susan and I. It was how we liked to see ourselves – part of our joint mystique. Together we could flap our free-spirited wings over the banal lives we saw set out for us. Apart, well, apart we were nothing. We felt ordinary.

'God,' he said, 'that's really quite scary.' He looked for a moment as though he meant it. And then he rallied himself. 'I mean,' he said, 'What I mean is, that could be scary to some men – that exclusionary thing – but only if you're not up to the challenge.' He grinned a pirate grin, filled with the clash of cutlass and the flash of steel.

Susan's smile disappeared and she flinched, perhaps at the loudness of his tone, or perhaps it was his brash machismo, which laid waste our gossamer web. She would have hated the implication that he thought the Sisterhood quaint. But I saw something else. Beneath his manhood, I glimpsed a naivety which made him think we would sigh and flutter at his masterful words. His ingenuousness softened his insensitivity, and touched a small nurturing nerve in me.

We wandered down the hill to where we had parked in the Bo-Kaap. The small squared houses of the Malay quarter were quiet with evening lights and the shadows of after-dinner activity. Below us lay downtown, desolate of humanity but for rare scuttling movements just glimpsed at the corner of one's eye. And everywhere, everywhere above and beyond us was the mountain, encircling and encroaching on all that we did and all that could be said and hinted at.

We reached his car first. He drove a beat-up *bakkie*, from which he drew a cheap, much-scratched guitar. Uncaring of the evening hush, he placed his foot on the running board and hunched his tall body over the guitar.

*'Spier-e-wit ga-poe-ier, het nie bê-ren-dous nie, het nie
bê-ren-dous nie . . . Spier-e-wit ga-poe-ier, het nie bê-ren-dous
nie, het nie bê-ren-dous nie . . . Bol-la wil sy dra, sy't nie
ha-re nie, het nie ha-re nie . . . Bolla wil sy
dra, sy't nie ha-re nie, het nie hare nie . . .*

'I know hundreds of Malay songs. That one's called a *ghommalied-
jie*. It's traditionally sung at picnics, after the food, when everyone
stands around in circles . . . well, just thought I'd continue your
cultural education for the evening.'

I laughed at his swagger and Susan, even Susan smiled a little. I
think she was drawn slightly out of her dislike by the charm of his
song. He swung into the next, without a glance at us. So restless of
spirit, he was not one to check for restlessness in others.

*'Spreek Kat-to-tjie se moeder haar aan: Ja, my-ne dog-ter
wat-ter skan-de't jy ge-daan . . .'*

We both burst into laughter, as he knew we would. '*Ja*,' said Susan,
'That one's for us – the lament of the Sisters' mothers . . .'

He had a way of disarming you, that man. Oh, I know he was a
much-married disaster area. But I don't think I ever thought him
through properly. He had a way of carrying you along on his
boisterous charm, against all judgement. His personality was so
rambunctious that, though you might cringe as he drew attention
to himself, it swept you along with him.

He followed us home, I don't think it was even discussed. He
just came. He came with his guitar and his exotic, Swazi gold
dope. He had a generosity of spirit, you see. What he had,
he shared. Even himself. When it seemed he was too large for
the room, too much for one, it was often all that he had of
himself.

He gave us his songs, singing into the early hours, entertaining
us with the Malay tales he had learnt – of picnics, of fasts and
feasting, of fishermen and their waiting wives. And he gave us
laughter. Even Susan was drawn into that at last – drawn into
stoned giggles over his fit of the munchies. His desperate gasps as
he searched for something, anything, to eat beyond a pair of
furred tomatoes.

'Oh God,' he cried, clutching at his throat. 'I'll die if I don't eat.

Anything. Anything. God, even if it's Jungle Oats.' And we collapsed in helpless hilarity.

He ate an entire bottle of *brinjal achar*, yelping with pain at the burn on his tongue. Laughter aching at our diaphragms, we rocked ourselves on the kitchen floor while he accused each spoonful of disguising its crocodile teeth in *brinjal* attire. And then we sang some more, and it sounded so good to us – old Beatles songs of which we knew all the words. He strummed his old guitar, his foot on Maud's dining-room chair, while we stood on either side of him, stridently yelling the choruses.

'Well, now you can't make me go home,' he said at last, laying his guitar on the table. 'It's too late and I'm too stoned. You don't want me to fall asleep on Victoria Road?'

We told him he could sleep on the couch, but he whimpered and whined and told us his back hurt. He said he'd keep his pants on and, laughing still, we allowed him into my bed.

'Behave,' said Susan, pointing her finger at him. And then she left.

I wore a tracksuit to bed, an old school tracksuit which slipped easily from my legs and shucked off my shoulders beneath his kiss. I think I made one small movement of resistance. And then I thought, oh what the hell. Let it flow, just let it flow. He fucked me all night long, or what was left of the darkness, with the same robust gusto he gave his guitar-playing. With the same giving of all of himself. All that he had to give, that is. He had no more for me. He had no patience for foreplay, little delicacy for gentleness. But in my need, in my clinging soul, I found him satisfying in the intensity of his focus. He made me feel bundled in his body and his encircling personality.

Just before dawn, as the mountain lay hidden in grey, he lay curled around me. 'Tell me a story,' he said, as a small boy would. 'Any story. Tell me about you.' That's when I felt his need, the intensity of his clutching for my mothering breasts and my woman's heart.

'Well . . .' I said, filled with confidence by his need of my nurture, '. . . once upon a time in Port Elizabeth there was a valley, a wide, wild valley filled with wondrous adventures and the smell of nasturtium. There beneath the wheeling *hadedas*, we kids would charge down from suburbs on either side. We were the battling hordes, the warring factions from Mill Park and Walmer . . .'

# Touching The Lighthouse

When the vision of the mountain poured in at the window, between the electric wires of the railway line, I left him spread across the bed and crept into Susan's room. I wanted to confess, because she hadn't liked him. I wanted her to say he wasn't so bad, while we giggled and chatted, as we had about all the others. I wanted to know that I could say horrible things about him without her agreeing with me.

She was already awake as I curled on her bed. 'Now you're well and truly fucked,' she said, the quirk of her mouth tempered just slightly by reproach. But it disappeared as she asked me: 'And now what're you going to do with him? He's not house-trained, you know.'

'I know,' I could feel the rueful corners of my mouth tugging my smile. That had always been the way of the Sisterhood. We had never criticized the other Sister's raving lunatics and pathetic wimps. We were there, we stood by to catch the scattered pieces, but we never chided the choice. 'I don't know really. I never intended it, so I never thought it through . . .'

I lit two cigarettes from the packet next to her bed. I was shy suddenly to place one between her lips. I thrust it at her fingers. 'You know, I think I'll just let it flow, for the moment. I'll think about it tomorrow, when I've got time to consider. For now, well, today I don't feel like thinking.' . . .

. . . 'Can't you leave it now, Mother?' She jerks me from my thoughts as I stand in the entrance hall, one hand on the telephone. 'I've been trying to ask you something for the past hour, and you've been on the telephone. You've no time left for us these days – it's just not fair.'

'Well, that's just too bad, isn't it,' I say, swinging to face her.

'Well really, I was just saying . . .' Her mouth moves and she licks her lips. She hasn't expected me to respond to her prodding.

For once, in the frustration of my quest, I have been shaken to sharpness by the truculence in her face. The trouble with being someone's life's work is that you grow to expect it as your birthright. That's my fault, I know, but suddenly it drives me to fury.

'Yes? What secrets of life do you, the all-knowing teenager, have to share with me?'

My anger fades as quickly as it came, in the shock of my own

149

response. In dying defiance, I reach for the cigarette packet on the telephone table and light one, looking directly into her eyes – those eyes which are so unlike mine.

'Oh, Mother, must you . . .' Her criticism dries as it reaches her lips. 'You know, golly, I was just trying to say something . . . we teenagers also have a right to our views . . . I've never known you like this. Now suddenly . . . I mean, maybe she doesn't want to be your friend any more. I mean, Daddy always says we shouldn't cling to things that are past and gone.'

'How very profound your father is. Oh . . .' I sigh, watching her eyes widen and fill at my unaccustomed jibe at her beloved father. 'I'm sorry . . . I didn't really mean that. He's probably right, for the most part. But . . . you know, Melissa, you haven't lived long enough to know, but sometimes you have to reach right into the past to heal the present. Sometimes, things don't heal and they sit there and spoil all the good things that could happen in the future.'

'What will happen when you find her? Will you . . . you won't leave, will you? Daddy says sometimes he thinks you hanker for South Africa. He says . . .'

'No, sweetheart . . .' the endearment tastes strange in my mouth. But I felt her need. These girls of mine range so often against me, they so often take their father's disdainful cue, that it sometimes takes me by surprise that this one still needs me. It shouldn't. They are still just children.

'No, I'll never leave you. I do . . . yes, I do hanker sometimes for South Africa. But I think that's because I ran away. I ran away from things I found too hard to face – just upped and came here before I'd had time to come to terms with . . . with everything. All the things I'd done and all I hadn't done.'

'What were they? What did happen? Daddy says he still doesn't really understand it all . . .'

'I . . . not now, Melissa. Please . . . I just have to do this in my own way. But I just think you should remember what I said. I think you can turn and walk from things that are gone and past, yes. But not from what is unfinished. And never run.

'If you run away, you'll always feel powerless.' . . .

. . . 'Once upon a time, when I was at school, I was the strange girl in the class who wrote poetry and practised spirit-writing. I never made it to the centre of anything.

'But one day – through an alliance with a new girl – I did claw my way to the in-group. She was cool, that girl. She came from Cape Town, and she had the kind of androgynous body that clothes just floated on. She smoked, you see – cigarettes and dope – and she'd had sex. And for some reason she allowed herself to be my friend.

'That's how I finally made it into the in-group. And that's why, I suppose, I could never manage to remain there for long. I was always being purged for overeagerness and having to claw my way back.

'The class bitch – there's always one of those. Every class has one. Anyway, she really wanted to be Angela's best friend – that was the cool girl – so she was always purging me for some or other reason.

'Once she purged me because I said that tissues with purple spots were pretty. She rolled her eyes and stuck her fingers in her mouth, pretending to puke. It took me two weeks, and a party at Angela's house, to get back in.

'And then, one day she said to me – in front of the entire group – that she could picture me in ten years' time. She said "You know, I can just see you getting out of your Beetle, pregnant, in your OK-print maternity dress with piles and piles of Checkers packets." I wept for weeks. I couldn't lose the awful humiliation of it. Even Angela had laughed, just a bit. My mother kept saying, in that exasperated way: "Why didn't you thank her for giving such a happy picture of you?" She just couldn't see.'

'I practised my spirit-writing, all by myself at break-time. I spoke to the Red Indian guide I'd chosen for myself, and I called up malevolent spirits to my pen, and wished every evil upon the class bitch. I wished she'd die.

'And you know what? She got pregnant. She got pregnant and had to leave the school. I never saw her again. Angela and I became inseparable and, right through to the end of matric, I was never purged again. She taught me to smoke and we lay on her bed smoking and said we'd be best friends for ever. But somehow, I always felt responsible for bringing that baby into the world. I always felt a bit guilty about causing the ruin of the class bitch. Anyway, that's it. That's the end of the story.'

'That was a good one,' he said, stretching in the calico

hammock. We were rocking quietly on his balcony, gazing down at the sweet-melon slice that was Llandudno beach. The day was whitened by mist and by the clouds which rolled over the mountains. This was Cape Town gentled by her muffling winter wraps. It was a day to read poetry before a fire, a day to borrow a faded art-school sweatshirt from the man one had met the night before.

He shifted his restless legs. '*Ja*, I enjoyed that story. It's just like you, you know that? I mean, even now I can see you're like that. I think I'll have to teach you to stop aching for people to accept you. It's slightly pathetic, you know? He brayed his laughter and granted me a small hug.

'Come!' he said. I didn't look at him. As I watched, splinters of light pierced the day's grey flesh, bleeding sunlight across the sea. 'Come on,' he said. 'I want to show you stuff. I want to give you crayfish for lunch.'

The light softened again as I went along with him. We walked on the beach, he talking and gesturing and pointing. I was swept along by it all. By the sea-dampened air which sprung tendrils of hair about our faces, by the sinking of the shoreline, the gritty clambering over boulders in our bare feet. By his sweeping view of everything, and the way he gave it to me with his wide-flung generosity.

'See the gannets, Jennifer,' – he never called me Jenny or Jen. We stopped, his restlessness held for a minute. I watched his jaw muscles clenching and unclenching, his eyes fixed intensely upon the yellow heads of the landing birds.

'Come, we must walk. We've got a long way to go.' It was also the immensity of that landscape which carried me. The way the mountain loomed above, wreathed in mist, and miniaturized our hand-holding figures – 'That's Klein Leeukop. See how like Lion's Head it is.'

And the sea, hurling itself at the rusted hulk that used once to be alive with seamen, filled with cargos from exotic places, far across the Atlantic.

'. . . Sunset Rocks. That's the wreck of the Romelia. It was being towed as scrap . . .'

I didn't care. But I liked to hear him talk, I liked to watch his wide gestures and his involvement with this place. I liked to hold his hand and allow myself to float along with it all. For once there were no hard choices for me, no decisions about life. That whole day, while the hems of our jeans soaked in salt, I never thought about Monday, about boys accused of murder, about James Hadley Chases and how I felt about it all. I never thought about Susan, and what she might be doing. I never gave a thought to the great creeping of violence and death which seemed to be everywhere – everywhere but there on that tranquil island, which wasn't an island.

'. . . really quite pretty, you know . . .'

The sun watered through, sharpening the planes of his face.

'Mm-mm,' I was watching the black-backed gulls, howling their wildness to the wind, and the nudging dance of kelp, given life by the wash of the waves.

'. . . if you really tried, know what I mean? I think you really should. It would give you more confidence. Then you wouldn't worry so much about what people—'

'What? What on earth are you talking about?'

'Yes, I thought you weren't listening, Jennifer. No really, I'm just saying that you could be quite pretty really. Like, if you wore some more make-up.'

'Martin, don't spoil this. Let it flow. Why're you trying to change me? This is how I look. This is my nature.'

'It's only for you that I'm speaking, you know. Although maybe you could do it for me just once as well. I just think that if you can be great-looking, why not? I just think you'd have more confidence . . .'

I have wondered upon occasion – whenever I have seen cormorants spread their wings and sand plovers skitter on the sand – I have remembered that day and wondered how I could have allowed him to do that to me. I know there was a seductiveness in being subsumed by his personality, something languid and easy about that lassitude I felt by his side. He was so sure, so beguilingly sure, that I was attracted to him with every uncertain breath which entered my body.

When I think of what he was, I know that he was nothing special. But he came into my life just when the foundation was knocked from it. It seemed so easy to focus on his encompassing spirit, which removed all my doubts and fears. For me, he was Cape Town, with its intriguing charm. Cape Town never felt as though it were involved in the real life business of Africa, and neither did he. They captivated, until you could spend your whole

153

life in the limbo of that great mountain. He gave it all to me, its sights and sounds and smells. But in return, he took little pieces of me. And I let him. To keep that pool of peace, I let him pick away at me. And the more I let him, the more needy for his seeming strength I became.

Just a small ache it gave me. Just a tiny chill in the pit of my stomach, each time. And then it was gone. Mostly, his need for me to be someone else was hidden. He disguised it in a great mass of ostensible caring. And even as I should have felt its lack of shelter, I found I could just believe it to be tangible.

He took me across the rocks at Hammersteen, and we paced it across Sandy Bay, his yellow diving bag slung across his shoulder. He never strolled. And when he stopped to gaze at something, his limbs twitched with the tension of inactivity. Through the tangle of dampened bushes he tugged on my hand, the words flying behind him as he pointed out the encroaching alien scrub, the gentle spread of the milkwood tree.

'Look!' he said, and stopped. Through the dishevelled screen of bush, I saw at first only the grey of the sea, the white of rocks and boulders. When I caught sight of the small dark head, I thought it was the bobbing of kelp. But it was a seal, the joyous sight of a seal, its whiskers thrust forward as it caught the swell and flew with the spray.

'No one really knows why they surf like that. Whether it's just for fun or . . .'

'Ssh. Shush for once, can't you, Martin? I don't care. It's just beautiful.'

When we got to a rocky peninsula, I watched as he put on his diving gear.

'I don't usually do this,' he said. 'I don't usually take crayfish out of season. But I'll only be taking two, and I want to do it for you.'

Slipping into the icy Atlantic, he became part of it. I sat and watched for him, tranquil in my dreams and wonderings. The sea was deceptively calm, fraudulently lapping at the edges of rocks. But just as it lulled, so it would burst forth a show of its might. The swell, far to the left, would power against the rocky ledge, flinging itself upward with a crash of triumph and a pillar of solid sea.

'Impressive, isn't it?' And he was towelling himself dry and pulling on his clothes. Two crayfish he placed in a large can – not

154

too many and not too few. He sat beside me on the rocks and I tasted the salt on his mouth and felt the drips fly from his hair.

'You're sweet,' he said and ran his fingers, sticky with sea water, through the tangle of my hair. 'I like to be with you. I like your stories and I like the way we fit together.'

'Yes,' I said, trying to memorize that mix – the spray from the towering wave with the smell of his skin, the rough feel of his jersey and the whip of the wind.

'Ja, you see, I never usually choose girls like you . . . I seem to've always gone for spectacular bitches. Beautiful girls, glamorous types . . . I felt good walking into places with them. But they were always more ambitious than I was . . .'

Another piece of me, a small crust of self-esteem, went flying off into the wind. I watched it winnow with the gulls, as they cried their desolation over our heads.

'. . . Oh sure, I've got a reputation with women. But, the last time I think it was me that got nailed. Amazing, considering how everyone warned her about me. God, she was beautiful! I think I'm still kind of fucked up over her.'

I watched his face as he brought his young wife to life before my eyes, the love that he had finally decided to settle with and adore. And I watched him try to squeeze me into her shape.

It wasn't only I who was clinging. With the clarity of the spray's sudden chill, I saw that the intensity of our suctioned relationship was in our mutual, smothering need to clutch at something else. His was nestled in a deceptive show of strength, but mine was there for all to see.

The sky seethed with suppressed light, exploding in sparks on the grey of the sea. And so, that day allowed me no space to consider. It swept me along with the wash of its waves.

In the smooth sand, we wrote the word EPHEMERAL in great loops, and watched as it washed away, along with our footprints. We laughed, leaping from waves, and thought ourselves clever.

We walked back more slowly, stopping for the rough hug of sweatshirt against jersey. We were slowed by the blood-racing need to show off, to cartwheel across the sand, to leap gull-like across rocks and swoop downward, to wrestle and kiss in the powdered embrace of dry sand.

I think I loved it, that day, probably as I loved him, though neither gave me the time to judge. They were both just there, the man and the day, overwhelming me with the sense of being – just being.

And back at his cottage, his housemate away, we licked crayfish from fingers in the huddle of rugs before a wood fire. We drank Cabernet to keep out the cold and made love, in his powerful, unconsidering way, with the fire heating the side of me and bursting blossoms through the wine . . .

. . . The fragile warmth of the winter sun didn't reach the chill of the courtroom. The boys huddled and slapped at each other in their new sweatshirts and *takkies*, bought for them by some funding body. The courtroom, rapt with waiting ritual, was shadowed by the looming coat of arms, untouched by the glow of the day before.

Somehow, I had remembered to raid the Observatory book exchange on Saturday for James Hadley Chases. The boys were flagrantly happy, knockabout-excited by the books and the half-naked women on their covers. But I felt uninvolved in the drama of them. It seemed a game – this shuffled nervousness to give me a letter, the giggles as I unfolded the many folds of exercise-book paper.

'That's you,' mumbled Jackson, as he ducked his head and looked down at his toe. 'I did it for you.' I smiled, finding a voluptuous, pink-pencilled caricature, copied from the cover of one of their books.

'Thank you,' I said, the sweetness of the grubby note bringing a lump to block the laughter in my chest. 'Thank you for that. I'll always keep it.'

I felt schizophrenic at having moved so suddenly to this, from the bed and the arms of a man who, so like Cape Town, despised reality. Who told me, in the cuddled hours stretching towards midnight, of winds and waves and inlets, of small buds of Erica on the heights of Table Mountain, of wrecks and the ghosts of sailors.

He had shushed me and told me these times, this Africa, were degrading to the spirit. They could only be transcended through creativity, he said. And I could picture his life, and what he did with it. I could see him in my mind – I see him still – stand naked on the shore to paint EPHEMERAL in the sand.

And then, that morning, I was flung so forcefully from our bubble, into the courtroom's distillation of the country's fury.

I saw him before the start of the morning's proceedings – the young man with ageing eyes and lined mouth. He came in with Ilsa and found a spot at the back of the public gallery. Mandla, the Botswana connection, who had placed his feet on the table without reproach.

The last thing I expected was that he would remember me, just one of the many voyeurs on his political life. But nonetheless he frowned slightly, and shifted across the public bench.

'Do I know you?' he asked, while the boys whispered and scattered, and I, shy to look at him, folded my scrap of paper. 'Have we met somewhere?'

'Well,' I said, my eyes leaping up in curiosity at last, 'We didn't actually meet. But I saw you . . . um, in Obs . . . you know, at the meeting. Um, I noticed you because you had your feet on the table and no one shouted at you.'

He looked amused. I wanted to die. I looked down again to hide the heat in my face.

'Oh yes, you noticed that, did you?'

He laughed and I gave up my struggle for invisibility. There was a warmth about him that made it seem unnecessary.

'I didn't know you were involved with this,' he said, nodding towards my boys. 'Part of the defence team?'

'Yes, I'm with the attorneys . . .'

'Hmm, it must be fascinating to be so close to it.'

'Yes, it is but . . . well, Mandla, um, can I call you Mandla?' He nodded. 'Jennifer,' I said. 'I just . . . I know I'm lucky, but I just feel so very confused about them, my clients, that is.'

'Why?' he asked me, his creased eyebrows quizzical.

'Well . . . because of what they did, I suppose. The strange thing is, they seem such kids. They're so nice, yet they're so very guilty.'

Mandla frowned. 'But I don't understand.'

Then he smiled, to take the bite from his words. 'What I mean is, I just don't understand why you have to find the good guys and the bad guys in all of this.'

I took a deep breath and glanced about us. The early-morning courtroom was muttering around us, people entering and leaving, bringing files, families chatting to their sons in the dock. The court orderly sat on his chair at the door, picking the spots on his face.

'Well, doesn't there always have to be a good and a bad? Isn't it just sometimes hard to find it?'

'It doesn't work here. It just doesn't.' He ran his hand over his exhausted eyes and reached out a finger to touch my clenched hand, again to soften the sting. 'We're a country of inevitabilities. And I think that you . . .' He was a nice man. He never could say 'you' without smiling and dipping his head apologetically. '. . . um, I think that you should have realized by now that here it is the children who get caught in the inevitabilities. The inevitability of people being pushed to the limit, and beginning to push back.'

It was past ten, but still the judge and assessors did not appear. The orderly, still picking at his face, was leaning forward, gazing down the judge's corridor.

It still makes me smile to remember Mandla – so committed, and yet able to be so patient with me and my ambivalence. He was easy to talk to, having about him no air of worthiness.

'You mean, they hit first so you're allowed to hit back as hard as you like?'

'Yes, well,' said Mandla, with a quick laugh. 'You see now, even you can understand that, from your schoolyard rules. No, but really, it's not so much a matter of "allowed" . . .'

The judge's clerk bustled in, placing a pile of files on his Bench.

'Judge Roberts apologizes, but says he is a little delayed,' she said. The orderly never took his eyes, glazed now, from the corridor as he moved his fingers over his chin, squeezing and scratching.

'You see,' said Mandla, 'these kids aren't trained revolutionaries, who made a considered choice. It's just that, from the time of their births, what they have seen and lived has led them to this. It is something . . .'

'Silence in court. *Stilte innie hof. Staan innie hof.*' . . .

. . . 'That you, Sister? How the fuck do you do a cable?'

'What are you talking about?' I was still at the front door, caught between perplexed irritation and guilt at not having seen her since Sunday morning.

I hadn't worked that out yet. It wasn't her aloneness that brought this guilt. Susan relished the high plane of sadness she gained from being solitary. It helped her piece together her parts and gauge perspectives. A day alone would often bring her closer to her creativity, even if she felt she couldn't use it. I often believed

I could see her talent nosing at her hands and licking at her thoughts. If she felt unable to take it out and pet it, it must nonetheless give her comfort to know that it was there, rubbing against her flank.

'This stupid jersey with a cable down the front,' she said as I stepped into the lounge. 'I thought these books would tell me how to knit, but they don't explain the cable.'

Around her was strewn the kaleidoscope pattern of a new Susan. Wools in different colours, knitting books from the library, needles freshly bought, scrumpled packets from the tiny haberdashery shop we visited sometimes in Woodstock, usually not to buy, but to pause and chat to the old German couple who still spoke hardly any English after all these years.

I perched on the arm of a chair and watched this new being within her feverishly trying, through its homely enthusiasm, to bring a contentment to our hearth.

'It won't work you know, Sister,' I said, amusement warming my voice.

'What, my cable?' It made me sad, this one. It had something to do with me.

'No, not your stupid cable, idiot. I mean the attempt to make the Sisterhood content to spend winter by the fire.'

'You think we can't?' She spoke cautiously – not so sure of her ground. She knew, in any case, that I was deliberately misunderstanding this new Susan. But that was OK, because I could never have faced it head-on. And I think I was doing what it wanted anyway – trying to pull things together.

'Idiot. Don't you know we're made that way – never to cope with contentment? Can't you see that we'll always be forcing ourselves to dance the razor's edge of intensity until, every single time, we cut our feet?'

'God, you are such a lunatic stuff-up, know that?' She laid down her knitting, but she was smiling. 'Let's make coffee. No, fuck that – let's have wine.'

And that was OK too. It was as it should be. And Susan's new self was pleased as we went through the ritual wine-pouring, the ceremonial lighting of cigarettes. It could see things coming together.

But Susan stretched the cigarette towards my hand. And I knew there was still a degree of distance between us, where before there

159

had been none. And there . . . there it was. There was the source of my guilt. Though it was Susan who had created the fight, it was I who had moved myself away from her – clinging to my infatuation – out of fear that she would someday take herself from me.

That was why Susan had needed this new self – not just to make us calm. It had been summoned in this last-ditch attempt to draw me back into what we had always been together.

'I must get this right,' she said as we returned to the couch. 'Read those instructions. Tell me what to do. There's a desperate knot here now . . .'

She struggled with it as I read aloud from the Woman's Weekly book of knitting. 'Pass the left needle over . . . no, fuckhead, not that way. Over the front. Where'd you get these – Rondebosch Library? Why the hell didn't you just get novels like everyone else?'

'Ja. I don't read novels . . . pass the right, no the left . . . I like to get books that I can do things with, that tell me things.'

I knew that. I was just teasing, trying to smother the space between us. Books were not the same for her as they were for other people. Susan saw books as props for her other selves. They were challenges – but quite often challenges that went unfaced when she returned to home and me. They seemed then too hard to bother with, or the mood turned and the enthusiasm scattered. I remembered the books on Savonarola and the Spanish Inquisition, during the time of the ascetic Susan, who longed for a rarefied spirituality; who wished to fathom the fervour of his time. And then it passed, and Savonarola went back, his spine unstretched beyond his first chapter.

'Tell me again, Sister,' she said. 'Read it again, slowly.'

'No Sister. It's impossible. It's too much for the Sisterhood. I'll tell you what. We'll take it across to Auntie. I bet you she knows how to knit.'

'Oh Sister, what genius.'

The delicate day was falling into the harsh chill of evening and we went back for jerseys before venturing to the street. It was hushed, the smell of unspecified stew lurking in doorways.

'Evening Mr Kennedy. I said: *Evening Mr Kennedy*!'

'Oh yes, evening. Yes. Evening girls. Cold enough for you?' He had stretched his tortoise head, indicating that he hadn't heard. Now he stood at the edge of his *stoep*, straining for the sounds of the street – the perimeter of his world. Mrs Kennedy was nowhere to be seen – too cold for her now.

I paused at the door for Susan, who had stopped to retrieve the unravelling balls of wool which kept falling into the street and having to be dusted off. Auntie stood behind the yellow light of the counter – hammy arms on hips, eyes scrunched to avoid the smoke from her cigarette. She seemed to survey something which displeased her on the floor.

'*Ja*, you old bugger,' she shrilled above the roar of the TV in the next room. 'If you would just once in your lazy life lay down the law a little. But no, you let all the bladdy suppliers walk all over you and then you complain we have no bladdy money . . . And everyone knows why you really have no money . . . Hello girls. Lazy old bugger, you know? That's what it's like to have a bladdy husband. No guts! Marry them, and they have no guts. Not in the shop and not under the sheets . . . You hear that, you old . . . oh, what the hell. He doesn't care. Hm-mm? So what you girls want from old Auntie today, hey?'

'Hey?' she said, as she heard of our quest. 'No, no my loveys, no, not old Auntie. Certainly not me.' Her voice had lowered to its usual brandied tone. 'You know where you must go? Auntie Celie. Down there by the very bottom of Crown Street, by Bellevliet. She's on the corner – the house stands alone – over the road from the bottom terrace.

'Oh, and girls?' she called as we left the café. 'Cats. You'll see hundreds of cats. Then you know it's the right house.'

And so, that chilling evening, we wandered past the terraces and semis, where people huddled indoors, and no trails of incense wisped past the closed sash windows.

And then we saw the cats – we'd seen them all before, but never isolated them to this particular house. They sat on pillars, wandered along walls, streaked across the road just ahead of the cars which trundled past.

I can picture Auntie-by-the-Café's harrumphing face to this day. Harshness is usually easier to remember than softness. And Auntie Celie was all softness. I remember her as silken white hair, soft skin falling into powdered folds. I remember her flowered dress and great soft lap, warm with sleeping cats. I can't picture her face, though. I can't see whether she wore glasses, or what colour her eyes were.

# Jo-Anne Richards

'Oh yes, my *skatties*. So Auntie sent you, did she? Oh, a cable – oh my *skatties*, that's easy for old Celie. Look . . . oh dear, I see there's a bit of a problem here. Well, you girls settle yourselves . . . oh, I see my cats like you. Well, that's a good sign. That's what I always say – when my cats like a person, it means . . .'

She chattered as she pulled out five rows of Susan's knitting and settled to knit, chattering as we sat in her lounge stroking cats.

'Well, Auntie – there by the café – always says to me: "You trust those cats far too much. One day you'll have a native come in to rob you, but your cats'll like him so you'll just . . ." '

Her needlework was spread over every surface. She had a tapestried fire screen, crocheted arm and back covers for her flowery chairs, knotted rug before the fireplace, cross-stitched traycloths and loopy crocheted doilies.

'But they've always been good to me, and we've always looked after each other. I know every one, you know?'

We were soothed, Susan and I. We smiled at each other as she expertly criss-crossed her needles and produced the cable.

'Here my *skat*,' she said, handing the needles back. 'Easy as pie. Come any time you have a problem, hear? I'm always in the house – my legs aren't too good any more. Auntie sends me packets down; she sends Willie. I don't mind the old pet. He talks about the war and that girl, Lily, they say up and left him when he came back not quite right in the head. But he's good to my cats. She sends eggs and bread for me, good for my teeth, you know? And pilchards for the kitties. You like pilchards, don't you my *skat-katte*? There, settle now Mimsy. Bye-bye girls, visit me again, you hear? I've always been the top knitter, even at school I was the best in Observatory, right up to . . .'

Her soft chattering followed us through the house. She didn't seem to mind our leaving. She wasn't really speaking to us any more. But Mimsy was listening. Mimsy sat straight-backed on her lap, gazing at her face as she explained that she'd been the champion knitter of Obs, way back before the war.

The phone was ringing as we reached the *stoep*. Wrestling with the door, we scrummaged into the house, giggling and fighting and dropping balls of wool. Susan reached it first.

'Hello. Yes, this is Susan. Yes . . .' she said. I watched her face for a sign that perhaps it was for me. She gave a small negatory flip of her hand, but reached out to pluck at my jersey before I could turn away. I was held by her look of astonishment. She gestured to the receiver and drew her face into exaggerated lines of disbelief and amusement. 'Yes . . . it so happens I am the blonde one . . .' I was amazed that the caller could so staunchly continue, given the scorn straining through her words. But her face – I couldn't take my eyes from her face. Despite the opprobrium in her voice, she was interested. I watched her homely self drain away. In its place skipped her own out-of-kilter, elfin look. Expressions skittered across her features. I noticed something like horror, yet it was laced with amusement. Then flickered interest, then horror again, then scorn. Finally, pure unadulterated delight.

'Well, yes . . .' she said, the laughter trying to tumble from between her teeth. 'I suppose I could manage that. Yes, why not? OK – tomorrow night? Do you know where we live . . . Yes I suppose you would, wouldn't you?' And then the laughter, winning the battle over her words, poured out. 'Yes . . . Yes, see you then. Bye.'

She collapsed to the floor, helpless with laughter as I shook and pushed at her, desperate for information. 'You just will not believe this . . . You just will not believe who just phoned . . .' she repeated between seizures of laughter.

'Well,' she said finally, rubbing at her eyes with her ruined hands. 'Can you believe this, or what? That was . . .' and again she collapsed in hilarity. 'That was Manie. You know! The Greenpoint Madam's new boyfriend.'

'I cannot believe this. So what on earth did . . .'

'He's heard about me from Maud, apparently – I'm the skinny blonde one. Fuck, can you believe that! Anyway, so he wanted to ask me out.'

'But Susan, you can't be serious. My God . . .' I was laughing now too, but nervously. 'You didn't accept, surely. You surely aren't fucking insane enough to have said yes. No, surely not even you . . .'

'Well,' she said. 'Perhaps I'm curious to see what a bi-ig man he is.' She used Maud's depiction of great, rounded buttocks.

'But, Jesus Christ, you can't. He sounds completely rough . . . I mean, it might not even be safe.'

'Oh, then you'll enjoy this. He actually admitted to being a police reservist – thought that'd make me feel safe, so I'd know he wasn't "just scum", he said.'

'Oh my God, Susan. You've accepted a date with a police reservist. What is it with you? What the hell's the matter with you?'

The smile dried from her mouth and the damp pools of her eyes. Within them, I could see the embroiled depths of her despair and her remaining hope.

'You don't understand,' she said, and I winced. The Sisters had never spoken those words. The two of us had always, always understood.

'You don't understand how sometimes . . .' she began her agonized dragging of each word from the depths of her. 'I have to . . . to kick at every last taboo that's placed in my way. Or else I'll . . . I'll just never be free . . . of my background, and everything that holds me down. Can't you see that the very fact that he scares me, and that the idea of him makes me *gril*, is why I have to do this?'

Her emotion had, in its expression, broken past her distaste of words. Suddenly she was fluent, more fluent than I had heard her in a long time.

'There's something erotic about mud-creeping. I don't expect you to see that, but there's a . . . I don't know . . . a sensuality in seeking out human beings who are the very furthest things from me and everything I grew up with. I know you'll never understand, but for me . . . I just know I have to explore the darkest side of myself that I can find, and . . . and everything else that comes in my way.'

I felt the darkness then, the darkness I had always sensed swirling in the depths of her well-like creativity. I felt it swirling through her fragile body and begin to threaten the exquisite balance of her mind. I feared for her. But there was nothing I could do. I had sensed it – that with the balance lost between us she no longer had a place of refuge. And I watched her having to batter at boundaries even here, before me. And I despaired. I despaired over what we had done to break the fragile threads, and I despaired, that in my own fear, I had removed myself from her. Now she had nothing – nothing but her wildness to push her on and on.

I looked down the passage and saw her knitting – her sanctified offer of love to me – lying where it had been dropped. The needles had pulled loose and it had begun to unravel, the beautiful cable untwining and springing free.

*Kalatter kalatter kalatter, kalatter kalatter kalatter skreee-ee-ee*

K I was rushed, late for work. And sick to my stomach as I finished my hairbrushing and – a small gesture to Martin – added lipstick. I wanted to catch a moment with Maud, to hear from her side how this had come about.

I grabbed my things and clattered down the stairs. I heard Susan behind me, scrabbling for school stuff and preparing to join me. I felt ill at the thought of him. I'd never met him – never even seen him, though we had peered into his life, and his most intimate relationships. But it wasn't just the person he was. He was also a symbol of Susan's breaking away from all that held her whole.

I had reached the kitchen and begun the coffee-spooning when I heard Maud's key and her measured steps. As she entered with her imperious nod, and sat herself in her chair, it seemed suddenly that she was magic.

She could be Fate itself in human form, with its love of mischief and its cosmic amusement at our expense. She was the universal Auntie Celie, cabling and knitting together all of our lives. I hadn't noticed it happening, and now it was done – our lives had become inextricably entwined with those of people we had never met.

I heard Susan come in behind me, greet Maud, and reach for the second cup of coffee I had poured. I gulped for the ordinariness of this morning ritual, but it tasted of strangeness.

'So,' said Maud to our silent figures. 'So, the Greenpoint Madam is upset. She says the new man, Master Manie, is no longer with her. She says she thinks he is seeing someone else. But I say nothing.'

We were both, I think, silenced by this other-side view. It had come too close, and lost its voyeuristic delight. Maud watched us

165

over her mug, sucking her tea past the bag as her eyes moved from one to the other. This morning, as my fears created fancies to flit about the room, I felt her strings upon our wrists and the binding of those powerful eyes.

'So . . . Master Manie, he asks me all about you. He is very interested to hear of the two. He says . . .' She rose and became the great-chested bear she had created previously.

Her voice gravelled: ' "So Maud? A teacher, hey? A teacher is a very smart thing. My mother wanted me to be one, but I didn't care for study so much. So, Maud? I think I would like to have been a teacher. A classy one. Hey?" '

She sank back into herself, and dropped to the creaking chair for a sip of tea. 'So he asks where you live, and I tell him. I think that we will now see what will happen.'

'We will indeed,' said Susan. 'So, listen Maud. Has the ex-wife been back?'

'Oh yes, she has come and she says I must watch out for him, that a black person cannot trust him. She says he is full of appetite.'

'Appetite!' exclaimed Susan. 'You mean sexual appetite?'

'No, I mean appetite! Appetite about black people.'

'Oh,' I said as it dawned on me. 'You mean apartheid.'

'Yes. In his house, I have a metal plate and mug. It is kept under the sink.'

I glanced at Susan, but her drawn face was fixed on her coffee. I wondered what she felt, and what she feared. I couldn't ask.

'But,' continued Maud, 'he has been a fair Master. And it is a good piecework. The work is not too hard. I think the old wife says this so I should rather trust her. She says I must watch him and tell her everything – and for the children, she says. She tells me about the children and I feel sorry, too sorry for the children.'

'Why?' I asked suddenly. 'Are they badly off?'

'No, there is money. No, but I can remember what it is like for children when all the men go away . . .' She paused to settle her feet, crossing them at the ankles.

I had to leave, but I could feel she was settling into a story that I compulsively had to hear – that would give us a little something of her, of the life which she had steadfastly refused to discuss since she first arrived. 'Can you remember that from when you were a child, Maudie?' I asked.

166

'Yes, I was a child in the district of Bizana in the Transkei.' For a moment I caught sight of the child, skipping barefoot in the dust. 'It is a poor place. No water. And too much cattle, too much. And no grazing for them. All the cattle were so thin. So, I remember the men must all leave, when they get big, to go to the mines. My father was gone, and my brother . . .' Her voice faded and she stared into her tea.

'So, Maudie? Did he leave? What happened to him?'

She shook herself and turned abruptly, her self returned to the adult. 'Yes, but that is enough. I do not like to speak of the Transkei. It is not good to think of things that are past. It is not good.

'Yes, and now?' she said, looking at both of us with disapproval. 'Must you two not be at the work?'

# 9

And so began a week that is embedded in the fibres of my life. And now I must lay it out, examine its parts and remove its magic by picking at it, piece by piece.

It was wonderful. It was a glowing thing. But it came in a time full of dread, a time of turbulence which rocked at the core of the country. And I was flung wildly between the two, sometimes feeling myself close to breakdown.

By day I was caught in the world my work threw at me, in which I had wrapped myself emotionally. As the court day ended, as I collected my things from the office and walked through the deadened streets of the vanishing city centre, I would meet him.

On the one side of each day, all was so clear and easy to discern. And on the other, the chill of doubts in a courtroom where the sun couldn't reach, the darkness of doom which clung like smoke about my accused boys.

In the dashing through this flickering strobe existence, I lost myself somewhere. I was left behind by the sweep of history, trying to keep up as, all the while, I watched over my shoulder for Susan.

It began . . . well, who knows where it began, but I remember that he drove me, on a Tuesday evening, to friends in Tamboerskloof. The mountain loomed, its face whitely lit, over the steep streets. Cottages huddled together in sash-windowed clusters, seemingly arrested mid-tumble.

I was shy of the settled cul-de-sac community which I sensed in that twisting road, so steep that I feared for his ancient *bakkie*. He, as usual, seemed entirely at ease, sure of his welcome and untouched by silent shiftings. It was the artiness of it that tongue-tied me, the carefully restored houses, the giddy, steepled lines of the church redesigned as a home, its soaring ceilings and art-bright walls peeking through arching windows. And the doors that were all open to each other, showing off halls with Afghan treasures or Mongolian statuary, or whatever.

We wandered into the house where I could smell a great steaming stew, and possibly lentils, and baking bread? And in the corner – where three intensely dark men discussed focal lengths – I could smell dope. As I was swooped upon in flashing embrace by our braceleted hostess, I was enveloped in something musky and exotic.

'My little *bokkie*,' she cooed over me, cradling my flushed face between her many rings. 'But Martin, how lovely and fresh she is. *Ag* my little *bokkie*. How did you end up with a jaded old creature like Martin? Come in, come in, my darling. You'll eat with us . . .'

'Well, I'm sorry,' I said as she released me. 'Martin just brought me. I mean, you didn't know we were coming for supper or anything.'

'*Ag* man, isn't it quaint? My darling, in this house I never know who'll be here. I'm basically just a common old thing from the Karoo. I like things very basic. People wander in day and night. That's just the kind of place this is. Now listen darlings, this is Martin's new little *bokkie* . . .'

I was flamboyantly and figuratively handled and passed along by each group in the tiny cottage, stuffed with the warmth of the hospitable stew and the accepting embraces. People wandered in and out, crossing between cottages and returning without ceremony, clutching an onion, a book or a drawing.

It was just there, all of it. It needed nothing from me. And yet, intensely, it enfolded me. I must confess to loving them as much for what they seemed, symbolically and picturesquely, as for who they really were. Much more, really. I can't say I ever knew any of them at all, except perhaps my volatile hostess. But that was later. That night, I loved the very idea of them. I loved offering my shy hand to a beetling poet, leaning against the wall – 'My trouble is that I look too much like a poet. I look as though I belong in a garret, so people romanticize me' – a group of photographers, who didn't say much, but stood comparing lenses and filters, and a pair of bickering actors – I think they must have been a couple, but I never was sure. I had seen them in something. I was still trying to place them, as a lumbering man hooked a grasping arm about my shoulders and demanded to meet me.

'A flower,' he said. He was famous. Even I, with my creaking knowledge of art, had heard his name spoken in awe by Susan's friends.

'A flower?' I asked him, confused. I thought perhaps he was being terribly esoteric, saying something obscurely clever that I was missing.

'Yes,' he said, lifting my chin with bony fingers. Bringing bulging eyes uncomfortably close to mine, he added, 'A flower. A fresh blossom of beauty, with the dew still on it.'

I felt myself blush, but everyone laughed and squeezed my hand, or nudged me, and told me to take no notice of him. He boomed with laughter and – with affected, but gentle intimacy – stroked and twirled the tendrils of hair about my face.

'*Ag* man, Martin, it's such a lovely *bokkie*,' said my hostess, pursing her mouth and pinching my cheek as she swept past me. I loved her instantly. She had the gravelly warmth of her Karoo childhood – which she played on with great pretentious effect for the interest it gave her. For she wasn't that at all. She was sophisticated Cape Town, swooping in skittish displays of excellent wine and classical music, providing a nesting place for artists and clever people. But it was still there, her background, slipping into her down-to-earth speech and her shoo-ing of children off to their beds.

But then she'd flit over to the record-player, flirting with choices. I watched as the man I'd rightly presumed to be her husband wandered over and pointed to an album. Ignored by all, they flew into volatile and gestured acrimony – I wasn't sure of the cause – and loudly decried each other's stupidity and insensitivity. I turned from them, embarrassed in my small-town way. But glancing back, I saw them embracing with a passion that thrilled me, which tightened in my chest. Arms around each other, they flicked the needle carelessly on to a record. It leapt to life in a sweeping embrace of voices which ached at my throat and instantly entwined itself around my memories of that house, and my happiness at being there.

'Oh yes, angel,' said my hostess as she passed. 'You like it, don't you? It's Puccini. Of course the romantic Italians are a little *passé*, but I don't care. I still think it's very special, don't you?'

'Oh yes. I'll never forget this . . .'

'You have a sensitive aura, my darling . . . So lovely to have a new face among us dissipated Sixties ravers. The rest of us've known each other since who knows when – early or mid-Sixties, you know?'

'How wonderful. You're so lucky,' I gushed, overwhelmed and overcome by this surfeit of the senses. 'I just love this – your home – and all these talented people. I mean, it's so thrilling.'

'Mm, well, if you'd seen what we've all seen together . . . Funny how so many of us've settled here, within walking distance. You know, my darling, in the Sixties, we all lived in those little Gardens boarding houses. You see Deb over there? She's a sculptor. And René – she writes children's books. She's married to the photographer, you see? Used to be married to Peter – my husband, you know? Anyway, the two of them used to live together in those days. They always had silver-painted legs, and short, short skirts . . .'

She glittered as she spoke – her rings, her mirrored scarf, her dark, vivacious eyes. ' . . . The times seemed somehow to lend themselves to more awareness of art and culture. Not so terribly depressing – we could rave, and dance, and paint all night. There were such a lot of creative ideas, and good theatre. Oh, of course, the police would raid us all periodically, and some of them . . .' she jerked her chin towards the photographers ' . . . would get arrested now and again. But somehow it wasn't so ugly . . . so ugly and basic. It was romantic. Like a campaign. There was a hope and a . . . a feeling that we could rush off and blow up pylons, come back and write poetry, and that everything would change. Now, there's a dark chill to it. It's all so terribly depressing . . . You know, my darling, I was once the most beautiful young actress to hit the Cape. You wouldn't believe it now to look at me, would you?'

'Oh, I would. You're still so beautiful. You look like a gypsy.'

She laughed, but I could see she was pleased. 'Oh, you sweet angel. Where did Martin find you? My sweetheart, listen! You must watch out for him. You can't marry him. He's a disaster, and far too well-used for you.'

'I know. I'm . . .' I glanced over at him. He seemed not really aware of me. It hurt me briefly, but then I supposed that no one could have felt shy there. He had no reason to hover. He was perched on the arm of a chair, tuning his guitar. ' . . . Well, I'm not really thinking that far. I'm just going with it for the moment.'

172

'OK . . .' she said, distracted suddenly. 'Oh Pieter, my sweet. You asked me to help frame for your exhibition. You must remember . . .' And she was gone, hands flying in illustrative swoops.

I curled myself in cosy delight between groups, not quite part of either. But I could eavesdrop on both, savouring their relationships, the incestuous repartee of people who had known each other so long, who had married and divorced each other, and had wild, choreographed affairs. Besides the famous artist, and the photographers, and the agonized poet, oh, and the actors, I think there were a couple of journalists there. And an architect, who lived next door. I suppose there must have been one or two, like me, who were scurriers among the talents, or just plain ornaments on the arm of some famous or clever person. But those I don't remember. I see, in my backward view of that night, just the patina of their flair, the flourishing of themselves in that symbolic parade of talents.

'I must tell you, I thought the stuff Johan read at his poetry reading last week absolutely powerful . . .'

I could feel Martin, having abandoned his guitar, squeezing himself beside me. I could smell the dark smell of his skin and feel his rough jersey scrub against my cheek.

'. . . the strength of his imagery when he writes in Afrikaans, it really gives a power . . . you know, from that staunch Calvinist background of his . . . to his agony. It's the contrast it gives his imageries of homosexual love.'

'Well, I still like his English stuff, but you know someone who had a reading recently, who I think is distinctly underrated . . .'

I rolled it around my senses, the whiff of dope, the rolling conversations, the bescarfed women in paint-splashed jeans and flowing tops. The men squatting in khaki chinos and white, collarless shirts. I loved their flower-child-like view of things as it had grown, vinelike and intertwined, in the shelter of their unthreatening mountain.

It was all so seductive – their incense-misted lives, their attachment to the spiritual optimism of the Sixties, which held them aloof from the harshness outside.

'. . . I wouldn't have thought of using anything but black and white for those township shots. But you'll notice, if you page through the book, that graininess which people seem to expect as part of my style, it just didn't seem adequate for the mood of

173

these. I thought it softened and flattened, kind of romanticized everything more than I wanted . . .'

Even that which had been ugly beyond the cottage walls had been filtered through their talents into something of artistry, or so it seemed that night. No one spoke of the boils of violence that were breaking out all over our country, as we scooped spicy, lentil stew with newly baked bread. And I didn't want them to.

Martin nuzzled my neck and cuddled me to his chest with intense arms. I wondered, briefly, how much his appearance at my side had to do with the attentions of the famous artist. But I didn't hold the thought. I let it slide into the serenity of the evening. He added his loud remarks, and laughed his belching laugh, pushing his overwhelming personality out in front, as he always did. And it was OK, they all accepted him, and me with him. But, while joints were passed and supper was eaten, I could feel the twitch of his muscles, and looking up at him, see the tautening of his jaw. After supper, he left his bowl where it lay and, not waiting to be asked, grabbed for his battered guitar.

'I'll play a bit,' he said to the room at large. No doubts touched a tentative tone to his voice. He just played, sure they would want him to. It embarrassed me briefly, in my connection to him – I, who thought that if one offered to play, one should have the grace and skill to bring goose bumps. He didn't play like that. He had a lovely voice and he used it well. But he played no more than a clumsy strum. I think we all forgot that though, in the conjuring act of his confidence.

Everyone sang, and laughed and joined in, whooping when he played what they liked and calling for others. As he skipped through images of San Francisco, and flowers in hair, and seasons for love, he became more whimsical, more attuned to their senti-mental mood.

They sang, and smiled gentle, down-turned smiles at each other. Wisps of hair swayed to the music and nostalgia rose among them like the melancholy smoke of the joints. Martin stopped and looked them over, watched their drift into faraway eyes and stroked heads in laps. I watched the quick drumming of his fingers, apprehensive over how he would channel the impatience trapped in the muscle beside his mouth.

'*Ag* pleez, Daddy won't you take us to the bioscope . . .'

He clanged it from his guitar, piercing their mood with his

suddenly strident voice. And then he laughed, dropping his guitar on the chair and throwing his head back in a gust of hilarity.

'Let's go!' he yelled, summoning me with the tilt of his head. I scurried through the sleepy bodies draped on the floor. We wandered without ceremony through the unlocked door, I turning with small nervous waves. But all their attention was inward, and no one noticed my anxious attempts at leave-taking.

He kissed me hard against the car, pressing the smell of his need into my mouth. And I wanted the whole of him. I wanted to disappear into the huge sureness of him.

'Tell me a story,' he whispered, under that icy moon. And I loved him. I loved him with an intensity that removed all my agonized doubts, and all my ugly fears . . .

. . . 'Yes, I remember that day in Langmanskraal Road . . . It was a day full of fear, a day full of blood.'

The prosecutor tugged at his slipping gown. 'Ah-hrumm. Yes, I see. Well, can you tell the court, a little more specifically, what it was you remember about that day?'

The man was old, his face a tumbleweed of dry lines, his hands, like rough twigs, clutching the edge of the witness box. But his eyes . . . eyes which flew to the escape of the door, to the high, high window where so little light fought its way through . . . his eyes were filled with the sheen of sights he had seen, of images too awful to be spoken of lightly.

'The dust.'

'The dust? Mr Mabuza, you must give us a little more detail than this. Please, now think very carefully . . .'

'You say I must remember that day. You ask me what I remember. Most, I remember the dust, which hung in the air from many feet, and much stamping. The dust and the hunger. Some were just hungry for food, but others were hungry for blood.'

'Fine. Now, Mr Mabuza, please explain to the court how it was you happened to be out in the street that day, an old man like you.'

'That is the day I see the blood of whites. Blood lying in the dust. It is the first time I see whites die. Before, I have seen many people die in our streets. Many neighbours, family, even children. But this is the first time I see a white man fall. The blood, it looks just the same, as it falls in the dust.'

'Mr Mabuza, do you need the interpreter?' The prosecutor

tugged at his gown again, twitching his shoulders in irritation at this witness of his. 'Please could you answer the question. I asked how it came to be—'

'I hear what you say. I will tell the whole story. I will tell it as it should be told. That day, my wife she has a terrible hunger. She is old, like me, and cannot work. She cannot walk so good. I see her sitting there with her suffering and I go out to find something for her. To try if I could beg or borrow some food for her.'

'Yes, thank you Mr Mabuza. So you went out to find some food. And what happened then?'

For once, all the boys and young men were caught by this testimony which brought all the sights and smells and hunger of that day to their bellies. They sat without shuffling, glancing to the empty seat beside them – the absent dignity of their lodestone, their yardstick. I felt it with them, that anxiety over Oupa's absence, and how they were to fare as the trial continued without him.

His advocate, at the start of the day's proceedings, had informed the court that Oupa was in hospital recovering from a minor stroke. The judge had given his permission for the trial to proceed without him for the time being, since it was not known how long he would be away.

Through the days and days of shuffled glances, through their giggles and exercise-book letters, through much-folded drawings of me and the endless buying of James Hadley Chases, I had somehow grafted a raw section of my emotions on to them. I felt twinned with my boys in some way.

I felt it that day, I could taste the dust in my mouth and smell the blood and the frenzy. And I could hear the roar of their sudden fear. I felt intuitively that, with Oupa alongside them, they hadn't had to think deeply of their doom. They could be children, they could shuffle and stomp each other's feet, because he was their grown-up and he would consider it all gravely. They gave him that responsibility – of watching out for their lives and deaths – so that, in the confines of their cage, they could play at being children just one more time.

And strangely, though I knew nothing of life as they knew it, they felt the connection too. On the mornings I spent in court, I walked past the dock to share a few words with them. Jackson and Thomas would reach down and hold my two hands, sometimes a panicked clutch of my wrist, sometimes an exploration of fingers, sometimes just a quick squeeze between two heartfelt hands. This morning, it had brought the prick of tears to the back of my eyes.

'. . . as I walked. I could see nobody in the streets. The streets were cold that morning, cold also from the quiet. The quiet hung on the streets. But in the distance, I could hear a great roar – as a great beast would roar.'

'Yes, Mr Mabuza? And then? Did you make for the noise you could hear?'

'Yes, then I wanted to see what is happening, so I walk towards Langmanskraal Road. I come out by the place where these boys make barricades with barrels and tyres.'

'Which boys are those that you saw? Do you recognize any of them here?'

My boys, I saw, skittered their eyes away from the old eyes that slowly travelled over them.

'No, no, these young boys they are all just the same to me. I cannot see which is which. No, I cannot say.'

'All right, Mr Mabuza. Perhaps you can tell us what happened then.' His exasperation sparked from his jerked shoulders, into the piano scales he drummed on the table. With his other hand, he twitched his gown further up his shoulders.

He was nearing the end of the State case. I could see him feeling that the end was in sight, this interminable year of presenting his side of the story. And now this irritating old man, this witness who seemed always on the verge of sinking him, would choose to go on and on about irrelevancies, like dust and blood and hunger.

I wanted to tap him on his twitching shoulder and say: 'But don't you see, that's what we should be talking about. That's where it all comes from. That's what that day in Langmanskraal Road was all about. You must taste it, you should feel it. Rub your hands in it.' Oh Jesus, I thought, I'm losing it. I'm not coping. I was no longer thinking like a lawyer. I was too much part of them. This whole thing had gone on too long, and too intensely.

'. . . pushed my way through, to see. And I see burning tyres and drums of fire in the road. Then I see a car travelling slowly along and the crowds making way. Then I see it is Oupa Kakaza in that car. So the boys at the barricade, they cheer and yell for him. The car stops and Oupa, he opens the door and stands up there, still in the car, but with his head out.'

'And so, Mr Mabuza? Did he say something?'

'Yes.'

'Well, what, Mr Mabuza? Please could you tell us? What did Mr Oupa Kakaza say to—'

'*Amandla!*' The old man bellowed it, an illustrative fist in the air. The prosecutor was taken aback, still caught somewhere in the middle of his biting sentence. The packed public benches erupted into laughter and an answering '*Awethu!*' A smattering of fists punched the air.

Two very young policemen had been chatting up two floralled and flounced girls in the back row, their hands only lightly on the rifles which they had leant, with great *savoir-faire*, against the wall. Now they sprang up, bristled heads darting across the laughing benches. The judge leant back, arms folded, a look of quiet amusement on his face. His clerk laughed openly but the pimpled orderly almost toppled his wooden chair in red-faced fury at this impertinence before him.

'Silence!' he yelled. 'Silence in court or you will be thrown out the court. Silence, now!' He glanced at the judge, who at last leant forward and addressed the subsiding courtroom.

'Please! Settle please! Settle down or you will be asked to leave. Mr Erasmus, that was an amusing interlude but please could you try to control your witness?'

'Yes My Lord. As it pleases Your Lordship. Mr Mabuza, no more of that, please. Just tell us in a quiet voice what they said that day.'

'Yes. Well then the crowd of people, they answered him "*Awethu*" . . .' Another ripple of laughter washed through the benches and the judge, his eyes on the old man, gave another distracted 'Settle! Settle please!'

'. . . And then he says to them . . .'

I heard the noonday gun fire above us on the mountain, marking the passage of the present, which was so preoccupied with what was past, and with retribution.

'. . . He says: "Sing my song!" '

'He said: "Sing my song!" I see! And what song was it that they sang for him? Was it "Suffer the little children", or "Onward Christian Soldiers"?'

I watched the languid shifting movement of Oupa's advocate making an effort to rise.

'Sustained!' said the judge, holding up his hand to show that he

178

needn't bother with the effort. 'Mr Erasmus, please! I don't want to have to tell you again. You don't impress my assessors and me with your dramatic ability and your irony.'

'As it pleases Your Lordship. Mr Mabuza, please tell the court what song it was the people sang for Oupa Kakaza that day? Which song did he regard as his?'

'They sang: "There are guns in Angola, Bring them!" '

' "There are guns in Angola"! Hmm-mm. Well, Mr Mabuza. What happened next, as you recall it?'

'Then Oupa drove away. He went away from there and I did not see him again that day. He was not involved with the thing that happened next.'

'And what was that, Mr Mabuza? What happened next, just after the people had sung Mr Kakaza's song of guns and war?'

'Yes, Mr Erasmus,' the judge said, his voice weary. 'We get the connection you're trying to make. Don't labour it.'

'Yes, My Lord. Mr Mabuza?'

'Well, cars were driving along the road to get out of the Camp . . .'

'That's the Langmanskraal Squatter Camp, is it?'

'Yes, and then I see, in the dust made by the people's fury, that the rocks fly. And then I see them, mouths screaming, rocking the cars. And I see the white men like this in the cars . . .' Arms over his head, he demonstrated cowering terror. '. . . And then, I do not see what happens with the one car. I think they say he tried to run and he was stabbed . . .'

'No, Mr Mabuza. Please don't tell us what you heard or didn't see. Only tell us what you yourself saw.'

'Yes, well my eyes were on the one car. And some of the youths gather round the car and they turn it over. I see the petrol begin to spill. And then I see flames.'

'Did you actually see who struck the match?'

'No, I was too far. I see only the flames. Then the white man was crawling from the car. He was cut and bleeding and the burn was falling from his bones like snakes. And he was crawling into a puddle in the road and splashing himself with water . . .'

There was absolute silence as he paused. My boys, oh my boys, what were they thinking? I couldn't see their eyes, turned down and away.

'. . . and his mouth was gaping pink as he was sobbing. And as

179

the crowd grew suddenly quiet, all you can hear is the sobbing.' . . .

. . . I stood on the balcony wrapped in Martin's jacket. It smelt of
sheepskin, dampened to wet dog by the misted drizzle. I stood
absolutely still, impaled by the sun's last shafts over the sea.

I had tried. I had tried to bring the two worlds together and to
make sense of my avid connection to both. I had tried to talk of the
day's evidence to Martin, but he hadn't listened. He had interrupted my tentative dripping of words with a flow of conversation
about tides and mussels and rocks. He was on university vac, and
had spent the day on the chilly beach. Finally, impatient with
solitude, he had driven into town and waited at my office for court
to end. He hadn't allowed me to settle to paperwork – that was so
much like him. What he wanted, he was so sure he could carry
away. And I let him. He whisked me off early and transported me
to Llandudno for the sunset.

And, on the way – stopping for wine in Sea Point – he had flung
away the *Argus*. I had bought it outside the court to read of the
violence, which was now exploding even on the Platteland. And
now I wouldn't know. And the truth was, I wasn't sure if I wanted
to, now that he had taken me away. I wanted the way he wrapped
me in the wholeness of him and the Cape he saw. When I was with
him, it seemed that he could replace everything – band-aid all the
anxieties, everything that hurt and tore at me. Even Susan.

So he gave me the sun, brilliantining the gulls, and the ship way
out over the sea. And then he took me to his large wooden bed.
And he fucked me there, in that consuming way of his, with his
sureness that I wanted him and that he could take over my every
cell.

Then I stood, sheepskinned, on his balcony, while he bustled in
his kitchen. At first unselfconsciously naked, he must have been
overcome by the damp chill because when I came back inside, he
was wearing his ancient, baggy tracksuit.

'Go back to bed,' he commanded me. 'I'll join you there just
now.'

It was an evening of mussels picked from the rocks, and cooked
in white wine. I waited in bed for him to bring his offering of
anointed shellfish. I accepted it as his proffered love in tangible
form, the only way he knew how to offer it.

# Touching The Lighthouse

That was how it was. Or how I made it seem that night, as I tangled with his cat beneath his duvet. Now, I'm not sure that anything went that deep with him. I don't know that he thought beyond the fact that we felt like mussels, and that he wanted to feel the warm breath of a human being in his solitary bed.

We lay and drank wine as the sun deserted the walls of his room. Growing desolate with darkness, we were illumined just once more. For one freak instant, a square beam of light shone through the high, western window. Dazzled by what seemed its consecrating glow, I quietly murmured:

'. . . Shine here to us, and thou art everywhere;
This bed thy centre is, these walls, thy sphere.'

'Hey, that's really cool,' said Martin. I looked up at him. 'No, not that stuff you're mumbling. Makes me think of bloody English I. No, see that? See the way the sun does that glowing thing?'

As it shifted, the dying light grew harsher, until it seemed to imprison us. As though a great ball-jar – the kind my grandmother would preserve peaches in – had dropped over our mouthing heads. As though, cut off from the world, even our screams might never be heard.

But then he cuddled my thoughts and my qualms. We listened to music on the radio and he pulled the duvet up to my chin.

'Tell me a story,' he said.

'Well,' I said, 'This is the once-upon-a-time story of a young girl, just out of school, and of how she lost her virginity. Longing to be rid of this burden, she conspired to lose it. And it's about how she choreographed its losing to fit all her romantic pictures of how it ought to be.

'So, once there was an artist, who sang in a band, and who kept an easel in the bay window of his room . . .'

He listened, as he always did to my stories, in absolute stillness. That was the only time that – slippery as a dolphin and with the same urge to leap – his thoughts could be held briefly by me. I was strangely held by him. I wasn't blind to him. I could see his insensitivity. I could still cringe in public when he spoke too loudly and blurted his laughter. And I never failed to be hurt by his need to remake me. But somehow, during the time I spent with him, it was as though nothing else existed.

'Well?' he said now, stretching arms above his head and pinioning my legs between his. 'And so? Was she pleased she had done it?'

'You know, years later, she could remember rising in the dark and wandering across to the window. It was only then that she could see the dust on the easel, and hardened paint on the brush. But she pushed that aside, because she wanted it to be as she had first seen it. And she went to the mirror to see if she looked different, and if her mother would be able to tell what she'd done. And she felt a . . . a pride in being a woman and a . . . sadness that it was so uninspiring.'

He burst into chuckles, rolled over and bit my neck.

'You know what I'd like you to do soon?' he asked, pulling my hair from my face in a style too sophisticated for me. 'I want to dress you up in something stunning. And I'd like to put some make-up on your face. And then I'd like to take you to some of the places I used to go before. I haven't been there in a while. You'll see how people react to you.'

'Oh Martin, don't!'

'What do you mean, "Oh Martin"? You've got no confidence. It'd be good for you.'

'No, it's good for you, not for me. You want to take me places you went with your ex-wife. You can't bear them to think you're with someone ordinary. I can't bear that, Martin.'

'Oh rot. It's got nothing to do with her . . .' He twisted away to grab his wine glass. His face was tight. From the side of him, I could see the muscle tic-ing in his jaw. And then he spun back to face me. His hands against my shoulders, he pressed himself down on me.

'You're mine – we belong together. Can you feel it? Can you feel how much I'm part of you?'

At last, sweating in the warmth of the bed, he subsided and – pushing the cat away from my side – lay heavily against me.

'Tell me another story,' he said . . .

. . . 'Can you feel it, Jennifer? Can you feel it in the air?'

'What? Feel what?' The boys seemed excited by something that I was missing. I could feel them squeezing my fingers, I, disoriented from being dropped into this play in Act II, with no prompt to help me with my lines.

'Can you feel it building?' asked Jackson. 'It is happening on the street. The people are all rising. Soon this country will be ungovernable. Truly.'

'Well,' I said, grasping for a foothold in this other intense life. 'Things certainly are happening. That's for sure. But does this violence . . . can it really be the beginning of the end? The government could just crush it – they've done it before.'

'How can they do that – if everyone stands together, in all parts of the country? Jennifer, here is my letter for you.'

I carried the damp, rumpled connection between us unopened through the morning. At the lunch adjournment, I took it and my morning newspaper to the steps of the Supreme Court building, where I could warm my feet in the sunlight. I read Jackson's letter first.

*Dear Friend Jennifer*

*In relation to my health, I'm still in good constitution, and I was very glad to hear you say the same from you. At this time in Pollsmoor, I would like to apprise you of my state of affairs. I must inform that at least life is bearable here. You will see how I am learning from others, and spending this long time in prison in the improvement of myself.*

*I have spoken with Oupa about many things and I learn much from him. When I have the chance I like to speak to the other political prisoners from whom there is much to learn. We have been talking much about the rest of this great country.*

*When we are finished with this trial, I think I would like to take up a job in Johannesburg. Jennifer, I have never been there. But I gather that it is a place of fast life. In my language we call it 'Egoli' which means the City of Gold. Many of my people from Nyanga and Gugulethu are to be found in that City. They work there every day of their lives and sleep in hostels and come back home to tell stories about it. Some do not come back. Someday when I can be able to walk and speak without fear I would like to visit this place.*

*If I am not given the chance to walk free from this place, the other men tell of the Island on which I may find myself. They tell me that life is bearable or rather interesting there. The conditions there are conducive for one to become an exponent of the hidden social processes which take place in the society. I should think it worth mentioning the fact that, knowledge becomes the material force, only if it highlights social processes. If I am sent to Robben Island, I hope* to do my Standard 8 Junior Certificate, that is the level I am at, and I hope to reach university level, because I will be in a very interesting intellectual environment. Meanwhile I am still trying to develop myself through other men with greater wisdom.

You see, Jennifer, when I think of you, I don't think of you just as an ordinary friend, but as a person to whom I'm emotionally part with. We must be destined for greater things, dear Jennifer, you and me. Please do pass my regards to all at home and to the comrades.

Your loving friend
Jackson

I was smiling, but I felt it tight against my teeth. He was learning – I could hear it in his letter. But he still had his innocence. It still lay like turned soil, in which his new political phrases were being planted.

I folded it into my bag and glanced at the *Cape Times*, trying to find at least some foothold in the country's reality.

*A delivery vehicle was set alight in Soweto. Arsonists in Oudtshoorn set fire . . .*

It was just a list, a long list – all that the press was allowed to report. I struggled through . . . *stoning of a vehicle in Veeplaas. In Port Elizabeth a national serviceman was burnt when a mob of youths threw a petrol bomb . . .*

I tried to concentrate on it all with fervency. But even as I tried to hold the anger, tried to see the horror, it was difficult to keep my mind focused on the inventory of all the places and all the stonings and all the arson.

*In Witbank, a pregnant woman was shot dead when police fired at a 'rampaging mob' stoning cars . . . petrol bomb into the home of a security policeman . . . petrol bombs in Soweto at the homes . . .*

So much horror, so much dust and blood and . . . Why couldn't I taste it? Why did it seem so flat?

'You are reading some more of our mounting inevitabilities, I see, Jennifer.' It was Mandla, plucking at the corner of my newspaper to grin his tired warmth at me.

'Hi,' I said.

'Oh no! Why so subdued today, Jennifer? That's what I like so much about you – you have such spirit.' He gazed quizzically down at me.

'I'm not sure. You know, I'm trying to kind of get a grip on all this unrest. But I'm just full up with feeling. I can't take any more in.'

'Why must you feel it?'

'I don't know. I think I need to make it feel real . . .'

'How could you really feel it? How could you ever know how it feels to live in fear every day, never knowing which of your children will lie dead in the street?'

'Oh God, Mandla . . .' I felt the trite, familiar guilt float down over my head.

'No, no, don't do that,' he said, laying his two hands on my shoulders over the newspaper I'd lowered between my knees. If I close my eyes I can still feel the warmth of his hands' pressure.

'I didn't mean you to take it like that.' He laughed his infectious *hee-hee-hee-hee*. 'No, I am saying only that your experience has been different. You can't really help that.'

He sat down beside me, his shoulder touching mine. 'If the time comes to choose a course of action, you will make choices . . . that is part of the inevitabilities. Some people never have to face them and for others – like those boys inside there – their choices almost seem to be made for them before they have the chance. But if the time comes, perhaps you will make the right choice. Who can say?'

He was silent and I watched his face. I should have seen him with greater clarity. I should have, when I had him there, seen his depths and asked what he'd been like as a child. I should have asked what lack of choices had brought him inevitably to becoming the 'Botswana connection' – whatever that meant. And then I should have wondered what agonies had stripped the conspicuous militancy from him and left him with that deep, slightly tired understanding of human nature.

'Do you smoke?' he asked. 'No, don't worry, have one of mine.' He crouched to light our cigarettes, struggling to shelter the match from the chill breeze.

I was too far into grappling with my own intensities. I needed him that day, but it wasn't as a person. I wish it had been. My one great regret is that I didn't know him more, as a person. Rather, I seemed intent on making him my sounding board.

'Come . . .' he said at last, blowing smoke into the wind. There go your advocates. It's nearly time to start again' . . .

. . . He was there when court finished, as always resentful of the work which held me apart when he was free. He whisked me

185

away, unmindful of my other life or of things I might have to do. And I let him.

I wonder now at what was I thinking, that I allowed myself to be led by the hand through those days, relinquishing even the tenuous grasp I had kept on my life. That week – when I think of those days in court and the nights with him – it is as though I lifted my hands in surrender, and handed myself over to other forces.

'I thought . . .' he said, and paused. He was holding my hand and weaving us through the late-afternoon crowds. I was forced to run every few steps to keep up with his unrelenting stride. 'I thought we'd sit in the Gardens while there's still some sun.'

We walked back past the Supreme Court and came out into Wale Street through the arch. The stone cathedral was buried in shadow, but strangely, not remote. It was so much part of the pavement and its life of beggars, loiterers, hurriers and chatterers – inviting the rush-hour scurry to sit upon its steps or hang about its coffee bar.

As we passed, two men stood beneath the scrawl of stained glass to play 'Daar kom die Alabama' again and again on a *blik-ghietaar* and a recorder.

A late-afternoon serenity drifted downward from the khaki mountain. But the pavements were filled with life – with movement and laughter and singing. It was the time for chatting to your girlfriend, for hurrying home to cook your husband's supper, for stopping just inside the Gardens avenue while your toddler searched for hibernating squirrels. Beside them all – beside the noise and the bustle, the clinking of coins into hats – stood the pedimented figure of a policeman. In full blue, he stood inside the curlicued fence of the Parliament building. He held a rifle to his chest.

> 'Daar kom die A-la-ba-ma
> Die Alabama, die kom oor die see-e-e . . .'

We strode firmly past the benches with wizened couples in coats and hats, past the children throwing hopeful nuts, through the almost ceilinged avenue of leafless oaks. Turning aside, we came out into an open glade, where nannies sat with chasing children, young girls smoked and giggled as they hunched over crossed legs, and couples lay on blankets to catch the last rays of the wintry sun.

'We'll sit here,' he said, and I wondered why. Why not the romantic grass, under the clustered trees? Why here on a bench, set in a circle of benches, within its borders of flowers? From beneath his coat, he drew a packet containing wine, a corkscrew and two carved wooden goblets. He opened the wine and poured, keeping the bottle within the packet.

> ' . . . die A-la-ba-ma
> Die A-la . . .'

'I like to sit here,' he answered my unspoken query. 'Here you can sit and be invisible but you can feel the whole heart of the city.'

It was true. It was quiet here, away from the traffic and the clumping of pavement feet. It was quiet with the hushed vastness of the mountain and the damping sun. But people gathered here, people who weren't rushing home from work, people with time to mingle, to flirt and to giggle.

'. . . It's a *plesha*,' said one of the laughing Malay schoolgirls beside us. *Doeked* and demure, they nudged each other, huddling together in the solidarity of their collective flirtation. Across the circle from us sat a group of young men, one perched on the back of the green bench.

'So what you doing tonight?'

'Du'know.'

'Du'know.'

'*Ag niks eintlik nie. Wat doen julle?*'

'Well, *ek het 'n kar*. So, you wanna do something with us?'

The girls giggled and whispered. The young guy leapt from the back of the bench and strutted, placing his foot on an adjoining bench where a young white woman read her book and ate her apple without looking up at him.

'*Ag, ja Meisies.* We're not *skollies* now, you know. You can go out with us.' He grinned his wicked grin at them, one tooth short. His buddies laughed, while the girls continued to giggle.

Strutting to the centre of the circle, the young man appealed to the bench alongside ours, where a courting couple held hands and murmured.

'*Ag ja*, my bra,' he said. 'So what d'you think? Are we nice *ous*?

Do you think these girls should go out with us?'

'I think,' countered the bridling young woman, with the self-righteous certainty of her flashing ring, 'That nice girls should *mos* go home and not bother with *skollies* like you.'

'*Ag* no,' he said. 'And you – *jy lyk* as green as these benches.'

The circle of joined strangers erupted into laughter. We laughed too, sipping our wine as the sun slid behind the blackened mountain.

'*Ja*,' he said, encouraged by the laughter, 'You should come in my car for a *jol*. *Dis nou* "out of this world".'

The girls whispered among themselves. But then they rose, brushing modest hands over their skirts and adjusting their head-scarves.

'We must now go,' said one and they linked arms to dart from the shadowed Gardens – no doubt racing to the Bo-Kaap before their mothers came home to find them gone. The strut seeped from the young man, who watched them go. Dispirited, he sank beside his buddies on the bench.

'What are you reading there, so si-lent and so lone-ly?' he addressed himself to the young white girl, nibbling at her apple core.

'Uh, what?' she asked, brushing her dishevelled fringe from her eyes. She wore the black-coated clothing of the student, her heavy coat too long on the arm, her small feet lost in Doc Martens. 'Uh, s'just a socio book. Have to read it for lectures tomorrow.'

'Oh *ja*? So you wanna *jol* with us tonight, hey?'

She gave a greenish half-smile. 'Uh no, thanks. I'm just waiting for my boyfriend.'

'Oh, a boyfriend *nog*. So is he an in-te-llec-tual, like you? *Ag*, why don't you rather come out with us tonight? Hey? What you say?'

'Listen! I find that really offensive. You know? Like I'm a feminist and I'm just like sitting here. You don't have to hit on me, you know.'

She moved off the benches as the young men howled with laughter and slapped at each other. Sitting on the grass, she crossed her legs and hunched over, her book open before her. The young engaged couple tutted and shook their heads.

'Hey, so what's your problem?' the strutting young man asked them, his chin jutting belligerently. But as the shadows crept heavily across the grass, he lost his force and slumped disconsolately back on to his bench.

Martin gave his shout of laughter and the young man grinned at him. He had his arm about my shoulders, clutching me to his great Aran pullover as the sun slowly tugged its warmth from us, like a rug that slips from the bed. He squeezed me beneath his arm, because I was there. He seemed not to notice that I was cold, inappropriately dressed for the evening outside. But it was a small discomfort, beside the silence of darkening paths and the gilding of bony branches. I could smell his unquestioning strength, or seeming strength, and I knew that he would order the night for me.

Martin shifted restlessly. I glanced at his leaping jaw muscle and his cracking knuckles.

'You want to go?' I asked, happy to sit in the twilight but anxious of his fitful unease.

'*Ja*, I think. It's nearly dark now. And the wine's finished . . .

. . . I watch the misty streamers drift past the window, overlooking the Norman church. Letting the phone ring five, six, seven times, I remember how I tried to phone Susan that week so long ago, letting it ring over and over, fifteen, sixteen times. I had worried and felt guilty about her, but felt unable to go home, to talk to her.

If I still had her, I suppose I could have talked through those two lives, as we had always done before. We would have sat on the couch and felt ourselves safe and together. And we could have placed our own weird perspective on those different lives.

But at that time, I still wasn't sure why I had moved away, and could never have articulated it. I could never have explained why I'd buried myself so deeply in that unworthy obsession with Martin. But now I could. If she asked me now, I could explain that it was because of her. It was because of the specialness of her, and the way our friendship had lit the night sky with starbursts of her passion, her exuberance for life and her wild creativity. The fear in that hint of loss was so strong that I could never have borne to watch it happen. I had to do it first, and I had to do it absolutely, embedding myself in something which brooked no other distraction.

'Alcon executive flat. Good morning?'

I suddenly can't remember her voice. I can't remember what she sounds like or how she speaks.

It was really in that interminable week that I lost her completely. As I frenziedly turned from her, she took up her headlong battle with boundaries. While our Observatory phone rang and rang, she was waging a war against me, against her family, against the world, but mostly against herself. In the ringing silence at the end of the telephone, I was unable to heal myself through protecting her. I lost perspective and I lost myself.

'Alcon. Hello? Can I help you?'

'Uh, Susan?'

'No, I'm afraid this is Mrs Wilkinson. Can I help you?'

'But that is the Alcon flat, um, the one that out-of-town executives would use?'

'Ye-es? But who is it you want, Madam? I'm the housekeeper here.'

'Oh I see. I'm trying to reach Susan Grant.' My hands are shaking. I switch the receiver to my other hand and wipe the sweat on my skirt.

'Oh, Mrs Grant. Oh yes. Well, you're just a little too early. Mr Grant is staying here already, but Mrs Grant has been doing a little travelling in Europe. Well, I do believe I heard Mr Grant telling a colleague – not that I was listening, mind! But . . .' she gave a small titter, '. . . sometimes it's hard not to hear things. Anyway, I understand that Mr Grant expects his wife the day after tomorrow. Will you be ringing back, Madam? Or should I leave your number for her?'

'Yes, I mean no. Mrs Wilkinson, thank you! I'll ring back.'

I feel buoyant suddenly. I have so many hopes bound up with this wished-for meeting with Susan. I have so much relying on it, as if everything else in my life lies merely in waiting.

I have used it – just the hope of it – to bolster my life and shaky marriage. And this seems an omen, a sign that things will come right. That all will be well, at last.

*Kalatter kalatter kalatter, kalatter kalatter kalatter skreee-ee-ee*
   I lay with my eyes closed, trying to picture the room next door. I was trying to feel, or hear, whether Susan was home. I had come in late the night before, had risen from his bed in the dark and, for once, insisted on going home.

I had needed to come home, to see Susan, just to see that she was all right. I needed to hear from her lips that she had just had coffee with Manie and left it at that. Or that she had phoned and cancelled their date. In my mind, it had the ice of disaster clinging to it. And I knew it was partly my fault.

I heard Maud's key, listened to her heavy footsteps creaking across the wooden floorboards, and strained for the kettle and tea noises. And yes, there it was. Susan's bed had creaked. Her footsteps groaned across the old floor and I could picture her tugging at the obsessively tight tie of her gown. I rose as she passed my door and went down more slowly. I wasn't sure what to say to her – that's how we had become. I felt I should apologize, but she would sniff and rub at her face in the dismissive way she had. And she'd probably say something like: 'Can't think what for.' And I wanted to beg her to look after herself, not to fling herself into destructive relationships. But I knew that I had joined her family – no, the whole world – ranged against her in her mind. And I knew that her very defiance could work upon itself and force her to push out the boundaries still more.

We needed Maud this morning. We needed her rituals to steady us and we needed her as intermediary. With Maud between us, we could make the coffee, smoke the cigarettes, even laugh, without delving any deeper into everything which made us so uneasy with each other.

191

Susan was gazing down into the cups she was stirring. Maud, her tea between her two sturdy hands, was watching her. A smile turned up just the edges of her mouth, but her eyes were watchful. No, not watchful – there was no wariness in them. It was more like an exultant watching.

'Morning Maud . . . Hello Susan. I tried to reach you during the week. What were you doing – you were still on school holiday, weren't you? I popped in once or twice for clean clothes, but you were never here.'

'*Ja*,' she said. 'Well, some of the time I was out. And sometimes I just didn't feel like answering the phone.'

'*Ag* Suze . . . um, Sister. I'm sorry. I'm sorry I hardly came home . . . and it was your holidays and everything.'

'Don't be pathetic. We're housemates, not lovers. We're not glued to each other's sides. You have a perfect right to sleep where you like – as I have.'

Maud gave a small choke of laughter. We both turned to look at her. Her eyes were still on Susan.

'I see your nightie . . .'

'Nightie?' countered Susan quickly. 'I don't sleep with a nightie.'

'I see your yellow nightie, with the ribbon . . .'

'Oh, you mean my other dressing gown? *Ja*?'

'Yes, I see that it hang in Master Manie's bathroom.'

Susan paused to light just one cigarette. Squinting against the trickle of smoke, she sucked hard. Then she raised her eyes, tough with truculence, and stared at Maud.

Maud gazed back unabashed. Her bearing was rigid with dignity, but her eyes were avid with delight.

'Yes, I believe I left it there. Was there something you wanted to tell me about it?'

Maud smiled. She was too astute to speak too directly, while Susan could still bolt.

'Master Manie's old wife comes around while I am working . . .' She fed Susan a titbit, and watched.

'Oh yes?'

'So, she comes and looks in the cupboards again. And in his drawers for letters. She opens the bathroom cupboards and she . . .' Maud made scuffling motions with her hands. '. . . she *froetels* about, looking for things.'

'And so . . .' Susan could see this was bait, but she couldn't resist it, '. . . did she see my gown?'

'No.' Maud laughed her deep *heh heh heh* at her own cleverness. 'I see her car arrive, and I hear the bell . . .' Maud rose, ostensibly to place her toast plate and cup into the sink. 'But then I run . . .' She mimed her clandestine scurrying, '. . . to the bathroom and I grab the nightie . . .'

'Gown, it's a gown. I don't sleep with a nightie . . .'

'. . . And I push it under the mattress, like this. Then I walk . . .' Now she walked with regal step, '. . . and I open the door for her.'

'Mm. So Maud, next time you're there, please bring it home for me.'

'But you may need the nightie there again . . .' The tilt of her head was innocently questioning.

'Gown . . . No. I don't think I will need it there again. Please bring it home for me.' Susan poured half her coffee into the sink and stubbed out her cigarette. She began to make for the door.

'He is a very strong man,' said Maud, but I could see she had lost her. Susan left the room without another word.

'Yes,' she repeated, to me this time. 'He is a strong man. Last week I tell him about my old Master at the other piecework. He fixes that up very quick.'

'What?' I asked, but I was distracted, listening to Susan mounting the stairs.

'That old Master he had no work. He would lie in the bed all day while the Madam she goes to work every day. She was tired, that Madam. All day I must bring coffee to the Master and he lifts up the blanket like this, and I see that he has no clothes.

'So then, one time he grabs my arm and he says: "Maudie, you a fine woman, you know that? Strong, very strong. I like strong women." ' Maud had hunched down to his level. And there he was before me, leering with his damp mouth and darting eyes.

'So what did you do?' I asked, drawn into the story.

Her face had become her own, and filled with disgust. 'So I pull away, I hit at him and I run from the house. Then I sit there on the step all day . . .'

She sat back on her chair. Her face now had the abiding patience of the eternal woman, the rock who could wait all day for water, stand in ceaseless queues, who could retain an essential stillness as the world turned about her.

'. . . And then the Madam she comes home and I tell her. She sighs like this and she gives me my money. She gives me extra and says she is sorry. But she says I must still come again because she needs me. She says if I don't come again she will tell my other Masters and Madams that I have let her down.'

'And so?' I asked. 'What did Manie have to do with this?'

'He fixed it all up. Next thing the Madam phones me at Master Manie's. And she is crying. And she says: "Who did you tell? Who did you tell? I gave you extra money and you told." '

'Why, what had happened?'

'The police came to him. They say to him that they're not looking for trouble with this black–white immorality thing any more. But they say he can still not do what he did. So they take him away.'

'And what happened to him?' I asked. I was suddenly stunned by Maud's reach, when she thought to use the extra arm's length of her puppets.

'The police take him away and charge him. But later, she says they let him go. But they hit him, she says. They hit him and punch him in the stomach. So she tells me she doesn't want me back.'

Maud had done now. I watched her subside. And as I wandered to the door, she began to sing a hymn.

# 10

Table Mountain was masked that day, obscured by smothering clouds. It seemed an omen. If I believed in omens. But as it happened, I liked them even less than fate.

Nonetheless, I remember noticing how closely it was cloaked by fierce cloud. I saw it as Martin and I drove around the point of Signal Hill, from the Llandudno side, into the nestling bowl that was Cape Town.

When you think about it, the night of that party in Gardens was in many ways a turning point. So I suppose it was fitting that there should have been some warning of the destructive chain which was to begin that night.

It was the photographer's birthday. He was the same photographer I'd eavesdropped on during grainy discussions of focal lengths the previous week. As we reached the *broekie*-laced veranda, I could hear the muffled boom of music.

There was some dancing in the corner, and some bobbing and ducking of shoulders, while still in earnest discussion, to old reggae. Many of the people I had met the previous week eased themselves incestuously into the crowd that clearly gathered, in some form or another, week after week. There were other people whom I didn't know, dressed either studiously leftie or flippantly avant-garde.

I was given a loosely guided tour of the party by a woman carrying a plate of raw carrot strips and mushrooms. I suppose I must have had that standing-by-the-door look. I had lost Martin, you see, almost as we arrived. My guide I remember only vaguely. But I know that she was dark, with a dimpled face which made me feel grateful. It was the art-school crowd who were dressed so flamboyantly bohemian, I discovered. The clusters of politics and industrial socio postgrads and lecturers were the ones in red-laced boots, leaning into well-worn arguments.

The night crackled with the warmth of burning pine cones and vine stalks in the wooden hearth, and with the blaze of political colour and vigorous fashion.

I was effusively greeted by the Tamboerskloof group, kissed on both cheeks and distractedly darlinged before they and a bunch of journalists fell back into the laying of bets.

'OK, so what's the odds on it lasting?'

There were about eight of them in the laughing circle. I had no idea who they were discussing, and I wasn't sure I could remember who was who, so I listened silently.

'Oh come on, you have to put a limit on what you mean by lasting.'

'Oh, is that because your last marriage only lasted eight months, or what?' Someone handed me a glass of wine. Slightly woody it was. I wasn't used to that, but it tasted outrageously sophisticated.

'Aw, fuck you, china. No, but seriously, how long are we going to wait to be paid out? I reckon we have to bet that it'll break up in the first year. That's a bloody sight longer than any of you lot can foresee this marriage lasting. If it lasts over a year, we optimists get paid out, OK?'

'OK, OK, but if he goes back to boys during that year – even if they're still married – then we get paid. Fair enough?'

I had noticed that the previous week. In between the talent talk which dazzled me, they gossiped incessantly about each other, about their marriages and divorces, their affairs and sexual preferences, about which of them was bearing the children of which. But the thing that disarmed me, just as my protestant breeding prepared to protest, was the lack of malice. No sanction was intended, no disapproval implied. Used with such delight, their gossip seemed aimed at perpetuating their picturesque image of themselves. I think it helped them to view their group as they wished to be seen – as wild, interesting and unconventional.

There were serious groups too. I could hear them – as I wandered off in search of Martin – discussing the significance of the last three days of violence. Yesterday, the unrest had finally reached Guguletu Township and Crossroads Squatter Camp, on the bleak Cape Flats.

Just at the kitchen door stood a small group of heavies. They took little notice of my attempts to squeeze past them. Oh God,

Martin, where the hell are you? The heavies were talking about the Eastern Cape activists who had been murdered that week and buried this morning in Cradock. It struck me particularly because they spoke as though they knew them.

'. . . not that Sparrow was. But I know that Matthew and Fort were involved with . . .'

I had heard of Matthew Goniwe, but not the others. I had never met anyone who had known them, until they were dead. But in the months that followed, before I left the country, I met many people who said they had known them well.

'*Ja*, see, it was always Matthew who used to say that the *boere* would get him one day. I don't believe in that shit, but . . .'

'Well shit, he was an activist, man. It doesn't exactly take great prescience – I mean, you know what it's like.'

'Uh, excuse me,' I murmured and they shifted slightly, allowing me to squeeze past.

The kitchen had burnt all the warmth from the white faces hanging in the fluorescent glare. Hands desultorily picked at sticks of celery and raw mushrooms, dipping them into what looked like tzatziki.

'. . . I really can't believe he's taken at all seriously. I find that work intensely self-indulgent . . .'

As my eyes adapted to the blast of light, I thought I recognized the older man, pronouncing on the state of Art to his encircling order of acolytes. I had seen newspaper pictures of him attending exhibitions. Martin's professor. And Martin, on the other side of the kitchen table, his eyes on the celery he was dipping with uncharacteristic care.

'. . . It's as though he's taken his emotions and smeared them all over his canvases. There is no intellectual basis or input at all. What you say, Martin? You see the exhibition?'

'*Ja*.' He was still gently rolling his celery in the dip, scrupulous about each ridge being covered. 'I saw it during the vac. Yes, no you're right. But I still think there's something appealing in that level of self-indulgence.'

Strange, I thought, as I watched his intent white face. How strange that, only this morning, we had walked along the shore and he had lectured me on that exhibition, on its power and cerebral profundity, shouting to be heard above the jacket-flapping gusts.

No one seemed to notice my uneasy hovering, not even Martin
– absorbed in the neat nibbles he was bestowing on his celery. I
should just withdraw. I should quietly slip my interloper self back
through the heavies, and the lesser lefties, back to my crowd of
leftover hippies and avant-garde freaks. But that would be a final
admission. It would mean that I knew I could never replace the
laughing blonde by his side.

I had found her once – hidden face down in Martin's bedside
drawer. I had come upon her captured vivacity during furtive
scrabbling while he showered. She had red-tipped fingers, the
upthrown arms and easy shrug of the Natal private schoolgirl – all
easy confidence, no substance. He could see that, surely he could
see it, that while I might not flounce into the kitchen with flirting
eyes, I had more depth. Surely now he would look up from that
fucking piece of celery.

There was silence as the high priest became aware of this
encroachment by an uninitiated one. I felt surveyed by the circle of
eyes. And Martin – oh God, Martin – he did it too. As my
unpainted nails made one humiliating clutch towards his hand,
and dropped again to my side, I saw him as I hadn't wanted to
before. I saw his strength as a deception. I saw weakness in his
unwillingness to lay claim to me.

Why couldn't he just show them what I was, get me talking,
show me as his storyteller, as attorney to the Kakaza accused? But
he had wanted to dress me up this evening, to recreate me in her
shadowed image. I had resisted because it was I . . . hey, come on,
this is me that you want to mess with.

She – all blonde flip and red-lipped assurance – had dumped
him. But it was I who would be punished for that, because she
could be replaced only by her equivalent.

'So . . .' said the professor, tiring of his scrutiny, '. . . anyway,
what can you expect? We're so cut off, here, from the outside
world. The cultural boycott is really killing us in terms of artistic
movement. The only things we keep producing are those intellec-
tually drought-stricken pieces, dripping with political relevance.'

Martin still did not acknowledge me. How could he possibly? I
had transformed in my own sight to a scruffy waif – vulnerability
breathing from between pain-bitten lips.

'Well,' said Martin. There was eagerness in his tone. 'Well,
perhaps when all is said and done, we will have created merit out

of protest art, something that . . . well, when the guilt and the bitterness are swept away . . . something that's become our own, that can be built on . . .'

It was hard to breathe, because the breath became entangled in the tears that blocked my throat. What I really wanted was to leave. I wanted to curl, knees to chest, on the *reimpie-bank* I had seen on the photographer's *stoep*. I wanted to sit there alone in the achingly pale light of the sickle moon. I wanted to listen to the wind and lick my entrails like the dog I had once seen slit from end to end by a baboon. But then, when I was a child, my uncle had lifted his vengeful rifle and shot the baboon between the eyes.

'. . . Anyway, the ideal, of course, is a sort of merging of influences – African and European – to produce our own level . . . what the fuck is going on?'

The music had stopped, with a grating of stylus, ripped from the record by a shaky hand. The roar of voices grew, but somewhere in its midst, other voices yelled: 'Shut up! For fuck's sake, shut up and listen!'

'What the hell . . .' said the professor, straightening from his languid lean against the sink, but still keen to show his cool, his lack of anxiety. 'D'you think it's a police raid?' He gave a little laugh. 'I suggest you all start pushing your illegal substances down the sink.' They all laughed as we moved towards the door.

'. . . so that's what it is. In thirty-six magisterial districts . . .' The young man was standing just inside the front door, running both hands through his hair. I was suddenly chilled by his mix of solemnity and fear, and of a shaking excitement. I had seen something was going to happen tonight. I had known, but hadn't wanted to acknowledge, the signs. And anyway, I had thought they had only to do with Martin.

Everyone was talking now, and shouting questions.

'*Ja*, we got the stuff from PW's office earlier this arvy,' he was saying. 'But it was embargoed for this evening. So it's only us Sunday papers that'll get it in.'

'What?' I heard myself cry. 'What is it? What's he talking about?'

'State of Emergency!' yelled someone in front of me. 'Fucking State of Emergency. I knew they'd crack down.'

'Oh Jesus.' My glittering hostess from the previous week was beside me. The glossy black of her mascara had wavered and spread under her eyes. I reached out and squeezed her arm, and she brought her other arm around to hug me.

'Fucking Nazis,' she said into my ear. 'Fucking Gestapo – he says they have unlimited powers of arrest and detention. There's nothing we can do. There's nothing anyone can do . . .'

I thought of my boys in Pollsmoor. At least they were safe there, safe from solitary confinement, from beatings, from standing hour after hour without sleep, with piss dribbling down their legs. There were rules for them.

'. . . still remember the last Emergency. But even that I don't remember being like this. That was after Sharpeville – you would have been only a baby.'

The crowd began to mill outward again, talking furiously in hard, low tones as more drinks were poured.

'OK, you guys . . .' An intense boy-man hovered by the front door, desperate for his leave-taking to be noticed. 'OK you guys, I'll be going then. Not sure when I'll see you all again. Good luck, OK?'

He flamboyantly swept his great coat about his shoulders, pouring the cold into the room as he swung the door with a flourish.

'Where are you going, Colin?' someone asked at last.

He turned in the doorway. A touch, just a touch, of surprise in his voice, he said: 'Well, I'll have to go and pack, if I'm to go into hiding. They'll be looking for me.'

Ripples of laughter followed him out.

'Why's everyone laughing?' I asked my former hostess. Her husband stood beside her, his arm about her shoulders. She shrugged him off as, recovering herself, she smeared the mascara from her face with the back of each hand.

'Haven't you come across him? He's a research assistant at some resource centre. He thinks he's very involved. His greatest tragedy is that no one's tried to detain him before . . .

. . . 'Hello, Susan Grant speaking.'

I forgot quite how flat it was, that voice of hers. Flat with Eastern Cape vowels and inflectionless tone. I smile, unable to stop all the edges of myself quirking upward at the familiar sound of her. I can't speak for a moment, but in any case I want to hear her do that again – that 'Hello' routine, in her funny, flat murmur.

'Hello? Uh, is anyone there?'

I want to weep and I want to laugh, sitting in my harmonious home in gently pastured England. It is the funny, sad, poignant sound of her, her accent compressed by Africa, the corners rubbed sheer by the pumice edges of her life.

'Say that again, oh go on, do the little routine again: "Hello, Susan Grant speaking".'

'Well, fuck me. It's the Sister. How did you find me?'

'It was hard, Sister. Very hard. But the Sisters will never be defeated. In the end, they will triumph over life itself and all the wicked Fates.'

And it feels right. It does. That Sisterhood we lost – I feel it on my tongue.

'Jesus Christ . . .' Her voice shakes slightly. I hear a long indrawn breath and I imagine her lighting one of her Camels. I smile again. Only we, after all, would be politically incorrect enough to continue smoking in these times.

'. . . Well, you know I tried to get you. I thought . . . um . . . I thought like perhaps you didn't want to meet, I mean, after the last time. It was kind of tortured, wasn't it?'

'Yes. I mean no,' I say. 'Yes, it was tortured, Sister. But I didn't get your message. Till you were gone. That husband of mine said he didn't think it was important.'

'Arsehole!'

I love to hear the relaxed vulgarity of her speech. We do not swear, here in our home in Kent. But I remember, oh I remember the roughness of our curse-scattered speech, in that tough and beautiful place.

'Ja, well fuckhead,' she says, 'you found me anyway.' Her gruffness grates at my insides and exposes a long-calloused light-ness in my soul, a sudden stillness in my searching spirit.

'Can we meet, do you think?' I ask. I hear her taking a drag on her cigarette as I grope for my packet.

'Yes,' she says. 'I still hate talking on the phone. I still have . . . uh, you know, even after all these years . . . um, I think it's a hangover from those days when we thought someone might be listening in. Now I suppose I just think it's my husband.'

'I'll come to London. Not tomorrow, I have a school meeting. I'll come the day after.'

I still can't quite believe that it is she. And not as we saw each other last time. Now I can feel that it is right. There is a time – it is true – for everything. And this, oh I'm sure that this must be the season for healing . . .

'Since the imposition of the State of Emergency at midnight last night, police report that one hundred and forty people have been taken into custody. As day one of the Emergency drew to a close, Commissioner of Police, General Johan Coetzee, said the sweeping Emergency regulations, giving security forces almost unlimited powers of arrest and detention, were a bold but necessary bid to quell the unrest which was killing people daily. Most law-abiding blacks, leading orderly lives, welcomed the measures, he said, as it was only a small, unruly percentage of township dwellers who wished to institute mob rule.

'In reaction to the drastic measures, the Leader of the Opposition, Dr Van Zyl Slabbert, said that this was supposed to be an era of negotiation and consensus. Instead, the country had drifted . . .'

Martin's hand shot from beneath my duvet and twisted the volume down.

'Shit,' he said. 'But I am sick of this fucking State of Emergency. It's all I've bloody heard about since last night.'

'So what did you do today?' I had intended it to sound casual – to show a passing interest, nothing more. But the tension bit the edges from the words and spat them from behind my teeth.

'Paddle ski-ing,' he said. 'Needed my time, you know. I needed to be out there on the sea. Tell me a story. Come on, quickly. Tell me a story.'

I shivered. Strange that, it wasn't at all cold. The room was warm from our breath, which concealed the mountain behind my fogged and drizzled window pane. And from our lovemaking – hard and pressing with the ragged desperation he had brought in with the damp and chill.

'Well, I'll have to think a minute. Funny, I can't quite think of one right now. Give me a minute, Martin . . .'

He had dropped me home after the party the night before. I really hadn't minded. I had never felt I had to see my boyfriends every minute. I really hadn't, before I met him. But then I had always had Susan. Susan to come home to. Susan to . . . to sit on the couch with . . . to giggle with, to discuss and relive every tiny detail of the night before with.

Since then, since I had transferred that responsibility to him, he seemed to have been there every minute. He had swallowed up my time and my self. He had twinned us absolutely, creating a Siamese partnership, unhealthily sharing each other's nourishment and each other's organs. So when he withdrew himself for the day, I felt how much I had lost the ability to survive without that dependency.

Later, as I had huddled by myself in the growing evening, I heard his car with the rush of receding panic. So sure of his welcome, he had swept me up the stairs, his nose and his hands still coated with the winter outside. His eyes closed, he had crushed himself to me that night, tattooed his personality on my entrails.

And then we lay, the radio on, while I felt his urgency to be free of her – the fey blonde who flitted between us – and to imprint me on his soul in her place.

'Tell me a story. Please, Jennifer. I want you to tell me one now.'

The news was over. There was nothing more to be said anyway. What more could be felt beyond the despair of the thing. It felt like defeat, like the war comics were all wrong – the good guys with smiling faces and curling hair hadn't won. It felt like the order of the universe had reversed itself, like the bad guys – the ones with bristled hair and scowls, had won their evil battle.

What could I think to do except cling to this strength? Oh yes, it was strength, I was sure, a strength regained in the healing salt of his sea. It had wavered only temporarily as, Delilah-like, she had touched his memory. But I could make her go away. If only I could think of a story.

'Well . . . once upon a time a winter covered the land. A snow fell which each day melted to mush but each night fell again, freezing the day's measly attempts to thaw . . .'

'No, no, on! Real stories, that's what you tell me. I want real stories that give me your childhood. I want you. Tell me a real story.'

The radio was tuned to Radio 5 – some golden oldie programme – and I could hear Jim Croce lamenting on the cruelty of women, who always want more than men can ever give them.

'Jesus, this song reminds me of her. You know, that's what she wanted from me. That's how I couldn't be. You know, she used . . .'

'Once upon a time . . .'

'. . . to make me wear things she thought would make me look . . .'

'. . . Once upon a time . . . there was a little girl who had a rabbit. This was a geek child, who spent break-times helping the school librarian rather than brave the bitch-girls outside. This was a girl who couldn't run the gauntlet out to the playground because the teacher had taught the children to chant: "Water Baby, Water Baby", thinking it would teach her not to cry . . .'

'No, Jesus Christ. But this is fucking dreadful. You always tell me funny stories filled with whimsy. This is just too fucking depressing. And what about the rabbit anyway? You got side-tracked onto "the horror, oh the horror" of school.'

'Well she got this rabbit because she was miserable at school, you see, and . . .'

'No, I don't think I could bear to hear a story about a rabbit. Really. Rather don't tell me a story then.'

The songs flowed through our desperate thoughts and desultory talk. I thought of Susan, with an ache of loss that made me want to clutch my belly. I had no idea where she was. She hadn't been in all day. Half of me had hoped she would be, and that we could grasp this new horror of the Emergency together. Sitting on the couch, we could have spoken of it with our hands just touching. We could have smoked cigarettes and – with our two backs against the wall – maybe it wouldn't have seemed quite so desolate. She would have laughed at the picture I would have painted of Martin, grovelling to his professor. But she wouldn't have slated him, nor torn him to pieces. We never did that to each other.

The other half of me had hoped she wouldn't come home – had known it wouldn't be like that and that we would grope for things to say, our eyes evasive and watchful. I hadn't wanted to see her that way, a travesty of the way we had been before.

'Oh Jesus, can you think of nothing, absolutely nothing to say to me?' he asked. But his eyes were on the window. 'Can't you see I need you now? How can you withdraw yourself like that, just when I need you? How can you be so bloody selfish?'

My mind, clutching about for my earlier life, could encompass none of it. No small encounter, not one whimsical adventure.

All I could hear, as I tried so hard to concentrate, was some dirge of lost love, trite with our own despair. I have never again been able to hear that old song without feeling the nausea of detentions and deaths, a numb helplessness over Martin and an aching longing for Susan.

We lay, as songs came and went, each of our bodies stiff with hurt, and distinct.

'Oh Jesus Christ, why do they have to play this song? Now, of all times. It's so much her. It's so very much her song.'

My mind had drifted from the radio and its mimicry of our misery. I listened now. I listened as his life and his strength faded from me.

'Oh Jesus, that was always her song. She played it . . .'

I made no more story attempts. He had moved too far beyond me.

Through that long night, I could smell his skin. He smelt like something of mine, like my clothes when they're washed in my mother's washing machine.

Around four or possibly closer to five, he rose very quietly in the chill of pre-dawn, and he left . . .

*. . . Dear Jennifer,*
*As you probably noticed, I left very early . . .*

I had found the note on my desk at work. He must have come to my office early and left it with the day-desk man just as he came on duty. Or perhaps the night watchman had received it. I'd have to ask him. But as I thought it, I knew that I never would.

*. . . left very early this morning. I'd been thinking all night. I'm sure you could see for yourself how screwed up I've been. You're so together that I know you'll understand.*

*I realize that, until I can fix myself up and come to terms with how I still am about my last marriage, I won't be able to have a proper relationship. I'm just not ready for the level of relationship we had.*

*I know you'll cope fine. So, be happy. See you sometime.*
*Martin.*

I carefully folded the note and placed it in my briefcase. I walked to court, thinking to myself . . . it's funny, I couldn't feel my feet,

walking in my dainty court shoes over the rough pavement . . .
that today would be the end of the State case, that some of the
other advocates would begin arguing for a discharge . . . My
hands felt odd too, slightly numb . . . Not our advocate, not our
clients. Our guys were too hellish guilty. No, it was the others, the
'common purpose' guys, caught there on their way to buying
butter, or buying a newspaper, or watching the others, or something . . . oh fuck, how could I manage? Why could I still not feel
my feet?

'Are you OK? My goodness dear, you look faint.'

'No . . . I don't know. I don't feel . . .' A few years later, I might
have known enough to ask that wavery woman for a paper bag to
breathe into, and she would probably have carried one, to deal
with hyperventilating strangers and occasions like these. Just then
I knew that I was dying.

I remember that she took me to the public toilet. My head was
pushed between my legs and I could smell the dirtiness of the
place. I never used the public toilet in court. I always asked for the
key to the lawyers' loo – always clean, and clear of all the fear and
tears of clients. And now I was as one of them.

Eventually she left me – burning face pressed to the smeared
tiles – and returned with one of the newspaper court reporters.

'Are you OK?' the reporter asked me. 'No, obviously not.
Never mind. I'll help you. It's OK now, I'll look after her.
Thanks, hey.'

After a while I was aware of being in a room with her. Table,
chairs – old-fashioned government issue, you know the kind. That
was about all it contained, but for the grimy kettle which stood on
the floor next to the plug. And the sunlight. I sat there alone for a
long time, staring at the column of balmy sunlight, the way it
yellowed the plain-wood table. I sat, picking at the blue leatherette
on my wooden chair.

She came back at the tea adjournment, bustling in to switch on
the kettle and spoon the coffee into the ill-assorted mugs, probably
brought from home by sundry reporters.

As the kettle boiled, she dialled the telephone and leafed
through her shorthand notebook.

'Ja, hello,' I heard her say. 'Copy typist, please. Ja howzit
Pammie. Di here. Ja OK. I've got just one short piece for you, OK?
Here goes: "The State completed its case in the marathon Kakaza

case this morning, after a year of evidence and debate over the admissability of statements.

' "Elderly community leader Mr Oupa Kakaza and sixteen others, many of them still youths, stand accused of murder and terrorism under the Internal Security Act in the trial, considered to be one of the most important political cases in recent history. It is also expected to become the longest-running Supreme Court trial ever, since it is anticipated that it will take at least another year to complete.

' "Advocates for several of the accused have given notice that they will begin argument tomorrow for the discharge of their clients. They claim that the State has failed to build a prima-facie case against the young men and that they should not have to face the lengthy case for the defence. This is particularly so, they say, since all the accused have remained in custody for the duration of the trial."

'That's it, Pammie. Can you put me through to the newsdesk please? Thanks. Say hi to your family for me. Bye. Oh hi, Markie. Listen, I've put through a very tiny piece on Kakaza. Not much happened there today – they've adjourned now till tomorrow – but I thought you'd like a para or two just because it's kind of important. I kept it short though. I'm sure the paper'll be packed with the Emergency. OK, see you later. Love ya lots. Bye.'

'Listen . . .' I said, my hands around my mug to warm my hands. It said *Best Mom in the World* in large black letters. 'I . . . listen, um, I'm really sorry . . .'

'Oh, it's OK. I've been there. Don't worry about it. But, now listen. I told your Counsel you were ill and had gone home, so you'd better go. You can't exactly go back to your office like that.'

'Thanks. Thanks for everything. I'm really . . .'

'Never mind now. Forget it, OK? I must go. I've other cases to follow up on. Just go home now, OK?'

Yes, but where was home? Where was it that I could go, where the crisp sheets smelt like they belonged to my past, where I could taste the safety of Bovril toast.

Almost without considering, I found myself bussing through town, watching the passing of Long Street's sedate Victorian shops. And up the steep hills, past the signs for the cable car, through all the hobbledy streets. I walked the last bit, past the squeezed rows of pastel cottages, sash windows white or bare

Oregon pine. Past the odd untouched one, where, no doubt, yuppies covetously beat on the door every other day – sensitive architects in tow.

There it was, that quiet little cul-de-sac. The doors were closed this time of the morning.

I had no idea if she would be there, or whether she worked. I just knew, with a quiet desperation, that she had to be there. I had nowhere else to go.

Almost as I knocked, the door opened and I was taken into her earthy embrace, washed in her exotic smells of Eastern oils and cigarettes and Indian cotton. She didn't ask. But she took me into her bedroom, where the sun soaked through the cottage panes. She wrapped me in flannel and tucked me under her great feather duvet. Tea, she brought me, tea with sugar in it. And brandy. I remembered that she climbed in next to me, and we sipped the last of the morning away with brandy and tea. Oh yes, and lots of Bovril toast. She knew about Bovril toast. Later, when I was stronger, she tempted me with other small delicacies: smoked oysters on Salticrax; salmon with cottage cheese. And all through the afternoon we watched the sun move over to the other side of the room and dim and douse itself behind the mountain. And we cuddled there under her duvet and drank brandy and smoked countless cigarettes.

As afternoon crept into evening, she told me stories about her childhood in the Karoo, about her previous marriage, about her nervous breakdown, about divorce, and about life . . .

*Kalatter kalatter kalatter, kalatter kalatter kalatter skreee-ee-ee*

K I stood still, brush in hand, listening to the wintry twitter of birds. I had come home late and crept into my bed. I thought Susan was there, but I wouldn't look. I would have to go to work today – at least make an appearance. My eyes were a disaster – swollen, reddened at the edges. I hadn't had the energy to take trouble over my clothing. I was wearing a baggy old winter dress that I had bought long ago when I was low, and fat from endless dope munchies.

I heard Maud's footsteps as I gave up on my hair. I didn't bother with mascara but – listening to those familiar kettle and tea noises – pressed cold toner under my eyes and a little cover stick over my reddened nose. Martin was right, I possessed very little useful make-up.

I went down the stairs tentatively and, averting my face, mumbled hello and began my coffee-making. Perhaps a short, sharp shot of caffeine would perk me up.

'What is wrong with your eyes? Is something wrong with you?'

'No, no Maud, it's nothing. I haven't been well, but I'm OK now. Really.'

'Heh heh heh. You were crying. I can see. You can't trick old Maud. Maud can see you are not really sick. You have been crying. Your man has left you?'

'Yes actually, Maud. But please, I really don't want to talk about it. I have to go to work.'

I watched the doorway, but Susan did not appear. I could hear some small scuffling noises but her door remained closed. Maud, stately profile intact, concentrated on her tea. I was silent, not wanting to attract her avid poring into my life. Somehow I had managed to avoid her interest up to now. Probably too boring,

Jo-Anne Richards

considering the material she usually had to work with.

'What is Susan saying about Master Manie?' she asked at last. Her eyes, as I looked up from my coffee, were still surveying her cup of tea. Casual, I thought. And for once, I felt irritated by her. In fact, I thought, it was a bloody outrage when you thought about it. So deceptively casual she was as she quietly inquired into our lives. So carefully she manipulated our actions through her selective sharing of our intimacies.

'Nothing,' I said at last, very quietly. I knew I looked challenging – my coffee cup placed overly carefully on the counter, my chin thrust like a rifle sight. 'Actually Maud, I really don't think he was important enough to mention. And I don't think it's really for me to tell you.'

Maud gave her dignified flip of the shoulders, and smiled. Shit, you'd think just once she might look abashed. I watched her smile gently at her cup, turning it between her two large hands.

'That is not what Master Manie says. He says she . . . oh, but maybe you don't want to hear, Miss Jennifer.' She placed her emphasis so carefully on the 'Miss' that I winced.

'Well . . .' I said, and I knew that I was caught. It was all the same game, after all. '. . . OK Maud, so what did he say? We've a right to know, after all. You got her into this.'

'Heh heh! He says she is nice in the bed. But he says these type of girls think they too good for a man like him. But in the end, all they can think about is a man like him. He says she loved it when he treated her rough, but she pretended he made her sick.'

'Well, pathetic! That's exactly what he would say, isn't it? Did you bring her gown home, by the way?'

'Yes, it is in my bag. The Greenpoint Madam, she asks me whose it is. So I say the old wife brought it for me. So she says I must take it away, then.'

'The Greenpoint Madam! So she's back ensconced there.'

'And you, Jennifer? Where is this man of yours gone?'

'Nowhere. Wasn't serious . . .' I took a gulp of coffee and tried to stare down the glint in her eyes. She was nodding gently, as though . . . Shit, she could irritate a person . . . as though she could see right down into me and read my every hurt. 'So . . . what's it like in Guguletu? I mean, what are people saying about the Emergency and everything?'

*Ka-cha.* With her resounding click, she switched instantly back into outraged dignity. She was prepared to allow me my little victory in changing the subject. Well, why not? She had her answers.

*Ka-cha*. 'The people are very angry. Yesterday, the Casspirs they were up and down, up and down. They have no right, those police, to treat people like that . . .'

'No, of course not. It's terrible. Was there much fighting, any shooting, where you were?'

'. . . of course, those young men, they are also very bad. No discipline, *ka-cha*! If I had children here, I would keep them controlled. What's the use of this fighting, fighting? The young people should keep quiet. What can they do against the guns? All they do is make their mothers weep. The mothers should lock them up. Yes *ka-cha*!'

In the past I might have teased her about that, said something like: 'Really, Maud. Don't you believe in the Struggle?' But now I felt too tired. I didn't have the heart. I think it was because there was no hope in it any more. The glory was gone – everything felt so filled with death and despair.

'Mm,' I said at last. 'Maybe you're right. Maud, I must go now. See you Saturday, OK?'

I was going to be late if I didn't get a train rather smartly. I couldn't be late – not after yesterday. I hung about briefly in the hall, fiddling with umbrella and raincoat. Part of me wanted to dawdle there to see if Susan would come down. But I was nervous of her. Nervous of disturbing her, ashamed of the way I had left her. And I couldn't bear to see her treat me like she did her mother, or to watch her exhaustion as she had to brazen out her defiant relationship with Manie. I couldn't bear that.

# 11

I had my life back.

I could cope. I was back in the office, and I was . . . well, I was back to normal. Enough, anyway, to be shamed by the way I had fallen to pieces the day before.

'Well,' I was saying, 'the arguments in Kakaza today have no bearing on our clients' cases, so I don't think Counsel will be needing me. If you want me to do something else, Philip . . .'

Yes, I was OK again. I was an independent woman, who could concentrate on work, whatever the circumstances.

'Mm, I thought that was probably the case. That's why I mentioned it,' Philip Wainstein said. 'Actually, there are a couple of urgent things . . . I really could use an extra body around today.'

'Well sure, whatever. I feel like being busy today . . .'

God, but I felt diminished – stupid! So stupid! Someone like Ilsa would never have behaved as I had. She would never, as I did even now, have seen his face before her so yearningly, with that leaping jaw muscle . . .

'. . . Anyway Philip, I have quite a lot of paperwork backed up here in the office, so it would probably suit me not to spend the day in court.'

'That's right. You've still got all those affidavits to do for the Malan brief. That's starting to become urgent now. Perhaps I should try and collar some other poor sucker.'

'No, I'll do it,' I said. 'I don't mind working late on Malan, really. I've nothing . . . I mean, I have no engagements on tonight.'

'Are you OK? You were sick yesterday, weren't you? Are you sure you're better? Perhaps you shouldn't be out in this weather. You know how Cape Town is in winter – four bloody seasons in one day.'

'I'm fine. Really.'

I was OK. It was all a matter of will. I could hold it down with these two hands . . . But as I thought it, I felt my hands flutter upward, weightless and will-less. I made them brush the hair from my forehead, to give them something to do.

'OK, if you're sure you can manage, I need some subpoenas taken to the sheriff in Wynberg. It's fairly urgent because . . .'

If I brought the sleeve of my jacket very lightly in front of my face, I could smell him. Brought too suddenly to my nose, it was lost. But if I brushed and brushed the hair from my face, I could catch the tiniest suggestion of his essence.

'. . . Did you get that, Jen? They have to be there by two o'clock. I'll drop them on your desk just now, OK?'

'*Ja*, that's fine – Wynberg sheriff, two o'clock.' The scent of him, I found, could conjure an emanence of him above my scribbled blotter. In the narrow column of sunlight which grew from my desk, he was created now like a spirit from ectoplasm.

'So here they are . . .' Philip's sudden voice made me jump, his solidity causing the image to waver and dissolve. My eyes tried to grasp one last sight of it. But it was gone.

'. . . Jen, are you all right? You still don't look well . . . Anyway, so don't forget. You must get to the sheriff with them by two. Oh by the way, don't suppose you've a car with you, have you?'

'No. I caught the train.' The loss of that image felt at that moment greater than the loss of the man. I had cut him off, I suppose. I had cut off all feeling. But visions – I hadn't guarded myself against visions.

'. . . So did you get that, Jen? Fetch the keys from my secretary when you want to go. It's in the garage under the building, level 3, green Merc, CA 42653.'

'OK.' I couldn't look up at him any more. The brightness which blazed across his face from the window stung my eyes and made them water. I heard Philip leave quietly. I drew the Malan brief towards me. This was good. I needed to concentrate on this. Then I'd be fine.

I worked, who knows how long. But I remember that my telephone rang, and I jumped.

'Hello?' I was tentative, fearful of having to face anything from real life right then.

'Jennifer? This is Nolene in reception. There's someone here for you . . . um, won't give a name but says you'll know . . .'

With a lightening of my temples, I knew that it was he. I had never really doubted. I had known he'd come back.

I knew it was Martin. I knew it, even as my eyes rushed and clambered around Reception, even as I saw a strange woman with her back to me. As she turned, I felt nothing but confusion. Where was he? Had he gone to the loo?

My eyes still scrabbled at the toilet door even as I slowly grasped that it was Ilsa. But an Ilsa I had never met before.

It was like one of those movies in which someone's long-lost twin arrives – an exact copy, but for the fact that they have developed in opposing directions. This couldn't be Ilsa. This was her twin, separated at birth, awarded different parents, a different house filled with different values. A twin who had experienced a quite different first sexual experience, who had read different books and developed a philosophy of life that Ilsa would find offensive.

Stockings. My God, she even had stockings over smooth, hair-less calves. My eyes dragged their way past the short leather skirt. The only leather to have come near her body before had been the uncompromising leather of her handmade shoes, always slightly curled at the toe.

Her hair was curled about her head – tortured from its usual lank freedom And she . . . Could this really be Ilsa, who had so often derided the need for artificial colours? . . . There she stood now with emphasized cheekbones and heavy smears of eyelid blue. My eyes kept straying downward, to the teetering feet on unfashionably high heels.

'Jennifer, uh Jennifer.' She was speaking softly, her urgency communicated in the hands which urged my sluggish shoulders to move, to respond. 'Can we go to your office?

'Yes, of course . . .'

'Don't!' Her voice rose as she said it. She glanced across at the desk, but the receptionist was giggling into the telephone, her eyes rolled upward to watch the smoke she had propelled towards the ceiling. 'Don't say my name. My name's Bridget, OK?' Ilsa's voice had dropped again to a murmur.

I led her to my office, where she sat opposite me and leant into my pillar of light. Her face gazed back at me in silence for a moment, eyebrows plucked into an expression of surprise.

'I'm in disguise,' she said at last. 'I've gone into hiding.'

I remember thinking that if my chest had not felt so bruised, I might have laughed. Not at the need for her to hide, but at the absurdity of the disguise she had chosen. It seemed as though she had always longed to dress like this, and now she had the opportunity. Now, at last, she could squeeze cracked feet into high-heeled pumps – as degrading and debilitating surely, as bound feet. I knew the line as well as she. But I had no energy for irony, that day.

At the same time, I could feel the poignancy of her disguise – because Ilsa was different. She was a real activist. She did real, brave stuff. But even she, I think, was moved as much by the drama she was acting out that day, as by the ice of reality. But any way she had a lot of time to think about it later. I wonder how much fantasy she had then, to make her Solitary survivable?

'Look,' she said to me as I lit a cigarette and tried to see only her, ambered in that square of light, 'I suppose you're wondering why I've come to you? Well, Mandla asked me to approach you.' She pursed her lips in exasperation. 'He has a mind of his own. The committee's always trying to tell him he's too independent, but . . .'

She sighed and I wondered what she was talking about. If I asked, she'd sigh and roll her eyes and explain it to me very precisely.

'So . . . Mandla asked you to approach me?' I asked carefully.

'Yes, he seems to think he'd be better off hiding out at your place. At first, the committee were very against it, they said maybe you two weren't, like, committed enough. But then they thought maybe that would be an advantage.'

'Gee thanks.'

She stared at me. 'So, will you have him?'

'Um, *ja*, of course.'

'OK then . . . Nigel's lent his car for the ferrying of people today. So, can you give us a key, or something?'

'There's no need . . .' She would leave now. She would take this other stuff, that I couldn't deal with right now, out of my office. I felt so very tired. '. . . Our char's there this morning. She'll be there till lunchtime. Her name's Maud. Just tell her I said to let him in.'

'OK, fine then. We'll speak to your domestic worker. It's actually quite lucky she'll be there 'cause he's only the one set of clothes.

Maybe she could throw them in the machine for him quickly, while he baths and stuff' . . .

. . . I wait for the scurry to be over, for my husband to smile over his book at his girls as, girded and booted, they burst from the house to attend the social in the church hall.

'Malcolm?'

'Mm-hmm.'

'Malcolm, please listen. I want to tell you something.'

'I'm listening, Jennifer. Do you want me to drop everything?'

'Well . . . this once I think perhaps I would.'

He draws his book down in one sharp stroke. His eyes are alert, surprised even.

It isn't that I don't sometimes feel the sting of his tone, and the bite of his disappointment in me. But somewhere along the line, I learnt never to confront life at its meanest. So I have always just held it inside, dragging hard on my smoke and building my own edifice of silent resentment. How it infuriates him, my lack of response. It gives me a small, mean-spirited triumph that I have struck a blow at his need for control, and to have his laughing circle in its doting place. A triumph of a kind.

'OK, Thank you,' I say. 'I want to tell you something, Malcolm, Yes, I'm . . . I'm afraid I'm not going to ask you. This is just too important to me. The day after tomorrow, I'm going to London.'

'Well!' he says, trying to recover, shoulders shrugging his bewilderment, face composing itself into charming rue. He has tried to pad the exclamation with laughter, to muffle his loss of control, but it emerges waveringly. 'Well, there's not much I can say then, is there? You seem to have decided.'

'Yes, but Malcolm, you had a right to know. I'll be sleeping over, you see, and coming back the next day. And, in case you're wondering, I'm meeting Susan. I found her.'

'I see. Well, that's up to you. But you know, I was really only trying to protect you. Last time you saw her, it seemed to affect you so badly.'

'Well perhaps that's what I need. Perhaps I need to be affected by something . . .'

'But what is it you still want from this? It's been such a long time, and you've never got over it. Do you want to go back? Do you want to leave us?'

217

Us. Yes of course. He would make sure of that.

'No . . . no, I don't think so. I just know that it's time I started to deal with things in my own way.'

He shrugs, and tilts his head to demonstrate what he thinks of my peculiar way of dealing with things. I feel a sudden spurt of fury at him for never looking beneath the surface of me, never trying to understand what has tamed me to this pathological level of docility.

'This is my life . . .' I say, my voice rising. '. . . This is no life.'

'Oh come now,' he says in the soothe-the-lunatic voice he adopts with people he considers to be hysterical. 'Don't be so dramatic.'

He pauses to sip at his whisky. Carefully replacing the amber glass, he gives a small kick at the book he has dropped at his feet – a controlled manifestation of his anger at me.

I feel tired, so very tired. He has missed so much of the movie. But his eyes – which so often seem to flow over me in the rush of arguments – are caught mid-eddy. They have stuck on something I've said, or perhaps just on the fact that I am participating.

Perhaps it is his sudden interest, or the fact that I have broken my own pattern of silence, but all at once I would like to talk to him about it all. If he'd listen. After all the time we've wasted in cyclical rancour, I think that perhaps I would.

I take a deep breath and watch him give an almost impercepti-ble nod, as if to indicate that I should go on, and that he is listening.

'I suppose it was fear,' I say, trying to gather my thoughts and my words.

'Fear of what? You were always safe here. What was there to fear?'

'Not that sort of fear. Not fear for myself. But fear at the terrible things one can cause, without even being aware. It was that . . . and those trite old feelings of guilt . . . which haven't allowed me to accept all this, or take this life, or enjoy the fortune of my baby girls.'

I stop and light a cigarette. His eyes steady on mine, he gives a small upward beckoning gesture, as if to tell me to continue. I drop my eyes to watch the other hand as it lies in my lap.

'Malcolm?' I say. 'Do you . . . I mean, can you understand at least why I've carried all that baggage?'

'Well, I've always found it hard, I suppose. I mean, I know I'm not perfect, but I try to live my life with the best possible intentions. I try not to carry regrets. And you know, your Man-dla . . . he was an activist. He knew what lay in wait and, in a way, he courted it.'

'No, no he didn't. He had no choices. He did what he had to do. It was the two of us, Susan and I, who failed him.'

'Well I can't say that I find that easy to accept, Jennifer, but . . .'

'I know. But you never had the same life experience . . .'

'. . . perhaps it was hard for me because it so closely concerned my life. I might have been . . . well I could, I suppose, have allowed a touch of resentment or . . . or even jealousy, to affect my reaction to your feelings.'

We are silent, staring at each other in unaccustomed amaze-ment. For years there has been no room for surprise in this, our predictable choreography of mutual reaction and withdrawal. I would like to thank him for that – for that admission of frailty, of a loosening of control. But I fear to break the spell.

'And now? What do you want us to do?' he asks, breaking our breath-held silence.

'I don't know. I'm not sure any more. We've let so much slip. I feel such a sadness about that. Sometimes I think that, if I could've just grieved – if I could've felt OK to grieve here – then perhaps I could've let go of it all and we would've been different.'

'Is that how you felt? That you couldn't allow yourself to grieve properly? But . . . I never did that to you . . . I never meant to. I . . .'

'Well, perhaps I might have projected some of that. I don't know. All I know is that I never got it out. And I never healed. And it spoilt what was here.'

'Yes, but what does that mean now? What I'm trying to get to is: are you seeing this as the end of us? Is that it for you?'

'No . . . I don't know . . . I don't think so.'

'Well that's nice to know,' he murmurs. But he is smiling – a small, rueful smile.

'Is it?' I ask, my face still serious. 'Is it really nice to know? I mean, is it nice because of me? Or just because it would seem such a failure to you?'

'Don't you know, Jennifer? Don't you understand that we both still care for each other? Hell, why else do you think two people would bother to spend years sniping and trying to hurt and score

219

small points off each other? I mean, why bother . . . if we had no feelings . . .?'

'*Ja* well,' I smile back at last. 'I suppose that if we do both still care a bit – if you do, that is – then perhaps we might be able to try with each other.'

'Well, I've faced challenges before, all right. But this one . . .' And he grins suddenly – just a grin. A light-hearted boyish lilt of the mouth. Then he gives a short, sharp nod.

'Perhaps we could. Who knows? You know, at first I did think I was being patient with you. But perhaps, deep down, I knew I wasn't really. And . . . I suppose much of my . . . um irritation with you, much of my . . . my occasional jibing, was really more of an attempt to get a reaction from you than anything else.'

'Perhaps I never did give you much of a chance to understand.'

'Jennifer? If we did . . . if we could give it another try, where on earth would we begin? I've never done anything like this before. Where would we start, do you think?'

'With me, I think. I brought all this baggage with me. I suppose we should deal with that first. Well, I should deal with it, really. I just know that now, I have the strongest feeling that I should try to forgive myself. I think that needs to happen before we can deal with us. I need to forgive myself and I want to forgive Susan. And more than anything, I want her to forgive me.'

He lifts his whisky to his lips without taking grave eyes from my face. At last he nods.

'Very well,' he says. 'Fine. I'll tell the girls you'll be gone overnight. Perhaps . . . perhaps you'll let me know how it goes.'

'I'd like that,' I say. And I mean it. If he won't scoff at Susan and me, and the children we were. Then I think perhaps I would . . .


. . . It was just as well that it hadn't been Martin in Reception. It would be better if he were to come tomorrow. Tomorrow I could remember to wear some lipstick. Today, with lank hair and white face, I was wearing my brownest of brown dresses – a dress easy to pull over my head without the considering of belts or coordinating tops.

I was slinking down Burg Street, avoiding the eyes of passersby. It was nearly lunchtime and I was in search of stodgy comfort to fill the void in my belly. I turned down into Church Street, the narrow lane that held the Café Royal, where journalists and arty people hung out.

Baked potatoes, I thought, with cheese and mushrooms . . . and there was Martin. Head-on, unavoidable, it really was he, caught on his way through the door of the Café Royal. Oh God, why did I come down here when I knew he often lunched with that crowd? As much as I had earlier hoped and hankered, I now cringed and died, feeling every strand of my unwashed hair, every inch of my brown body.

He was laughing, looking down at the careless toss of curls he was ushering through the door. Aware of every brown button on my brown, brown dress, I watched his face speak of surprise, of dismay, of a hint of panic – as though he feared I had followed him – and then an attempt at a smile.

'Hey Jennifer,' he said, one languid arm leaning on the door. 'What are you doing here?'

'Buying lunch,' I said.

His jaw muscle tic-ed and his sinews leapt to be gone.

'Martin!' I said, and it came out too loud. He turned back, but his poised leg shivered his impatience. 'Martin, couldn't we talk? Couldn't we see . . . I mean don't you think we could just discuss what the problems were? It just seems so senseless to have ended this way, I mean, without even talking.'

At that moment, I wanted nothing but to sit on the beach with him, eat crayfish and lick each other's fingers. I wanted to hear him rave egotistically about art, or fish quotas, or anything, while the red wine glinted ruby in the firelight.

'Well . . . well OK. But I don't come right into town every day. I'll phone you. Maybe if I'm coming in then perhaps we could have coffee or something. OK?'

'Yes. Leave a message if I'm in court.'

And then he was gone. The wooden doors were closed on its initiates and I was left on the pavement, found wanting . . .

. . . Sash windows let in the first warmth for days – flung high to allow the escaping wisps of U2 and the mingling haze of cigarettes. Philip's Merc felt too wide for my higgledy street.

I was searching for a parking spot between the oddment cars. Slowly, slowly I cruised past my neighbours, who had moved their lives out on to their *stoeps* with the first sign of this flighty sunlight. Caught like that by my voyeuristic passage, they looked up from books, paused in the exchange of records or textbooks, screened hands full of 'bankies', mid-transaction with the dope Mert. Young girls drying their hair flung hanks of it back from their faces. And there was Uncle Willie, berating an amused group of Rastas. They were giggling, while he articulated his fury with spiralling arms. Mr Kennedy was stretching over his rail to see. Uncle Willie, probably tired out by the Rastas' lack of response, completed his tirade and left them to search for another household to mooch off.

'Ha. That told them, Willie. That told them all right,' Mr Kennedy yelled to the military figure returning from his campaign of pride. '. . . Hello there, my girl. Warm enough for you?' he called out as I passed him. I inquired after his ancient wife, and had my hand pumped before I could reach my steps. This was just a quick stop-off, a quick check on Mandla – if Ilsa'd got it together to bring him – on my way back to the office from the Wynberg Magistrate's Court. I could probably manage a quick cup of tea, but then I really did have to take Philip's car back, and complete those bloody affidavits.

Our house, locked sash windows like mirrored walls, seemed to reflect the life of the street, but to give nothing back. Oh, he had probably not even come. That would be typical, wouldn't it.

The house had an air of neglect in the thin veil of order – as yet undisturbed – which Maud laid over the chaos twice a week. It seemed deserted, although in the empty lounge I could smell . . . what was it? A hint of smoke and a trace of Mum for Men.

The stairs creaked their emphasis of the silence. Why would he go upstairs? My room had the brief tidiness of Tuesdays, my junk piled instead of scattered. I paused before Susan's door and – though I knew she would be at school – knocked and flustered my hands a bit before entering.

Here it was empty too, the sunlight from her balcony doors imprisoning the room in golden bars. A breeze sifted and sighed across the balcony and her balcony door stirred and tapped against its frame – it was difficult to close, that door. You had to know it well to tug and lift it into place.

I eased it open and there I saw him, crouched futilely behind the large empty plant pot – a reminder of one of Susan's past enthusiasms. His cowering shocked me. He had always seemed so assured, so filled with languid ease . . . I hated that. I hated that he should be so lowered by his dread of whatever he had conjured in my stead.

'Oh . . . oh God . . . Jennifer. I thought . . . oh my God. I saw, I saw through the window, I saw that Mercedes and I thought they'd come . . . Shit, man . . .'

He rose, brushing leaves and tangled cobwebs from his pants. He grinned at me sideways – acknowledgement of the ridiculousness of his ineffectual huddling.

'I'm really sorry, Mandla. It's my boss's car. I wanted to check . . . well, I just wanted to see if you were OK. I had to go to Wynberg. For the firm, I mean. So I thought I'd stop by. Are you OK?'

'Yes, yes. Sorry. It was stupid, I suppose. I saw that car through the lounge window. It seemed to be cruising by so slowly. I just panicked, I suppose. It looked out of place to me.'

'Well it is,' I smiled and gave his arm a small squeeze. 'You should have seen me trying to park it.'

We moved down the stairs, laughing with relieved tension and embarrassment. The laughter, and the steam of our shared coffee, opened up our reserved selves – shy of divergent lives – as we perched on the kitchen table. Or, that's what I like to think, although I know that Mandla was a better listener than he was a talker, and that he could give the impression of sharing while he gave very little of himself. But still, I like to think that he shared a bit, or perhaps the intention was there, although the habit of the close-mouthed activist lay at odds with this, there between us on the table.

'That's the first time,' I began tentatively, 'that I've seen you look anything other than confident. I suppose it's the first time I could actually see that you might sometimes be scared.' He paused and appeared to consider.

'Actually Jennifer, there are many things that scare me. And that is one of them. Though I prepare myself for it day by day – for being taken – when it comes that close I can smell my own fear.'

'Why did you come here, Mandla?' I asked him suddenly. 'To us? Ilsa said you asked to come to us. Why? You've lived so very differently that our lives must seem . . . I don't know . . . so directionless, I suppose.'

He leant away from me, sitting beside him on the table, so that I could see the smile he toyed with.

'Oh, I don't know . . . Perhaps there is something restful in being directionless – perhaps even a little frivolous – for a while.'

He erupted into high-pitched laughter, slopping his coffee on his thigh. I felt the sting of his teasing in my tearducts. I sniffed and rubbed my hand across my nose, before he noticed.

'Oh,' he said, 'of course I am joking with you.' With the tips of his fingers, he tapped me lightly beneath the chin – but becoming aware of his gesture, withdrew it too suddenly. It was a display of perfect equality. And perhaps, in that instant, he became aware that we were not yet equal. He, in hiding in my house, was entirely within my power. I hoped he didn't think of that.

There was a knock. I was sure I heard a knock – but quiet, unobtrusive. His lunch would be finished by now. Perhaps he felt bad . . . I leapt from the table, and started into the passage.

'Wait! Jennifer, wait!'

He hissed it, clutching at the kitchen doorway as though it could shelter him, as though he could duck into its lee and hide there.

'Oh,' I said stupidly, my hand still reaching prematurely for the door.

'Check first. Out the window.' He followed as I crept down the long passage, skirting the floorboards I knew would creak. Mandla stopped and hovered, in the lounge doorway this time, as I crouched before our sash window and peered around its edge.

'Oh,' I said, louder. 'I remember them from the meeting, Mandla. Tall guy – Indian, you know? – and that, um, black guy – the cool one with the jeans and Docs.'

'Oh them.' His face slumped into a smile as he reached for the door. 'Well, of course,' he said, as it opened, 'you would arrive now and scare me shitless, wouldn't you?'

The two men glanced at me and smiled distractedly. They didn't laugh. Mandla looked at me and laughed, shrugging with lifted arms. 'Again,' he seemed to say.

'Mandla, come bro.' The black man gestured into the house with his chin. 'We've got things to talk about.' He looked angry, his face clutched in frowns. His companion seemed merely austere.

'Come Jennifer,' Mandla said, still looking at me. 'Come and have coffee with us. This is your house, you should join us.'

'Ey listen, man,' said the austere one. 'Come on. We have things to talk about. It's not safe.'

'She can join us for a while. She'll be going back to the office in a little, anyway, won't you Jennifer?'

I nodded, but he'd already turned, leading the three of us in odd formation down the narrow passage. I was grateful for Mandla's inclusive gesture but I felt distracted again. Their arrival had drawn me back into trawling the air for knocks, and for signs that he might come.

A car roared and clattered down Crown Street, but screeched to a revving halt at the stop sign.

'. . . details of, you know, where you'll cross the border and stuff.' The angry one was speaking. Lighting a cigarette, he flicked the spent match at the open window and missed. It lay on the window sill and bothered me, the way a skewed picture can irritate and obsess one. But if I crossed the kitchen to retrieve it, I'd be seen to be making a point – about my house, about my values, and probably about my skin colour too. I sat and stared at it.

'But I won't go into that now,' he continued, turning his head to fling his fury in my direction. He had the unmistakeable mark of the private school about him, in the way he wore his jeans – expensively rumpled over the tops of his Docs – and in his accent.

Mandla, leaning in the doorway – he had this thing with doorways – had on pants that were ill-fitting and slightly shiny. They were slung unfashionably low on the hip and they fell too short on the ankle. He said nothing, but brought his face down to suck at the last of his cigarette, holding it within the shelter of his palm. 'Well . . .' he said, and pinched the end of the *stompie*, '. . . OK then. But we have time to go through that some other time. I mean, as far as I understood, they can't move me out immediately, anyway. It'll take a while.'

The angry one took a long drag on his Marlboro. That bothered me too that day, as every small irrelevancy seemed filled with meaning. The brand was so all-American cowboy. What on earth, in that image, had appealed to this young man, who had spent his life moving between rain-rutted roads of townships and green-matted gyms of school?

225

'*Ja* . . .' said the angry one. 'Soon you'll be gone. We're fucking decimated, man . . .'

The intense one was rummaging in the kitchen cupboard, presumably for coffee mugs. He drew out a green-rimmed enamel dish, stared at it perplexedly for a minute before returning it. I wanted to say: 'It's for mixing, and taking the bones out of pilchards.' I wanted to tell him: 'It's not for the maid. We don't keep it there for the maid to eat off.' But he hadn't said anything, so neither could I.

'. . . have to keep up the momentum. The *boere* are obviously running scared, judging by the reaction. See, Mandla, with every-one of any significance in hiding or being smuggled out, we still have to keep things moving.'

The intense one was switching the kettle on. Mandla, still leaning in the doorway, had inadvertently pressed the bathroom light on with his shoulder. He made no attempt to turn it off again. And there he stood, the light glistening off his shirt, shimmering on the shine of his pants.

He seemed detached, watching the angry one pace the floor between the back door and the sink. I had perched myself on the kitchen table, where I was doing a quick mental inventory of my clothes cupboard. I couldn't possibly wear those yellow pants for coffee with Martin. They were flattering, but they needed a carefully matched top . . . I couldn't look as though I had dressed up specially . . .

'. . . of course. What we really need now is another Kakaza figure. The old fart's always gone his own way, of course, but he's loyal and he's been controllable. And he carries weight with the youth and that's what we need right now. Someone to keep the youth where we want them, to keep them fighting . . .'

'*Ja* no,' said Mandla, suddenly straightening in his doorway, reaching thumb and forefinger into shirt pocket for cigarettes. 'Why do you always talk like that – about the youth?'

'What do you mean? Where do you come with this shit sud-denly?'

'I just mean you never really knew . . . not the same as I did. You just talk like you give no consideration to the tragedy of those kids.'

'Jesus, Mandla,' said the angry one. 'What the fuck are you saying? You of all people understand the necessity for mobilizing the youth?'

'You just speak of them so callously,' I butted in, resentful of the angry one's pacing, by his sureness of everything.

'*Ja*, but you have no right either,' said Mandla, suddenly sharp. 'No right, from your position, to judge or comment on his.' He held his look fastened on me for a minute. I shrugged and looked down. Feeling slapped and scolded, I withdrew myself again, back to my clothes cupboard.

Mandla put a match to his still unlit cigarette, guarding the flame with cupped hands. The intense one was making coffee, sloshing milk and sugar into all four mugs. Should I tell him I took sweetener? Just above his head in the cupboard? No, I could never do that.

'Well,' I said, truculent in my refusal to look at Mandla. 'I suppose I'd better go – I don't really have the time for coffee.' I was hurt by his castigation. Somehow I'd got the idea that he liked me.

In the safety of the doorway, I turned and muttered resentfully: 'Well, at least I've always had some idealism. He's already a politician – he's all hidden agendas. He doesn't have idealism.'

'He does, you know,' said Mandla, smiling at me. 'But it's just a little postponed – you know? He's just channelled it into his distant view of society.'

Putting my coat on, I could hear the intense one: '. . . really shouldn't be staying here, you know.'

'No, she's OK.' That was Mandla. So, at last, he was protecting me, just a bit.

I glanced back through the kitchen door, to where he still hung about in his doorway, backlit by the yellowed glow.

I never really knew Mandla – never really knew what he did or how he felt, beneath the glass ceiling he had built in his emotional life. Once – when, I can't remember – I had asked what it meant to be the 'Botswana connection'. 'I've no idea what that means,' I had said. And he had laughed and said: 'Neither do I, really. No, but seriously, Jennifer, I can't tell you. Obviously, I can't – you can see that.'

Another time he had said: 'No one can ever ask me to choose, Jennifer. I don't have that choice, to choose emotionally – a person over the Cause.'

But mostly, I didn't try hard enough. And now, I wish I had known him, so that he could have become grubbied by the life we

227

all lived. So that, when I think of what happened, I wouldn't feel as if I had torn down the world . . .

. . . I sat and read. No, not really. I could hear the tinkle and trill of Obs life through the evening outside, snatches of songs carrying its hopes and its enthusiasms. I had thought that I would read. But I sat, my eyes covering and recovering the empty page, listening. I have never felt it since. That desperate intensity of listening, as though one's whole being were oozing into one's ears.

Cars came down Crown Street a lot. They cruised, or they raced, they stopped for conversations, or they found parking spaces just outside our window. And I listened to them, every single one, unable to let them be. I listened for that particular revving, that careless changing of gears by someone who had to prove his independence from machines. I listened for the sewing-machine clatter of his *bakkie* when it idled.

The radio was on, but I kept turning it softer so that I could hear the cars more clearly. From the kitchen, where Mandla was holding some dead-secret meeting, came the hushed hum of closed-door discussions. Every half an hour the music's low drone broke for the news – absolutely audible in the silence.

'. . . Four hundred and forty-one people have been detained since South Africa entered a State of Emergency at midnight on Saturday, according to the Police Directorate of Public Relations. A statement from the office of the State President, Mr P. W. Botha, said the wide powers given to the police, railway police and the Defence Force in the affected areas – mainly the Witwatersrand and Eastern Cape – were necessary to quell the unrest. The statement said that, in a rising tide of violence, three hundred people had died this year in bloody clashes. Mr Botha said, in his statement, that the Emergency crackdown was not aimed at law-abiding South Africans – whatever their colour – but at those who wished to overthrow the elected government by force. It would heavily affect the activities of the United Democratic Front, Azapo and other political organizations, whose stated aim was to make the country ungovernable . . .'

At any other time, I would have been thrilled by the idea of having Mandla in the house, and by my picture of ourselves in relation to him. We would have loved having his meetings at our kitchen table, and by the furtiveness of the participants, who arrived one by one in hour-long trickles.

But that night by the lounge window, I just wished that I could keep it all in my head without my mind wandering out of the window. Without Mandla transmuting into Martin. I wished that I could dispel the haze which seemed to descend on me, like a dropped mosquito net, each time I lost concentration. And I wished, I wished so hard that I could feel the excitement which, at any other time, would have come to me with the sound of their secretive drone.

Susan had come home finally. I wasn't sure where she'd been these past few days – I no longer felt entitled to ask. I hoped she hadn't been with the police reservist.

I had never seen Manie, but I felt the nausea of foreboding in all thought of him. I thought then it had to do with Susan, her delicate parts shuddering into self-destruction.

I hoped she hadn't been with him again, using him as some grotesque and unknowing accomplice to her kamikaze act. Oh, I hoped that she hadn't felt it psychically necessary to fling herself into further defiant revolt against me. I didn't think she could stand much more of that – the self-hatred she drew down over herself, as she struggled to separate her self-castigation from her punishment of me.

It was gone. That winsome flutter of Sisterhood, of alighted girlish hope, it was irrevocably lost.

We hadn't spoken yet since she had come home and, to be honest, I wasn't quite sure what we would say. I wasn't sure what she was feeling. But I knew that she also knew the Sisterhood was crushed. I think she felt its loss, in her guilt and her sorrow, but also in her anger. We both knew that, in the end, I had done it. Oh, she had flirted with that delicate spirit, she had toyed with it, tossing it carelessly into jeopardy. But I think she had thought it stronger. And I think she had placed greater faith in the wistful threads spun between us in all the whimsy of our laughter, all our wallowing and tears. Now that I was grown, I could look back at the two we had been and understand that, in the end, it was I who had irrevocably torn it to pieces.

From the hall, I could hear the murmur of her voice – even then it made me smile. But I could also hear her anguish. I could hear it in the defiance she spat into the phone in her small, tough-guy voice. I could almost conjure her through the wall – rigidly holding her parts in check, her fisted hands clutching at her escaping wisps of normality.

I could taste my own betrayal. And I recall that, in listening to her voice, I thought I could hear the spirit leaving the body of our friendship. What a barren word that is, born of moderation. It hadn't been a friendship. A hurricane rather, it had blown together our most unfettered thoughts and the most pagan of our fears and made them, in their fusion, whole and manageable.

I knew what it was that she was doing, there in the hall at the bottom of the stairs. There was not a human being – save me, and I was lost to her – to whom she could pour out her words so fluently and for so long. Together we had done the same thing many times, but always with a theatrical flourish to show that we did not take it quite seriously. Giggling, and with wrists to foreheads, we had used it to release what Susan had found hard to force through reluctant vocal cords. 'Let's tell it all to the Uncle,' she would say, and I would know that she needed to tell me something. Fighting over who would speak to him first, we would dial 1026 and all that fear, or anguish, or humiliation – whatever it was – would gush out to the machine which told the time.

'Susan?' I was tentative. She looked up, her mouth twisted in defiance. Impatiently, she gestured to the telephone, her frown telling me *You arsehole. Can't you see I'm on the phone?*

'Susan,' I said again. 'I know it's just the Uncle you're talking to.'

She shrugged, a tossed, uncaring shrug, as her eyes repeated the challenge. 'OK, fuck off then, Uncle. Yes? And so, what is it you want . . .'

'Susan, I just wanted to ask . . . Susan, are you OK? You look all pinched and thin. You . . . you haven't been seeing that Manie again, have you?'

'None of your business, oh Self-righteous One. Oh Bastion of Cool, Guardian of the Lapsed Leftie.'

'OK, OK, it's just that I was worried . . .'

'Oh how terribly touching . . .'

'. . . about you, but OK, I won't ask. Listen, I just wanted to know if it was OK, I mean that Mandla's staying . . . he had nowhere else. Actually, he asked to stay here.'

'Why do you ask, Jennifer? Do you think I've turned suddenly into a rabid reactionary because I fucked one? Do you think that, because I have a desire to go mud-wrestling, I'll never be able to shift the mud from my body for the rest of my life?'

'No. I just wondered, because the house . . .'

'Well fine. Oh yes, and while we're about it, there's something I want to tell you. At the end of the month, I'll be moving. I've found a flat . . . in Mowbray' . . .

*Kalatter kalatter kalatter, kalatter kalatter kalatter skreee-ee-ee*

K I was downstairs early for a Saturday. If I stood on tiptoe at the kitchen window, I could just see, over our back wall, the top of Maud's train as it slowed into the station. The white walls of our courtyard blinded me in the sunlight – creating a glowing pediment for the mountain glooming darkly above.

I turned back to our trashed sink, weakly considering which of the mugs – crusted with sugar or filled with *stompies* – to wash for my coffee. I was procrastinating, of course, in the hope that Maud would arrive and offer to do it for me.

But that was only because it wasn't our mess. In the intertwined complexities of our own guilts, Susan and I would have woken at five to run brooms and wash cloths through this clutter, had we caused it to look like this. Nothing could have prevailed upon us to suffer Maud's tongue, deeply entwined in clicks. I didn't feel the same obligatory guilt over Mandla's meeting mess.

I heard Maud's key in the door as I trickled cold, desultory water into what seemed the least sordid mug. I heard two heavy footsteps before she halted. Oh, she must have seen Mandla asleep on the couch.

'Maud? That you, Maudie?' I called, moving to the kitchen door, still clutching the sugar-frosted mug. She didn't answer me, but stood in the doorway to the lounge, quivering.

In her weekly retelling of urban tales, Maud had always been a consummate proponent of method acting. But at other times, like now, she was a star of the silent movies, doing facial renditions of shock, surprise, outrage and rabid disapproval. And then, as she reached the kitchen and saw the mess, despair. Despair and betrayal, there in the hand clutched to her forehead, in the low moan, followed by her *Mm-mm-mm-mm-mm*, and in the seeming weakness of her knees, which caused her to clutch at the wall for balance.

'I am afraid, Mama . . .' Mandla had followed her in, roughly buckling the belt of his pants,' . . . that this is from the meeting I had here last night. I am sorry for that.' He lowered his head slightly, rubbing at it with one hand – caught, clearly, between amusement and discomfort.

'What is this boy still doing in the house?' she gestured behind her sweepingly, her other hand still propping her against the wall.

'Mama?' Mandla said tentatively. He was smiling now.

'Why must you have this boy sleeping in your lounge? What kind of house is this?'

'Maud . . .' I said. I felt presumptuous and ridiculous trying to explain the moral reasons for having Mandla in the house. And in front of Mandla, who didn't know us, nor the tyrant Maud could be, I feared it would sound patronizing rather than argumentative.

'Maudie,' I said eventually, before the pause became paralysingly hard to break, 'We've asked him to stay. He needs a place . . . He's a friend . . .'

I glanced over at Mandla, feeling idiotic, stilted by my own constraining desire for his approval.

Mandla ducked his head again, masking his chagrined smile, and disappeared into the bathroom. Maud sniffed. *Ka-cha*. I heard her resounding disapproval in the click sent echoing around the room.

I finished my washing of mugs. 'Um,' I said, to Maud's staunch back view. 'Shall I make you some tea, Maudie?'

'No,' she said. 'How can I sit to drink tea, when there is this mess? First I must clean this . . . this terrible room . . . Mm-mm-mm-mm-mm.'

I finished making my coffee in silence. Overhead, I could hear the shuffling sounds of Susan dressing. I knew her. I knew that, unable to still the disorganized flitting of her inner self, she tried so hard to order her physical world. I knew the steps – from the bed to the table where she flung her gown at night. Pause to slip it on and tie it fiercely around her middle. From there to the chest of drawers for panties and bra. Back to the bed to make a small pile of what she would wear. Then to the cupboard for jeans. Back to the bed . . .

'It is not right,' Maud muttered into the sink, as Susan entered, still in her dressing gown. Having made her small pile upstairs, she would now want coffee. From there she would wash, before returning to her readied clothing.

'Morning,' Susan said, with hurtful abstraction. 'What's not right, Maud?'

'It is not right. This boy to stay in the house. What makes him think it is right for him to stay here, right inside the house? And this mess – this terrible mess. It is not right.'

She sniffed as Mandla emerged sheepish and damp from the shower.

'Coffee?' Susan asked, glancing briefly at him. He nodded and leant against the fridge, sweet with Mum for Men. 'But Maudie, this isn't our mess, after all. Don't forget it's a very worthy mess . . . one could almost say a relevant mess. This isn't, you understand, just some hedonistic mess. This here is a leftist mess – probably a Stalinist mess, I should think.'

Susan glanced at him archly as she poured water into his mug. I watched his silent shake of laughter as his grin closed over a cigarette. Then his mouth was hidden from me by the masking hands held firmly over his smoke.

'So you see, Maudie . . .'

'*Ag, ka-cha.*'

'No really, Maudie,' continued Susan. 'Today you should feel proud at having the opportunity to do something for the Struggle. This is your contribution. From each according to his or her abilities and all that, hey Maudie?'

'*Ag ka-cha*' told us she was partly mollified by Susan's mockery of Mandla. But only partly. I knew she would still punish us one way or another.

'Mama?' said Mandla, still grinning, 'I am sorry for the mess. But you don't want me to take over the washing, do you? I am still so tired from the running and the hiding from the *boere*. But I thank you for the extra work you have had to do.'

'Hmm,' said Maud, scrubbing ferociously at a pot which looked as though it might have held burnt beans.

Turning to me suddenly, she said: 'Finish that coffee. Give me that mug so I can wash . . . Madam.'

And there it came, with a wash of burning cringe. My punishment.

# 12

*Dear Jennifer,*

*Well, concerning health I'm still in good state. I wish you the same over there.*

*Well, Jennifer, it has been quite a considerable period now since I've last seen you. I have passed through difficult times searching for the reasons underlying your sudden quietness, yet I could find none. I thought that I might be the cause. But I could not get anything to back this up. I am writing now to your old address, in hope that wherever you are, someone might send this letter on to you.*

*I am hoping, dear friend Jennifer, that you can find it in your heart to write to your old friend Jackson, here on the Island. It's because of the uncountable generous things you've done for me. Not only that but because of our friendship I shall not forget you for the rest of my life.*

*You were gone from us for the rest of the trial, which dragged still longer on and on. In the end, as you may know, some were acquitted of these things of which we were accused. I myself was sent here for 15 years for having the matches. My friend, Thomas, I think you will remember him. He got 20 years because he was the one with the knife that killed the one white man. Some others, they also got 15 years and some others, only 7 years for being a part of this. The old man, Oupa, he got sentenced only for the terrorism, not for the murder. He got 5 years but they never send him here. They gave him easy bail so he could make appeal. He is now very old and sick. The judge was giving us these sentences because we are young, and because we already have spent 3 years in Pollsmoor for the trial. He told us this in his sentencing.*

*Where are you, Jennifer? Where are you working now? Our advocate told me at the end of everything that you cannot take this country. He told us you were too soft to take our harshness. Is this true, Jennifer? Is it true that you are in another country, far over the sea?*

*I'm learning here, continuing with my academic education. Please don't worry. I'm always with you. I think I will have much to say only after I have received your reply.*

*Your friend,*

*Jackson*

This was the last letter I received from my boys. It was forwarded painstakingly from Crown Street to my parents' home in the Eastern Cape, and from there to England.

How far it all seems from everything I live now, here in this gentle landscape. I am reading it, to remind myself, on the surreal train journey through Kent's undulating green, on this journey into my South African past.

I wasn't there for the end of my boys' story, that was true. I fled all my failures and all my fears in the way that so many of us did. After my week with Mandla, after the shame and horror of it all, I resigned. I just couldn't cope any more. It was as simple as that. I couldn't see the Supreme Court without panic, couldn't answer the phone. I couldn't face Crown Street and the house we'd been so happy in. And I couldn't, I just could not face my boys and their fate.

Clutching my meagre savings, diminished still further by the plunging exchange rate, I crossed to England, where I scraped and scrimped for illegal employment – for washing and waitressing, scrubbing and barmaiding. Until I met Malcolm, who saved me, who lifted me into his life so matter-of-factly, and saved me with his ordinariness – and with his passport.

I wasn't there for my boys' defence, to hear them questioned on why they were there that day or why they'd done the things they did. But I knew already that their evidence would have enlightened no one. My boys, my overly guilty, obviously there boys, weren't about to lay bare their emotions at the time of lighting a match, or tugging at a reluctant knife blade, frothy with blood.

Anyway, in the end it didn't matter. Little about their trial – so filled with sound and fury at the time – mattered in the end. They were all released. I think it was in 1990 that they received amnesty – just a few years after the last letter I received. So few years later and yet I bet that, after the euphoria of change and the troubles of transition, no one remembered the political significance of that unending trial, and the intensity of energy that was aimed at it.

All existence is just cyclical; it seems to me – caught here in the endless round of village bazaars and the church's greedy need for flowers. As I sat in England, and read of those changes, I felt the world as a recurring cycle of renewal and destruction. Things are born and then grow old – as my hands seem to have done, lying in my lap before me – and then die.

We struggle along, trying to see life as having linear meaning, and humans as a developing species, through profound threads of time stretching from our forefathers and beyond, to our own lives and beyond. We believe and believe it, as we wait for our own cycles of destruction and despair to end, meaningless as they began.

But my unshakeable guilt has to do, not so much with the meaningfulness of those events, or what happened to Mandla. I was never very good at meaningful things. I never managed to give anything of any significance to what were considered the most important events of our age. My only skill was a human one. People sometimes seemed drawn to me and I could give something with my life. And perhaps that was what I should have tried to do – not search for significance, for how I should feel about things.

Perhaps the best I could have done would have been to reach someone, to ease them through their own cycle of destruction and despair. But in the end, I failed in that too. I failed those boys, I failed Susan and I failed Mandla. In a strange way, I probably also failed Martin. And because of them all, up to now I have failed my husband and children too . . .

. . . Lipstick! I had to find some. Why on earth had I been so stupid as to leave mine at home?

We had spoken at last, he and I, on the telephone. Oh hell, OK, so I phoned him. I just felt that if he saw me . . . if he spoke to me . . . I just knew that if he would listen . . .

I had awoken during the night. That was why I had weakened. I had awoken to the sound of a train – it was too dark to make out the time. And I had lain listening to my own night terrors. What would become of me? Whatever would I do, now that I was grown? Now that I had felt the intimation that I wasn't really special, or charmed? How desolate a city can sound, in the silence after the passing of a train. I didn't sleep again.

And so, in the morning, I had phoned. And he had sounded cool, slightly irritated by the intrusion. But I didn't care. It was only as I left my office to meet him in the late afternoon that I remembered I had no make-up. I couldn't go, of course – I remember that. It suddenly seemed the centre of everything, the symbol of all that I wasn't, and couldn't be, for him. And it seemed that I shouldn't bother at all, if I couldn't find some camouflage for my unsophisticated face.

'Andrea, Andrea, have you some lipstick I could borrow. Please? I have a . . . I have to meet someone. I . . .'

'Yes, of course I have. What do you think – I'd come to work without my lipstick? Are you *mal*?' She was the secretary of one of the partners – she'd worked her way up from Reception. My mother would have called her common, the way she dressed in fake leopard skin and kohled her eyes. I went to her then, all panicked and intense, knowing she would help me with this stuff.

'Come here,' she said. 'Purse up, like this. There . . . that's better, sweetie. I've told you before. You could be really pretty with some make-up. No wait, you're a bit pale. Hang on a seccie. There, now you've got some colour. Go'n knock his socks off, sweetie.'

Through the rush-hour crowds I held my mouth still and dry, careful not to lick or gnaw on my lower lip. I kept it smooth and unsmudged, checking it again in the window of a shop, just before crossing St George's Street to the coffee shop. I saw him at the back of the coffee bar, his face in its tensile planes, his leg jittering its taut-muscled dance.

'Oh . . . hi,' he said, his eyes sweeping over me to Joyce, who always served here. 'Another coffee, please Joycie . . .' He gave her the benefit of his charming grin, '. . . you gorgeous thing, you.'

She – all of fifty-five and without a hint of make-up – tittered a bit, ducking her head and shaking a finger at him. But he wouldn't look at me. He gazed at the teaspoon and rolled-up packets of sugar he was playing with. I could feel the table shaking gently in time with his leg's jitter.

'Here's your coffee, dearie,' said Joyce. 'He's a charmer all right, this one. Enjoy!'

I don't remember what we spoke of. But I remember feeling my grown-up veneer washing from me with each sip of that coffee. And still he chatted to me, of this and that, of nothing at all, while his eyes flitted about the table, following the fingers which grabbed and twisted at packets of sugar and sweetener, pressed and lifted grains of sugar.

At last he said: 'Come, I'd better give you a lift home now. It's pitch dark.'

We travelled in silence, I watching the tautening of his jaw muscle, he driving frenetically, over-revving and swerving into his turns. We stopped in Crown Street, gusted free of people by the icy, funnelled wind which wailed through the *stoeps* and rushed old papers and plastic bags past the car.

He looked at me at last, at my face rubbed clean by anxious hands. He looked at me, and took a breath, and then looked back at his hands, drumming on the steering wheel.

'Yes?' I asked. 'What were you going to say?'

'Nothing really,' he said, drumming still. 'Nothing . . . except, you shouldn't be sorry about me and you. I'm really very screwed up at the moment. I can't really give anything to anyone. I seem to have fucked up every relationship I've had.'

'But it was good, wasn't it? We were so close. Wasn't it good for you? I gave you stuff you needed. I told you stories and . . .'

'*Ja,*' he said, his mouth twisting into a reluctant smile. '*Ja,* we were good together. The stories were great. I always enjoyed your stories.'

He was silent and I, sensing there was more to be said, tried to hold in my tumbling words.

'. . . And your body. That was one thing that was always good between us.' We were both silent again, and I watched his stress uncoil as the centre of his tension moved. I listened as his breath changed quality, and his eyes adjusted the way they looked at me. I didn't match his sudden lust. I was too tired, too tense, too watchful of his every move and mood. And I didn't know how to use this suddenly handed power, if it was power. I just wanted to give him something, make him feel good, so he would remember that about me.

And so . . . And so all I am left with is this picture of myself with nothing left; with the last of my pride smeared from my lips, all over his triumphant cock.

I gave him that. I asked nothing for me. And as I slipped from the car and crossed the shivery road, I understood at last that, to have met him bare-lipped and naked-faced – now that would have been pride . . .

. . . 'Here I am, Sister.' She is leaning towards the match the waiter proffers. 'Thank you,' she says to him, but her eyes are on me. Her face – that small pixie face with its still delicate lines – holds the sardonic tension she uses when she doesn't know what to expect, or how she will be received. After all these years, I can still read her.

'You called me "Sister",' I say, slipping into the seat directly opposite hers.

She is silent, her derisive look in place. 'Here,' she says, and gives me the cigarette she has just brought down from her lips. Slowly, not taking her eyes from my face, she withdraws another cigarette. I light it for her. And then, like the sun baking the Atlantic from sea-chilled bones, she smiles.

'Sister,' I say, and the seat I have chosen feels suddenly wrong. Clumsily, I stand and move my chair so that I am in triangle formation with her, so that our arms nearly touch and I can smell her perfume.

She hasn't changed that much – her nose perhaps a little more harshly aquiline, the delicate spray of broken veins just a little more obvious, her eyes further emphasized by the underlining the years have given them. But her face . . . it is all there. That aching vulnerability, that delicacy I always feared might shatter her from her sanity, the toughness she shows the world in the tautness of her mouth and the way she sucks at her cigarette.

'You still bite your nails,' I say.

'Hm,' she says. 'You thought I would stop?'

'I'm glad,' I say. 'It's almost as though nothing has changed, nothing has passed.'

'Mm,' she says. 'You still dress as though your mother bought your clothes from Woolie's.'

I laugh suddenly, unable to hold it in. I can see myself in my skirt and shirt at once so sensible, and so silly in what they say about me. She laughs with me, the two of us leaning our heads together, blowing our rebellious smoke over the disapproving tables, our laughter breaking at last into the gulping giggles of girls.

Glancing around, I see all around us averted eyes. How odd we must seem, framed here by our environment. I don't know why I suggested the Ritz for tea. It just seemed so neutral and apart from everything we'd come to speak of and consider. Everything is muted, discreetly curlicued, delicately ordered. No corners. There are no angles here, no contrasts. Everything is rounded, excluding of all the world's harsh edges, and all its wild edge-dancers.

And here we are – middle-aged and middle-brow, ordinary as hell. And yet we aren't ordinary. There is something about us that doesn't fit. Something that – in me, anyway – wasn't there when I came in, and which speaks of all the edges we have danced in our time. Among all those powder-coloured jackets and powdery clouds of hair, we – in the joy of our sudden singularity – laugh again. Susan snorts, blowing her smoke from her nose. We laugh in raucous revolt, losing our breath till our eyes stream and ... and suddenly I am weeping.

Susan is looking away, the heel of her hand pressed to the bridge of her nose. 'Let's get out of here,' she says and rises, toppling the layered tray with all those scones and little finger sandwiches. And I see that her eyes have rimmed themselves with the rosy hue of her emotion.

I watch the rigid back of her as I pay and follow her out. Still, she holds her unbending arms to her sides, her hands coiled. Still her mix of clothing is incongruous. But where before the gauche softness of her face and her wisped blonde hair made the articles merely unmatched, now the tight planes of her cheekbones, the sharpness of her nose and the harsh cut of her hair, give it all a style. Her disjointed personality, her complex creativity and her tough, fragile self, make her mix seem matched.

We wander the streets, talking and listening, holding each other's silences and clutching at each other's arms.

'Why did we wait so long?' I ask her, as we stop beside the gates to Green Park to light two cigarettes. Through those great gates, the sky is lacy with bare trees, a fretwork of misted branches.

'Why did it seem so insoluble, with so much between us that could never be bridged?'

She doesn't answer just then, and I know that most of that stuff is still between us. We have reached over the top of it, but it is still there. She leads me across the street and I don't question as she steers me through Mayfair, to the flat where she is staying, where there is a couch.

The streets loom dark with boots and black coats. And as the sky drips on our damp faces, umbrellas burst open – a kaleidoscope display, as all my senses run together through my tear-blurred vision.

I marvel at the feel and the smell of this damp London street, as though I am here for the first time, a dry-bred South African girl. As though this time-travel journey has taken me so far back that all this is suddenly unfamiliar. I expect the mountain, I expect *fynbos* rippled by the south-easter, and bobbing brown kelp heads in the sprinkling of sunlight. I expect the corner café and Auntie and Uncle still fighting over the money, or the sex. Suddenly I long for it all . . . for the lighthouse and the foghorn. I long for that wind-whipped wildness of our youth and the Cape which fueled it. My wrist is damp and, without thinking, I lick it, disorientated by its lack of salt.

Susan leads me through the cultural balance of the place, the assured display of its continuum of time and of culture, in the gentle symmetry of the buildings, each behind low railings. A marking of territory, I think distractedly, as she leads me into Hill Street. Not a desperate, manic holding of the world at bay, as we used to do, but a discreet sign that 'this is ours' – this house, this street, this culture, this country.

She leads me . . . this is wrong. God knows, I don't really know how we are with each other now. But I need her to lean on me again, as she used to, in the pretence that I am the stronger.

As I smile at the absurdity of my ever being the practical one, she steps from the pavement in her unwary way. I catch her, my left arm about her thinness, my right clutching for her arm. And I feel the bursting of strength within me. We walk that way, I leading her by the shoulders through the jostling raindrops.

Damp and warm, we reach the flat – and the couch, with the bottle of Cape wine that Susan has brought, and the small twist of Durban Poison she has smuggled through. We sit on the couch, she and I, listening to the Tim Hardin CD she has brought – a special, commemorative CD . . . 'Here,' she says, 'I found this . . . um, I looked, well anyway, I just found this in a CD shop and I got it for you.'

My throat feels blocked by all the tears of our past and of our future, still unshed. So I nod and, giving that small, tight smile of hers, she nods back and pours the wine. She knows that I understand how she must have searched, to bring me this offering.

And she knows that I know that this is more than a gift. It is a ritual offering of runic charms. It is a Celtic dream-bringer, filled with the covenly secrets of Sisters. It is an offering, as was the parcel I had left on her bed so many years before.

We sit on the couch, her hand spread so that her fingertips reach mine. We listen to Tim Hardin and pass the gentle haze of a joint to and fro, to and fro.

'Look . . .' she says, struggling to pass the words through the tension in her throat, fighting, as she always did, to bring up the bitter words. '. . . Look Sister, I feel . . . I hurt still and feel kind of fragile with you. I don't . . . the bad stuff hasn't just vanished.'

She turns her head sideways to suck at the joint's last misty power to hold us calm and bring us together. We sit in silence – it's become hard to judge its length – but it is a healing silence of touching fingers and the smell of her skin alongside me. She crumbles the last of the joint into an ashtray and lights two cigarettes.

'But . . .' I say, and she knows where we left off, 'at the same time, I don't think anything could really kill the spirit of the Sisterhood. It was too magical.'

'Funny, yes, I always felt like it came from beyond us, in a way, and shouldn't just die like that.'

'Ja . . .' I smile and, in my most special storytelling voice, intone: 'It was an arcane force from out of our women's selves – from the creativity of our fertility and our animistic sense of being one with nature.'

We giggle now, pleased with ourselves and our cleverness, but half believing it all nonetheless. Believing, at last and again, in ourselves as slightly special – but only in relation to each other. In our togetherness, we are each more than we are apart – each of us is singular and, I think as we sit upon our couch, quite extraordinary.

And that makes me ache. There is an awful sadness still, inside me. Through all this trying, this playing at the Sisterhood, I haven't forgiven her yet. And I still don't know if I can.

'It just came upon me,' she says at last and, miraculously, I know what she is speaking of. 'My life has been such a mess. You know my . . . shit, my marriage is falling apart. I suddenly realized how much I'd been missing without the Sisterhood. And that we needed to talk. So I phoned. But I didn't have much hope. I didn't really know if you would . . . well, it's not as if all the anger and hurt went away.'

'*Ja*, but I think it was time, for both of us. I think we both needed to do this now, to try to understand at least . . .'

'Mm . . .' We put out our cigarettes and sipped quietly at our wine before I lit another two smokes and placed one between her lips.

'I just don't know why,' she says, 'that I . . . well, we . . . were so reckless with everything. With life. With ourselves and even the Sisterhood. I just remember that time, and think of how wild I felt all the time. It was that kind of bursting-out desperation that had nowhere to go, no channel.'

We sit for a while in our bubble of silence. But I know I'll have to break it. I know that there is still something that hangs between us. Something I will have to ask her.

'Sister? You know, it wasn't . . . it wasn't just what we did to each other. In the end, it was what happened to Mandla that made me go away. I blamed myself, but I blamed you more. And I never could forgive us. I suppose I couldn't forgive you because I was never able to forgive myself.'

'I took it hard too, you know. I know you always thought he was your preserve. But I . . . I also found it hard.'

'But there's just one last thing I have to ask you. Forgive me, I have to.'

She smiles, but her wariness begins to bolt out the openness I saw in her earlier. I hate to watch it happen. I want to stand before her and protect her from the world. But I have to. I just have to ask, or it will burst out sometime, some angry time.

'I just have to ask . . . we had him in the house, and you were still seeing that . . .'

'Manie . . . yes.' She shudders. 'I must really have hated myself, mustn't I?'

'It's just . . . I mean . . . I need to ask whether you told Manie about Mandla.'

She drops her eyes to the cigarette packet and withdraws two. A slight smile twists her mouth – so tragically twisted a smile, it seems to me, who has put it there.

'Perhaps I can't blame you, considering the way we were with each other. But Sister, you should know! You . . . you at least should know that no matter how little I cared for myself, I would never . . . Sister, you should know that I would never have told.'

'You see, Sister, it had to be him – Manie, I mean – because I saw him . . .'

'I know. I know it was him. That's what still gives me such a sense of horror and pain. Not that low-life disgust it pleased me to toy with then. I mean the true horror of him. But don't you realize, even now . . . who it must have been?'

And suddenly I did.

'I thought . . . I just thought it had to have been you.'

'I knew, I knew in the end. But only because I knew it hadn't been me. At first I thought it couldn't be her, because . . . well you know, it just seemed impossible. And also, of course we somehow thought she never carried our stuff . . .'

'Ja, I know. We thought we were special. We thought she only told us those stories because she liked us.'

'No Sister, she just carried, she couldn't help herself. She carried everything. Every story, every piece of *skinner*. From us as well. That was her talent.'

'I suppose she may have resented Mandla. And perhaps we should have seen that – not just made assumptions. Perhaps he was making opportunities that had never been there for her. Or something. But in any case, he wasn't standing for what she'd put up with – and she could've disliked him for that.'

'I don't know, Sister. Somehow I think it just bubbled out of her in storytelling frenzy. You know, unthinkingly . . . You really thought it was me, didn't you?'

'I'm sorry Sister. But I'm really, really glad it wasn't. Not that I think it really exonerates us, or anything.'

'No, I still live with it . . . I think we'll both probably always live with it.'

'We should have thought of her, we should have thought of everything. We just let everything happen.'

# Jo-Anne Richards

Susan flusters her hands a bit, tucking her perfectly styled hair behind her ears and crushing out her cigarette.

'But at least . . .' she says, 'at least it means . . . I think it means we can be together with each other again. I mean . . . you couldn't have been, Sister, could you?'

'Thinking it was you? No, Sister. I . . . I'm really sorry but I don't think I could.'

'No, I suppose I couldn't have either.'

We sit together, a quietness at last between us, listening to Tim Hardin going on about Susan Moore, who always dressed in lace, and whose daddy read the law. A princess like we once were . . .

. . . I sat for some time in the silent room, smoking alone on the couch. I had no heart for tapes.

I had tried to eat but couldn't, my mouth refusing to dampen its texture of dust. I had tried, thinking food might comfort me.

We had gone through our girl depressions, Susan and I. We had laughed – close to tears – as we scraped out eight avocado pears, or raided the fridge for leftovers. But never this – beyond avocado pears. Beyond all that.

This was the first time I had come upon the reflection of my own ordinariness. Before, I had waited for my belated adulthood to bloom with a charmed future. And because of the times we grew up in, it had seemed linked with somebody else. Some man, white-horsed by cleverness, knighted by insight, had always been just out of sight, ready to release it from suburban spell.

And now I was grown. Dry-grown into a sense that this – not some wonder just around the corner – was my life.

'Do you want to sit here, alone in the dark, or can anyone join in?'

It was Mandla in the doorway against the filtered light from the hall.

'Please don't turn the light on.' I don't know why I bothered. He could hear the thickening of tears in my throat.

'I'm sorry. Is there anything I can do?'

'No . . . No, Mandla, but thanks. It's . . . it's me, just me.'

'I have lived so much alone. It has shown me the value of being able to talk about things. Perhaps it would help if you could talk to me.'

'I don't know that I can talk now. My throat's closed up.'

246

'Here, I brought you coffee . . . I heard you come in. Perhaps it'll help your throat.'

'Thanks. Really, thank you . . . Oh Mandla, I've been so fucked up. Everything I've been concentrating on is so . . . so nothing.'

He offered me a cigarette before sitting – in Susan's place – on the couch.

'I just feel so appalled at how I've turned out, you know, Mandla. Not so much what I was doing, or should've been doing, but the kind of things my attention has been stuck on instead.'

'Do you really think everybody is fixedly concerned with the state of the country right now? Life isn't like that. They're mostly worrying about their leaking roofs or their wives or lovers.'

'You're not, though. You're utterly fixed on what's going on.'

'Not entirely. But to an extent I can't help it. I mean, it impinges on my life and liberty, wouldn't you say?'

'I suppose. But at least your life's had purpose.'

'Yes, but as I've told you, I had little room for choices. And sometimes . . . sometimes late at night it seems a very lonely thing to do. In the early hours of the morning, that is the time that I sometimes wonder if there is a purpose to it all. But perhaps a person should not ponder his path too deeply. It could make him mad.'

We sat in silence, smoking his last two cigarettes. I crept my hand along the couch to his and curled it inside his calloused palm. He squeezed it.

'I'm a person too, though, Jennifer. Please remember that. I don't only talk Struggle talk.'

I noticed, probably for the first time, the dangling quality of his eyes. There was a vulnerability there. And I understood in that moment that I had failed him. He, in his fear, had come here for the ordinariness, for the homely sense of human touching. And I had bounced all my own insecurities off him. I had used him as a benchmark to test if I was OK.

I turned towards him. 'Oh Mandla, I'm so sorry.'

And I wept on his chest, smelling sweetly of Mum for Men. I shuddered, my face a wet mass of tears and saliva, which fell into my hair. He didn't say anything for a long time, until I calmed to spasmed hiccups.

'Don't cry for me Argentina,' he said. 'Remember not to make me a symbol. I'm just one small actor in all of this.'

I'd always hated that song. It reminded me of my hall of residence at university, and of the walls too thin to close it out as it played relentlessly on fifty-odd transistor radios.

'I couldn't get into Rhodes,' he said when I told him. 'Even though I lived in Grahamstown. I had to go to Fort Hare because the bush college had the courses I wanted to do. Couldn't go to a "white" university if I could do the same thing at the bush college.'

'I'm sorry.'

'OK,' he said. 'I don't really care any more.'

'D'you have another cigarette?'

'No, those were my last. Why don't we get a bit of air? I think you need to get that face into the wind. We'll just go across to the café and get some – not far. I'm sure it'll be OK.'

'Oh yes, I'll be fine. I don't really care if Auntie and Uncle see me like this.'

'I meant . . .' he said and laughed his high, rolling chuckle, '. . . I meant for me. I meant I'm sure no one'll see me at this time. It's so close.'

'Oh God, I did it again.'

'That's OK. It takes a while to remember to live like a fugitive. But I'm starting to feel a little closed-in here.'

We hunched against the wind that hit us as we left the *stoep*. I thought I could faintly smell the sea, and its kelpy reminders of the life it held in its depths.

'I don't suppose you've ever snorkelled, or dived at all, have you Mandla?'

'I can't swim.' He draped his arm loosely about my shoulders, squeezing me to the warmth of him. He let me go as we reached the corner.

We bought two packets of cigarettes from Auntie in her curlers and housecoat, her meaty arms drooping with tiredness. She said nothing as she slapped the packets on the counter, her eyes narrowed in contemplation of Mandla.

'Oh,' I said, 'wait a minute. We need butter. There's not a scrap.'

'OK hurry. It's freezing. Catch up with me.'

I bought the butter from the sphinx-like Auntie, her face yellowed by the counter lights and misty with smoke from the cigarette between her lips.

'Thanks Auntie,' I called, and darted for the door. I'd catch up

248

with him before he crossed the road. I was in a hurry now. I'd like to ask him about his childhood, about his parents and where he went to school. I'd like him to explain to me all about—

The cars were there. The cold blue light had transformed them into a tableau. They stood facing him, he with his head bent and his arms spread to show he was not armed.

In the years since then, I have hardly thought of Martin – he means so little to me and my life. And yet hardly a day goes by that I don't think of Mandla. For years I wrote letters that I knew I'd never send, because I knew they'd never reach him. That writing again and again: 'Are you all right? It wasn't me. Dear God, Mandla, it wasn't me that brought them – except perhaps by carelessness.'

From England I wrote and wrote. To him and to organizations I thought might find where he was held, and check on him. When it became clear he would never come out, I continued to write letters in my head: How did you die, Mandla? I don't care about the symbolism. I just want to know. Were you cold? Did you shiver? Did you hurt, and bleed? Did you think of me, fixated upon you and your death? Fixed, not on my life or my marriage or my children, but year after year on you, in atonement for not doing so when it mattered?

But in the end, this wasn't my tragedy, mine and Susan's. In the end, it was Mandla's – the terrible waste of him. We just had to go on living with it.

That night, I stood unmoving, held in the deep shadow of the café's side wall. I stood without coming to his aid, without speaking for him. Even then, at the end of it all, I hadn't the courage to face them alongside him. I watched it all. I watched Manie – that great, fat police reservist who had seemed amusing once.

He slapped Mandla – just once. I knew from the great bulk of him that it was Manie, even before the shouts of 'Go f'r it, Manie.'

'Don't cry for me Argentina!' Mandla yelled it, just before his head was shoved down to enter the police car.

Oh God, why did he say that stupid thing? Reminding me of all those stupid girlish things – and of the university he couldn't get into. Why did he have to quote that, from a song he knew I hated? How I've ached over the years to remember something profound, some message he could have given me.

But, I suppose it was profound. And I suppose the message was there.